Unconquered Path

Path Series

By: Neri Lopez

Other books by this author:

Path Series

Book 1: Red Path

Book 2: Unconquered Path

Book 3: Wagering Path
(Coming Soon Summer 2024)

Book 4: Unexpected Path
(2024)

Book 5: Twisted Path
(2025)

Book 6: Blue Path
(2025)

To join my mailing list please email me at:
sirenbookandcraft@gmail.com

or
follow me on:
Facebook: Neri Lopez - Author
Instagram: neri_lopez_author

Unconquered Path

Path Series

by:
Neri Lopez

This work includes themes of sexual assault and rape
that some readers may find disturbing or triggering.
Reader discretion is advised.
If you or someone you know has been sexually assaulted, please know that
you are not alone and that there are resources that can help you through
this difficult time. If you are or have been a victim of sexual assault,
you can contact your local police department
as well as call the number below.

National Sexual Assault Hotline:

800-656-4673

Or chat online at: http://www.rainn.org

RAINN (Rape, Abuse & Incest National Network)
is the nation's largest anti-sexual violence organization.
RAINN created and operated the
National Sexual Assault Hotline
in partnership with more than
1,000 sexual assault service providers
across the country.

For victims of a roofie assault, please contact: 844-960-2939
http://www.theedgetreatment.com

Help is available 24/7 on the Suicide and Crisis Lifeline.
You can call or text in English or Spanish.

The number is: 988 or reach out to them online

American Indian Cultural Center

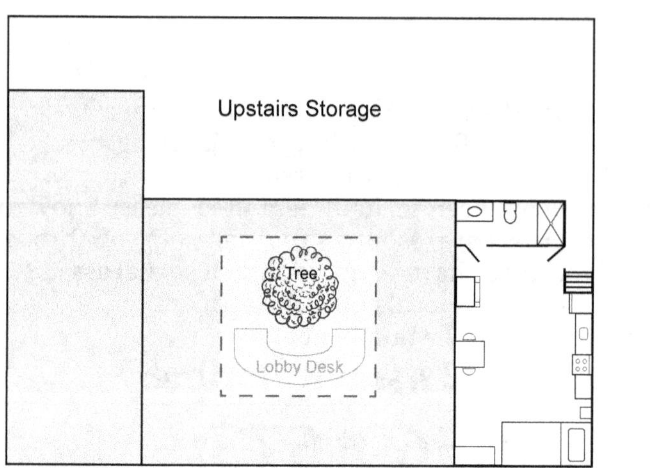

Second Floor

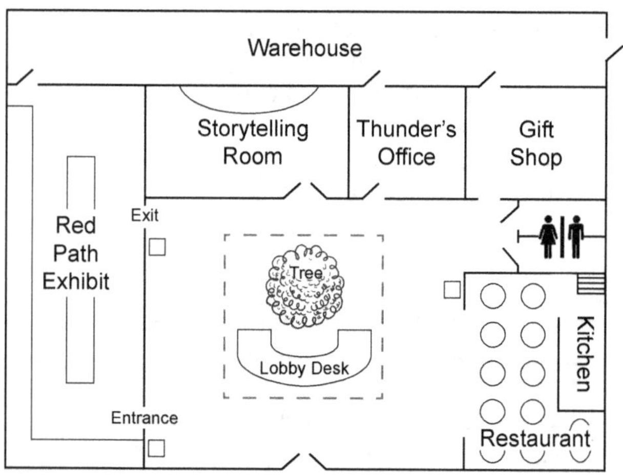

First Floor

Rock 'n' Roll Resort & Casino

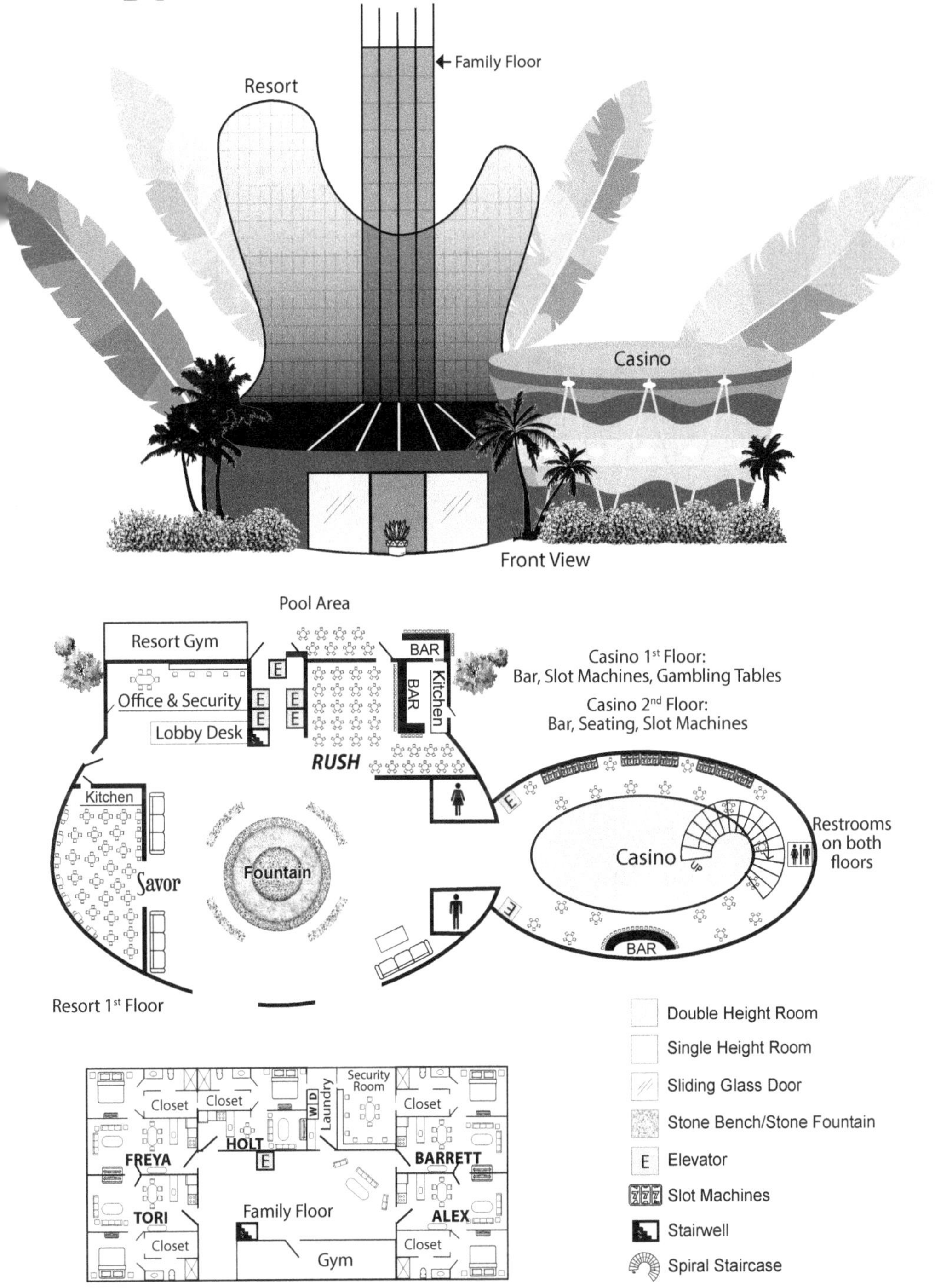

Pool Area

Lakota Translations

aké waŋcíŋyaŋkiŋ ktélo – goodbye, I'll see you soon

até – father

ciŋkší - son

cuŋkší - daughter (his)

cuŋwítku- daugher (her)

haŋ – yes

hau – hello, you're welcome, or good morning

higná – husband

híŋhaŋni wašté tibló – fine morning big brother

hiyá – no

iná – mother

inala – aunt

lekší – uncle

Mató Háŋska - Tall Bear

mitáwicu – wife

mitáwicu thečhíhila – I love you, my wife

mitáwicu caŋté thečhíhila – I love you, my wife, my heart

pilámaya – thank you

tojáŋ - niece

tcuŋšká – nephew

šicé - brother-in-law

suŋkáku – younger brother

Wakaŋ Táŋka - Great Spirit

Wakíyaŋ Hotóŋpi - Thunder

wówaštelaka mitáwa – my love

wíŋyaŋ mitáwa– my woman

Zintkála Wakíyaŋ Hotóŋpi - Thunderbird

Lakota Translations were found in the book:
Everyday Lakota: An English-Sioux Dictionary for Beginners.

Seminole Translations

chackshosti - daughter

chacteka - father

chakpootsi - son

chastalay - watermelon

chatski - mother

cheh moka is cheh - I love you

enca - yes

efeki - heart

eny - my or mine

estonko - hello

famechalatka - canteloupe

foinsampi - honey

helittah ma hich - handsome, very

isteameheilst - love

pacaneah - peach

Spanish Translations

abuela – grandmother

adiós – goodbye

¡Ay! ¡Dios mîo! - Oh my God

gracias – thank you

mami – mommy

por nada, mi niño - Your welcome, my boy

qué guapos – how handsome

Seminole Translations were found in the book:
English / Seminole Vocabulary As documented during the Second
Seminole War

Spanish Translations were done by Neri Lopez.

Table of Contents

Chapter 1

Times are Tough
Thunder

Marriage to Isa was a dream come true, but the struggles maintaining the cultural center were real. Sarah had called Thunder and set up a meeting with him. Thunder was sure he knew what the conversation would be about.

"*Híŋhaŋni wašté tibló,*" Sarah strolled into his office, walking behind his desk for a hug.

"*Taŋkši,*" Thunder stood up for his hug, "how is my favorite sister."

"You're funny," Sarah frowned since she was his only sister. "What's up?"

"I think we need to ask the council for help." Sarah sat down in the chair across from Thunder and sighed. "You need someone to replace Rachel sooner rather than later. I love coming in and helping you, but I'm running ragged between here and taking care of Lilly."

Thunder's sister Sarah had given birth to her second child, Lilly, just a few months ago. On school field trip days at the American Indian Cultural Center, when Thunder needed Sarah's help with the students, Sarah left Lilly with Minnie Morris, her neighbor. The Red Path Exhibit was turning into a huge success, causing several elementary, middle, and high schools to call and book field trips daily.

"You're right, I'm sorry I haven't reached out sooner. I know you have done a lot to help around here."

"I've loved helping you. Teaching our dances to the young girls has been a lot of fun. Watching those little middle and high school girls staring at you with stars in their eyes while you are practically naked has been quite entertaining. Now I understand why you always had Rachel teach the girls, and you taught the boys."

Rachel was Thunder's previous assistant who, unbeknown to him, was still harboring feelings for Thunder after they had broken up. Long story short, Rachel and Joseph (Thunder's jealous cousin) had kidnapped Isa (Thunder's now wife). When Joseph no longer considered Rachel necessary in his plan to hurt Thunder, he stabbed her, killing her, and kept Isa captive, making her watch.

"I'm not naked *taŋkši*, I'm wearing a loincloth and bathing suit underneath."

"Yeah, well, you might as well be naked," Sarah laughed. "That speedo is tiny."

"Better than the loin cloth without the speedo."

"Well Yeah! Those girls would probably faint, and the police would arrest you for indecent exposure."

"Valid point. Perhaps it's time for me to consider wearing pants beneath my loin cloth."

"I don't know *tibló*, you are pretty hot with your long hair and muscles."

"Uh, *taŋkši*, stop. This conversation is over. Let's talk about why you came here to meet with me today, without my beautiful niece."

Thunder knew he attracted female attention, but he was humble enough to not want to talk about it with his sister.

"Fine," Sarah smirked at him, "I'm exhausted. Please call Tall Bear and ask for another assistant."

"Done," Thunder acknowledged, "I will call him as soon as you leave."

"Thank you. I didn't bring your niece because I had to do the groceries—and wanted some alone time. Minnie is watching her."

Minnie and Skip Morris were older and didn't have kids. They enjoyed watching Lilly and Tommy whenever Sarah needed a break.

"What's your next exhibit going to be about? I know it's been nice continuing this one, but it's time for a change."

"I agree." Thunder folded his arms and leaned forward on his desk. "I'm gonna highlight the Seminole Tribe of Florida and title the exhibit 'Unconquered Path'. I need to talk to our council about that as well."

"That's a great idea, since they are one of the local tribes."

"Once our council agrees, then I need to hire a new chef."

Sarah sat back in her chair, "I'm sure George and Mary Grayfeather will be happy to go back home."

George and Mary Grayfeather were the Lakota chefs that moved down with Thunder to help him in the American Indian Cultural Center restaurant.

"Yeah, I think so too. I'm waiting to tell them after our council approves."

"Have you spoken to Uncle Spirit?"

"When Isa and I went up there for our wedding, I made sure to have a conversation with Uncle Spirit." Thunder ran his hands over his face, "he was still devastated over Joseph's actions, but he's glad we are all safe now. He wished Joseph had talked to him about his issues. I wish Rachel and

Joseph had made different choices. It never occurred to me how deep their feelings were toward me."

"There is nothing you could have done—they were filled with jealousy and hate. Now we need to move forward."

"Hey Thunder," George Smith (Thunder's shelter kid, who he mentored) knocked on his open office door, "do you have a minute? Hi Sarah."

"Hey George," Sarah stood and gave him a hug. "I was just leaving. Thunder, talk to the council and let me know what's going on."

"Will do. George, come on in," Thunder stepped around his desk and slapped him on his back. "It's good to see you. Have a seat and tell me what's on your mind."

"Thunder, you know I appreciate all you've done for me. Putting a roof over my head after the halfway house, paying for bartending school, and helping me get a job bartending at Giovanni's. But I didn't want to be a bartender for the rest of my life, not that it's an awful job, I simply wanted more. So, a few months ago, I joined the Police Academy. I applied and was admitted."

"Wow, congratulations. That's fantastic. That's a noble cause. I think you can do anything you want and be successful."

"At first, I wasn't sure if they would accept me since I wasn't a stellar teenager and had several encounters with some officers every time I ran away from the shelter. But I met with those same officers, and they encouraged me to apply since I've been a model citizen since turning eighteen. Not having any felonies and convictions helped. They gave me a physical fitness test, and I took a polygraph test—I passed both. I'm sorry I didn't tell you sooner, but I wanted to make sure I could cut it."

"Of course you could. You've grown into an incredible young man. It took a lot of courage to find those officers and ask for their help. Do you need any money while you are in the academy?"

"No, I'm still bartending at night and saving money. Honestly, between the academy and working, I haven't had much time to do anything else. One of the officers, Detective Sean O'Reilly, has taken me under his wing and is allowing me to partner with him while I'm in the last stages of my training. They rarely do that, but he knows me from when I was in the shelter. I guess you can say he has a soft spot for me and wants to see me succeed. If everything continues to go well, I will be a part of the Sunrise Police Department in a couple of weeks."

Thunder stood up and moved around his desk to George. "I am so proud of you. If you need anything at all, please come to me."

"I will." George stood up and hugged Thunder. "I can't thank you enough for everything you have ever done for me."

"It has been my pleasure. Mentoring you has been just as rewarding for me."

"Thanks, Thunder. I'll talk to you later. It sounds like you have a lot to do."

"I have some phone calls to make, but let me know when you graduate, and Isa and I will take you to dinner to celebrate."

"Will do, bye Thunder."

"Talk to you soon."

Thunder sat back down at his desk and picked up the phone. He had several phone calls to make.

Johnny "Thunder" Thunderbird (part owner and manager of the American Indian Cultural Center) and Osceola Panther (a member of the Seminole Tribal Council and Manager of the Rock 'n' Roll Resort & Casino) had been friends since the Lakota Tribal Council built the American Indian Cultural Center near the casino four years ago.

During that first visit, Osceola introduced Thunder to his eldest son Alex (the head chef at the resort restaurants), twin daughter Freya (a dealer who ran one of the many blackjack tables), younger twin son Barrett (a security guard at the casino) and his wife Sehoy (hospitality desk manager for the resort area of the casino). Osceola and Thunder tried to get together once every couple of months to catch up on each other's lives. They constantly advertised for each other, helping to promote their businesses.

Osceola's help was crucial to Thunder finding contractors for the AICC building, as well as assisting him to acclimate to South Florida. Thunder was only accustomed to South Dakota, a place with distinct differences in people, weather, and landscape compared to home. For one, not seeing mountains was something he wasn't used to. Everything was very flat with lots of Palm Trees. Living in Fort Lauderdale was hot, but the winds off the coastline helped which was why he bought a house by the beach. After much deliberation with the Lakota Tribal Council, Thunder knew he wanted his next exhibit to feature The Seminole Tribe of Florida. It would be a great way to thank Osceola and familiarize the people in the area with this wonderful local tribe.

Tall Bear, a Lakota council member, volunteered to reach out to Osceola and their tribal council to ask them if they were interested in this opportunity. The Seminole Tribe of Florida started with 300 descendants who eluded capture to become the unconquered people. This Seminole Tribe was a federally recognized Indian Tribe and the only Tribe in America who never signed a peace treaty. Thunder and the Lakota tribal council felt it was time to educate and highlight the Seminole culture at the AICC.

After Tall Bear's meeting with Osceola, Tall Bear called Thunder to let him know the Seminole Tribe agreed to exhibit their culture and history. Osceola Panther would be their contact for the tribe. Artifacts, paintings, pottery, and jewelry had arrived at the cultural center daily. Osceola also sent paintings, pottery, and jewelry from their Seminole Artisans to be sold.

Thunder and Mark had been cataloging all the items and placing them in the warehouse as they were being delivered. They couldn't display the items until The Red Path Exhibit was taken down, but they could organize it in the warehouse. It was time to call Osceola and ask about a chef. Thunder took his cell phone out of his back pocket, sat at his desk, and made the call.

"*Estonko*," Osceola answered his ringing cell phone. "Thunder, my friend, how are you?"

"Great, my friend, how are you?" Thunder smiled and sat back in his chair.

"Busy, like always," Osceola replied, and Thunder heard slot machine sounds in the background quickly fading. Osceola must have been in the casino and walked out to the lobby.

"I get that." Thunder leaned forward, placing his cell phone on his desk and pushing the speaker button. "I have a favor to ask of you. I'm hoping you can help me."

"I'll try. What do you need?"

"First, I'd like to express my gratitude for all the items you've been sending us for the exhibit." Thunder said with genuine affection. "Everything is falling into place perfectly."

"Thank you, Thunder. It is a privilege that you have chosen to highlight our tribe. I attended your Red Path Exhibit and am familiar with your displays. The way you teach the culture and heritage of the tribes is admirable."

"It's our honor to showcase and educate non-natives about American Indian culture and history," Thunder said. "Now for the favor part. Do you have a chef that cooks traditional Seminole food? In two and a half weeks, when the Red Path Exhibit comes to an end, my Lakota chef will be leaving."

"I have several chefs. My son is our head chef here. I will talk to him and see if he has any suggestions," Osceola answered.

Thunder remembered Alex ran impeccably clean and efficient kitchens. He hoped Alex had a chef he could either share with him or recommend. During the day, the Rock 'n' Roll Resort & Casino only had their casual dining restaurant RUSH open for business. Their fine dining restaurant Savor was open for breakfast and dinner. Thunder only needed a chef for lunch. He didn't serve breakfast or dinner.

"Thank you, my friend," Thunder continued with the specifics of his job, "our restaurant is open for lunch from 11:30 am to 1:00 pm. I would need a chef from 10:30 am to 2:00 pm on Tuesdays through Saturday. The allotted time for preparation and cleanup should be sufficient, but the hours can be discussed. I want to run this exhibit for six months, so this would be a temporary job, but we could revisit this contract at the end of the exhibit. George and Mary Grayfeather never wanted to stay longer than the Red Path Exhibit. If I had a chef who wanted to experiment with other native tribe foods, we could make this job permanent."

"Okay, sounds good. Let me talk to Alex and I will get back to you."

"Perfect," Thunder checked off Osceola's name on his list. Thunder was all about his lists and he had already checked off 'conversation with Lakota Tribal Council'. "I look forward to your call."

"Bye Thunder."

"Bye Osceola."

Thunder hung up and sent a quick prayer to *Wakan Tanka* to answer his prayers for a Seminole Chef.

Chapter 2

Opportunity of a Lifetime
Alex

Alex was busy in the kitchen prepping all the fruits and vegetables for the dinner rush. Cutting everything up ahead of time helped at night when he and his other chef and sous chefs were putting together the dishes. He dusted off his hands as he finally finished cutting up all the items he needed for dinner. Now he could help Bernie with the breakfast orders.

During the day RUSH served a continental breakfast and full coffee bar switching at lunch to American bar food such as nachos, burgers, sandwiches, wraps, and wings with an assortment of coffees, tea, sodas, and alcoholic beverages so their die-hard casino patrons could walk in and get a quick bite to eat between gambling. He had been debating leaving RUSH open for dinner as well. At their fine dining restaurant, Savor patrons enjoyed a full sit-down breakfast cuisine and an array of gourmet Italian, Spanish, and Seminole delicacies for dinner. Alex preferred to work in Savor, although he couldn't alter the menu too much. His father really wanted to cater to the area's demographics along with introducing them to their traditional Seminole cuisine.

"Alex." Osceola walked into Savor's kitchen.

"*Chacteka*, what's up?" Alex looked up from his cutting board.

"Remember when I told you Thunder wanted to highlight our tribe in his next exhibit?" Osceola clapped and rubbed his hands together.

"Yeah?" Alex stopped chopping and stared at Osceola. His mouth dropped open. He was happily shocked, "that's great *Chacteka*." Alex knew his dad was hoping Thunder would do a Seminole exhibit but didn't want to take advantage of their friendship enough to ask. In the beginning, Thunder showcased several tribes during each exhibit. Then he narrowed it down to his Lakota tribe, which was understandable. Now choosing to showcase their tribe would make Alex and his family happy. Alex would've been upset if Thunder had chosen another tribe before theirs. An irrational thought, but one he'd wrestled with.

"Anyway, he wants a chef who is familiar with Seminole foods. Do you know of someone who would want to work for Thunder from around ten thirty to two on Tuesday through Saturday? I don't really want to lose one of our chefs, but this is a great opportunity for us." Osceola bounced on his feet rubbing his hands, barely containing his excitement. "They would only work there during lunch and could keep their jobs here in the morning or night shifts. I know it would be hectic for them, but I would consider it a great favor. I could compensate them for any pay they lose with the travel time. Thunder would pay them for their time there and I would also keep them on our payroll until the exhibit was over. Once the exhibit ends, they could continue to work here full time like before. Thunder recruits chefs who excel in a specific tribe's cuisine, but if they show interest in exploring other American Indian culinary traditions, they may have the opportunity to continue working there." Osceola spread his arms wide, "What do you think?"

"I think this is a great opportunity for us. How long does the exhibit run?" Alex inquired while chopping the peppers.

"He wants this exhibit to run for six months. I know this is a good amount of time for someone to work in two locations, but I would make it worth their while–again, they would not lose their pay. This is important to me and our people, Alex. I want to make this work; they can come back here full time if it doesn't work out with Thunder. If you have any questions, don't hesitate to contact Thunder. I can give you his number if you want to talk to him yourself."

"That would be great, *chacteka*. This is exciting news. I'll call Thunder and talk to him about the job offer." Alex turned around and spoke to the other chef, "Bernie, can you please finish the prepping while I step out to make a phone call? I've already cut up the fruits and veggies. If you can cut the meat, that would be great."

"Absolutely, Alex." Bernie walked to the cutting station and took over for Alex.

"*Chacteka*, can I have your phone and I'll get Thunder's number?" Alex washed his hands and held his hand out after drying them.

"Here do whatever you need to do. Your generation knows how to work these phones better than us old folks," Osceola laughed and handed him his phone.

"You're not that old, *chacteka*. You're not even fifty yet." Alex smirked at his dad, saved the contact, and dialed the AICC number while walking out of the kitchen and into the empty restaurant. Osceola followed his son and listened to Alex's side of the conversation.

"*Hau*," Thunder answered. "American Indian Cultural Center, can I help you?"

"Hello, is this Thunder?" Alex asked. He had only talked to Thunder once, so he didn't recognize his voice.

"Yes, this is he." Thunder sounded confused, "How can I help you?"

"Hi Thunder. This is Alex Panther, Osceola's son."

"Yes, Alex. How are you?"

"I'm good Mr. Thunderbird. My dad was telling me you need a chef with Seminole cuisine experience." Alex leaned up against his counter, crossing his legs.

"Please call me Thunder and yes, we want to highlight the Seminole Tribe of Florida in our next exhibit. I would like to have someone who could cook authentic Seminole cuisine. They could choose their own menu. My only requirement would be for them to include a fry bread recipe any way they choose. It has become a common staple at all our exhibits," Thunder explained. "Also, if things work out, we can discuss future employment options."

"That sounds reasonable. Let me think about who would be the best fit for you. Can I call you tomorrow?" Alex asked.

"Of course, our next exhibit won't open for another two and a half weeks. Since your tribe is one of our local ones, we want to run this exhibit for six months."

"Sounds great," Alex answered. "I'll call you tomorrow."

"Thank you, Alex."

"No…Thank you Thunder for thinking of us and wanting to teach the people in our area about our tribe."

"It's my pleasure," Thunder stated. "I'll talk to you tomorrow. Have a great day."

"Sounds good, bye."

"Bye Alex."

Alex hung up the phone and looked at his dad, who was standing next to him. This was a great opportunity for any of his chefs. He truly believed that any of his chefs would consider it an honor to work at the American Indian Cultural Center. They had three chefs and four sous chefs working at the casino. In truth, he would love to go there and be Thunder's chef. It would give him a chance to cook his peoples cuisine exclusively and other American Indian cuisines in the future. Alex loved a challenge. He could add somewhat of his own style to their traditional dishes.

According to Thunder, if he had Indian fry bread, he was good to go. He could make Indian fry bread in his sleep. That was the first recipe he perfected as a child. When Barrett and Holt were running around pretending to be security officers, Alex was learning everything he could from his mom and other chefs at the restaurants.

"So?" Osceola looked at Alex questioningly.

"Well, *chacteka*, if I'm being honest. I would like to be his chef." Alex looked his dad in the eyes to gauge his reaction.

"Really?" Osceola looked puzzled. "You don't want to be here anymore? I thought you liked it here?"

"I do love it here *chacteka*,"Alex side-hugged his father. "But this would give me an opportunity to add a little something to our traditional dishes and test them out in another environment. I wouldn't change them all, but it would be nice to cook some of our dishes instead of continually cooking

American, Italian, and Spanish cuisine. It would be a nice, challenging change of pace for the next six months. I would reevaluate after the exhibit closes. I would work for Thunder until two and then come here and work until nine. Bernie is an excellent chef and could handle working breakfast and dinner at Savor. I could also promote Sam to chef at RUSH. What do you think?"

"I'm fine with that, but I know you. You will go in early and stay late so everything is perfect." Osceola squinted at Alex. "You are an overachiever, but you might end up burning the candle at both ends and what about if you decide to stay?"

"It'll be okay, *chacteka*." Alex squeezed his shoulder. "I usually work here every day from 6:00 am to 10:00 pm. Now, instead of being here all day, I'll be there from ten thirty to two, but my hours are the same. Don't worry, it will be fine. As far as staying there, we'll cross that bridge when we get to it."

"Okay, if you really want to do this, I won't stop you." Osceola hugged Alex. "I'm proud of you Alex. I can't think of a better chef to showcase our cuisine to the non-natives. You're a superb chef. I know if you stayed there, you would do your best to cook the other natives' foods to perfection."

"Thanks, *chacteka*." Alex patted Osceola on the back at the end of the hug. "Your support means a lot to me."

"You have my support. I love you son. I'll leave you in your kitchen," Osceola walked away, stopped, and spun around. "You will call Thunder?"

"Yes, I'll call him, but I want to talk to my staff first."

"Okay." Osceola nodded. "I'm going out to the casino. See you later."

"Bye *chacteka*." Alex nodded.

Alex thought about the logistics of his decision. Sam and Bernie could fill in for him with the breakfast and lunch crowds. Alex was aware Sam needed the money now that his wife was pregnant, and they had taken in his mom to live with them. He had been an exceptional sous chef for Alex. It was time for him to be the chef at RUSH. Sam would really appreciate the increase in pay.

Bernie would be happy to pick up more hours as well, since his daughter was in college and extra money would come in handy. If this became permanent, he would have to speak to Bernie and Sam again to rework the schedules and maybe hire another chef. Alex texted an impromptu meeting for today at three, ensuring the lunch crew hadn't left yet and the dinner crew was just arriving. It would have to be a quick meeting.

> Alex: Meeting today @3pm in Savor Kitchen.
> Sorry for the late notice.

As soon as he sent the text, his kitchen crew texted back their responses. He wanted everyone who worked for him to know what was going on if they didn't see him during the day. The kitchen crew was like family to him. He believed in complete transparency with them. The crew

knew Alex's door was open to them with any issues or concerns. It helped
that   Alex worked beside them daily and didn't sit behind a desk
telling them what to do.

Alex sent individual texts to Sam and Bernie. It would be good to talk to
them before he brought it up to his entire kitchen crew, just in case they
weren't on board. Alex didn't want to cause them any embarrassment if
they didn't want to fill in for him. Not knowing all their family dynamics,
he wasn't totally sure Bernie or Sam would accept their new hours and
positions. If they didn't want these promotions, he would have to hire
another chef, promote another sous chef, or lose this opportunity for
himself.

> Alex: Can you guys meet with me @2:45? Before the entire crew meeting?
>
> Sam: Absolutely. See you then.
>
> Bernie: Of course.
>
> Alex: Thank you, meet me in Savor's dining room.

Great, now he had a couple of hours of prepping before the meeting.
Time to get back to work.

Chapter 3

A Change of Scenery
Tori

Victoria "Tori" Tall Bear was a caring and nurturing twenty-seven-year-old beautiful Lakota woman who loved her job at the preschool on the reservation. Tori had lived her entire life on the Pine Ridge Reservation with her father, Adam Tall Bear, Mother Dyani, and younger sister Elizabeth "Lizzy".

She loved reading to the little ones and helping them create art with paints, shaving cream, and play doh. This morning she was helping them paint their families as pumpkins with water-based paints on paper. She waited until they went to lunch and hung up the children's artwork. Once that was done, she sat at one of the kiddie tables and ate her peanut butter and jelly sandwich.

"Hey sis." Lizzy walked into the room and plopped down at the table with Tori.

"Hey," Tori said between bites.

"Can you go on a double date with me tonight?"

"No." Tori shook her head. "I thought we agreed I didn't have to go anymore."

"Please Tori," Lizzy begged. "Larry's cousin thinks you're hot, and he wants to double date."

"Jim?" Tori stared at Lizzy. "The guy that doesn't have a job and hangs out at the gas station all day talking to Larry?"

"He's really nice Tori."

"No, I'm not interested. If you want to go out with Larry, tonight take mom and dad."

"Larry's tired of having mom and dad staring at him during our dates.

None of our other friends have chaperones. Why do we?"

"Because dad is very overprotective. Plus, you change boyfriends like underwear. It's hard to keep up and I'm sure dad wants to know what's going on with you. Sorry Lizzy, talk to mom and dad and maybe you guys can figure out another solution to your incessant dating."

"That's not fair," Lizzy stood up abruptly, hitting the table with her knees, "Ouch. I would do it for you."

"Are you okay?"

"Yes, but I'd be better if you agreed to help me."

"I've had to put up with your double dates for years. I'm done. I'm sorry."

"Fine!" Lizzy stomped away. "Be that way."

Tori felt bad, but the last thing she wanted to do tonight was go on a date with Jim. The way he stared at her was a little creepy. Lost in her thoughts, she recalled the time she convinced her parents to let her skip double dating with Lizzy.

Every once in a while, Lizzy would have a date or a friend come to the preschool. It was Lizzy's way of vetting out guys for Tori. Several times Tori gave in to her sister, but not as much as she used to.

Dating was hard for Tori. Between working a lot of hours, her overprotective parents, and a sister setting up blind dates for her—most of which were not her type—Tori's virginity was intact even though several boys tried to claim it.

Tori was part of the approximately 29% of the population on the rez that graduated from high school but didn't attend college. Tori's parents didn't allow her to leave the reservation when she turned eighteen because they felt she wasn't ready to be on her own with no money. It would be very hard for her to make her own way. Their reservation was one of the poorest in the United States and only about 11% of the population attained a bachelor's degree or higher. Being from a poor reservation with only a high school degree makes it very difficult to get out and live anywhere else.

So instead, Tori worked at the preschool on the reservation and loved every minute of working with the little ones. Although she wasn't paid a lot, Tori found the work she did at the preschool on the reservation rewarding enough. Not thinking she would ever leave the reservation, Tori accepted and was happy with her lot in life. She was kind with the children, endearing herself to the parents and the little ones. All the parents loved her and would ask her to Babysit some evenings. Throughout the day, you could find Tori sitting crisscross applesauce on the floor with a small child on her lap while she read to them.

That was where Lizzy found her during afternoon recess time.

"Tori," Lizzy walked over, "*até* is here. He wants to talk to you."

Tori wrinkled her brow, confused because her father usually came to get them, not right after lunch.

"Lizzy, do you know why he's here?" Tori shut the book she was reading to Katie.

"Nope," Lizzy shook her head, "he just asked me to come get you."

"Okay." Tori lifted the little girl off her lap. "Katie, I'll finish the story later."

"Okay, Ms. Tori," Katie said and ran away to play with her friends at the train table.

Tori stood up and followed Lizzy to the front office of the preschool. Her father never came to her job during the day. She hoped everything was okay.

"Lizzy, are you still mad at me?"

"Yes." Lizzy shoulder bumped her. "I told Larry you didn't want to go, and he said Jim would be disappointed, but he still insisted on going out with me tonight."

"That's good. You guys will have some quality time. I just wanted to make sure you and I are okay."

"Yeah, we're good. Deep down, I understand." Lizzy stopped and hugged Tori before rounding the corner toward the front office.

Tori was relieved Lizzy never held a grudge. She would have to agree to chaperone one of their dates in the future without Jim.

"*Hau até.*" Tori hugged her father, Tall Bear. "Is something wrong?"

"*Hiyá c'unksh.* I have an opportunity for you." Tall Bear kissed Tori on her forehead and held her hands in between them.

"Okay." Tori stared at her father. He looked so serious.

"Do you remember Johnny Thunderbird?" Tall Bear asked.

"Of course." Tori nodded. "He is Sarah's brother."

"*Haŋ.*" Tall Bear squeezed her hands. "Thunder direly needs of some help at the cultural center in South Florida. He really depended on having a female there to assist with the local children. Losing Rachel was quite a hit and Sarah had been scrambling to help him, but it was hard for her since she had just had a little girl. I've spoken to the tribal council; we think you would be the best candidate to help Thunder. You are great with our children, you are friends with Sarah, and I know you will listen to Thunder's instructions." Tall Bear stared into Tori's eyes. "But if you don't want to do this, I understand and I will find someone else."

Tori's mouth dropped open when she heard her father was going to let her go to Florida. She knew Tall Bear trusted Thunder and the Rachel issue had been quite a cluster mess, but she never in her wildest dreams thought he would allow her to go that far. After all, he never let her go anywhere without him. Tall Bear was vigilant in watching over his girls.

"Why Tori?" Lizzy whined. "*Até*, I want to go."

"Tori is older and more mature, Lizzy." Tall Bear turned to Lizzy and patiently stated, "It is time for her to find her wings and fly."

"Really, *até*? You're being serious?" Tori whispered, with tears in her eyes.

"*Haŋ, c'unksh.* The vote from the tribal council was unanimous." Tall Bear hugged Tori. "I also discussed it with your *iná*. We agreed you are the best person for this job. We trust you and know you will do a great job."

"I don't know what to say, *até*." Tori pulled back from her dad, "I would be honored and proud to be a part of the American Indian Cultural Center. When do I leave?"

"You can fly out in two days on Sunday. I have spoken with my friend Osceola Panther, he is the manager of the Rock 'n' Roll Resort & Casino. He will have a room ready for you with a connecting door to his daughter Freya's room. Freya will help you get acclimated. You can also reach out to Sarah for more female companionship. I'm sure Thunder will let her know you are coming. If you decide to stay and you don't want to live in the resort, we will find you an apartment. However, you will have more people to watch over you and help you at the resort." Tall Bear explained.

"Okay. It will be great to see Sarah. I haven't really seen her since she left the rez and moved to South Florida. I've missed her. Working at the preschool has been different without her. Thank you for setting up a place for me to live. I would feel uncomfortable in a new apartment in a new town."

Tall Bear raised an eyebrow questioningly, "So, it is settled?"

"*Haŋ*," Tori stood up straight and smiled at her father. "I am ready for this adventure, *até*. I will not let you down."

"I know you won't *c'unksh*," Tall Bear smiled. "I wouldn't have volunteered your name to the tribal council if I wasn't 100% sure you could do it."

"Are you sure I can't go with Tori?" Lizzy begged. "I could keep her out of trouble."

"*Hijá*," Tall Bear laughed, "this is your sister's journey. Besides, I think it would be her keeping you out of trouble, not the other way around."

"Okay, but when I turn twenty-seven *até*, I hope you have an amazing journey for me too." Lizzy crossed her arms and pouted.

"Lizzy," Tori hugged her sister, "let's finish out the day and then you can help me pack. Who knows if you behave maybe *até* will let you visit me." Tori turned around and looked at her father pleadingly.

"Oh," Lizzy jumped up and down facing her father. "Please, please, *até* can I go visit?"

"We will see, *c'unksh*. Let's allow Tori to get settled and then we will discuss a visit." Tall Bear patted her back to comfort her.

"Okay, *até*," Lizzy stood up on her tippy toes and kissed her father's cheek.

Tori laughed at her sister's antics as she tried to convince her father to let her go. Lizzy begged and pleaded for something from their parents. Tori wished she had the courage to be more like Lizzy and embrace new experiences without fear. Now her wish was coming true. She was not only leaving her family behind, but she was also going to n unknown place and meeting new people. Truth be told, she felt very nervous, but excited at the same time. Luckily, Sarah would be there, so she knew she had at least one friend.

Sighing, Tori realized she had a lot to do before she could get on that flight to South Florida. Shockingly, she still couldn't believe her father had volunteered her for this adventure so far away. Tall Bear was not abusive. He'd never raised a hand at his girls, If she wanted to move away, he would've let her go, but she loved living at home with her family. Tori loved having family dinners together. Family and her daily routine were a comfort to her. Never in her wildest dreams would she have thought her father would help to push her into a future outside of the reservation.

"I need to go." Tall Bear kissed both his girls. "I'll come back once both of you are done for the day. I need to talk to the tribal council and let them know Tori has accepted their decision."

"*Pilámaya até,*" Tori thanked him. "We will be done by five today. Laura is taking the late parent pickup time. We'll wait outside."

"*Hiyá,*" Tall Bear looked them both in the eye, "do not wait outside. I will come in to get you."

"*Haŋ até,*" Tori and Lizzy both said at the same time.

"We'll wait in here and be ready to go when you get here," Tori nodded.

"*Pilámaya,*" Tall Bear shook his head, "*aké waŋcíŋyaŋkiŋ ktélo.*"

"*Aké waŋcíŋyaŋkiŋ ktélo,*" both girls said before going back to work.

Feeling invigorated with excitement, and a little fear, Tori finished out her day and went home to prepare for her trip.

Chapter 4

The Call that Changed His Life
Alex

Alex met Sam and Bernie at one table in the back left corner of the dining room. Savor was closed until dinner at four. He knew his staff would be there in about fifteen minutes and he wanted to have some privacy with Sam and Bernie in case that meeting ran a couple of minutes late.

"I called both of you here early because I have something to discuss with you before everyone else gets here," Alex began. "For the next six months, I will work at the American Indian Cultural Center's restaurant during lunch. I know this will put a strain on you both here, so I came up with a plan that will benefit us all."

"Sam," Alex looked at Sam, "I would like to promote you to head chef in RUSH. You will now work the breakfast and lunch crowd. I've been watching you as Bernie's sous chef and I know you are ready to move up."

"Are you serious?" Sam's mouth was hanging open in shock. "I don't know what to say."

"Say you'll take the promotion," Alex laughed. "It will come with more hours, but higher pay."

"Alex," Sam recovered from his shock. "I would love to accept your offer. The extra money will help with the new baby and my mom moving in. Angie and I were thinking I would have to pick up another job, and I really didn't want to have to find a second job."

"Bernie," Alex turned to face him, "I would like to move you to Savor as their head chef. You will now work breakfast and dinner with a break in between unless you want to help Sam, then you can put in a long day. You will also receive an increase in pay."

"I am honored," Bernie accepted immediately, "I know Savor is your baby, and I promise to make you proud in there."

"I know you both will do a great job in your new positions," Alex commented. "I could not have had better candidates for these positions."

"This will help me send money to Callie in college," Bernie confirmed Alex's suspicions about helping his daughter. "She works too hard and pulls all-nighters all the time. Maybe now she can take fewer hours at her job and have more time to study."

"Will you work here at all?" Sam looked panicked. "Are you leaving us?"

"No," Alex shook his head. "I will work there for lunch and then come here. I've been wanting to open RUSH for dinner for a while so when I come back from working there, I'll work here in RUSH. They are closed on Sunday and Monday, so I can fill in wherever you guys need me on those days. We can also rotate our other chefs whenever you need a day off. I'll set up a schedule, but I think we will play it by ear."

"How about when the six months are up?" Sam asked.

"Nothing will change. You will keep your new jobs, and I will become a floater," Alex confirmed, wanting to make them secure in their new pay. "Thunder might keep me on there, but I'm not sure yet. I'm going to take it one day at a time."

"Do we start this schedule next week?" Bernie asked.

"We can start it tomorrow if you guys want," Alex answered.

"Tomorrow would be great," Sam interjected.

"Yes, I would love to start tomorrow." Bernie nodded.

"Tomorrow it is then." Alex stood up to shake their hands, but Bernie pulled Alex into his arms for a big hug. Sam followed suit with a hug after Bernie. Alex had noticed several crew members walking into the kitchen during their meeting.

"Let's go meet with everyone else and tell them our good news." They walked into the kitchen and greeted the crew that was present. As soon as they all arrived, Alex began the meeting.

"Hello, everyone. Thank you all for coming on such short notice." Alex nodded to everyone. "The American Indian Cultural Center will feature an exhibit on the Seminole Tribe of Florida, and I'm going to be their lunchtime chef for the next six months. I won't leave any of you empty-handed." Alex waved his hand toward Sam and Bernie.

"Sam has been promoted to chef in RUSH for breakfast and lunch and Bernie is head chef in Savor. I'll be at AICC from ten thirty to two. I want to have enough prep and cleanup time there. Some of our guests have been requesting a quick bite to eat at dinnertime between gambling, and I want to offer that to them. Therefore, when I finish my shift there, I'll come back here and keep RUSH open for a quick dinner meal. I'm excited I get to do this for the cultural center. I appreciate all of you helping me to make this happen. Although there will be a period of adjustment, we will handle it as we always do. You are all magnificent at your jobs, and I have no worries or concerns. If any of the wait staff would like some extra hours, come see me. I will need three of you to help me in RUSH for the new dinner hours. Does anyone have questions or concerns?" Alex looked around at his employees, watching as they shook their heads no.

"Alex, if we can help you with anything, please let us know," Bernie volunteered. "It sounds like you will be very busy. We are more than happy to lighten your load."

"Thank you all so much." Alex patted Bernie on the back. "This will be something new to me. I appreciate your support. I've never had a better kitchen crew than all of you. We are family, so please, if during these six months something comes up, talk to me and we'll work it out. You all have my cell number. You can call me anytime, even if I'm not here."

"You're the best, boss," Sam cheered.

"Yeah, the best," everyone said as they took turns walking up to Alex hugging and congratulating him. Sam and Bernie also received their fair share of congratulatory hugs and pats on the back.

After Alex thanked everyone, some of his wait staff asked for extra hours. He needed three per shift. Six stepped forward, so he took them all and said he would create a rotation schedule, making sure everyone received an equal number of hours. Once Alex finished talking to everyone, he stepped out to call Thunder.

"*Hau*," Thunder answered, "American Indian Cultural Center, can I help you?"

"Hi Thunder. It's Alex Panther."

"Hi Alex. You found someone already?" Thunder asked, "That was fast."

"Yes, I would like to do it." Alex stated.

"Really? That's great," Thunder sounded stunned. "You working here would be an honor," Thunder expressed. "I couldn't have asked for a better chef. I've tried your food at Savor and it's delicious."

"Thank you." Alex felt humbled. "It sounds like a great opportunity for me to cook my cultural cuisine with some of my own personal flair."

"I'm so glad," Thunder reiterated. "Like I said before. You can set up the menu, but please include Indian fry bread. We have always had that on the menu and our guests love eating it. When can you start? I know the Grayfeather's would love to return home as soon as possible."

"I can start next Monday."

"Great, then you can learn the Lakota cuisine from George Grayfeather. This will allow them to leave before the exhibit ends. They will appreciate that since the Red Path exhibit was only supposed to last four months. My wedding and family issues caused me to extend it."

"I heard about all that. I'm sorry about what happened and I'm glad Isa is doing well. Please let George Grayfeather know I will be there on Monday. What time should I arrive?"

"George and Mary typically come by at approximately ten o'clock, so any time after that works."

"Sounds good. The timing is perfect. My staff is amazing, so I'll only need a couple of days to prepare their new schedules. I'm eager to plan my menu and run it by you before I place the order for the food I need. Your approval would be appreciated. Thank you for the opportunity, Thunder."

"You're welcome. Thank you for wanting to be our chef. I'm looking forward to tasting your meals."

"See you next week."

"Yup, see you then." Thunder replied.

Alex hung up the phone, feeling a burst of energy. He hadn't felt this good about cooking in a long time. After years of cooking the same cuisine, he had been in a rut. This new opportunity was exhilarating. He couldn't wait to plan the menu. He had so many ideas running through his head. Tonight, he would focus on Savor. Tomorrow morning, he would set up the new schedules for his workers and on Monday, he would be ready to go to AICC and talk to George Grayfeather. Bernie and Sam were already eager and familiar with the shifts. Sam had been working with Bernie in RUSH as his sous chef and knew what to do. Bernie sometimes filled in for Alex in Savor. He was aware of the job. Alex knew he could not have taken on this new job if he didn't have Bernie and Sam.

Time to stop daydreaming. Dinner would not cook itself.

Chapter 5

A New Journey Begins
Tori

Sunday, Tori arrived in Fort Lauderdale International Airport on time. For the last two days, she'd told herself she was going to be more social, courageous, and adventurous. Presented with an amazing opportunity, she didn't want to waste any time in her new life.

On her flight, her excitement was so contagious, her seatmates were all congratulating her on her new job by the time they disembarked. Tall Bear told Tori to look for Thunder. He was her ride to the resort. Tori had extra pep to her step as she walked out of the gate heading toward the luggage claim. She had seen Thunder when he went to the rez for his wedding to Isa. She knew she could recognize him. How could you miss a tall, long-haired Oglala Lakota warrior?

She looked around once she arrived in the airport's lobby but didn't see Thunder. Several people were holding signs for fellow travelers. She looked at all the signs and smiled when she saw her name. Beaming, she looked up from the sign, only to see a stranger where Thunder should have been. Not sure how she could have missed him. Surprisingly, Thunder was not holding the sign but a tall, attractive man with brown hair in a man bun and the sides shaved. His brown eyes and nicely trimmed beard and mustache combo covered his face. His bulging muscles were so large his shirt stretched tightly over his arms and chest. Tori could see tattoos on both his arms as he held the sign in front of him. Drawn to him, not just because of the sign, Tori walked forward.

"Hi," the sexy man smiled, "Are you Tori?"

"Hi, yes. Who are you?"

"I'm Alex. Thunder was going to get you, but Isa, his wife, is pregnant and was feeling sick, so he asked me to come get you since I have to drive to the resort, anyway."

"Oh, okay." Tori wasn't sure if he was telling the truth. Without being rude or obvious, she wanted to call Thunder to verify this Alex person but didn't know how to do it without being rude and obvious. Despite her longing for adventure, she also valued her safety. She did not want to get in a car with a sexy stranger that could hurt her.

"I'm assuming you have luggage since you're moving down here?" Alex inquired.

"Yes, I do," Tori walked toward the luggage claim suddenly stopping when she saw the restroom sign. It was a godsend. She would go in there and call Thunder. "Do you mind if I use the restroom?"

"Not at all," Alex replied. "I'll wait for you right here."

"Great," Tori smiled and walked into the restroom. This was a good place to make her call and verify her driver.

"*Hau,*" Thunder answered his cell phone.

"Hi Thunder, it's Tori."

"Tori, I'm so sorry I couldn't come get you. Isa is feeling sick, I didn't want to leave her alone. Is Alex there?" Thunder asked.

"I think so. Does he have brown hair in a man bun, tall, a lot of muscles and tattoos on his arms?" Tori verified.

"Yes. I'm sorry I should've sent a photo of him to you. He usually wears his hair up and is over six-foot, muscular, brown eyes has a mustache and beard."

"Whew," Tori released her breath. "I'm sorry I'm acting crazy."

"You are not acting crazy," Thunder said, "It's good that you're careful. To double check him, look at the back of the poster he's holding. Tommy made your poster and wrote you a message."

"Okay, I'll look at the poster. Thank you, Thunder. I hope Isa feels better soon."

"You and me both," Thunder sighed. "Thank you for understanding. I'll see you tomorrow at nine at the center."

"Sounds good."

Tori used the restroom since she was already there and walked out to find Alex leaning up against the wall people watching.

"Alex," Tori stood in front of him and shifted her weight from one foot to the other, "Can I see the poster?"

"Okayyy," Alex looked at her like she was a loon and handed her the poster.

Tori turned the poster over and saw the message in pencil from Tommy. *Hi Tori, Welcome to Florida. Can't wait to see you. Love Tommy.* Tori smiled at the message.

"What are you smiling at?" Alex asked as he looked at the back of the poster with her.

"Tommy, Thunder's nephew wrote me a message." Tori pointed at the message.

"How did you know?" Alex really looked confused.

"Uh," Tori stared at the floor and winced. "I called Thunder to verify you were who you said you were."

"Smart," Alex pointed a finger at Tori. "I'm glad you're careful."

"You're not mad?" Tori avoided eye contact with Alex.

"Nope." Alex placed his hand under her chin and raised her head to look into her eyes. "It's good to be careful. Now let's go get your luggage."

"Sounds good." Tori said as she followed Alex to the luggage claim.

"When we get there, just point out your bags and I'll get them for you." Alex said.

"Okay," Tori nodded. "Thank you."

Tori stood by the luggage carousel and pointed out her bags. She only had two, which shocked Alex. Tori never bought more than she needed. She spent her money wisely and until now she needed little clothes. That might change since now she worked in a more professional environment and didn't have to worry about babies throwing up on her. Tori followed Alex as he wheeled her luggage to his car. Once there, he unlocked his car and placed her luggage in his trunk. Tori walked to the passenger side and got into his car, waiting for Alex to finish loading her luggage into the trunk.

"So, Tori." Alex started his car, backed up and pulled out of the lot. "Tell me about yourself. It would be nice to know about you since we will work together."

"You work at AICC?" Tori looked at Alex.

"Yes." Alex nodded and merged into traffic. "Thunder hired me as their chef."

"Oh, I guess I knew Thunder would hire a new chef now that the Red Path Exhibit was ending, but I didn't realize he chose someone. Do you know what the new exhibit is about? What tribe are you from?" Tori turned in her seat, fully facing Alex for his answer.

"I'm from the Seminole Tribe of Florida. I live and work at the Rock 'n' Roll Resort & Casino. My father is a member of our tribal council, which runs the resort and casino. I'm the head chef, my mom runs our hospitality desk for the hotel, my sister is a dealer, and my brother is part of our security team. Hence why Thunder asked me to come get you since we're heading to the same place." Alex glanced at her while focusing on traffic.

"Wow, it's a family affair. I've heard of the casino from my dad, Tall Bear. If you are the head chef at the casino, how are you going to be our chef?" Tori asked, puzzled.

Tori turned to watch the scenery outside her window. Having never been to Florida, Tori found everything outside her window to be so different from what she was used to on the reservation. So many differences exist between the two unique landscapes. The reservation had the Badland mountains and no palm trees. Here she didn't see any mountains. The terrain was flat with many palm trees. There were countless exits on the busy highway. On the rez, they didn't have a highway, just one road in and out with other roads as you came closer to the center part of town.

"I didn't realize you were Tall Bear's daughter." Alex nodded. "I've met him several times when he was at the resort, and I was head chef at Savor. Currently, I promoted two of my other chefs so I could focus on the AICC. I love working with my family, but this will be a great opportunity for me. I'll work the lunchtime food service for Thunder and the dinner service at one of our restaurants at the casino," Alex explained.

"Wow, busy guy." Tori was stunned by his work ethic. He must really love his job. Tori kept glancing at Alex out of the corner of her eye. How could she not? He was so handsome and masculine. "What about after the six months are up?"

"Not sure," Alex exited the highway, "I told my employees I would not demote them, so I'll just be a floating chef or maybe I'll stay on with Thunder. We'll figure it out. How do you know Thunder?" Alex asked.

"I'm Oglala Lakota and grew up on the same rez with Thunder and his sister Sarah. As a matter of fact, Sarah and I worked at the preschool together. I've missed her since she left and moved down here. I can see why she wanted to move here. It's so pretty and sunny. Really, I know Sarah better than Thunder. Anyway, my father is the president of our tribal council. He thought I would be the best fit to be Thunder's assistant. So here I am," Tori shrugged after she quit rambling.

"Well, welcome. Let me park the car around the side and I'll help you get your luggage to the front desk so my mom can check you in."

"Don't you have to get to work? You can drop me off at the front. I can carry my luggage." Tori protested while Alex parked.

"It's not a problem." Alex stepped out of the car and pulled her luggage out of the trunk. "This won't take long. I can take your luggage to your room and get back to work. These are the perks of being a floating chef." Alex smiled and waved her ahead of him.

Chapter 6

How Lucky was She?
Tori

Alex opened the side door to let Tori enter before him and led her to the front desk.

"*Chatski,*" Alex greeted his mother behind the desk. "This is Tori, Tall Bear's daughter. She's working for Thunder and her dad said you had a room for her."

"Hi Tori. Yes, we do. We've been expecting you. She'll be staying with us for as long as she wants." Sehoy came out from around the desk and hugged Tori. "It's so good to meet you. I've heard so many wonderful things about you from your father. We love when he comes and stays with us."

"Hi Mrs. Panther." Tori stepped back from the hug.

"Oh, please call me Sehoy." Sehoy held Tori's hand in both of hers while she spoke to her.

"Alex," Sehoy turned to her son. "Can you take her to the adjoining suite next to your sister? Tori, if you need anything, my daughter Freya will be there. She has the night off so she can give you a grand tour of our beautiful resort and casino."

"That is so kind of you, Sehoy. Thank you so much for letting me stay here. My father has always spoken so highly of all of you and your beautiful resort and casino."

"Oh, my sweet girl, it is our pleasure." Sehoy released Tori and spoke to her son. "Alex, after you drop off her luggage, knock on your sister's door. She is expecting Tori. Give me one second and I'll give you the keycard to your room."

Sehoy walked behind the desk and worked her magic on the computer to generate Tori's keycard. Tori looked around the lobby while Sehoy was tapping away on her computer. Everything was so elegant and beautiful. She noticed the beautiful stone fountain in the center of the lobby separating the two restaurants. One restaurant looked fancier than the other one. Next to the casual dining restaurant, she saw the women's restroom and an entrance to the casino.

"Here you go Tori." Sehoy handed her the card. Tori turned when she heard Sehoy's voice.

"Thank you again, Sehoy." Tori smiled widely at Sehoy.

"Thanks, *chatski*." Alex grabbed Tori's luggage and headed toward the elevators.

"Tori, make sure you use this elevator." Alex pointed to the one at the end of the hallway. This is the only one that goes to our floor. My siblings and I are all on the top floor, the penthouse floor. To access our floor, you MUST scan your keycard before you push the floor number. If you don't do that, you can't get to our floor. We put this in place for security reasons." Alex escorted Tori into the elevator and held out his hand. "Let's use your keycard so we can make sure it works."

Tori handed her new keycard to Alex, observing what he did.

"You all live here?"

"We do." Alex gave her the keycard back. "We work a lot of long hours and since we're all single, we here together. At one time, my parents used the room you're staying in, but they moved into a house a few years ago."

When the elevator doors opened, Alex stepped out and waited for Tori to follow him.

"Your room is the last door on the right. In case of emergency, the stairs across your room in front of the gym." Alex pointed toward each room as he pointed them out. "Next to you is Frey, my sister. You both share an adjoining door. The door here to my right is Holt's room. He's Barrett's best friend and works security with him." Alex left her luggage in front of the elevator and turned to the left.

"This door is the laundry room with access to our 'family only' security room with monitors to watch the cameras around the resort and casino. We programmed this door to only open for family members. Try your keycard and make sure it works so you can wash your clothes." Alex waited and watched her keycard open the door.

"Perfect." Alex stood outside while Tori walked in, looked around, and walked back out. "When the laundry room door closes, it locks automatically. The last two doors are Barrett, my brother, who monitors the security cameras—hence the security room—and my room is at the end. This gym is for family only the same as this sitting area.

"There are automatic blinds you can activate, but since it's only us using it, we usually leave the blinds open. Try your keycard here too. This door works just like the laundry room." Alex followed her into the gym and pointed out the different equipment. "We have a yoga mat, free weights, treadmills, and ellipticals in here. On that counter is the remote for the TV. Come in and use this room anytime you want."

"Wow." Tori looked around in awe of what she was seeing. "This is really nice, thank you."

"You're welcome." Alex held the door open for her. "Let's get you to your room now that you've seen our floor."

Alex retrieved her luggage from where he left it in front of the elevator and met Tori by her door as she used her keycard and held it open for Alex to roll in her suitcases. Tori had never been in a hotel room, let alone a beautiful one like this one. The room had an open floor plan. On the right was a small kitchenette.

"It's nice to have a full-size refrigerator and stove/oven combo. Unfortunately, I'm not a great cook."

"Well, lucky for you, I'm a talented chef and I can help you with that."

"Skilled chef?"

"My cuisine has earned Savor great reviews from food critics and made it one of the top-rated eating restaurants."

"That's impressive. I didn't realize we have such a skilled chef at the cultural center."

Directly in front of the kitchenette was a long island with the sink facing a dining room table with seating for six. On the left, there was a long, narrow foyer table with a vase of beautiful flowers. Continuing straight in was the living room with two couches, two end tables with lamps, one cocktail table, a large screen TV, and floor to ceiling glass windows with a breathtaking view of Sunrise, Florida.

"This is a great surprise. I thought I would only have a bedroom with a bathroom. I never thought I'd have a suite."

"We aim to please." Alex shrugged.

Alex left her luggage in the living room. Opening the door to her left, Tori walked into a room with a queen size bed, two nightstands, a smaller-size TV, and those beautiful windows facing outside on the side and back of the bed making the room feel like it was floating in the sky. Continuing into the room, she saw the large closet on the left before the door to the bathroom. Despite the bedroom being surrounded by glass on all sides, the bathroom had a wall for complete privacy. The bathroom had a modern design with light tile flooring, a silver quartz counter, and black cabinets underneath. This design was the same as the kitchen design. A beautifully tiled white with silver accents shower at the end with a rain shower and regular shower head. The bathroom had a pocket door with access to the closet.

Tori left the bedroom and headed to Alex in the living room with her mouth open. She was stunned by her living quarters.

"By the smile on your face, I'm going to assume you like your accommodations?" Alex asked.

"What's not to like? It's all so beautiful."

"Come here. Let me show you how the blinds work." Alex reached for the remote on the cocktail table and waited for Tori. "If all the windows make you feel weird, push this button. It closes the automated blinds, and the room will feel enclosed. It will give you more privacy whenever you want it. These are the same blinds that are in your bedroom and in the gym."

"Alex, this suite is beautiful," Tori whispered. "I'm honored your family is putting me up in this room on your family floor."

"We're happy to have you."

Alex walked to the door between the TV and dining room table and opened it. Tori saw another door and realized it must be the adjoining door to Freya's room.

"Frey," Alex knocked loudly.

"Coming." Freya's voice echoed as she unlocked her door.

"Hey bro." Freya opened the door, tucking her shirt into her pants, and hugged Alex.

"Meet Tori," Alex kissed Freya on the cheek. "Tori, this is Freya. Sorry to leave you ladies, but I must get to work downstairs. Frey, I showed Tori around this floor, so you can give her a tour of everything else."

"Hi Tori," Freya walked to Tori. "I'm so glad to have a suite mate."

"Hi Freya," Tori hugged Freya back. "I can't believe you live here. This is so beautiful." Tori spun around the room quickly and caught Alex staring at her backside. Was he checking her out?

"Tori, I'll see you tomorrow at the cultural center. What time do you have to be there? I'll give you a ride." Alex offered as he stood by Tori's front door.

"Thunder said to be there at nine in the morning." Tori looked at Alex.

"Okay, I'll take you. I need to get an early start, anyway. I'll knock on your door around eight-thirty. It should only take us fifteen to twenty minutes to get there." Alex opened the door and turned around. "Is that okay with you?"

"Yes, that would be great." Tori smiled at Alex. "Thank you."

"Sure, no problem." Alex nodded. "See you tomorrow. Bye Frey."

"Bye, bro," Freya hollered back.

Alex

Shit, Tori was so beautiful and sexy. His life was looking up. Not only did he have a great job, but he would be working with a beautiful woman. Tori was very petite with beautiful, light brown skin. Her long, silky black hair and her dark brown eyes were stunning. She took his breath away when he first laid eyes on her. Alex would enjoy being her chauffeur for as long as she needed one.

Work for him at the AICC didn't start until ten thirty, but he would start early without pay just to see her and spend some time with her. He could familiarize himself with the kitchen and clean it up if necessary while he waited for George and Mary. Alex had never fallen so hard for a woman so quickly. He dated, but nothing serious because he was constantly working. Candice was his one serious relationship, but she dumped him after a year because of his lack of commitment. He wasn't a commitment-phoebe. He was more focused on furthering his career. Candice didn't want to wait for him to make a name for himself as a well-sought chef, and he wasn't ready to rush into a marriage. They agreed to split up, and these days he mostly engaged in one-night stands in his dating life.

Tori had awoken feelings in him he'd never felt before. He wanted to take care of her, protect her from anything and anyone, and just be around her. She had such a calming, tender way about her that was endearing. The abundance of feelings he had for her in such a short time shocked him. Lucky for him, he could offer his carpooling services and work with her. That would give him plenty of time to get to know her.

Alex walked down to the casino floor to find his brother Barrett before he had to go to work and let him know Tori was here. Barrett and Freya were twins and a few years younger than him. As the older brother, he looked out for them. Barrett worked with the security team, and Freya was a blackjack dealer. Barrett and Holt alternated between the Family Only security room and the casino floor. Barrett liked to know who was on the family floor for safety purposes, hence why Alex was trying to find him. All the other security guards used the monitors in the lobby behind the lobby desk.

Alex and Barrett had adjoining suites and often left their doors open because Alex liked to see the security footage when he wasn't in the kitchen. However, if either was entertaining, they would close and lock their door. That was their code for 'Do Not Disturb'. Having two ladies on their floor meant they would have to be more vigilant about any visitors. The brothers were both raised to care for and protect women. They took it seriously. No one was getting hurt on their watch if they could help it.

"Barrett," Alex called out before he walked up behind his brother on the casino floor.

"Hey bro," Barrett turned around and greeted Alex, "What's up? What are you doing here? Shouldn't you be cooking something?"

"I'm heading to the kitchen now, but I wanted you to know Tori arrived and is staying in Frey's adjoining suite. Mom and Dad gave Frey the night off so she can give Tori a tour. I'm sure you'll see them later." Alex stood with his arms crossed, watching everyone playing.

"Is she hot?" Barrett wiggled his eyebrows.

"Yes," Alex smirked, "but I saw her first."

"Ah, I see how it is. You like her."

"I do," Alex grinned, "so hands off Romeo."

"Okay, okay." Barrett held up his hands in a stop motion. "I'll keep my hands to myself and watch over her for you."

"Thanks bro," Alex nodded and slapped Barrett on the back. "See you later."

"Later."

Alex headed to Savor's kitchen and worked.

Chapter 7

Resort Tour Time
Tori

"He's pretty cute, huh?" Freya nudged Tori's shoulder.

"Huh?" Tori turned to look at Freya as soon as Alex left the room.

"Alex. You think he's cute," Freya insisted.

"What makes you think that?" Tori mumbled.

"Duh, the way you look at him." Freya snorted. "All the girls look at him like that."

"He is very handsome, but I'm not looking for a relationship. I want to focus on my new job. It's important for me to make my family proud while I'm down here helping Thunder. Sending me here is such an honor and I feel a lot of pressure to succeed."

"I totally understand feeling pressure from your family to succeed and make them proud. I feel that every day." Freya smirked and wrapped her arm around Tori's arm, leading her toward the front door. "But I still think you like Alex. Let's unpack later. Since Alex showed you this floor, I'll give you a tour of the casino, restaurants, and the pool."

"That would be great. Thank you, Freya."

"Of course. Before we leave, did Alex let you know you need your keycard to enter this floor?" Freya asked.

"He did."

"Perfect. Now let's go downstairs. Are you hungry? It'll be dinner soon." Freya spoke as they entered the elevator to go down. "We have two restaurants. Savor serves a full breakfast menu and gourmet dinners while RUSH serves a continental quick breakfast with a full coffee bar and American bar foods for lunch and now dinner. Alex told us a couple days ago he would open RUSH for a quick dinner. So before if you wanted to see

Alex for dinner you had to go to Savor, but now he'll be in RUSH. Although knowing Alex, he'll probably jump between RUSH and Savor." Freya glanced at Tori. "Just saying."

Tori didn't miss the mischievous glance Freya sent her way, but ignored it. Alex was a sexy, nice guy, but she needed to stay focused.

"I am a little hungry. Can we go to the casual dining for something quick and light?" Tori asked.

"Of course. First let's stop by Savor so you can see it and then we'll eat in RUSH. After we eat, we'll see the pool since there is a door from RUSH to the pool and then wander around the casino." Freya led Tori to Savor.

"Hi Amy," Freya spoke to the hostess. "This is Tori. She is one of our special guests who will live with us for a while. I just wanted to give her a tour."

"Hi Frey." Amy waved, "Tour away. It's nice to meet you, Tori."

"Nice to meet you as well, Amy."

Tori looked around the elegantly decorated dining area. All the tables had a candlelit centerpiece atop a pressed black tablecloth. The interior design had a modern look with black walls above the light gray wainscoting panels. Looking around, she saw many paintings of American Indians and Florida landscapes. Several chandeliers hung from the ceilings around the room to give a romantic setting. Tori listened to Freya's explanation of the foods served there and the atmosphere they tried to achieve. Freya continued to walk by the staff and introduce Tori while she spoke, leading her into the kitchen.

Tori walked into a spotless but active kitchen. Freya introduced her to everyone in the kitchen, including the head chef, Bernie.

"Bernie." Freya side hugged a big, large middle-aged man wearing an apron while he plated the food. "This is Tori. She'll be staying with us on the family floor for a while. Tori, this is Bernie, our new head chef at Savor."

"Hi Bernie." Tori stuck out her hand to shake his. "It's nice to meet you."

"You too," Bernie raised his hands and replied, "sorry I can't shake your hand since right now, but I look forward to making you a meal sometime."

"Is Alex in RUSH tonight?" Freya asked him.

"Yep," Bernie smiled down at Freya. "That boy is going to wear himself out running from here to there all night."

"Don't let him fool you. Alex thrives on challenges. He is the most hard-working person I know. He loves going between restaurants." Freya kissed his cheek. "We are heading over there now. See you later."

"Bye Frey. Nice to meet you Tori," Bernie waved, "I hope to see you eating here soon."

"I will some other night," waved back. "Tonight, I'm tired from my flight, and I just want to grab a quick bite to eat and unpack."

"I totally understand." Bernie turned around to grab the head of lettuce for the salad he was preparing. "Talk to you later."

Tori and Freya said goodbye and walked to RUSH. Freya introduced her to Tiffany, John, and Jane, the wait staff working at RUSH tonight, as she headed into the kitchen. She spotted Alex behind the center counter making sandwiches. He was wearing his white chef's shirt—sans hat—and black slacks. Freya grabbed her arm and dragged her over to him.

"Freya, he's busy. Let's not interrupt him," Tori whispered and tried to get out of Freya's grip.

"Nah, I come in here all the time," Freya said loudly as they approached Alex. "He is so talented he can multitask. Right Alex?"

"Yup." Alex glanced up. "I see Frey is giving you the full tour. Are you hungry?"

"We were just going to get a quick bite to eat." Freya smiled brightly at Alex.

"I can make you ladies something." Alex was piling cheese into a turkey sandwich. "What would you like?"

"One of those would be great." Tori pointed to the sandwich. "Is that a turkey and cheese sandwich?"

"Yup." Alex grinned. "I'll make you a fresh one. Order up!" Alex yelled and placed his finished dish on the top shelf ready to be picked up and served.

"Tori," Alex grabbed a sub roll and sliced it. "What do you want on your sandwich?"

"Can I get turkey, cheese, lettuce, tomato, and a little mayo?" Tori inquired.

"Yup," Alex grabbed the turkey. "What kind of cheese do you want?"

"Provolone, please." Tori was fascinated watching Alex. It wasn't like he was making her beef wellington, but he cooked with such ease, and he had such manly hands. Hands that would feel so nice on her body. *Whoa, where did that thought come from?* Tori wasn't a skilled cook. She never had to cook since she lived at home, and her mom cooked all their meals. Sometimes she helped her mom in the kitchen on the weekends, but during the week, dinners were already done by the time she arrived home from work. She didn't hate cooking, just didn't get the chance to cook very often.

"Got it." Alex finished her sandwich. "Anything else you want on it?"

"No, that's good." Tori reached for her plate. "Thank you."

"No problem," Alex grinned. "If you want chips, they are behind you on the counter. Frey, what do you want?"

"I'll have the same." Frey kissed his cheek. "It looks good."

"Done." Alex prepared Freya's sandwich and handed her the plate.

"Alright, well, I wanted Tori to see you in all your glory. See you later, bro." Freya winked at Alex and turned around. Tori's eyes widened at Freya's comment, and her mouth dropped open.

"All my glory, huh?" Alex pointed to himself, giving Tori a sexy grin.

Oh, my lord, Tori thought as she felt heat rising on her face and stared at Freya. Tori couldn't believe Freya had said that to Alex.

Alex chuckled. "See you later, girls. Don't do anything I wouldn't do on your day off."

"Well, that means we can do just about anything, Tori." Freya laughed as she pulled Tori out of the kitchen.

"Not what I meant, Frey!" Alex shouted.

Freya opened the door to the outside seating. "Let me show you the poolside eating area. You can sit out here at a table or the bar." Freya pointed everything out as they held their plates and walked around outside. "There's our exceptional pool with a hot tub hidden behind those bushes on the right."

"This resort is so spectacular." Tori didn't know where to look. Lounge chairs and tables with umbrellas for shade surrounded the pool. The kidney-shaped pool had a cascading waterfall in the middle, with a slide on the side leading into the pool. She couldn't see the hot tub, but would look for it later.

"It's hot out. Let's eat inside. I like to eat outside when it's cooler or if I'm in my bathing suit. After we finish eating, I'll give you a tour of the casino," Freya led Tori back into RUSH and chose a table for them.

"Hey Frey." Tiffany walked up to their table. "What do you ladies want to drink?"

"I'll have water please," Tori answered.

"Water for me too," Freya repeated. "Thanks Tiffany."

"So, tell me something about yourself," Freya said before taking a bite of her sandwich.

"Well," Tori opened her bag of chips and dumped them onto her plate. "I've never lived off of the reservation. This is all so new to me."

"Wow, I lived on our reservation when I was little, but as soon as this resort opened, we moved into the penthouse. My mom and dad lived in your room and kept the door open to my room. My brother Barrett and I are twins and we stayed in the same room until he was around sixteen, then his friend Holt moved here, and they roomed together. Alex, being the eldest, had his own room."

"Did Holt lose his parents? Why did he move here?"

"No," Freya sighed. "It's a long story. They ignored him and were glad when my dad stepped in and took over his care."

"I can't even imagine not having supportive parents." Tori drank some water.

"Yeah, Holt is more reserved than Barrett, but a nice guy. I'll introduce you to them when we go inside the casino. Of course, none of them is as attractive as Alex." Freya wiggled her eyebrows.

"Have you ever dated Holt?" Tori chose that moment to change the subject. She wasn't falling for Freya's attempt to find out how much Tori found Alex attractive.

"Uh…no." Freya bumped her. "He's like a brother to me. I don't think he likes me that way."

Continuing to get to know each other, they both realized they were twenty-seven and had similar interests in hobbies, books, and boys. Once they finished eating, Freya let Tori know the food was on the house.

"What do you mean on the house?" Tori asked.

"Anytime you eat in one of our restaurants, you don't have to pay." Freya smiled. "We consider you our special guest and we will make sure you feel like part of the family."

"Wow," Tori's eyes widened in disbelief, "that is so nice of all of you."

"Your father has spent a considerable amount of money gambling here, and my father holds their friendship and Thunder's in high regard."

"Thank you, Freya. This is all very kind of you and your parents."

"Call me Frey. That's what my closest friends and family call me."

"Okay, thanks Frey."

They thanked Tiffany for clearing their plates. Leaving the restaurant after eating and not paying was a strange custom for Tori. Even though Tori lived nowhere other than the reservation, her family took some trips to surrounding areas, eating at various restaurants. It was a strange feeling to not pay for the food provided.

"Now, follow me to the heart of our home."

Chapter 8

Overwhelming Energy and Excitement
Tori

Freya guided Tori out of RUSH, through the lobby, and opened the door to the casino. Tori stopped short inside the casino. She had never been inside a large casino like this one. All the noise from the slot machines was overwhelming as soon as they opened the door. The door into the casino must be soundproof because it was so quiet and soothing in the lobby. Then, when she walked into the casino, she heard a hubbub of noises and activity. So much excitement and energy flowed from within this room. Walking in, Tori noticed it was two floors with a large opening in the middle to view the extravagantly elegant chandelier hanging from the ceiling.

The room displayed a decoration of rich variations of dark brown carpet with intricate, muted American Indian patterns. Tori could see groupings of eight slot machines back-to-back in a circle with comfortable chairs for seating. As they continued to walk to the center of the room, Tori saw all the gambling tables.

"Frey." Tori looked around, taking everything in. "This is all so beautiful. What are they playing? I've never been to a casino."

"Okay," Freya said, "let's walk around and I'll tell you what game they are playing on each table and give you a brief explanation."

Freya walked Tori around and explained Baccarat, Craps, Poker, Blackjack, Roulette, and the slots. Again, Freya introduced her to everyone they passed and showed Tori the table where she usually worked.

Tori felt overwhelmed as she tried to remember everyone's names in the restaurants and casino and understand the gambling game rules, causing her head to spin. After they finished on the first floor, Freya pointed out the restrooms by the staircase and let her know they were in the same location on the second floor before they climbed the stairs. The second floor, which was also carpeted, had a bar and seating with slot machines along one wall. Tori went to the center, leaned on the wrought iron fencing, and looked down onto the gaming tables on the first floor. She didn't gamble, but it was hard not to feel everyone's excitement.

"This is cool," Tori mumbled. "I can't believe I'm going to be living here."

"It is," Freya sighed. "I forget how incredible it is to live here. I guess you take things for granted when you have them every day. Come on, let's get a drink from the bar." Tori followed Freya to the bar.

"Tori, this is Carl." Freya introduced Tori to the Bartender working behind the bar upstairs.

"Hi Tori." Carl put down a napkin on the bar in front of them. "What can I get you ladies?"

"I'll have a frozen Strawberry Margarita with a pretty umbrella," Freya replied immediately.

"You do like your pretty drinks." Carl laughed. "Tori, what would you like?"

"I've never had a drink." Tori looked to Freya for help.

"She'll have the same, but not too strong," Freya told Carl, then turned to Tori, "I think you'll like it. It's sweet and Carl won't add too much alcohol since it's your first time."

"Thanks, Frey." Tori smiled and glanced around. "It's fun just people watching."

"It is. Unfortunately, I don't get to do that often." Freya turned around to see who was on the floor. "When I'm here, I'm usually working. I used to gamble sometimes when I was younger, but now I hate losing my money. Have you ever gambled?" Frey asked.

"No." Tori shook her head. "My dad is the only gambler in the family."

"Yup," Freya laughed. "He's played at my blackjack table. He's won, he just loses more than he wins."

"Here you go, ladies." Carl placed their drinks on the napkins in front of them. "Let me know if you need anything else."

"Thank you." Tori smiled and faced Carl. "This is really pretty."

"Thanks, Carl." Freya picked up her drink. "A toast to my new BFF. I think we will be great friends."

"You make me feel so welcome Frey, thank you." Tori clinked her glass. "I'll drink to that."

"Hey sis, whatcha doin'?" Tori heard a voice behind her and turned around. First thing she noticed was a sexy muscular man dressed in a suit that was straining against his muscles and bore a strong resemblance to Alex.

"Hey little bro," Freya said and hugged him.

"By only a minute," Barrett huffed.

"Tori." Freya put her arm around Tori. "This is our little brother, Barrett. Barrett...Tori."

"Hi Tori." Barrett stuck out his hand for a handshake. "We're twins, technically we're the same age. But because I came out of the womb one minute after her, Frey seems to think I am her little brother." Barrett shoulder bumped Freya. "Tori, it's nice to meet you. Alex told me you were here and Frey's suite mate."

"Hi Barrett. It's nice to meet you."

"Are you girls going to play?" Barrett crossed his arms and widened his stance.

"No," Tori said at the same time Freya said yes.

Tori and Freya both stared at each other and burst out laughing.

"No, Frey," Tori looked at Freya and shook her head, "I still need to unpack and get ready for my first day tomorrow at the cultural center. Maybe another time."

"I think you should call it a night too, Frey." Tori heard another voice coming from behind her and turned around. Did they breed sexy, muscular guys here?"

"Tori, this is Holt." Freya rolled her eyes at Tori and pointed toward him. "He grew up with us and is my third overprotective brother."

Tori didn't miss the longing look in Holt's eyes when he looked at Freya. Tori didn't think he thought of Freya as a sister. There was no doubt in Tori's mind—he was into Freya, and she was oblivious. What a shame. They made a cute couple.

"Hi Tori," Holt held out his hand to shake Tori's.

"Hi Holt. Nice to meet you."

"You too," Holt turned to Freya. "Why don't you help Tori unpack?"

"Ugh, fine," Freya sighed. "Let's go Tori, we'll finish our drinks in your room. Their overprotective meter is off the chain tonight."

Freya turned and stormed off grabbing Tori's hand on her way. Tori looked over her shoulder to raise her glass goodbye and saw Barrett had already walked away, but Holt was staring at Freya.

They went back to Tori's room and Freya helped her unpack her luggage while they drank their margaritas before falling back on the bed when they finished.

"Tori," Freya turned her head toward her, "This has been a great night. Are you okay if we leave the adjoining door open? I love knowing I have a friend next door."

"I would like that," Tori looked at Freya and nodded. "I'm not used to being all alone in a quiet room."

"Great." Freya swung her legs to the side and stood. "You look tired. I'll leave you alone so you can get to sleep. Give me your empty glass. I'll take it down tomorrow."

"Thank you, Frey." Tori handed her the glass. "I'm so glad I have you here to help me out."

"You're welcome." Freya placed both glasses in her hand and hugged Tori. "Get some sleep and good luck on your first day tomorrow. Have fun with Alex on your way to work." Freya wiggled her eyebrows.

"There's nothing going on." Tori raised her hands in frustration. "I've just met him."

"Thou dost protest too much," Freya smirked. "There is such a thing as love at first sight."

"You're crazy." Tori shook her head and changed the subject. "What about you and Holt?"

"Me and Holt?" Freya's eyes widened. "Growing up, Barrett and Holt were thicker than thieves, and I tagged along. I told you he doesn't think of me that way. You'd know if you saw how many girls he dates and fucks. I had a crush on him when we were in high school, but he never gave me the time of day, so I moved on."

"Well, I think he's changed his mind." Tori followed Frey to the adjoining door.

"Not likely," Freya sighed, "anyway, have a great day tomorrow. When do you get off work?"

"I think five," Tori said as she pulled her door open all the way.

"Come get me when you get home." Freya opened her door all the way as well. "I go to work around six and work until around two in the morning. I want to hear about how your first day went."

"Okay." Tori hugged Freya. Leaving their doors open, they both headed toward their respective bedrooms.

Tori walked into the bathroom to wash her face and brush her teeth. Walking into the closet, she put on her pajamas and headed to bed. As a going away present, her dad had bought her an inexpensive kindle so she wouldn't have to take all her books on the plane. The day before she left home, she set up a Kindle Unlimited account and downloaded books to read. Grabbing her kindle from her nightstand, she curled up in bed and chose a new smutty alpha male romance novel. Just because she was a virgin didn't mean she didn't know how to pleasure herself. Some of her books were very steamy and put her in the mood for a sexy time. Book boyfriends were the best. They never let you down and always put you first. Not to mention the hot covers.

Alex's image popped into her head. No, she couldn't date someone she worked with even though she felt a pull toward Alex. Today, when Alex's hand had touched hers on her luggage handle, she'd felt a tingle in her hand and butterflies in her stomach. She felt a powerful attraction to Alex, but she would never act on it. It could never work out between them.

What if something happened, and they broke up? Then they would have to work together and that would be uncomfortable. If it became awkward, she wouldn't be able to do her job properly. No, she couldn't date Alex—no matter how attractive she thought he was.

Chapter 9

The First Day of a Great Adventure
Alex

Alex woke up at five every day and went to the family gym to work out. The resort had a gym on the first floor, but they preferred to stumble into their gym in their running shorts and no shirt to work out in private. When Barrett and Holt were sophomores in high school, they shared the same suite. Holt's parents divorced, and neither of them paid attention to him. Holt's mom and Sehoy had a conversation, and Sehoy offered to have Holt stay with Barrett. Holt's parents agreed. They both wanted to date other people and not having to take care of a teenage boy was a relief to them.

During that time, Osceola and Sehoy were living on the family floor. They stayed on the family floor until Barrett and Freya turned twenty-one. Before Barrett and Holt turned eighteen, the casino floor did not allow them access since they were minors, but they loved watching the monitors to spot potential cheating customers. Osceola didn't want them to bother the security team, so he turned the kid's playroom into the 'family only' security room. It kept them out of the way, and if they saw something strange, they would notify the security officers on the first floor so they could investigate the situation.

Once Barrett and Holt turned twenty-one, Holt moved into his own suite next to Freya and they joined the security team. Physical fitness was a requirement and their early morning workouts became a routine. Barrett and Holt joined Alex in the gym around six unless they had a late night, then Alex worked out alone with his ear buds. Not only did working out keep them in shape, but the ladies loved to see a buff chef and security officers. Alex didn't take advantage of his physique, but Barrett and Holt were constantly being propositioned.

"Hey Bro," Barrett said as he stepped into the gym with Holt.

"Hey," Alex answered from his run on the treadmill.

"I met your Tori last night." Barrett stepped onto another treadmill and began his run.

"She's hot." Holt climbed on the elliptical.

"Hands off buddy," Alex smirked at Holt.

"Yeah, Holt," Barrett looked at Holt, "she's mine."

"Fucker," Alex stared at Barrett, "she's not yours."

"Ooooh, are you guys going to fight it out?" Holt egged them on.

"Nope," Alex sounded confident, "nothing to fight out. She's mine and Romeo over there knows it." Alex pointed at Barrett.

"I got it, bro," Barrett shook his head, smiling, "it's nice to see you are so excited about a girl."

"Yeah," Holt busted out laughing, "Barrett told me. We just wanted to bust your balls."

"Figures," Alex grumbled, running faster.

Holt and Barrett followed suit, and they all placed their ear buds in one ear to listen to their own types of music.

Alex finished his five-mile run and moved onto the floor mats for his daily 200 pushups and 300 crunches. He switched between one handed, knuckle, and regular pushups. The last exercise he did was fifty burpees. Despite his dislike for burpees, he appreciated the outcome.

"Alright boys," Alex called out after his workout and waved, "have a great day."

"See ya'," Holt and Barrett hollered.

Entering his room, Alex showered and dressed in one of his white chef shirts, black slacks and black comfortable work shoes for the day. At 8:30 am, he wasted no time and immediately knocked on Tori's door.

"Good morning," Alex said when Tori opened her door. He'd leaned his shoulder on the door frame with his hands in his pockets and legs crossed at the ankles.

Alex couldn't believe he wasn't drooling after seeing Tori in her sexy tight skirt and fitted blouse. It was going to be hard staying away from her today. Luckily, he would be in the kitchen, and there was a wall between them. She would be an enormous distraction if he could see her from the kitchen. He would hate to lose a finger while prepping his food on the cutting board.

"Good morning," Tori answered, dressed in a nice blouse, skirt, and black high heels. "Let me just get my jacket and purse."

"Of course," Alex stepped away from the door, "I'll be by the elevator."

Tori grabbed her items and joined Alex.

"You look very nice," Alex looked down her body and complimented Tori.

"Thank you." Tori looked down at herself. "I wasn't sure what to wear, and I thought it would be best to go with professional rather than sloppy."

"Somehow," Alex held the elevator door open for her, "I don't think you could ever dress sloppy."

"Well," Tori blushed, "you should have seen what I wore to work at the preschool."

"Get thrown up on a lot?" Alex smirked.

"Daily," Tori laughed. "If I'm being honest, I only own one other blouse and skirt." Tori stared straight ahead. "I think shopping is in my future, and I don't really know where to go."

"That's a no brainer," Alex stepped out of the elevator and held the door open for her, "Frey would love to go shopping with you. It's her favorite pastime. She loves the big mall down the street."

"I would like that," Tori smiled. "I'll have to ask her and maybe we can go on her next day off."

Alex led Tori to the lobby desk and opened the side door on their way to his car. Alex felt a jolt as Tori lightly brushed by him on her way out. The heat of her shoulder against his chest sent shockwaves throughout his body. He couldn't wait to explore these feelings with her.

Chivalry was not dead within Alex. He opened the car door, helped her into the seat, and shut the door. Sehoy would be disappointed with his behavior if he didn't act like a gentleman. She prided herself on raising him and Barrett to look after women and treat them with respect.

He would love to drive Tori to work every day and see her radiant smile for the rest of his life. Whoa! Alex stumbled on his way to the driver's side. Where did that thought come from? I'd just met her yesterday. How could he have thoughts like that about her when he hadn't even kissed her yet?

Chapter 10

Co-worker Zoning
Tori

"What time do you get off work, Tori?" Alex asked while he drove.

"I'm not sure, but I think five. When do you get off work?" Tori looked at Alex.

"I wanted to be at the casino at four, but maybe I can talk to my kitchen crew and start at 5:15." Alex glanced at Tori before the light turned green.

"Oh, Alex," Tori stared at him, "You don't have to change your schedule for me. I can get a ride from Thunder or call a car service. Eventually I'll have to buy a used car. I was just waiting to make some money first. I don't want to ask Thunder for any more money. He's already been so generous by giving me a clothing allowance so I could purchase professional work clothes."

"I would rather you not get a car service," Alex said wryly, "it's not safe as a single female and you don't know the route. They could take you a long way and charge you an arm and a leg. No, I'll figure something out and I'll be your driver."

"I understand, but it's not your call. You're not my father or my boyfriend," Tori huffed. "I can do things for myself." Tori would prove to everyone she could do this. She was a grown woman. Granted, she had little life experience, but she was smart.

"Okay." Alex slowed down at another light. "I'm not sure where that came from, but I only want to help and look out for you."

"Well, you don't have to. I'm good." Tori closed her eyes and released her breath. "I'm not trying to offend you. I appreciate your help, but I want to prove to my dad and myself that I can do this on my own."

"I understand," Alex murmured. "I'm sorry if I made you mad. My only intention is to offer help. Let's get to know each other better since we work and live in the same place. It's easier and cheaper if we carpool."

"Okay," Tori looked at Alex, "thank you. It would be nice to have a friend. I'm more than happy to pay you for carpooling, and when I get my car, we can take turns driving to work. Let me know later if you can leave with me at five."

"Sounds good." Alex parked the car and looked at Tori. "I would like to take you out for dinner sometime."

"I don't think that's a good idea Alex," Tori was shifting in her seat and reached for the door to get out of the car, "since we work together."

"Okay," Alex sighed, "but let me know if you change your mind."

"Yeah, okay," Tori said and quickly climbed out of the car.

Tori hurried to the front door and prayed it was already open, since they were a few minutes early. She liked Alex, but she didn't want to continue their uncomfortable conversation. Tori wished he wasn't so sexy because it would make it easier for her to focus on work and not daydream about him. As she rushed to the door to put distance between them, she didn't realize the door was locked and she didn't have a key to open it.

"Here," Alex stepped around her, "I have a key. Wait outside for a minute until I turn off the alarm."

"Oh, okay," Tori startled as Alex brushed his chest on her arm as he tried to get around her to the door. Darn his chest felt solid against her arm.

Alex opened the door and turned off the alarm before letting her in.

"I'll lock it back again until Thunder gets here since I'll be in the kitchen, and I can't see who comes in." Alex motioned for her to go to the kitchen. "Do you want to come into the kitchen with me?"

"Uh, no," Tori looked around, "I'll go into the exhibit and familiarize myself with the displays."

"Okay," Alex said, "After you talk to Thunder today, let me know when you need a ride home. I can leave here any time after three."

"I'll let you know," Tori answered, watching disappointment in Alex's eyes, "thank you for the ride, Alex. I really appreciate it."

"Anytime." Alex nodded and walked toward the restaurant.

Tori walked to the exhibit, but at the last minute, placed her hand on the doorway and turned around before entering. She watched Alex walking into the restaurant, his shoulders slumped and his hands in his pockets. She didn't enjoy rejecting him. It made her feel bad when he had done so much to make her feel comfortable. However, a relationship right now would be a distraction she couldn't afford. Being away from family for the first time was weighing on her. Her father trusted her to make smart choices.

Tori jolted out of her thoughts when she heard the lock on the front door.

"*Hau*, Tori," Thunder greeted her as he walked to her for a hug.

"*Hau*, Thunder." Thunder's hug felt like home. Thunder was four years older than her. He'd always treated her like a little sister on the rez.

"I'm sorry I couldn't get you yesterday," Thunder kept his arm around her and guided her toward his office. "Isa was feeling sick and throwing up. They say it's just a symptom of the first trimester. She just entered her second trimester, so we're hoping it ends soon. Anyway, she was doing better this morning and took the day off to relax at home. Have a seat and let's go over what this job entails. I gotta say, I'm glad your father sent you down here to us. I think you will fit in well and enjoy yourself."

"Don't worry about yesterday," Tori sat in the chair opposite Thunder's desk, "Alex took me to the casino and his sister showed me around."

"Good," Thunder sat behind his desk, "Okay, you know what happened to Rachel?"

"*Haŋ, até* told me," Tori looked down at her hands, "I'm so sorry Thunder."

"Nothing to be sorry about. None of us saw it coming." Thunder sighed, "I'm just glad it's all over and Isa is okay. Rachel was my assistant; she ran the place because I usually visit the schools and do a lot of promoting. I'm not usually in the office during the day. Mark works the front desk and will help you with phone calls and welcoming walk-in guests. Most Friday's we have kids from a local boy's shelter come in to see the exhibit and eat some fry bread. Rachel and I called them 'Our Kids' because we didn't want to call them shelter kids."

"That's really nice of you guys," Tori nodded.

"Well, we love to have them. They are our extended family. We also have school field trips throughout the year. I would love for you to wear your traditional regalia as we teach the kids about our history and culture. Rachel taught the girls the Jingle Dress Dance and I teach the boys the Fancy Dance. With our new exhibit, we will need to learn the Seminole Stomp Dances. I think Alex and his family can help us. I know you will do great with the kids since you come highly recommended by Tall Bear and Sarah. Which, by the way"–Thunder pointed at her– "She can't wait to see you and introduce you to Lilly."

"I can't wait to see them," Tori smiled.

"We can go over things as they come up. This week I want you to familiarize yourself with the Red Path Exhibit. I will show you all the spreadsheets and information you need to know about it. Next week, we will take an inventory of the items we didn't sell and make sure we have enough boxes to ship those items back. I'll show you where the inventory files are stored on this computer, and we'll walk around together so you know what to do. Every day, we get new items for the upcoming Unconquered Path Exhibit. We need to keep them separate." Thunder stated.

"So, the Unconquered Path Exhibit is about Alex's tribe?" Tori inquired.

"Yes, we will feature the Seminoles with an emphasis on the Seminole Tribe of Florida. We will promote and teach our guests about their history and culture," Thunder answered as he pulled up the flyer on his computer. "Teramar Studio already finished our flyers and brochures. Come around and take a look."

Tori walked around Thunder's desk and saw the flyer on his computer.

"Wow, that looks magnificent," Tori couldn't help but be impressed by the flyer's vivid colors and captivating artwork.

"Isa worked on it when we came back from our honeymoon."

"Well, she did a great job. Now it also makes sense why you wanted Alex as your chef." Tori walked back to her seat.

"Yup, we're honored to have him. He's an excellent chef," Thunder nodded and pointed to his monitor. "So, first things first; Grayhorse, Sarah, you, and I will deliver these posters to our usual business partners. Sarah and Grayhorse are on their way over after they drop off Tommy at school. Sarah is bringing Lilly so you can meet her. She will drive and you can deliver the posters. This way, she doesn't have to get Lilly out at every location. Your hours will be from nine to five unless it's Opening Night for one of our exhibits. On those nights, we stay until closing at ten. You can wear business casual clothes to work, please no holes in your jeans and crop tops. We wear our regalia during our openings and field trips. Do you have questions for me so far?"

"Not right now. I'm sure I'll have questions as things come up," Tori said.

"Not a problem." Thunder pulled out some paperwork with her salary. "I have some papers for you to sign so you can receive health care and tax information. As an assistant museum curator, we will pay you an annual salary of $40,000, which amounts to approximately $3,300 per month before deducting taxes. If we work well together, you'll get a raise at the end of the year."

"Thank you, that's more than I've ever been paid, and since I am living for free, I can save some money to buy a used car and eventually get an apartment," Tori looked over the forms and signed in the highlighted areas that Thunder had pointed out.

Thunder continued while she signed the papers. "Some of your duties include managing contacts and correspondence, budget tracking, inventory, writing and editing our curatorial-related copy, some research, materials and exhibition documentation. Is that okay?"

Tori could tell Thunder knew she was a little scared about this new job. She'd never had so many responsibilities, but she was ready for the challenge.

"To be honest," Tori said, "I haven't done some of those things, but I'm willing to put in the effort and learn. I love what you're doing here, and I'm so happy to be a part of it."

Thunder explained her responsibilities. It was a lot, but she was up for the challenge.

"I know you will do great. You come highly recommended from our council. They had a lot of nice things to say about you. We have a lot to do before Unconquered Path opens in two and a half weeks. But I know we can get it all done."

"Hey, anybody home?" Sarah screamed from the front door.

"Well, Sarah's here," Thunder grinned.

Tori finished signing the paperwork and turned in time to see Sarah running toward her.

"Girl, I've missed you." Sarah ran to Tori and hugged her.

"I've missed you, too." Tori hugged her back. It was so good to see her friend again. Being the same age, they were in the same grade in school, but didn't really get to know each other until they both worked at the preschool.

"Where is my beautiful *tojáŋ*?" Thunder stood up from behind his desk and walked toward Grayhorse.

"What am I chopped liver?" Grayhorse said wryly as he held his daughter in her car seat carrier.

"Nope, you are the courier," Thunder laughed at Grayhorse's dumbfounded expression, "just kidding *suŋkáku*. I love my niece's baby daddy."

"Fucker," Grayhorse murmured before Sarah slapped his shoulder, "Sorry."

"Hah," Thunder laughed, "she's got you trained."

"She'd slap you too if you cursed in front of the kids." Grayhorse rolled his eyes.

"Tori, ignore them and come meet my beautiful daughter Lilly," Sarah stated proudly, pulling Tori toward Lilly.

"Oh, Sarah," Tori rubbed Lilly's head, "she is absolutely beautiful. You are so lucky."

"Do you want to hold her?" Sarah asked Tori.

"I would love to." Tori reached out to get her out of the car seat as soon as Sarah unbuckled Lilly.

Tori placed her close to her chest while she held Lilly's head toward her shoulder. Bending her head down toward Lilly's neck, Tori could smell that sweet baby smell. Tori loved kids and couldn't wait to someday have one of her own someday.

"Thunder," Alex said, standing at the office door with George and Mary Grayfeather, "I'm sorry. Are we interrupting?"

"Alex, George, Mary, no come in," Thunder motioned for him to enter his office.

"Alex, I'd like you to meet my sister Sarah, her husband Grayhorse, and my niece Lilly."

"Ahh," Mary beelined toward Lilly, "I love seeing my little Lillybell."

Mary rubbed Lilly's back and kissed her head while she was being held by Tori.

"Hi," Alex greeted them and shook hands with them while constantly staring at Tori.

"Hi Alex," Sarah said and moved closer to Lilly and Tori, "it's nice to meet you. I hear you are an excellent chef. I can't wait to taste your food."

"Not only is he a talented chef, but he is picking up our cuisine really fast," George Grayfeather nodded, "at this rate, Mary and I will be able to leave in a couple of days. Is that okay with you?"

"I'm fine with that Grayfeather," Thunder smiled. "I know you both didn't expect to be here this long. As soon as Alex is ready, you can both head home."

"We will miss you," Sarah hugged George Grayfeather.

"We will miss you too, but hopefully you will come home for a visit soon." Grayfeather hugged her back.

"Hey man," Grayhorse shook Alex's hand, "Thunder told me you were here as his new chef. He raves about your food. I can't wait to try it."

"Thanks," Alex nodded to both. "I appreciate that."

"Did you want to ask me something?" Thunder asked him.

"Yes, I've placed the order for the food I want to serve during Opening Night. I wanted to give you the copy of the order. Everything should arrive at the end of next week. Grayfeather said you serve wine at the openings. Do you need me to order it for you?" Alex handed Thunder the sheet of paper, his gaze wandering toward Tori.

"Nope, I'll get the wine." Thunder took the receipt from Alex. "You don't have to worry about that."

"Wait until you see what Alex has planned for your opening. I think you will really like it," Grayfeather slapped Thunder on the back.

"Thank you Grayfeather, I appreciate your support. Thunder, I'll be done with Grayfeather by three today. Is there anything you need? I can stay until five and drive Tori to the casino." Alex quickly added, "You don't have to pay me. I can volunteer my time from three to five."

Tori looked up when she heard her name and noticed Alex looking at her with a strange intensity. She held his gaze for a moment, unable to look away before she forced herself to avert her eyes.

"I can use a car service," Tori looked at Thunder.

"No!" Thunder, Grayhorse, Grayfeather, and Alex all said at the same time and Tori jolted, startling Lilly, who cried, "Shh Baby, I'm so sorry." Tori mumbled and rocked her to calm her down.

"You are not using a car service," Alex looked mad, "we already talked about that."

"Ah, Tori," Sarah whispered, "these alpha males are full of testosterone. They will not allow you to use a car service by yourself."

"Alex," Thunder stared at Alex, "That is very generous and kind of you. We can use your help to distribute these flyers and then it would be great if you could drive Tori home after work."

"Absolutely, no problem," Alex confirmed.

"We are going out now, but I'll leave some flyers and a list of places on the lobby desk with Mark. Most of those places are near your casino, so it won't be too far out of your way."

"Of course." Alex nodded. "I'll take care of it."

"We will be back by two since we have to get Tommy, so Tori, you can go with Alex and make his runs." Sarah smiled at Tori.

Tori noticed the look Grayhorse gave Sarah. Clearly, she loved matchmaking.

"That's good," Thunder looked for his list on his desk, "by then we will know which places we could deliver to and the ones we are missing, so I can leave you an updated list. Okay, Grayhorse, you're with me. Here's our list. Sarah, you're with Tori, here's your list. George, Mary, and Alex, we'll see you later."

Tori handed Lilly back to Grayhorse so he could buckle her into the Baby carrier, and everyone left Thunder's office.

"Mark," Thunder called out, "we're going to deliver the flyers for the new exhibit and opening night. We'll be back by two. Are you good here?"

"Yup." Mark nodded.

"Okay, Alex, George and Mary are in the kitchen if you need anything." Thunder pointed toward the kitchen. "See you later."

"Alright." Mark waved to them. "Good luck."

Chapter 11

The Inquisition
Sarah

"*Pilámaya, higná,*" Sarah thanked Grayhorse with a kiss for getting Lilly's car seat in the van.

"*Hau, wówaštelaka mitáwa.*" Grayhorse hugged his wife. "Please drive carefully."

"I will. I promise."

Grayhorse escorted Sarah to the driver's side and closed the door.

"He is so sweet," Tori sighed.

"He sure is." Sarah waved at him. "Grayhorse is the best thing that ever happened to me. He was my rock after my parents died and Thunder came home. Thunder was busy trying to make ends meet. Grayhorse was there for me every night since Thunder worked two jobs. As a father and husband, I couldn't ask for a better man." Sarah started the car and looked up. Grayhorse was still standing in front of her car with his hands in his jean pockets. Sarah smiled when Grayhorse winked at her. "Now, I'd like to know what is going on with you and our new chef, Alex."

"Uh…nothing," Tori fidgeted with her hands and stared out the window in the passenger seat.

"Oh, I don't think it's nothing," Sarah pulled out of the parking lot. "The way he was staring at you while you held Lilly is not nothing. He looked like he was ready to wrap both of you up in his arms."

"I didn't see that." Tori kept staring out the window.

"How could you miss it?" Sarah glanced at Tori with a raised eyebrow, "he was practically salivating at you holding my little girl. Probably picturing you as the momma to his baby."

"Sarah, stop," Tori laughed at Sarah's outrageous comment, "we're just friends."

"Has he asked you out?" Sarah put on her blinker.

"Yes, sort of. But I told him we should be friends since we work together."

"Girrll," Sarah pulled into an elementary school parking lot, "you are crazy. That man is so hot, and he wants to go out with you. You two would make a beautiful couple. I think you should go out with him. It's not like you have to marry him tomorrow. Just get to know him. Thunder says he's a talented chef. How nice would it be to have someone cook for you?"

"I don't know Sarah," Tori whined, "wait your perfect husband doesn't cook for you?"

"He works a full-time job training horses and taking care of our farm animals, but if I asked him or felt sick or run down, he'd cook for me." Sarah came to Grayhorse's defense. "It's just easier for me to cook since I'm home with the kids. I make a lot of casseroles that last several days. He never complains about leftovers and even eats cereal for dinner if I had a hard day."

"He is the perfect guy, Sarah. I'm so happy for you. You are so lucky to have found him."

"Just think about dating Alex. He seems like a nice guy too. Okay, I'll stop for now because this is our first stop," Sarah pointed toward the elementary school, "they advertise our exhibits and set up field trips. All you need to do is give these ten flyers to the lady at the front desk and she'll know where to post them throughout the school. I'll wait here so I don't have to take Lilly out of her seat."

"Okay." Tori took the flyers into the school.

Sarah had to get Alex and Tori together. He really seemed like a good guy, and being sexy was just a bonus. Mind you, Sarah didn't think anyone was sexier than Grayhorse, but she could appreciate eye candy when she saw it. Sarah checked on Lilly through her rearview mirror and saw her baby girl sleeping soundly.

"Alright." Tori returned to the van and slammed the door shut. "They will take care of it. Where to next? Oh Sarah, I'm sorry I forgot about Lilly."

"Are you kidding?" Sarah snorted. "Lilly can sleep through anything, especially a door being slammed. Tommy has cured her of being a light sleeper. The only reason she cried in your arms earlier was because your body jolted while you were holding her. But as soon as you calmed down, so did she. Obviously, she can sense people's feelings when they're holding her. Like most perceptive babies."

"Okay, but I'll be quieter next time just in case," Tori glanced back at Lilly, "Do you guys go to the same places to deliver the flyers?"

"Pretty much. I go to the schools and Thunder goes to the local businesses, malls, restaurants, and the casino. But now we have Alex, he can deliver some of those for us. After today's deliveries, we usually all take some and deliver them throughout other parts of town. Isa's ad agency does a fantastic job of promoting us on our social media accounts— that really helps."

"How many people do you expect to come to the opening?" Tori grabbed ten more flyers.

"We keep getting more every time. The Red Path Exhibit had over 300 guests attend Opening Night. That's the most we've ever had. I think it also helped that Isa and Teramar did such a good job with the flyers and promotions."

"Wow, that's an incredible turnout.
Sarah stopped at the next school, Tori delivered their flyers, and off they went to the next location.

"Okay, two down," Tori announced, "so that opening sounds so exciting."

"It sure was," Sarah laughed, "not only did we have a lot of guests, but Isa ran out in Thunder's shirt and no shoes."

"Wait," Tori turned toward Sarah, "what?"

"It's a long story and one that Isa should tell. So, we need to set up a Girls' night. Usually it's Isa, her friend Maggie and me. Oh, and sometimes Isa's sister-in-law Gaby joins us. We like to get pedicures or just hang out at my house and drink. If we drink too much, then we either have a sleepover or Thunder drives Maggie and Isa home."

"That sounds like fun," Tori smiled. "I would love that. I've never had a lot of girlfriends, let alone a girls' night out. Honestly, after you left, I kept to myself and worked more hours. Well, unless Lizzy would try to set me up on dates."

"I forgot how protective your dad was." Sarah wished her dad was alive. He would have been just as overprotective as Tall Bear. Sarah's parents had died when she was in high school from a head on collision on the rez. They died instantly.

"Dad told Lizzy the only way she could date was if him, mom, or I chaperoned," Tori explained. "After several bad double dates, one with especially busy hands, I begged dad to not make me go to any more of her dates. I hated every minute of those dates. I was going because it made Lizzy happy and in the beginning that's all that mattered to me, but after so many, I just couldn't' do it anymore. We all agreed on mom and dad chaperoning Lizzy. They sat close enough to watch, but far enough for Lizzy's dates to escape dad's inquisition. Unfortunately, over the last few months, Lizzy brought the double dates to the preschool with her dates and guilted me into going. Sometimes I cancelled, but most times I went. This opportunity could not have come at a better time."

"You are such a good sport for doing it at all," Sarah turned into another school. "It shows how much you love your sister. Being willing to sit through horrible dates is a labor of love. I would not have wanted to go out with losers for Thunder."

"Somehow I feel Thunder would not have set you up with a guy with wandering hands."

"Very true," Sarah parked in a visitor spot, "you're up." Tori grabbed more flyers on her way out of the car. Sarah was glad Tori was in town. It was nice to have someone from the rez here to talk to and share stories. Sarah took her phone out of her purse so Tori could add her number when she returned.

"Next!" Tori exclaimed.

"You're enjoying this, aren't you?" Sarah noticed the excitement in Tori's voice.

"Yes, this is so much fun," Tori smiled, "everyone is so nice."

"Let's go through a drive thru," Sarah suggested. "I'm getting hungry."

"Sounds good to me." Tori reached into her purse, but Sarah placed her hand over Tori's.

"Tori, I got this. You haven't even gotten your first paycheck yet."

"I know, but my dad sent me with some money," Tori sighed while Sarah shook her head no. "Fine, but it will be my treat after I get my paycheck."

"Deal. Hey, my phone is in the cup holder." Sarah pointed toward it. "Add your number. I already unlocked it. When we get to the next stop, I'll add you to the group chat for a girls' night out."

"Sounds great," Tori added her number to Sarah's phone, "Thank you so much for including me, Sarah."

"You will fit right in with us, Tori. Oooh, there's a place where I can get chicken nuggets and eat them while I drive. Let's get something from there." Sarah pulled into the drive-through.

"Great idea," Tori agreed.

Sarah placed the order for two chicken nugget combo meals and paid. Tori distributed their food as they drove to the next school. While Tori delivered the flyers, Sarah texted the group to give them a heads up.

Sarah: Hey ladies, we have one more to add to our Girls' Night Out. Tori is Rachel's replacement; she really needs some girlfriends. Do you guys mind if I invite her to our next GNO?

Maggie: The more the merrier.

Gaby: I really need a night out ladies. Invite her.

Isa: Oh, my goodness, yes, invite her! I've heard so much about her. Can't wait to meet her.

Sarah: You guys are awesome!

"How many more can we do before you have to get Tommy?" Tori asked while checking her watch.

"I think we have time for a couple more," Sarah answered while eating her nuggets. "Oh, by the way, I texted the girls and they are good with you joining us. I'll add you and send out a date and time when we get to the next stop.

"Perfect," Tori ate until Sarah stopped.

Sarah: How about this Saturday, my house, 4pm? We can make sandwiches and watch a movie while we drink. Sorry Isa.

Isa: No worries. I'd rather be pregnant than be able to drink.

Maggie: I'll be there and drink enough for me and Isa.

Isa: Of course, you will Mags…LOL

Gaby: I'll ask Aurora and see if she can Babysit. *Abuela* rarely misses an opportunity to spoil her grandbabies.

"Another one down." Tori announced, getting back in the car and reaching for her nuggets.

"I just texted the group." Sarah took a drink before she pulled out of the parking lot. "Check your messages."

"Okay," Tori pulled out her phone.

Tori: Thank you all for inviting me. I can't wait to meet you guys. I'll have to get a ride.

Isa: Can't wait to meet you either.

Maggie: So glad to have another in our group.

Gaby: See you soon.

"Alright Tori," Sarah sighed, "this is our last one."
"Got it," Tori knew the drill.

Sarah: You can get Alex to drive you to my house.

Maggie: Oooh, who's Alex. I feel like I'm missing a meet-cute story.

Isa: The new chef at the cultural center?

Gaby: The cultural center has a new chef?

Sarah: Yes, to your questions. I think he has the hots for Tori, and he is HOT! Caliente!

Isa: LOL, I can't wait to hear this story.

"They said they would also post it up on their school website," Tori said when she sat and looked at her phone. "My phone is beeping like crazy. Oh my God Sarah, I can't ask Alex."

"Why not?" Sarah asked.

"He might work, and I just told him we were friends! I don't want to give him mixed signals. What if he thinks I'm a tease?"

"He will not think you are a tease. Besides, friends help each other out. What could it hurt to ask?"

"No, I'm not asking him. I have a week to figure something out because I really want to go." Tori finished her nuggets.

"Well, worse comes to worse. I'll get Grayhorse to go pick you up," Sarah volunteered her hubby. She knew without a doubt he would do that for her so Tori could attend.

"I'll let you know." Tori finished her lunch and put the trash in the original food bag.

Sarah was getting drowsy and yawned as she drove them back to the cultural center. Her post pregnancy hormones were making her exhausted after simple tasks. Pulling into the parking lot, Sarah was grateful to see Thunder's truck was already there. That meant Grayhorse and her brother were finished with their deliveries.

"Tori, I'm gonna leave the van running for Lilly. Can you please go tell Grayhorse I'm ready to go?" Sarah looked back and saw Lilly was still asleep.

"Of course," Tori grabbed the bag with all the trash, "I'll take this and throw it out inside. Thank you for today, Sarah. I had a lot of fun and I'm really looking forward to our Girls' Night Out."

"My pleasure," Sarah finished her nuggets before handing Tori more trash, "leave the rest of those flyers in the car. Grayhorse and I will deliver them tomorrow."

"Okay. I'll see you on Saturday. Oh, text me your address."

Sarah waved to Tori and waited in the van for Grayhorse while she texted Tori her address. She didn't have to wait long before he confidently strolled over to her on the driver's side, raising an eyebrow when she yawned.

"*Wíŋyaŋ mitáwa*," Grayhorse said when he opened the door, "Get in the passenger side, I'll drive. You look sleepy."

"You don't have to ask me twice," Sarah got out and brushed nugget debris off her shirt.

"Chicken nuggets?" Grayhorse quirked one eyebrow at her.

"Yup," Sarah gave him a peck on the lips, "no judging."

"Nope." Grayhorse held up his hands in surrender and walked Sarah to the passenger's side.

"How did it go?" Grayhorse asked after he helped her into the passenger seat.

"Good," Sarah yawned again, "I'm tired."

"I'll drop you off at home and go get Tommy," Grayhorse grabbed Sarah's hand and kissed it, "It will give you some time to take a nap. Besides, Lilly is sleeping peacefully in the back."

"You are the best husband EVER!" Sarah moaned, and Grayhorse walked to the driver's side and drove home.

Chapter 12

My Turn to Deliver Flyers
Alex

Once Alex told George and Mary they could leave, he cleaned up the kitchen after they showed him their recipes and made some fry bread together. Alex preferred to come into a clean kitchen every day, and he could tell George and Mary were tired. Alex was sure he would only need one more day to work with them, then he could tell Thunder he was ready, and George and Mary could go home.

"Mark," Alex walked to the lobby desk, "Is Tori back yet?"

"Yes, she's with Thunder in the warehouse, going over the new exhibit."

"Thank you." Alex turned and walked to Thunder's office. Seeing the door to the warehouse open, he walked through and immediately saw Thunder and Tori unpacking a box.

"Sorry to interrupt," Alex walked toward them. "Thunder, George and Mary are gone, and I'm done in the kitchen and ready to deliver some of your flyers."

"Hey Alex," Thunder looked up. "Tori, I can keep unpacking these boxes and we can begin the labeling process tomorrow. You should go with Alex.

"Are you sure?" Tori questioned.

"Yup, it's more important right now to deliver our flyers while the businesses are open. It gives people a week and a half to add this to their calendar." Thunder emptied the box and put it to the side. "I can work late if push comes to shove. Mark has the extra flyers on his desk. Grab at least half. If you don't deliver all of them today, just bring them back. Thank you for doing this, guys. I really appreciate it."

"Not a problem." Alex nodded. "Thunder, I think after tomorrow you can send George and Mary home. I'll be good in the kitchen."

"Really?" Thunder grinned. "that would be great. I know they are ready to go. I'll make all their travel arrangements and call them. Thank you so much Alex."

"Sure," Alex nodded, "no problem."

Tori and Alex left the warehouse, making their way to Mark.

"Mark," Tori stood in front of Mark and grabbed a flyer, "Can I get some of these flyers to deliver to the casino and any other businesses on the way?"

"How many do you need?" Mark reached into a drawer.

"Thunder said to take half of your pile?" Tori looked at Alex.

"We can return our leftovers tomorrow," Alex nodded, "or I'll drive around in the morning and finish delivering them."

"I sorted these in packs of 25, so here's about 100." Mark gave Tori the flyers.

"Sounds good," Alex turned toward Tori, "Do you need to grab your purse or anything before we leave?"

"Yes, I'll be right back" Tori handed Alex the flyers and went into Thunder's office to get her purse.

Alex waited for Tori before heading out to his car. Once they were situated inside, he noticed the awkward silence in the car.

"How did the morning go with Sarah?" Alex asked.

"It was good. We delivered to several schools," Tori continued to stare out the window, fidgeting with the flyers on her lap.

"That's good. Did Sarah get Lilly out or did she drive you around?" Alex was trying to engage Tori in a conversation, but she was not elaborating. He wondered if he had done anything wrong. How could she be upset with him when all he did this morning was drop her off at work? Was she upset because he'd asked her out?

"She drove, and I got out," Tori continued with her short answers.

"Tori," Alex thought he might as well just flat out ask her, "Did I do something?"

"No," Tori's smile seemed forced.

Alex drove her to several office buildings and strip malls on their way to the casino. It was the same every time. He offered to go in with her, she declined, came back, said done, and Alex drove her to the next location. At the strip mall, Alex walked with her, but every time she went into a store, she informed him he could wait outside. He couldn't figure out what he had done wrong. She seemed much more open with Sarah, Grayhorse, Thunder, and Mark.

"Tori," Alex pulled into the casino, "are you okay?"

"Yes," Tori answered quickly, "I'm fine. Thank you for the ride."

"Okayy," Alex parked his car by the side entrance again, "Let's get these to my mom. She'll place them all over the hotel and casino."

"I can take them," Tori jumped at the chance to take the flyers, "it's my job, anyway."

Alex was stunned at Tori's attitude. It seemed like she couldn't wait to get away from him. He really didn't understand this woman. Usually, women were throwing themselves at him, not running away from him. As far as he knew, he had done nothing wrong. Unless asking her out was a crime. Alex let her take the flyers and quietly followed her to his mom.

"Tori," Sehoy smiled, "how was your first day?"

"It was great, thank you for asking," Tori smiled back. "Thunder wanted me to bring you the new flyers for the Unconquered Path Exhibit so you could put them up and help him market opening night in two weeks."

Alex walked behind the desk and gave his mom a kiss on the cheek. Watching Tori smiling genuinely at his mom, he wished he could be on the receiving end.

"Okay," Sehoy hugged Alex, "I will let the staff know where to place them. I want to put one on every floor for maximum exposure. Thank you for bringing them to us. I'm so excited to see the exhibit. It is the first time he is showcasing our tribe."

"He told me. We are so excited. If you need more, let me know. Thanks again for the ride, Alex," Tori waved, ready to turn around and leave.

"Tori," Alex called out to her, "8:30 tomorrow morning?"

"Sure," Tori finally looked at him, "see you all later."

"Alex," Sehoy turned to her son, "is there something I should know? Is she mad at you for something?"

"Mom," Alex kissed her on the cheek again, "I really don't know. She won't talk to me. I've got to get to work. I'll try to talk to her tomorrow." Sometimes Alex hated how observant his mother was.

"Okay, be nice," Sehoy pleaded with Alex, "she is here all by herself and this is an adjustment for her. You need to be gentle with her."

"Mom," Alex stared wide eyed at her, "I would never hurt her. How could you think that?"

"Alex," Sehoy put her hands on Alex's face, "I don't think that. You just look mean sometimes when you are serious about your overbearing stance and tattoos. I just don't want you to scare her."

Alex sighed, "I'm well aware of what I look like. It's worked in my favor on several occasions while working here. I've had my tats covered up all day with my chef shirt, so I'm sure that's not it. I promise you I'll be on my best and kindest behavior."

"That's my sweet boy," Sehoy squeezed his cheeks, "Now get to work, the food isn't going to cook itself."

"Yes, ma'am," Alex hugged his mom and headed toward RUSH.

Chapter 13

Pulling Freya into Her Web of Friends
Tori

Tori took the elevator to her room. After talking to Sarah, Tori really wanted to have a girls' night out. Back home, she never received invitations to take part in anything like that back home because she typically went to work and returned home. She was close with her sister, but Lizzy was more interested in double dating and boys than hanging out just the two of them.

Tori didn't want to ask Alex for a ride. She didn't want to feel indebted to him or give him the impression she liked him. He was so nice, but she didn't want to get involved with someone from work. When she entered her room, she started pacing and wondered how she could get to Sarah's. Snapping her fingers when she came up with a possible idea. Maybe Freya wanted to go. She sat down and sent a quick text to Sarah to make sure it would be okay.

Tori: Can I invite Freya to our Girls' Night Out?

Sarah: Sure, who's Freya?

Tori: She's Alex's sister and has been showing me the ropes around here.

Sarah: That's nice. Absolutely invite her.

Tori: Thx Sarah

Sarah: np, see you Saturday.

Tori got up off her couch and walked to her adjoining door knocking on Freya's open door.

"Hey." Freya walked out of her bedroom in a towel. "What's up? Did you just get home?"

"I did," Tori answered, "Do you work tonight?"

"I do." Freya turned around. "Come in. I gotta get dressed and put on makeup. I gotta be on the floor at my table in thirty minutes."

"Oh, I don't want to bother you, Frey," Tori hesitated before she entered Freya's room.

"Nonsense," Freya waved her off, "you are not bothering me. I can talk to you and get ready at the same time. I'm good at multi-tasking. Now, what did you need? Oh, and how was your first day?"

Tori stayed in the living room while Freya dressed in the bedroom.

"My first day was great, but I have a lot to learn. I wanted to know what you are doing Saturday at four?" Tori spoke loudly so Freya could hear her.

"Come in here," Freya screamed, "I'm dressed, and I gotta go into the bathroom to do my makeup. No need to be screaming across my apartment."

"Okay," Tori walked into Freya's bathroom and leaned on the doorframe, "do you have plans for Saturday?"

"Nope. What did you want to do?" Freya asked while applying eyeshadow.

"Sarah Grayhorse invited me to a Girls' Night Out at her place, and I was wondering if you wanted to go with me?" Tori walked to the toilet and sat down.

"Who's Sarah Grayhorse?" Freya looked at Tori through the mirror.

"Do you know Thunder who runs the American Indian Cultural Center?" Tori asked.

"Yup, I met him once. He's not much of a gambler unlike your dad." Freya teased.

"Ugh, it's bad enough dad plays when he comes here, but it would be nice if he ever won," Tori laughed. "Anyway, Sarah is Thunder's sister. She and I worked at the preschool on the rez before she moved here. Sarah wanted to include me in her circle of friends to make me feel more at home here, and since you are my newest friend, I wanted to include you."

"Okay," Freya applied her mascara, "I'm game. Anyone else coming?"

"Yes, there are others, but I don't know who. We've been texting, but I only see the numbers since I don't have them in my contacts." Tori watched as Freya finished her look with a bright red lipstick.

"What are you going to do tonight?" Freya asked.

"I'm going to go to RUSH and get dinner, then shower and read."

"Sounds good," Freya stepped into her closet and slipped on her shoes, "come on, I'll walk with you downstairs."

Freya and Tori walked into RUSH and grabbed a table.

"Hi Frey, Tori," Jane the waitress walked up to their table and gave them menus. "What do you guys want to drink?"

"Water, please," Tori looked up and smiled at Jane.

"Nothing for me Jane, I have to get to the casino."

"Okay, I'll be back with your water, Tori."

"You don't have time to eat something before work?" Tori asked Freya.

"Nope." Freya pulled a granola bar out of her pocket. "I'll eat this and then take a dinner break around ten."

"Wow, that's really late to eat dinner. How do you stay so thin?" Tori wondered.

"Good metabolism," Freya smirked before she took another bite. "I could ask you the same question."

"It wasn't hard to stay thin on the rez, not a lot of food. Here I'm gonna have to run on the treadmill," Tori started laughing.

"Tori, what would you like?" Jane asked after she placed the glass of water in front of Tori.

"I'll just have a turkey sandwich with chips, please." Tori handed the menu back to Jane.

"You want to go see Alex in the kitchen?" Freya wiggled her eyebrows at Tori.

"No, I'm pretty sure he thinks I'm mad at him and I'm not. I just don't know how to talk to a cute guy. Stop grinning Frey, I can't date him, and I don't want to lead him on."

"Just talk to him. It's not like he's asked you out?" Freya watched Tori blush and look away. "Oh my goodness, he asked you out already?"

"Yes," Tori shook her head.

"Huh," Freya looked stunned with her mouth open, "he moves fast."

"So now I don't know what to say to him," Tori sighed. "I really like him, but I just can't right now. If we broke up, I would still have to work with him for six months."

"Wow, you haven't even dated him and you're already talking about breaking up."

"You know what I mean."

"Okay, I get it, but I still think you should give him a shot. I know I'm biased because he is my brother, but he would treat you right."

"I'll think about it."

"Good, now I need to get to work," Freya checked her watch. "I'll talk to you tomorrow."

"Hey ladies," Alex placed Tori's food in front of her, "Jane said you were here. I should have known since you ordered the turkey sandwich with chips. I made it like last time. Is that okay?"

"Yes," Tori nodded, "thank you Alex."

"Bye Tori, bye bro," Freya kissed Alex's cheek, "gotta go. See you all later. Alex, keep Tori company while she eats."

Tori squinted at Freya as she turned around and laughed her way out of the restaurant.

"I can stay for a little, but I might have to cut out if they need me," Alex sat down in the chair Freya had vacated.

"You don't have to babysit me Alex," Tori sighed, "I know you have to work."

"I do," Alex nodded, "but I can take a fifteen-minute break. Besides, I'm right here. If they need me, they'll come get me. How are you doing being away from home?"

"I miss my family and the kids at the preschool, but everyone has been so nice here and made me feel welcome."

"I'm glad I know what it feels like to miss family. I went to culinary school in New York and lived there working in different restaurants for a few years. Once I learned different cuisines, I moved back and started working here."

"I didn't realize you lived anywhere else."

"I did." Alex crossed his arms over the table. "I loved the city with all the lively activity at all hours of the day, but I love my family more. I knew I'd move back home and work here for my dad to be close to family. What about you? Do you see yourself staying here, or are you ready to go back?"

"It's kind of hard to say since I've only been here two days, but I do like it here. Believe it or not, I'm looking forward to a year of sunshine and no snow." Tori laughed.

"I can understand that," Alex chuckled. "I love to visit the snowy states in the winter, but I wouldn't want to live there."

"Well, thanks for keeping me company," Tori finished her dinner, wiped her mouth and hands. "I think I'm going to head up to relax and read."

"No problem," Alex stood up and cleared the table for Jane. "Maybe next time you'll let me make you something else for dinner."

"I don't know Alex," Tori pointed to her empty plate, "it's hard to beat a good turkey sandwich."

"Pretty sure I can beat that," Alex laughed.

"See you tomorrow?" Tori asked.

"Yup," Alex nodded, "see you at 8:30 am. Goodnight. Enjoy your book."

"Thanks," Tori smiled, "don't work too hard. Goodnight."

"Hey when you love what you do, it doesn't feel like work."

"Bye Alex."

"Bye Tori."

Tori stepped into the elevator and headed up to her room. She had a great romance novel waiting for her with a sexy, book boyfriend who now seemed to morph into Alex.

Chapter 14

Boys will be Boys
Tori

Tori woke up energized to check out the gym on her floor. Tori ran in high school and about two to three times a week at the rez before work. She didn't feel comfortable running outside here, she wasn't familiar with the area but the treadmill on this floor was calling her name.

Putting on her tight bike shorts, tank top, and running shoes she headed out to the gym. Opening the door, she noticed Alex and Barrett running on the treadmill while Holt used the elliptical machine. Alex faltered his step when he saw Tori in the doorway.

"Hey." Alex slowed his run. "Good morning. What's up?"

"I wanted to come in and run on the treadmill," Tori stared at the sweat running down Alex's washboard abs, "but I can do it later today."

"No, no." Alex turned off the treadmill. "I'm done with my run. You can use this one."

"Are you sure, Alex? I don't want to stop you from your workout."

"Hey Tori," Barrett hollered while running, "he's been in here for just about an hour, believe me he's done running."

"Hi Barrett, Holt," Tori looked toward them. Holt waved a hand up in acknowledgement.

"Barrett's right," Alex got off the treadmill and draped a towel around his neck wiping his face. "I'm done running. Let me know if you need any help setting it up."

"That would be great," Tori stepped onto the treadmill, "I've never run on a treadmill before so I don't know what to do."

Alex helped her with the settings. They chose a program that started slow, increased speed and ended with a cooldown walk.

"Thank you, Alex," Tori began her walk.

"Sure," Alex nodded, "if you ever want to run outside, let me know and I'll go with you."

"Or I can go with you if Alex is busy," Barrett grinned at Alex.

"I think my hours are more flexible than yours Barrett," Alex blurted.

"Okay," Tori felt so grateful to have friends that were so accommodating, "thank you both. I really appreciate that."

Tori stayed focused on the treadmill, she didn't want to trip and fall. She barely paid attention to the boys' conversation. Mostly they were teasing each other.

"Tori," Barrett looked over at her, "look up, you can see the sun rise."

"Wow, that is so beautiful," Tori looked up and tripped. She would have fallen had Alex not placed his arm under her legs and picked her up off the treadmill.

"Are you okay?" Alex asked.

"I guess I really need to pay attention, but that looks so beautiful," Tori placed her arms around Alex's neck. Being held by a strong, sweaty sexy chef while watching a beautiful sun rise was a great way to start the day.

"It looks really beautiful when you watch it rise over the ocean," Alex murmured snapping Tori out of her daze.

"Oh, my goodness," Tori scrambled to get down from Alex's arms, "I'm so sorry."

"It's not a problem Tori, it's not as if you weigh much," Alex leaned down and whispered in her ear, "besides you felt good in my arms."

"Tori, if Alex can't hold you for too long, I know I can," Barrett winked at her.

"Fucker," Alex grunted, "get off that treadmill and I'll show you how much I can carry."

"Come on old man," Barrett stopped the treadmill and jumped off, "let's see what you got."

Before the words were even out of Barrett's mouth Alex ran toward Barrett tackling and turning him toward the mat on the floor. Both went down hard.

"Ah, oh my God," Tori screamed as they wrestled on the floor, "Holt, stop them!"

"Nah," Holt stopped the elliptical and walked over to the free weights, "they're good."

"How can you say that?" Tori continued screaming, "Alex stop, you're hurting Barrett."

"Nope, this fucker is fine, he's just trying to put on a show for you."

"But he's groaning in pain," Tori tried pushing Alex off of Barrett. "Alex Panther, you stop right now!" Tori screamed and punched his arm. Everyone froze and stared at Tori.

"Shit Tori," Alex murmured as he rolled off Barrett, "that hurt."

"I'm sorry," Tori covered her mouth with both hands, "Barrett, are you laughing?"

"Yup," Barrett was holding his sides, "I've never seen Alex punched in the arm by a girl before. Tori you are my favorite person right now."

"But wasn't he hurting you?" Tori looked between Alex's icy glare and Barrett's laughing face.

"No babe," Barrett stopped long enough to say, "we wrestle around to stay in shape and stay sharp with take downs. Holt and I gotta stay fit to work security here."

"Do not call her babe," Alex pointed at Barrett, "or I will really kick your ass."

"Sorry bro," Barrett stood and walked over to Holt to spot him on the weight bar.

"You guys are crazy," Tori said with tears in her eyes, "I'm gonna go get ready for work."

"I'll walk you to your room," Alex turned around and glared at Barrett, "see you later."

"Yup," Barrett smiled back.

Tori had gotten to her door when she felt Alex's hand on her back.

"Tori, are you okay?"

"I'm not gonna lie Alex, that scared me. I didn't realize you guys were messing around."

"I'm sorry. Barrett, Holt and I spar all the time and I didn't realize you were really concerned. I love my family. I would never hurt them."

"I know. I just don't have brothers and I've never seen that before. My sister and I might argue, but we were never physical with each other."

"Come here." Alex pulled her into his arms. "We'll keep our wrestling away from you. Please don't let that keep you from using the treadmill."

"Okay," Tori stepped back when she felt his shaft hardening against her stomach. Clearly, she was as turned on as Alex, but this had to end. Alex was her friend and co-worker and they had to stay in their lanes. Tori placed her hands on his chest and gently pushed him away. Alex wiped her face with a clean edge of his towel. "Thank you for explaining, it's nice to have a great co-worker. I'll see you soon."

"Yup," Alex kissed her forehead, "I'll be back to get you for work."

"Thanks Alex," Tori quickly turned around and entered her room leaning back against her door she sighed and wondered how she was going to stay away from him. She kept trying to call him a friend and co-worker, but he was still acting like a doting date. Realizing Tori would have to face this head on, she finally pushed off the door and went into the bathroom to shower and change for work.

Alex was constantly punctual, and this morning Tori was ready with her purse as soon as she opened the door.

"Hello, again," Alex smiled when she opened the door.

"Good morning." Tori stepped out and they walked to the elevator.

"Are we good?" Alex leaned down and looked Tori in the eyes.

"Yes," Tori nodded, "I understand you guys were playing around this morning."

"Good." Alex held the door open for Tori to step out when they reached the lobby. Tori felt Alex's hand in the middle of her back as they walked by his mom at the front desk. They all waved to each other but didn't stop to talk. Sehoy was busy registering guests and they had to get to work.

"Do you have a key for the center?" Alex glanced at Tori.

"Yes, Thunder gave me one yesterday and taught me how to turn the alarm on and off."

"Great. I'm gonna drop you off at work and deliver more flyers before George and Mary show up."

"Okay, thank you Alex."

"Tori, you don't have to keep thanking me. It's what friends do, right?"

"Yes."

They continued their short drive to work in silence which Tori appreciated. She didn't know what to say and didn't want to get too attached to or dependent on Alex. Tori could have started the conversation as soon as they sat in the car, but she wasn't a confrontational person and didn't know how to approach the subject. By the time she talked herself into it, they were already at work and Alex had pulled into the handicap parking spot.

"I'll wait here until you get inside. It looks like Thunder is already here." Alex pointed at Thunder's truck, "can you let him know I'm delivering flyers and I'll be back by ten?"

"I'll tell him." Tori opened her door, stepped out and leaned down. "See you soon."

Tori walked to the door. Pulling it open she saw Mark sitting at the lobby desk.

"Good morning, Mark."

"Mornin' Tori." Mark looked up from the computer. "I see we haven't scared you off yet."

"Nope," Tori laughed, "I'm back and ready to learn."

"Great, Thunder is in his office. Check in with him for your next job."

"Sounds good, see you later."

Thunder had an open-door policy. He wanted his employees and guests to feel comfortable if they wanted to talk to him. Tori walked in.

"Good morning, Alex dropped me off and wanted me to let you know he is out delivering flyers and will be back by around ten."

"That's awesome." Thunder waved her over to his computer. "Come over here and bring that chair. I'm gonna show you how to input our inventory."

Tori pulled the chair over, and they worked on the computer most of the day. Once Tori got the hang of it, Thunder began making marketing calls to local schools about setting up field trips. Time flew by and before she knew it, Alex was at Thunder's office door.

"Is Thunder in the warehouse?"

"Yes." Tori looked up. "He's making some calls."

"I'll be ready to go as soon as I finish talking to him. Are you about ready?"

"Wow, it's already five o'clock?" Tori was totally blown away.

"Yup."

"I'll save my work and be ready when you come back."

"Okay." Alex went into the warehouse.

Tori saved everything she was working on and organized the files on the desk, so she knew where to start tomorrow. She also had a lot to file tomorrow. She finished just in time to see Thunder and Alex walking in.

"That sounds great, Alex." Thunder slapped him on the back. "George and Mary will fly out tomorrow. However, if you have any questions, I'm sure you can still reach out to George."

"I already got his number, but I think I'll be okay. Tori, are you ready?"

"Yes." Tori stood behind the desk. "Thunder, I'll finish the rest tomorrow and then file everything."

"No problem," Thunder smiled, "remember I told you about the shelter kids 'Our kids'?" Tori nodded and Thunder continued, "they won't be able to come in this Friday but want to see the Red Path Exhibit one more time before we take it down, so they will come the following Friday."

"Sounds great. I can't wait to meet them." Tori grabbed her purse.

"Who are you talking about?" Alex asked Thunder.

"Since we opened this cultural center, I wanted to help young men who have lost their way in life. So, I mentored a young man named George from the local boy's shelter. It didn't take long for me to mentor all the boys there. Anyway, they come in practically every Friday, and I show them the exhibit and we hang out and talk about anything they want to discuss. Some boys have graduated out, but the ones that are still there bring the younger ones, and the cycle continues. I love when they visit. Grayfeather made them Indian Fry Bread every time and they love it. Will you be able to make it for them?"

"Absolutely," Alex confirmed. "Grayfeather mentioned something about making bread for the boys, but he didn't say they were from a shelter. I will make extra for them to take."

"That would be great. I can't wait for them to meet you both."

"I've heard so much about them," Tori nodded. "I can't wait."

"Great," Thunder switched places with Tori behind his desk and sat down, "have a good night."

"See you tomorrow." Tori and Alex said, as they walked out the door.

"Bye, Mark." Tori waved on her way out.

"Bye man, see ya tomorrow." Alex knocked twice on the lobby desk.

"Bye guys, see ya," Mark answered back.

Tori followed Alex to his car so he could drive them home. Funny how she already thought of the resort as home.

"Are you coming in again for another turkey sandwich tonight?" Alex grinned at her.

"Maybe I'll pick a ham sandwich?"

"Oooh, walking on the wild side tonight, huh?" Alex laughed.

"I'm still coming in," Tori laughed with him. "I'll look at the menu and pick something different. Will that make you happy?"

"Seeing you and making you anything you want will make me happy."

"Alex," Tori sighed, "you know we are only friends, right?"

"Yes, unfortunately I do," Alex stared ahead as he drove, "but you can't fault a guy for trying."

"I can't right now. I'm sorry."

"Sure."

Tori knew she'd hurt his feelings again. She hated doing that. Maybe she should try dating Alex and let the cards fall where they may. Both of them lost in their own thoughts, the rest of the trip passed in awkward silence. When they pulled in and parked, Tori got out of the car and headed inside.

"Tori, wait." Alex gently gripped her arm. "Look I understand. We can just be friends."

"Thanks Alex." Tori relaxed. "I'll see you later in RUSH?"

"Sure." Alex released her arm and followed her inside.

They both waved to Sehoy and headed up to their respective rooms.

Chapter 15

The Lipstick Bet
Tori

"Frey?" Tori immediately walked into Freya's room.

"In here," Freya screamed, "come back here."

Tori followed the voice into her bathroom.

"How was your second day?"

"Busy, but really great." Tori watched Frey apply her lipstick. "I'm finally getting the hang of inventory. Then I'll be ready to learn something else. Wow, Freya," Tori sighed, "that red looks good on you. I wish I could wear that color."

"You can." Freya motioned for her to step close to her. "Come here."

Tori stepped up to Freya.

"I don't think it will look as good on me," Tori stated.

"Shh, open your mouth so I can apply it." Freya painted Tori's lips red. "Okay, close your lips and rub them together."

Tori did as Freya instructed.

"Now look." Freya gently nudged Tori toward the mirror. "It looks great on you. You can borrow it anytime you want."

"You think I can pull this off, really?" Tori stared at herself in the mirror.

"Absolutely." Freya nodded. "I'll make you a deal. You go downstairs with this lipstick on and get a drink at the bar in RUSH before you order dinner. I bet you a man will come sit with you because you look hot."

"I don't think I can do that, Frey," Tori blushed.

"If you don't do that and report back to me," Freya tapped her lips, thinking of something to bet, "then I won't go with you on Saturday. Meet all those girls on your own."

"Frey," Tori's mouth dropped open, realizing Freya was a little sassy, "are you blackmailing me?"

"Nope," Freya wiggled her eyebrows, "just a friendly bet. What do you say?"

"Fine." Tori's shoulders drooped. "How long do I have to hang out at the bar?"

"Hm, fifteen minutes," Freya announced.

"Funny," Tori smirked, "you really think I can pick up a guy in fifteen minutes?"

"Yup, you look beautiful and since it's dinnertime, we have a lot of men in RUSH." Freya put on her shoes. "Now let's go before you chicken out. I'll walk you to the bar on my way to the casino."

"Bossy," Tori murmured.

"Yep." Freya grabbed Tori's arm and dragged her out of her room toward the elevator. "After fifteen minutes or after the magic happens, make sure you come see me at my table and let me know what happened. I don't get off until two in the morning, and I don't want to wait until you get home tomorrow to get the update. And I don't think you would appreciate me waking you up when I get off work," Freya grinned.

Freya walked Tori up to the bar and made sure she sat on the stool.

"Okay, Tori. Time to get your sexy on." Freya winked at her and left.

"Hi Tori," Carl greeted her and placed a napkin down like last time.

"Hi Carl," Tori smiled. "Are you working down here tonight?"

"Yes ma'am," Carl answered her, "I rotate around with the other bartenders. What would you like to drink?"

"Can I have one of your frozen Strawberry Margaritas?" Tori inquired.

"Yup," Carl nodded, "like last time, not too much alcohol?"

"Yes please," Tori looked around, "do you have a menu?"

"Here you go," Carl pulled out a menu from under the bar.

"Thank you." Tori looked at the menu. She told Alex she was going to try something else.

"Did you want to order food?" Carl asked after he set her drink on the napkin.

"I do," Tori looked and took a sip, "but I think I need another minute to decide."

"No problem. Call me over when you're ready."

"Thanks, Carl." Tori took another sip and put her drink down.

As she was studying the menu, a nicely dressed blonde hair blue eyed man sat down next to her.

"Is this seat taken?" he asked Tori.

"Um, no," Tori answered between sips.

"Can I get you something?" Carl appeared in front of the man.

"Whiskey on the rocks, please," the man answered.

The man turned his body toward Tori.

"Can I buy you a refill?" Tori looked at him and then her glass and realized her nervousness had caused her to nearly finish her drink quickly.

"No, thank you," Tori smiled. "I'm about to order dinner."

"My name is Winston," he smiled and held out his hand toward her, "mind if I join you? I haven't eaten dinner yet. We can get a table and eat together, if that is okay with you?"

"Sure." Tori stood up and shook his hand.

"Get a table for us. I'm gonna wait for my drink, and I'll meet you there, Beautiful."

"Okay." Tori blushed and walked to a table. She couldn't wait to tell Frey about this cute guy that had asked her out. I guess the red lipstick worked, Tori thought.

"Hey Beautiful," Winston said as he sat down opposite Tori. "What is your name?"

"Victoria, but everyone calls me Tori," Tori gazed into his lovely blue eyes.

"Hi Tori," Winston smiled, "it's very nice to meet you. Are you new here? I come here often, and I've never seen you before?"

"I just moved to town." Tori looked at the menu.

"Hey, Tori." The waitress came over. "Can I take your order?"

"Hi, Tiffany." Tori handed her the menu. "Can I get the Chef Salad please?"

"Sure." Tiffany looked at Winston. "What can I get you?"

"I'll have the burger and fries, please." Winston handed over their menus. "This will all be in one check."

"Oh, Tori doesn't pay here," Tiffany grinned at Tori. "Do you all want something else to drink?"

"Can…," Tori tried to speak, but Winston cut her off.

"We'll both have a glass of water." Winston folded his hands on the table.

"Okay." Tiffany placed her pad and pen in her apron. "I'll put your order in and get you your waters."

"Thanks Tiffany." Tori was confused when Winston ordered her water for her, but she assumed he was trying to keep her hydrated after her drink. Little did he know, her drinks were more or less non-alcoholic. *Winston was being thoughtful, not controlling*, she thought.

"So, you don't pay here?" Winston raised his eyebrow at her. "What's that about?"

"My father is a member of the Lakota Tribal Council, and he made a deal with Mr. Panther, the manager, here to provide me with food and rent." Tori unwrapped her napkin and placed it in her lap.

"Well, that was very kind. How long are you here for, Beautiful?" Winston reached across the table and held her hand.

Tiffany came over and dropped off two glasses of water.

"Thank you." Tori acknowledged Tiffany.

"Of course. Your food should be ready soon." Tiffany turned and walked to another customer.

"Winston, I'm not visiting. I work at the American Indian Cultural Center." Tori gazed into his eyes.

"That's good." Winston squeezed her hand. "I was afraid I had met the woman of my dreams, and I would only get to spend a few days with her."

"What do you do?" Tori blushed.

"I'm a self-employed financial advisor." Winston let go of her hand when Alex delivered their food.

"I heard you were dining with us and a guest tonight." Alex placed the plates in front of them. "Who is your guest?"

"Alex, this is Winston." Tori released Winston's hand and placed hers back on her lap. "Winston, this is Alex. He is the chef here."

"Winston James." Winston stood to shake Alex's hand. "Nice to meet you."

"Alex Panther," Alex released Winston's hand, "like Tori said I am one of the chefs here at the Rock 'n' Roll Resort & Casino. How do you both know each other?"

"I just met him," Tori smiled at Winston.

"I couldn't leave a beautiful woman sitting at a bar by herself." Winston took a sip of his drink, looking at Tori over the rim. "She mentioned she was getting dinner and invited me to join her."

"Outstanding," Alex mumbled. "Well, enjoy your dinner. Let Tiffany know if you need anything else."

"We will." Winston said dismissively and reached for Tori's hand again.

Winston mesmerized Tori so much, she didn't realize Alex had stepped away from the table. Impressed by Winston's occupation, looks and manners, she felt lucky to have met such a nice man on her first flirtatious attempt. She'd hit the jackpot with her first date in Florida. Tori saw Barrett walking toward her out of the corner of her eye walking toward her.

"Hey, Tori," Barrett stopped at her table.

"Hi, Barrett," Tori smiled, "how are you?"

"I'm good, working." Barrett pointed to Winston. "Who is your friend?"

"I'm Winston James." Winston stood up and shook Barrett's hand.

"Nice to meet you," Barrett nodded. "Tori, will I see you later?"

"Yes, I'm going to see Frey when I finish eating." Tori nodded.

"Great." Barrett placed his hand on Tori's shoulder. "I'll see you then. Enjoy your dinner."

Tori and Winston said goodbye to Barrett and continued with their dinner.

"You seem to know everyone here, don't you?" Winston asked.

"I've been meeting everyone." Tori noticed Alex had cut up her lettuce into bite-size pieces. "They are all very nice."

"You said you just moved here, where are you from?" Winston picked up his burger and took a bite.

"I was born on the Pine Ridge Reservation in South Dakota. I'm an Oglala Lakota American Indian," Tori answered. "Have you always lived here?"

"So, you are my beautiful Indian princess." Winston winked at her. "I grew up in Fort Lauderdale. My parents were very wealthy bankers before they retired. We own a house on the beach."

"Do you live with your parents?" Tori asked. She loved he was a family man.

"No." Winston looked offended. "They live with me. I've done well for myself, and I bought their house so they could travel during their retirement."

"That's really nice of you, Winston." Tori smiled and took a drink of water. "I love that you help your parents. While I was on the reservation, I lived with my parents."

"Really." Winston sat closer to the table and reached for Tori's hand. "We have something in common. I'm sure the more we get to know each other, the more commonalities we'll share. I have a feeling we'll be very compatible and get along wonderfully."

Tori felt enamored with everything Winston was telling her. He was a good listener, engaging in their conversation, and a family man. What more could she ask for? Enjoying her dinner immensely, she hoped he asked her out. She couldn't wait to tell Frey all about it.

"Would you like some dessert?" Winston wiped his mouth. "Although you are sweet enough."

"No, thank you." Tori looked down at her lap and felt heat rising in her cheeks. "I'm full and really need to go see my friend in the casino."

"Can I get you all anything else?" Tiffany came by and cleared their plates.

"No thank you, Tiffany." Winston sat back in his chair. "Everything was delicious. Can I please have my check?"

"Coming right up." Tiffany walked away with their plates.

"Thank you for a nice evening," Tori looked up into his eyes.

"You're welcome, Beautiful." Winston reached for her hand again. "Think maybe we can do this again. Tomorrow night?"

"That would be great." Tori sat up and leaned against the table.

"We can eat in Savor so you can get to know me better before we venture to a restaurant outside of this resort." Winston raised her hand to his lips and kissed the back of her hand.

Tori didn't get the same warm and fuzzies she did with Alex, but she wanted to give Winston a chance since he was acting romantic and sensitive toward her feelings. Dating Winston would be better, since they didn't work together. Workplace romances were tough, from what she'd been told about Thunder and Rachel's relationship. Working at a preschool she'd never had to worry about being in that situation.

"I would really like that," Tori said, watching Winston pay his bill in cash.

"I'll walk you to the casino." Winston stood up and walked behind Tori to help her up. "I have to get back to work for about another hour."

"Thank you." Tori was being swept off her feet, and she loved every minute. Winston placed her hand in the crook of his arm and guided her to the casino entrance.

"Well, here we are," Winston gently tugged Tori around to face him, "I will see you tomorrow night, Beautiful." Winston gave her a quick kiss on her cheek. "How about I meet you here in the lobby at 6:00 pm?"

"Perfect. I can't wait," Tori whispered, "see you tomorrow."

Tori turned around quickly and entered the casino, practically skipping all the way to Freya's table. Tori saw Freya look up before she approached her and wave to another dealer. She noticed Freya swapped places with the other dealer.

"You look thrilled." Freya grabbed her arm and led her toward the bathroom.

"I met someone," Tori sighed, opening the bathroom door.

"I knew you would." Freya slapped her arm. "How long did it take?"

"He showed up about five minutes after you left. I checked my watch because I knew you would ask me." Tori walked into a stall.

"Hey, I want details." Freya knocked on her stall door. "I didn't have to go to the bathroom. I just wanted some privacy for this conversation."

"Well, I did." Tori flushed the toilet and walked out to wash her hands. "He was so sweet, cute, charming, considerate, and hot with stunning blue eyes."

"Don't stop now," Freya laughed. "You are smitten. I can't wait to meet him."

"Well, you are in luck." Tori leaned back onto the counter. "He's meeting me at Savor tomorrow for dinner. He said this way I could get to know him better before he takes me to another restaurant outside this resort. Isn't that sweet of him?"

"Smooth." Freya reapplied her lipstick.

"He was very flirtatious and charming." Tori pointed to the lipstick. "I may have to borrow that tomorrow night. Oh, now you must come with me to girls' night."

"Okay, okay, I'll go with you to your Girls' Night Out." Freya walked into a stall. "I guess I'll use the potty since I'm here. What time are you meeting Mr. Perfect?"

"In the lobby at six," Tori said over the sound of the toilet flushing.

"I will be there." Freya straightened her blouse and washed her hands. "I start at six, but I'll have another dealer cover for me for the first few minutes. I MUST meet this dreamy guy. Just so you know, I was going to go to girls' night, anyway. A girl can't have too many girlfriends."

They both laughed and hung onto each other as they walked to Freya's table. Tori waved to Holt on her way out of the casino. She needed to shower and wanted to relive the wonderful night with Winston while she laid in bed.

Chapter 16

Shady Deal
Winston

Winston left the casino and couldn't believe his luck. For months, he'd been trying to get close to Freya. He did a lot of business deals in the casino and wanted some leverage with the manager. Unfortunately, Freya never gave him the time of day. She was a cold bitch. He'd watched Freya walk with a beautiful woman into RUSH and followed her.

Just his luck, Freya left her alone at the bar in the restaurant and went to work. Winston had hoped this new girl would be amenable. Meeting Tori was a gift from up above. It was a sign that everything was going to work out. If he believed in that which he didn't. He made his own fate. The idea of growing his business and making more money excited him.

Tori could help him conduct his business at the casino. She seemed to have perks, and he was more than willing to take advantage of them. He just needed to ease her into his business. Once he charmed her into being an active participant in one of his deals, she would have to keep her mouth shut and help him. She seemed too naïve to catch on to his plans.

Winston was a large supplier of drugs in the area, and he "financially advised" his sellers to work hard or die. When he received the drugs from the cartel, they would give him a week to sell them and deliver their money. Several times he'd paid for the drugs out of his parent's money to buy him time, but he couldn't do that every time. The more drugs he moved for the cartel, the more they upped the quantity. It was getting harder and harder to sell those large quantities as quickly as they provided them. Selling drugs to the tourist patrons of the casino was becoming a necessity. Or at least he thought it might solve that problem.

He usually sold the drugs to the two violent motorcycle clubs in the area; Lucifer's Renegades MC and Los Lobos de Muerte MC. Winston never told them he was working both clubs. He played the clubs against each other, driving up the prices. Each club thought they were Winston's exclusive dealer. Lucifer's Renegades were dependable since the one time they took too long to make their payments for the drugs and Winston shot one of their prospects. He had to reinforce the importance and urgency in paying their debt. He had convinced both MCs if they worked with him—they stood to make a fortune. Time to call Reaper, Prez of Lucifer's Renegades, and his most profitable buyer.

"Reaper, this is Win. Are you ready for another pickup Friday night?"

"Hey man," Reaper answered, "We'll be ready for more on Friday. Same price?"

"Yup." Winston opened his safe and checked his drug stash. "I have several bricks of Fen, Coke, and Pot laced with LSD."

"Let me check with Numbers to see how much we can purchase," Reaper stated. "I'll text you tomorrow."

"Let me know by tomorrow or I'll sell it to 'Los Lobos de Muerte'," Winston knew mentioning them would light a fire under Reaper to talk to Numbers.

"I will discuss it with Numbers tonight and text you ASAP, Win. Just give me a few hours."

"You got it Reaper," Winston hung up the phone.

Winston preferred dealing with Lucifer's Renegades. Their pipeline moved a lot more drugs than Los Lobos. Which was why he usually sold the majority of his drugs to Lucifer's Renegades. He was leery of Los Lobos. They spoke Spanish constantly in front of him and once they'd tried to steal from him. Unfortunately for them, Winston knew some words, and that biker ended up eating a bullet. Los Lobos President, Machete, let it slide since he wasn't behind stealing from the dealers and didn't want to lose a supplier. Los Lobos knew Winston sold the best stuff. After that, Winston still sold them some drugs, but he double checked the payment on site. Those fuckers were bat shit crazy and unstable. He knew Machete could turn on him at any time, so he tried to ensure that Machete remained unaware that Lucifer's Renegades were supplied with most of his drugs.

On a different thought, Winston couldn't wait for his date with Tori. She was beautiful and didn't seem too bright. Getting her into a predicament was going to be a piece of cake. Where Freya was hard to manipulate, he felt Tori would be putty in his hands. Every time he said something flirtatious, she blushed. He would bet any amount of money she was still a virgin. He loved deflowering virgins. With his money and his parent's prestige, women would throw themselves at him, not realizing he would fuck them and leave them. He just liked the chase and the catch. After that, he would grow bored.

He might keep Tori since she could prove profitable for him. Not to mention if they ate at the resort, he never had to pay for her. Maybe eventually, he could eat for free as well. He wondered if she could play in the casino for free and keep the winning money. Yes, Tori was a keeper… for now.

Chapter 17

W.T.F. Happened
Alex

Last night Tiffany came into the kitchen and told him Tori was there with a date and all he saw was red. So, she was okay dating someone else, just not him. What was wrong with him? He was a nice guy, held doors open for women, could cook, and kept a clean apartment. What the fuck had happened between yesterday morning and afternoon?

He'd tried to be nice to her date, but Winston was an asshole. It also didn't help that Barrett gave him shit this morning in the gym about his girl being on a date with another guy. That sucked. After he showered and changed, he was looking forward to talking to Tori. He wanted to get back on the right footing with her.

Alex knocked on her door.

"Good morning," Tori's greeted with her sing-song voice as she swung the door open and walked to the elevator.

"Good morning." Alex joined her in the elevator. "You're happy this morning."

"I am," Tori beamed at him. "I have a date tonight."

Alex's stomach twisted at her declaration. What the fuck? What did he miss?

"Uh, a date?" Alex muttered and walked into the elevator.

"Yes," Tori glanced at him, "with Winston."

"Winston, huh?" Alex tried to be nice and get as much information as possible. "How did you guys meet at RUSH?"

Tori didn't answer him right away, since they were walking out to his car. Once they got in, Alex asked her again.

"Tori," Alex focused on the road, "how did you meet Winston?"

"Winston," Tori sighed breathlessly.

"Yes, Winston." Alex was getting annoyed with her behavior toward this guy she just met.

"Frey dared me to wear this bright red lipstick," Tori started rambling, "saying if I wore it, I would pick up a guy. I didn't believe her at first, of course. I mean, I'm not beautiful, but she said if I went through with it and picked up a guy in fifteen minutes while I sat at the bar, she would go with me to Sarah's on Saturday for Girls' Night Out. So, I wore it and BAM! I got a date."

Alex was trying to process all the information Tori had just spewed. He was going to have a serious conversation with Frey about this bet.

"Okay, first off," Alex tried to address all her comments, "you don't need red lipstick to attract a guy. You are beautiful, just as you are. Second, why the hell would Frey bet you to hook up at a bar, and third, where is this girls' night?"

"Like I said, it's at Sarah's house. Sarah is Thunder's sister. It's nothing you need to worry about, Alex," Tori breathed out heavily. "None of this concerns you. We're just co-workers."

"Wow, Tori," Alex glanced at Tori, "I thought we were friends. Now I'm just a co-worker. Even as just a co-worker, I would be worried about you. You're new to this town, and I want nothing to happen to you. Shit, shoot me for caring."

"I'm sorry, Alex," Tori kept looking anywhere except at Alex, "let's just drop it."

"Fine, Princess," Alex's calm demeanor just went out the window. Again, what the fuck just happened?

"Don't call me that." Tori huffed and crossed her arms.

"Well, you're acting all high and mighty about everything." Alex couldn't stop the angry comments coming out of his mouth. So much for telling his mom he would be nice to Tori. "I'm trying to look out for you, and you can't see that. You haven't been here long enough to figure out where to go and with whom. That guy Winston seemed like a jackass. Why would you go out with him? Do you not see he's not a nice guy? What do you really know about him? How naïve are you?"

"You're acting like a jerk," Tori mumbled.

Alex agreed with Tori. He was acting like a jerk. He couldn't seem to stop his mouth from saying all the shit in his head. Dammit, it hurt how easily she turned him down and turned to another man just because they worked together. He could tell she was getting frustrated with him. Maybe it was best he kept his mouth shut the rest of the way to work.

Once they arrived, Tori once again stormed out of the car and slammed her door before walking to the front door. This was becoming a habit he didn't like. Unfortunately, now she had a key and knew the alarm code so she could open the cultural center and scurry away from him.

Alex walked into the kitchen and slammed his hand on his prepping table. Except for this morning, he had tried to do so much for this girl, and she wasn't giving him the time of day. Who the hell was this Winston person to just come in and sweep her off her feet in just a few hours?

Working with her had been a disadvantage. Who knew that would be a hard no for her? Many people met at their workplace and made it work. Why couldn't she at least give him a shot, like she gave that fucker Winston?

He knew Freya had worked until two and would still be asleep, but he was waking her ass up right now. Alex dialed her number. He knew when she saw it was him, she would answer the phone.

"Hello," Freya mumbled.

"What the fuck did you do?" Alex screamed into the phone.

"Alex," Freya whispered, "I worked late, and I was sleeping. What the hell are you talking about?"

"Really, Frey?" Alex paced and mimicked Freya's voice, "*wear red lipstick pick up a guy. I bet you can.* What the fuck was that?"

"Are you talking about Tori?" Freya still sounded sleepy.

"Well, duh! Of course, I'm talking about Tori." Alex rubbed his hand over his face. "She could've gotten hurt. She's too nice and naïve, and he's an asshole."

"I wouldn't let her hear you say that," Freya yawned. "Besides, she was safe. She stayed in RUSH the whole date. Barrett kept watch."

"Barrett? You told him, but not me, about your crazy ass bet?" Alex screamed into the phone. "I had to walk out and watch them together at the table. It sucked, Frey."

"I knew you were in the kitchen working, and Barrett could walk anywhere he wants." Freya explained, "I didn't know she met anyone when I sent him over there. I just wanted to make sure she was okay since I gave her fifteen minutes to hook up."

"Hook Up!" Alex screamed into the phone, "What the Fuck! I am so pissed at you right now," Alex growled.

"Relax, big brother, she's fine," Freya said calmly. "Barrett said he wore a business suit and appeared to be okay. I thought they would just have a drink and she would walk away. I had no idea she was gonna go out with him again. If I knew you were into her, I would have sent her your way with the red lipstick, not to the bar. Be honest with me next time. This isn't just my fault. Wait a minute, you've fallen for her."

"Yes, I like her a lot, dammit," Alex hollered.

"Alex," Freya sighed, "I didn't know you should have told me."

"How was I supposed to tell you I was interested when I haven't seen you except when I introduced you guys?" Alex grumbled. "I have no clue what's happening. I've never liked a girl so quickly and now she is dating that asshole. I don't trust him."

"I'm so sorry, Alex. Tori told me she's meeting him again tonight in the lobby at six, and they are going to eat at Savor. Are you still mad at me? What can I do to help?"

Alex stayed quiet for a few minutes, making his sister sweat before he answered her question. If he had known Freya's intent, he would have unquestionably had Tori sent to him in the kitchen with the red lipstick and not some crazy ass bet with a stranger. At least he had known Tori for three days, and their families were friends.

"How could I be mad at my favorite sister?" Alex sighed. "I should have told you. I forgive you, but I'm still pissed at you for doing that. Maybe you can ask her questions about Winston. She won't talk to me."

"Alex," Freya spoke cautiously, "she's the nicest person I know. What did you do to make her mad?"

"I sort of lost my temper and talked shit," Alex mumbled.

"Oh Alex," Freya sounded concerned, "you really need to control your temper and your mouth. Personally, I would love for you to hook up with her, so let me know what I can do to help."

"Right now, I just need information so I can keep her safe. Where does Sarah live? Do you know who else will be there? I'm assuming since she hasn't asked me to take her and you guys are quickly becoming thick as thieves, you're driving her."

"Yeah, I'm driving her. I'm so excited to meet more girls, I feel like I'm constantly surrounded by testosterone. It will be a pleasant change for me. Sarah lives on a farm with her husband and two kids. We are meeting there on Saturday at four. My goodness, you are worse than dad."

"Hey, I take that as a compliment because dad cares about his family." Alex grabbed the flour to make fresh Indian Fry Bread. "I gotta go. I have to make some fresh fry bread for today and I want to try out some new recipes."

"Okay," Freya whispered, "I'm sorry. I truly didn't realize how much you liked her."

"Ugh, she friend zoned me, Frey. Or rather, co-worker zoned me." Alex pinched the bridge of his nose. "I just…really like her and worry about her."

"Okay, I'll see what I can do on my end. I'll see you later."

"Yup." Alex placed the oil on the counter and disconnected his call.

Since there was nothing he could do about Tori's dating situation at the moment, Alex focused on working with his sample menu items. Alex wanted to try a couple of different recipes for the opening. Thunder told him they served the Indian Fry Bread with honey. He wanted to make something a little different. Most people love tacos and pizza, so he thought he would make bite size Indian Fry Bread Tacos and Pizza appetizers. He would substitute the flour tortilla and pizza crust with Indian Fry Bread. They were a couple weeks away from the opening, and if Thunder liked these appetizers, he needed to make sure he had all the ingredients and perfected the recipe.

Chapter 18

Second Date with Mr. Perfect
Tori

Tori walked into the center, leaving the door unlocked for Alex, and headed to the office to wait for Thunder. Apparently, Alex didn't want to talk to her, and she needed to do some filing. She wanted to stay busy and away from Alex, although truth be told, she really missed their friendship even if they only had it for a few days.

When Thunder arrived, Tori went with him into the warehouse and labeled the new artifacts and paintings. They organized all the new items and decided how to display them. They agreed to leave the Red Path Exhibit until the end of the following week, while they organized the artifacts in the warehouse for the Unconquered Path Exhibit. Some of the Lakota artifacts stayed in the center display case, but everything else had to be shipped back to whichever tribal council had lent the cultural center the artifact.

"So, I hear my sister is having a Girls' Night Out at her house." Thunder placed another empty box to the side.

"She is, and I told her I would be there, not realizing I work until five on Saturday," Tori huffed. "I'm sorry. I will let her know I'll get there after work."

"It's okay Tori," Thunder shook his head, "Mark and I can stay until five. You can leave at four."

"Thank you, Thunder," Tori said gratefully, "I won't do it again."

"You won't, but I'm sure my sister will. Sarah and Isa would give me so much shit if I didn't let you go." Thunder laughed. "Do you have a ride?"

"Yes, Alex's sister, Freya, is coming with me." Tori put another artifact on the table. They continued to work in companionable silence until lunchtime.

"Hey guys," Alex interrupted, "I wanted to try something different for the Unconquered Path Opening so I made these bite size appetizers and I want your opinion."

"Okay," Thunder walked toward Alex, "what do you have?"

"I made bite size Indian Fry Bread Tacos and Indian Fry Bread Pizzas," Alex stared at Thunder as he took one of each. "If you don't like it, I can still make plain fry bread with honey like last time."

"Oh, wow!" Thunder exclaimed as he bit into the bite size taco, "These are delicious. Tori come try one. Are you going to add a full-size version to the restaurant?"

"I would love to if you approve," Alex watched Tori.

"I approve. These toppings are delicious on fry bread." Thunder took another one.

"I was going to make two variations of each. For the Tacos, I can make chicken and beef and for the pizza, I can make cheese and sausage," Alex explained.

"I love it." Thunder ate a third one. "Okay, take these away before I eat them all."

"Oh, I have more," Alex informed them. "I made enough for all of us to have them for lunch."

"These are fantastic Alex," Tori said between bites. She didn't know why Alex seemed so nervous for them to try his food. It was delicious.

"I'll get some more and meet you guys in the restaurant so you can finish these for lunch." Alex announced as he turned to leave.

"Sounds good," Thunder called out, "Tell Mark so he can join us."

"Will do," Alex backed out of the warehouse.

"Tori," Thunder turned toward her, "let's stop for now and eat lunch. I love those and I want to eat them while they're fresh out of the oven."

"Sounds good," Tori laughed, "Alex outdid himself."

Tori followed Thunder to the restaurant where Alex had laid out his fry bread selection on a couple of different tables and bottles of water for them.

"I could get used to this." Thunder covered his mouth to talk in between bites. "I think I'll be eating your food for lunch every day like I did Grayfeather's. Test out any recipes you want if there's some Seminole twist to it. I'm so glad we have you as our chef."

"Thanks, I'm excited about this opportunity," Alex nodded. "I'm grateful for the chance to try new foods. Seminole recipes and ingredients will always be a part of the menu."

"Thank you, Alex." Tori tried to be nice and get their friendship back on track. "I agree with Thunder. I'll be eating lunch here as well."

"Yup," Mark nodded before standing up, "make that three."

"Thanks guys," Alex stood up and began clearing tables.

They finished all of Alex's lunch while they raved about it. Alex had done a great job with his blend of American Indian, Mexican and Italian cuisine. All the variations were delicious. Thunder and Mark left the restaurant to go back to work. Tori grabbed a couple of dishes, but Alex stopped her.

"Tori," Alex placed his hand over hers, "I got this. I know you have things to do."

"Okay." Tori grinned, "thank you again. It was delicious."

"See you later. Come get me when you're ready to go."

"Okay," Tori removed her hand and walked back to the warehouse.

Thunder wanted to break down all the boxes because they'd reuse them to send the previous exhibit items back. By five, Tori was dragging her feet as she made her way to Alex in the kitchen so they could go home.

"Are you ready?" Tori asked from the doorway.

"Yup," Alex wiped down his prepping counter, "I just finished cleaning up. You have perfect timing. Let's go."

Alex grabbed his keys from the counter and guided Tori out with his hand on her lower back. Tori felt a tingle run up her spine from Alex's hand. She hadn't felt that with Winston, but maybe she would feel it tonight after their more romantic dinner. Saying goodbye to Mark and Thunder, they walked by the lobby toward Alex's car.

"How was your day?" Alex asked as he pulled out of the parking lot.

"It was busy," Tori looked at Alex, "but good. I loved your food. It was creatively, unique and delicious. I've never tried fry bread like that before."

"Thanks," Alex glanced at her, "I got the idea last night and really wanted to get in today to try it. I'm glad you liked it."

Tori was getting nervous about her date. She sat on her hands to stop fidgeting and stared out the window.

"Are you excited about your date?" Alex was drumming his fingers on the steering wheel.

"I am," Tori smiled, "and a little nervous, to be honest. I haven't been on a date in a long time. Plus, usually my mom, dad, or little sister were with me. This will be my first solo date."

"Wait," Alex stopped at a light and stared at her, "what? You've never been on a date alone?"

"Nope." Tori felt the heat rising in her cheeks.

"Tori," Alex turned back towards the light, "you can stay at the resort, so you feel safe and comfortable."

"Actually," Tori mumbled, "I am. We are eating at Savor. Winston wanted me to get to know him better before he takes me somewhere else for dinner."

"That sounds really nice of him," Alex cleared his throat.

They stayed silent the rest of the way to the resort. Once there, Tori said bye and headed to her room to shower and change. She wanted to look nice for her dinner.

Tori put on light makeup and a black tight wrap around dress she'd brought from home. Maybe Sunday she could convince Frey to go clothes shopping with her and she could finally break into the clothes bonus Thunder gave her. He must have assumed she wouldn't have professional clothes. He would know, since Sarah had worked with her for a couple of those years. Maybe it had been Sarah's idea for the clothes' allowance. That would make more sense. Checking her watch, she saw it was almost six o'clock. She had better hurry and head downstairs.

She left her room and rode the elevator down to the lobby. She immediately spotted Winston in the lobby by the waterfall fountain. Winston made his way to Tori.

"Hi Beautiful." Winston kissed her on the cheek. "You look stunning."

"Thank you, Winston," Tori blushed, "you look very handsome."

"Ladies first." Winston waved his arm for Tori to walk ahead of him.

Once Tori passed him, she felt his hand at the small of her back, but no tingles up her spine. That was weird. She really thought she would feel something with Winston like she'd felt with Alex. Was she making a mistake by dating Winston? Tori snapped out of her thoughts as they approached the hostess stand.

"We have a reservation for Mr. James," Winston informed Tess.

"Hi Tori," Tess smiled, "Of course, right this way."

Tess escorted them to a secluded table near the kitchen. Winston pulled out the chair for Tori and placed the napkin in her lap.

"Thank you, Winston." Tori scooted in.

"Our chef has selected a wine for the table," Tess winked at Tori, "I'll get it for you."

"Actually," Winston interrupted her, "Tess, I would like to choose our wine. Can we please see the wine list?"

"Of course." Tess bowed her head and backed away from the table.

"Winston." Tori didn't want to be confrontational. "I'm sure the chef would have provided a superb wine for us. I've heard Bernie is an exceptional chef."

"I'm sure he is," Winston nodded, "But you are my lady tonight and I want to choose for you."

"Oh, okay." Tori looked at the menu.

"Here is our wine menu selection," Tori looked up when she heard Alex's voice, "I hear you would like to choose your own. Please select whichever one you want. It's on the house."

"Alex," Tori said with surprise as she saw him, "Are you working here tonight?"

"Yes," Alex responded. "I gave Bernie the night off."

"We would like to have the 2017 Opus One Red Wine." Winston didn't even look at the wine list or at Alex. "Do you all carry that? Only the best for my girl."

"Of course," Alex nodded.

Tori noticed Alex's jawline harden before he looked at her with a raised eyebrow.

"Winston." Tori waved at Winston. "You remember Chef Alex."

"Mr. James." Alex held out his hand. "Pleased to see you again dining in our other establishment."

"Nice to see you too, Alex," Winston nodded. "Thanks for stopping by."

Winston dismissed Alex and reached for Tori's hand. Winston's rude behavior surprised Tori.

"Thank you, Alex," Tori tried to soften the blow.

"No problem," Alex said through gritted teeth, "I'll have your waitress bring your wine. Enjoy your dinner.”

Tori watched Alex back away and walk toward Tess before he glanced at her one more time and headed into the kitchen.

“Winston.” Tori pulled her hand out from Winston’s grip. “That was kind of rude. Alex was just trying to be nice.”

“I know, Beautiful,” Winston softened his gaze. “I’m sorry. I wanted to take care of you tonight since it is our first official date, and I’m hoping you will go out with me again tomorrow. I just want to have your undivided attention.”

Tess came by with the wine, uncorked it, and gave a sample to Winston. Winston nodded his acceptance of the wine, and Tess poured out two glasses.

“Thank you, Tess.” Tori acknowledged and took a sip of wine.

“So tomorrow night?” Winston drank some wine.

“Wow, two nights in a row.” Tori placed her glass on the table. “I would love to. This wine is delicious.”

“Only the best for my girl,” Winston raised his glass. “I can meet you again at six in the lobby. I’ll make a reservation at Jack’s Steakhouse. They serve the best steak in town.”

“That sounds lovely,” Tori smiled.

“Hi,” Freya surprised Tori from behind, causing her to jump in her seat.

“Hey.” Tori stood up to hug Freya. “I want you to meet Winston.”

“Hello Winston,” Freya looked stiff as she said his name, “I know Winston. I’ve seen him in the casino.”

“Hello Freya,” Winston stood up and put his hand out, “it’s nice to see you.”

“You too.” Freya shook his hand. “Can I talk to you for a minute, Tori?”

“Sure,” Tori looked at Winston, “I’ll be right back.”

Tori and Freya walked into the kitchen.

“Tori,” Freya whispered, “I don’t like him. I think he’s a player. He kept trying to ask me out and wouldn’t get the hint.”

Tori’s eyes widened. “I’ll be careful, but he is really nice to me.”

“I bet he is,” Freya mumbled under her breath.

“He’s been a real gentleman.” Tori placed her hand on Freya’s arm. “I think you’ll like him when you get to know him. Maybe he just didn’t understand you weren’t interested. I’m sure he didn’t mean to offend you.”

“Oh, Tori,” Freya closed her eyes briefly, “you are so nice. Just promise me you’ll be careful, and if he does anything you don’t like, you’ll run like hell.”

Tori smiled and hugged her. “You’re overreacting. Winston wouldn’t do anything to hurt me. But I’ll keep that in mind.”

“Okay,” Freya squeezed her hands, “I don’t like this, but if you really like him, there’s not really anything I can do about that. Just be careful, please.”

“What’s going on, ladies?” Alex asked them.

“Nothing,” Tori smiled and looked at Freya like they shared a secret, “Frey was just asking about our Girls’ Night Out. Right Frey?”

“Right,” Freya hugged Tori and whispered in her ear, “Wake me up in the morning and tell me about this date.” Then loudly said, “I gotta go to work, see you later."

Tori followed Freya closely, so Alex didn't have time to ask them again.

"Frey, Tori," Tori heard Alex's voice call out to them, but they both ignored him, and she returned to her date.

"Is everything okay?" Winston stood when Tori approached the table.

"Yes," Tori answered, "Freya just said you tried to ask her out?"

"I did," Winston agreed. "She's a beautiful woman, but she turned me down. I want you to know I don't date a lot and I have asked no one after that. Not because I still like her, but because I am very busy at work. But when I saw you sitting alone at the bar, well, I've never felt this way about anyone, Freya included. I'm sorry if it hurt you because I flirted with her, but we never did anything. I would never flirt with her or any other woman now that I am with you. I really like you and want us to get to know each other better."

"I understand," Tori smiled. "I really like you, too. It's not your fault I know one of the previous girls you flirted with."

"You are so good to me," Winston took her hand and kissed the back, "how did I get so lucky to meet you."'

Tori finished her lovely evening with Winston and allowed him to escort her to her room. Winston was a gentleman and kissed her on the cheek before he left.

Chapter 19

What does She see in That Guy?
Alex

Alex was fuming when he approached Tess and told her which bottle to send to their table. What a jackass! He would love to know what Tori saw in that fucker. He was going to send a nice bottle of wine and that fucker had to pick an exclusive bottle that cost almost five hundred dollars which he kept in stock for his affluent customers.

Alex knew the bastard had tried to test him with that specific bottle of wine. Little did he know, Alex had an entire wine cellar with several rare bottles of wine for his best customers. And Winston James was not one of them.

Alex stayed away from Tori and her date after that. He was afraid if he went out there again, he would punch her date in the face for being an asshole. When Freya came into the kitchen with Tori, he knew something was going on. Freya looked worried as she talked to her. He'd walked over to them, but they both left without telling him anything. As soon as he finished in the kitchen, he planned to track down Freya and have a talk.

Four hours later, Alex stormed into the casino straight toward Freya's table.

"Hey, bro," Barrett intercepted him, "what's going on? You look pissed."

"Have you seen Frey?" Alex looked around. Freya wasn't at her usual table.

"Yeah, she's in the break room," Barrett walked with him. "I gotta hear this."

Alex ignored him and walked into the break room. Holt was sitting with Freya at a nearby table.

"What was that about with Tori?" Alex demanded.

"What are you talking about?" Freya raised her eyebrows.

"Don't play coy with me, dammit," Alex pounded on the table, causing Freya to stand up and back up.

"Whoa, Alex," Holt stood up and moved in front of Freya, "what's going on?"

"Frey," Alex huffed and ran his hand over his face, "sorry. I didn't mean to scare you. What were you talking to Tori about? You looked worried."

"Tell him," Holt turned around to face Freya.

"Tell me what?" Alex raised his hands in frustration. "I really wish people would start talking to me around here."

"Alex," Freya stepped around Holt and placed her hand on Alex's arm, "I'm not keeping anything from you. I was going to talk to you about it. But, I didn't want to do it in the kitchen. I don't like that guy Tori's dating. Before hitting on her, he was hitting on me last week and wouldn't take no for an answer— well, until he met her."

"Did he hurt you?" Alex was fuming. "Because I'll kill him."

"No," Freya hugged him, "I just kept turning him down. The last time Holt stepped in, removed him from my table. I was warning Tori to be careful. But who knows? Maybe they are both really into each other. Just because he gives me the creeps doesn't mean he is a creep."

"Frey," Barrett interrupted, "what do you mean he gives you the creeps?"

"It's nothing," Freya rubbed her arms, "I just have a weird vibe from him."

"Can you talk to Tori?" Alex asked. "You're an excellent judge of character. If you tell her he gives you the creeps, she might listen and not go out with him again."

"I tried," Freya put on an apologetic smile, "she really likes him. I even told her he hit on me. He's convinced her he's a nice guy. I told her to wake me up in the morning and tell me about her date. I figure if she tells me what's going on, I can try to convince her not to date him again, before something happens."

"Shit, fuck!" Alex shouted. "What do you mean, if something happens? If he hurts her, I will track him down and make him suffer."

"I'll talk to her," Freya rubbed Alex's arm.

"Talk to her tomorrow morning, Frey. I need her to understand he is not a good person, he's a player. It might be too late by then. He may already have her snowed, but you gotta try. Please talk her into not seeing him again. She won't talk to me since I've been co-worker zoned."

"Co-worker, what?" Barrett asked, looking very confused.

"You know, like friend zoned," Alex waved his hands up in the air again, "when you want to keep someone as your friend and are afraid to date them because it could go wrong, and you can lose your friend. Well, she did that to me since we work together. She co-worker zoned me."

"Yeah," Holt placed his hands on his hips and shook his head no, "pretty sure that's not a thing."

"Well, it's a thing now. She won't go out with me."

"Alex," Freya rubbed his back, "I'll try to talk to talk to her."

"Thank you," Alex sighed.

"I'll keep an eye out on the floor in case I see him," Holt nodded.

"I'll check our video footage of the last couple days to make sure he did nothing fishy." Barrett slapped Alex on the back.

"Thanks guys," Alex turned around and headed to his room. He was done for the night. Hopefully, he could finally catch some z's after this shitshow of a day.

Chapter 20

Mr. Perfect May Not Be So Perfect
Tori

The next day, Tori was just finishing her makeup when she heard Frey.

"Good morning, Sunshine," Frey said before yawning into her hand.

"What are you doing up?" Tori asked.

"I wanted to know how your date went." Freya leaned up against the door.

"It was so good," Tori smiled. "Winston chose our bottle of wine and food. He is so considerate."

"Sounds a little domineering to me."

"Frey, please don't ruin this for me. I've never had someone really listen and pay attention to me, especially not a guy. Anyway, I can't talk right now because Alex will be here soon."

"Okay," Freya sighed, "will you come talk to me when you get home?"

"Of course," Tori hugged Freya, then heard the knock on the door, "that's Alex. I'll see you later."

"Have a good day," Frey yawned again.

"Go back to sleep," Tori smiled and walked away.

Tori grabbed her keys and purse before opening the door, "Good Morning."

"Good morning, you ready to go?"

"Yes." Tori followed Alex to his car. Once inside, she wanted to talk about last night at Savor.

"I'm sorry for Winston's behavior last night."

"You don't need to apologize for him."

"He was just nervous and wanted to show me his chivalrous side."

"By being an asshole to his chef?"

"He didn't mean to come across as rude to you. We talked about it right after you walked away. I'm sure if you had come back, he would have apologized."

"Yeah, right," Alex mumbled under his breath.

"Alex," sighed and turned to look at him, "don't be like that. I want you guys to get along."

"Why?"

"Because I don't have a lot of friends here and I want my boyfriend to get along with my friends."

"So now he's your boyfriend?"

"Well, we have gone out several times, and he kissed me."

"Right," Alex pulled into the parking lot, "Did Frey talk to you this morning? You know, he gives her the creeps."

"Frey said Winston asked her out, and he was a Romeo Joe, but she never told me he gave her the creeps."

Alex turned toward her and reached for her hand, grabbing her attention. "Frey told Barrett, Holt, and me when I spoke to her last night that he gave her the creeps. Please reconsider going out with him. Frey is an excellent judge of character."

"You think I'm not a good judge of character?" Tori was fuming. How dare he belittle her!

"No," Alex began backtracking his words, "no. I just meant she is fantastic at reading people, since she does it daily at work."

"I will be fine. I'll be careful and show you all what a great guy Winston is."

Tori yanked her hand away from Alex. "Let's get to work. I don't want to be late. I'll see you later."

Tori walked in and greeted Mark on her way to the office. Today she needed to price new items for the Gift Shop. She took a break at lunch to eat with Thunder, Mark, and Alex. They kept the conversation about the opening, which was great. Tori didn't want everyone to know about her new boyfriend. After lunch, Tori went back into the gift shop with Mark. She loved working with Mark. He was very easygoing and laid back. Nothing seemed to bother him as far as she could tell. They liked to talk about music and running. The time passed quickly and before she knew it—she heard Alex's voice.

"Tori," Alex asked from the doorway, "Are you ready to go?"

"Yes," Tori closed the glass counter which displayed the jewelry for sale, "I'll grab my purse and meet you at your car."

"Okay," Alex left.

"Bye Mark, I'll see you tomorrow?"

"Yup, I'll be there," Mark smiled.

Tori grabbed her stuff and headed out.

"I'm ready," Tori said as she pulled the car door shut.

"Do you want to get dinner?" Alex pulled out into traffic. "I'm not working tonight."

"Uh, I'm sorry. I can't." Tori looked down and fidgeted with her purse. "I have a date with Winston, and I have some work to do." Tori held up the folder in her lap.

"Wow. Three days in a row, huh?" Alex gritted his teeth. "You must really like this guy."

"I do," Tori sighed, "He's nice and a proper gentleman."

"Really?" Alex raised an eyebrow and looked at Tori. "A proper gentleman?"

"I know he was rude to you, Alex, but he just wanted to be the one to choose our food and wine for dinner."

"How does it not bother you he flirted with Frey?"

"It did at first, but then he explained she wasn't interested. He hasn't flirted with anyone else after that until he met me." Tori told Alex what Winston had told her.

"Tori, there's something about him I don't like." Alex parked his car in his usual spot at the resort.

"Alex," Tori turned to look at him, "I know what I'm doing. He's a nice guy."

Alex faced Tori after parking and placed his hand on her knee, accidentally knocking the folder she had in her lap on the floor.

"I don't think he is, and I don't think you see him for the player he is," Alex raised his voice, "you're so nice and naïve, you wouldn't know a serial killer if he asked you out."

"How dare you?" Tori slapped his hand off her knee. "I am not an idiot, and what's wrong with being a nice person? I've been nice to you and you're turning into a jerk. You and Frey need to back off. I know what I'm doing. Come to think of it, this arrangement is not working for me. I'll get Winston to drive me back and forth from work. He already offered. I just didn't want to put him out since we were going in the same direction." Tori hurried out of the car.

"Tori, wait," Alex tried to grab her arm before she got out.

"Bye, Alex." Tori slammed the door and stormed off.

"Fuck!" Tori heard Alex scream behind her.

Tori'd had enough of Alex's comments. She thought he was her friend. They had been getting along. Apparently, she was wrong. They weren't friends…again. Alex just wanted to ruin her happiness. Well, she was done with that and didn't want to hear any more negative thoughts about Winston. True, Winston didn't give her a little tingle in her belly like Alex did. But how could she have any feelings for someone who kept pissing her off? It seemed like all she and Alex did was argue. Right now, the only thing tingling in her body was her anger toward Alex.

Tori stormed into her room and headed toward the shower, stripping off her clothes as she went. Later, she would come to pick them up. She was going to call out to Frey, but she didn't want to take her anger out on her friend. She'd calm down and then go see if she was home. As soon as the water was at the right temperature, she stepped in and washed her hair.

"Oh Shit!" Tori screamed out. She had totally forgotten to bring in the folder she brought home from work. She had to add the AICC surcharge to all the items for sale in the gift shop from the Seminole Tribes. Not only did they have paintings and jewelry from several artists from the Seminole

Tribe of Florida, but also from all the Seminole Tribes around the country. Tori preferred to do the calculations in writing tonight so she could enter them on the computer tomorrow. Her previous dates with Winston usually ended by nine, giving her plenty of time to work tonight without staying up too late.

"Ugh!" Tori grunted, stomping her foot on the tile floor. Now she had to go see Alex and get his car keys. He said he was off work tonight. First, she would knock on his door and hope he was there. If not, then she could ask Frey to call him because she didn't have his number. Tori would have to get the folder, return his keys, and bring it to her room before she could meet with Winston.

Finishing up, she put on another nice dress and applied minimal makeup— time was of the essence. Tori grabbed her purse and knocked on Alex's door. Alex didn't answer, so she knocked harder.

"Coming," Tori could hear his voice coming closer to the door, "geez, hold your horses."

Alex whipped the door open, and Tori's mouth dropped open. *Oh, my goodness gracious.* Alex answered the door dripping wet with only a loosely tied towel wrapped low on his hips. Tori could see his tattoos all over his chiseled chest.

"Ahem," Alex cleared his throat, "Tori, did you need something?"

"Ah, yeah." Tori continued to stare at his chest and followed it down to his growing erection that loosened his knot.

"Tori," Alex grabbed the knot with one of his hands, "Did you need something?"

Alex repeated the question, but Tori was not paying attention. She was making little moaning noises. Alex bent down to look her in the eyes.

"Tori," Alex smirked and waved his hand in front of her face, "What's up?"

"Oh, uh," Tori placed her hands on her cheeks and could feel them burning up, "sorry. Um, can I borrow your keys? I left something in your car."

"Sure." Alex left the door open, turned around and grabbed the keys from his foyer table.

Tori reached out to get the keys from his hand, but Alex closed his hand over hers.

"If you give me a minute, I'll get it for you." Alex squeezed her hand.

"No." Tori pulled back her hand with the keys. "I got it. I gotta come back up here to drop off my folder, so I'll return them when I'm done. But Thanks."

Tori gave him a small smile and spun around to head to the elevator. Holey. She was not expecting him to look that good under his shirt. Tori knew he had muscles because his shirts stretched over his chest, but she was not expecting such a work of art. When Tori stepped into the elevator, she turned around to punch in the floor number. Looking up she noticed Alex was still staring at her from his door. Tori gave him a small smile and held up her hand with a wave and a nod.

Tori walked out to Alex's car and leaned down to get the folder from the floor of the passenger seat. She was so angry with Alex when she had gotten out of the car, but now all she could think about was that tiny towel with its precarious knot. As she was getting up from grabbing the folder, she looked through the back window and saw Winston standing with a man who wore a leather jacket with no sleeves. She had seen similar jackets worn by motorcycle clubs back home. Was Winston giving him a small white brick? Why would Winston be carrying a white brick? Tori didn't think he was in construction. Strange. Tori sat down and watched for a few minutes–confused–when Winston handed the man what looked to be a bag of gummies. It was nice of Winston to think of the other man's kids and send gummies to them. He was a nice guy, and Alex just didn't see this considerate side of him. The man then gave Winston cash.

Tori got out of the car and closed the door. Making her way to Winston, she noticed the man in the leather jacket leering at her. Before she could reach them, they both shook hands and the leather jacket man left. Winston looked angry as he looked at Tori.

"Hi Winston," Tori said when she stood in front of him, "what are you doing back here?"

"What did you see?" Winston grabbed her arm and pulled her up to his face.

"Winston," Tori cried out, "Why are you mad? You're hurting me. I just saw you give that man some gummies for his kids and shake his hand."

"Okay," Winston immediately released his grip and held her by her shoulders, "He's one of my clients and I had to meet with him tonight before our date. He's not the nicest guy, so I was trying to butter him up with candy for his kids. What are you doing out here? We were supposed to meet inside."

"I left something in the car." Tori lifted her folder. "I need to do some work tonight after our date, so I came out to get it. Why were you meeting him out here?"

"You are so beautiful and perfect; I didn't want his savory character to taint you. So, I scheduled to meet with him outside before coming in to get you." Winston kissed her cheek. "Are you ready to go?"

"Okay." Tori rubbed her arm. "Please don't grab me like that again. I'll be back in a minute; I just have to take this to my room and give Alex back his keys." Tori held up the folder.

"I'll come with you." Winston put his arm around Tori's shoulders and guided her inside.

"Okay." Tori was still tense, but Winston was being a gentleman again, so maybe that was just a difficult client he was trying to save her from.

Tori and Winston took the elevator to her room.

"Can I come in?" Winston asked when Tori opened her door.

"Of course." Tori opened the door wider to let him in behind her.

"Do you leave this door open all day?" Winston walked to the adjoining door.

"Yes, Frey and I like to go back and forth," Tori answered as she placed the folder on the dining room table. "I'm just going to use the restroom and we can go."

"Okay." Winston walked to the couch. "Take your time."

Tori picked up her clothes from her bedroom floor and walked into her bathroom to finish getting ready. Winston stood up from the couch when she entered the room.

"I'm ready." Tori grabbed her purse. "I just need to give Alex his keys back."

"Lead the way, beautiful," Winston placed his hand behind her back.

Tori closed her door and knocked on Alex's door.

"Hey," Alex answered and stiffened when he saw Winston, "Mr. James, how are you?"

"Couldn't be better." Winston kissed Tori's cheek and draped his arm around her shoulders.

"Here's your keys, Alex." Tori tried to step away from Winston, but his arm tightened around her shoulder. Winston surprised Tori by snatching the keys from her hand and moving in front of her to pass them to Alex.

"Thank you." Alex lifted the corner of his mouth. "Where are you guys going tonight?"

"I'm taking my beautiful girlfriend to a nice dinner." Winston kissed Tori again.

"Great." Alex smiled wryly, "Have a good night."

"Oh," Winston winked at him, "we will."

Winston gently shoved Tori backward toward the elevator.

"Thank you," Tori leaned around Winston and waved. "See you tomorrow."

Chapter 21

Caught Red-Handed
Freya

Freya was in her room when she heard voices coming from Tori's. She was going to say hello, but as she walked closer to the door, she heard a man's voice, and it wasn't Alex. She stayed hidden behind the door and peeked into Tori's room. The man got up from the couch and looked in the folder Tori put on her table. Freya didn't know what was in there, but she saw his eyes widen with shock and smirk with interest. Freya waited until she heard them leave her apartment and slowly opened her door, noticing everything that had happened in front of Alex's door. Once the elevator doors closed, Freya knocked on Alex's room.

"Yes," Alex answered irritated, "Oh sorry Frey, I thought it might be Tori or her new beau Winston."

"Alex." Freya pushed him aside as she walked into his room. "What is going on? I thought she was your girl, and you were going to talk to her? I told you, that guy gives me the creeps."

"Ah, no," Alex sighed heavily as he closed his door, "You were supposed to talk to her this morning, remember? You never told her that fucker gives you the creeps."

"True, but that's because she wouldn't listen to me and kept raving about how perfect he is. I thought maybe since you have her undivided attention when you drive to work, you would've talked to her. You're charming. Girls continually fall all over you, make it happen!"

"I think you're confusing me with Barrett," Alex mumbled. "He charms the pants off the girls daily. Besides, did you not hear me yesterday when I told you she co-worker zoned me? Every time we're together, she clams up, ignores me, or argues with me."

"Ugh, men! Like Holt said, "There is no such thing." Besides, you can also charm the pants of girls. I've watched you do it. Anyway, back to what I came to tell you. I heard her voice a few minutes ago, but before I could go into her room to say hello, I saw Winston snooping."

"This is all your fault, you know." Alex pointed at her.

"My fault," Freya points to herself, insulted by his accusation. "How is this my fault?"

"She's with him because of your damn red lipstick bet!"

"Fine," Freya placed her hands on her hip, "I'm trying to fix it."

"Try harder." Alex ran his hand over his face. "Wait, what did you mean he was snooping?"

"Tori had a folder on her dining room table, and he opened it to look inside. Whatever is in there fascinated him."

"Shit!" Alex was running on a short fuse since his encounter with Winston. "Tell me everything you know about Winston."

"Well, when he wasn't flirting with me, he was hanging around the tables. Sometimes he met with some members of Lucifer's Renegades MC. I never saw an exchange of items. Mostly they were whispering to each other and looking around nervously."

"Have you told Barrett or Holt?" Alex walked to his adjoining door and knocked.

"I've told them about him. That's why Holt escorted him away from my table," Freya followed Alex, "but now that he's dating Tori, I'm sure they will be more vigilant."

"Hey, bro," Barrett opened his door, "What's up? Hey Frey."

"What have you found out about Winston James?" Alex cut to the chase.

"Not much." Barrett walked back into his room. "We think he is dealing in our casino, but we haven't been able to catch him on film. He's a sneaky bastard. Why?"

"He's out on another date with Tori," Alex huffed, while pacing in Barrett's room. "She's under the impression that he's a good guy."

"Wait," Barrett looked from Freya to Alex, "I thought you guys were going to talk to her. She's your girl. Why haven't you convinced her of that?"

"That's what I said," Freya threw her arms up in the air.

"Remember, I was co-worker zoned. Have you guys not been paying attention to me? What the Fuck!" Alex explained, exasperated with both of them.

Barrett winced. "Shit, I heard you, but with your reputation, I figured you'd already convinced her to drop jackass and date you." Barrett winced.

"In one day? And what the hell do you mean by 'my reputation'?" Alex stared at Barrett, confused.

"You know. You call me Romeo, but all you gotta do is open your mouth and cook something for them and they fall right into your bed." Barrett shrugged.

"That was years ago. I haven't fucked around in a long time," Alex stated.

"Okay, okay," Barrett held up his hands, "Sorry man. I thought you had straightened it all out. That sucks. I know how much you like her from our daily talks."

"Daily talks," Freya screeched, "why are you not talking to me, your twin, daily, huh?"

"Well, I see him every day," Alex pointed toward the door, "we usually leave the door cracked open since neither one of us is getting any action right now."

"True," Freya sat down on the couch, "I talk to Tori every day when she comes home from work. After our talk this morning, I was going to convince her to cancel her dinner with him, but she never woke me up. Which is why today, before I started work, I went to say hello. That's how I saw that creeper looking at a folder on her table. Normally, it wouldn't be a big deal, but he looked nervous while he did it. He kept glancing toward her bedroom and was stunned when he saw whatever was in the folder."

"What was in it?" Alex stopped pacing.

"I didn't look," Freya stood up from the couch, "I came to you."

"Well shit," Barrett headed toward the front door, "Let's go see what it is."

"Isn't that an invasion of privacy?" Freya shouted as she followed them to her room.

"Frey," Alex placed his hands on his hips, "it's not as if it can give us a clue to what is going on with Winston. Plus, I work at the cultural center, so it shouldn't be a big deal for me to look in the folder."

"Okay, fine," Freya opened her door, and they all walked into Tori's room. Alex opened the folder.

"It just looks like a list of items," Freya commented when she saw the sheet of paper.

"Yes, but look." Alex pointed toward the paper. "It lists the prices of these items. Some of this jewelry is silver with turquoise or silver with an Azurite stone. Check out the value."

"You think he wants to steal it?" Barrett voiced his opinion.

"If the look on his face was any sign," Freya looked at Barrett, "yes. Alex, I think you need to tell Thunder, especially after what happened a few months ago with the theft and kidnapping of Isa."

"How do you know about all that?" Alex asked.

"One, it was all over the paper and two," Freya smirked at them, "dad told me. Did he not tell you?"

"I can't remember. Honestly, I've been so busy," Alex sighed. "Alright, I'll talk to Thunder tomorrow. Now I'm concerned about Tori. Frey, do you know where they were going?"

"No, I was going to ask her when she came home, but I didn't get the chance," Freya widened her eyes. "Do you think she's in trouble?"

"I don't know," Alex sighed, "but keep your eyes out for her. I'll try to talk to her tomorrow."

"I'll keep our doors open and check on her when I get off work," Freya pushed their doors open all the way.

"Okay," Alex walked to Freya's room, "please call me if you hear anything. I should've given her my number. I'll fix that tomorrow."

Barrett and Alex left and went back to their rooms.

Chapter 22

I Feel Woozy
Tori

"Winston," Tori looked around after being seated, "this place is really nice."

"I'm glad you like it."

"Good evening." The waiter came to their table. "May I get you something to drink?"

"We'll both have waters and a glass of your house white wine," Winston answered for them.

"Very well," the waiter gave them each a menu. "Please look over the menu. I will be back with your waters and wine. Let me know if you have any questions."

"Great," Winston spoke up again, "thank you."

"Winston," Tori leaned forward and whispered after the waiter left, "I wasn't going to drink tonight. I still have to work when I get home."

"One glass will just relax you during dinner, Beautiful," Winston winked. "Now tell me about your job. It sounds interesting."

"I'm the assistant museum curator for the American Indian Cultural Center," Tori said proudly. "I help run the exhibits."

"Here are your waters and wine," the waiter set them down on the table, "are you ready to order?"

"Yes," Winston spoke up quickly, "I'll have the Filet Mignon with mashed potatoes and side salad with Ranch Dressing and my beautiful date will have a Chef Salad with Balsamic Vinaigrette."

"Great," the waiter directed his gaze at Tori, "Ma'am, would you like your salad when we bring his salad is delivered or with his meal?"

"She'll have it when you deliver my meal," Winston answered again for

Tori. Tori was really confused—she was looking forward to eating a steak tonight.

"Sounds good," the waiter backed away, "Let me know if you need anything else."

"Winston," Tori whispered, "I was going to order a steak. I was really looking forward to trying one here tonight."

"Well, beautiful," Winston widened his eyes and placed a hand over his heart, "I was just looking out for you. If you eat a heavy dinner, you will get sleepy and not be able to get your work done."

"Oh, I hadn't thought about that." Tori relaxed. "Thank you for looking out for me."

"Of course. I will look out for you." Winston nodded, leaned forward, and grabbed her hand. "I've never been to your cultural center. Tell me about it. Is it only one room with an exhibit?"

"Oh no," Tori leaned in, pumped to share information about her workplace. She loved her job.

"I work with Thunder. He is the manager, and we share an office. Not only do we have the exhibit room, we also have a storytelling room, gift shop, and a restaurant."

"That's a lot of rooms for you to be in charge of," Winston asked. "Is this Thunder guy there all the time?"

"Most of the time, but he visits schools and businesses promoting our center." Tori took a sip of wine, "but I'm never alone. Mark and Alex work there also."

"Alex," Winston raised his eyebrow questioningly, "the chef at the resort? I think he likes you."

"Yes, the chef at the resort," Tori confirmed, "but no, Alex and I are just co-workers. There's nothing between us."

"Good," Winston squeezed her hand, "I don't like to share my woman."

"Your food will be ready in just a few minutes," the waiter said as he placed Winston's salad in front of him.

"Thank you," Tori smiled at the waiter.

"Do you ever worry about what's going on in the museum when you're in the office? I just want you to be safe, Beautiful. I don't know what I would do without you."

"That's sweet Winston," Tori smiled dreamily at him. "I like you too. I don't worry when I'm at work because from the office I can see into the storytelling room, gift shop and lobby. The office has blinds that face the lobby, and the side windows have a reflective film so I can see what is going on, but no one can see me while I'm in there. We always keep the warehouse in the back locked, and it has an alarm."

"Here's your meal," the waiter placed their meals on the table and took away the salad, "is there anything else you need?"

"No," Winston answered, "we are good. Thank you."

"How do you get to the warehouse?" Winston asked, while he was cutting his steak.

"There are two doors into the warehouse," Tori explained, "one from the office and another from the gift shop. That's where I've been working this week with all our inventory."

"In the warehouse?" Winston asked.

"Yes, and the gift shop," Tori answered while she cut up her salad. Tori wanted to make sure her salad fit in her mouth with small bites. If Tori had ordered this from Alex, he would have already cut it up for her. She'd have to let Alex know what a generous chef he was for providing that service to his customers.

"Have you received all your shipments for the exhibit?" Winston asked.

"I don't think so, since we are still two weeks away." Tori swallowed and took a sip of wine. "I think we will still receive items until the day of the opening."

"When is your opening?"

"Not next Thursday, but the one after that," Tori was glad Winston was so interested in her job, "would you like to come? I would love to introduce you to everyone."

"I would like that," Winston smiled back. "What time does it start?"

"It starts at seven," Tori couldn't contain her excitement, "I'm so glad you will attend."

"When do you have to be there, Beautiful?"

"Mark, Thunder, and I will be there in the morning to finish setting up." Tori grabbed another forkful of salad. "Alex will also be there awaiting a food shipment in the warehouse. After we double check everything, we'll all go home and get ready so we can be back by five for a final run-through."

"Sounds like a busy day," Winston murmured.

"Busy, but exciting," Tori nodded. "Oh, you'll get to see me in my Lakota regalia clothing."

"I can't wait to see that," Winston smiled. "I bet you look beautiful in it."

Tori looked down, but could feel the heat rising in her cheeks. She had finished her salad and her wine.

"Will you excuse me, Winston? That wine has gone through me," Tori giggled. "I'm going to use the restroom."

"Of course. Would you like another glass of wine?" Winston asked before she left the table. "I hate to end this evening so soon."

"No more wine for me." Tori grabbed her purse. "Maybe coffee?"

Tori walked into the restroom thinking about how great her date was going. Winston's interest in her job made her feel very accomplished and special. It was strange he ordered for her, but after his explanation, she went with the flow. After Tori used the restroom and came back, a fresh glass of wine was already waiting for her.

"Winston, this was sweet of you," Tori gestured toward the wine, "but I really wanted a cup of coffee."

"I know, Beautiful," Winston grabbed her hand, "I just like to see you relaxed and enjoying your wine."

"Enough about me." Tori took a sip of wine. "What about you? Do you think that difficult client will like the gummies you gave him for his kids?"

"I think so," Winston smiled wryly.

"Why did you give him a white brick?" Tori asked inquisitively, "Was that for his kids also?"

"Drink up, Beautiful. You don't need to worry about my difficult clients," Winston chuckled. "I didn't realize you saw all that. Yes, all of it was for his kids."

"He is lucky to have you," Tori was having a hard time keeping her eyes open, "not everyone would give their client something for their children."

"I'm so glad you forgive me for flirting with Freya," Winston grabbed Tori's hand again. "I will never do that again. When do you see Freya? It seems like you guys have different schedules."

"We do, but I see her before her shift when I get home from work," Tori blinked.

"When is her shift?"

"She usually works from six to two in the morning," Tori answered. "She never talks to me when she gets off work, since she knows I have to get up at seven."

"Finish your wine, Beautiful," Winston was staring at her, "you look exhausted."

"Winstonnn," Tori slurred her words, "IIII think IIII need tooo leave. IIII don't feellll right."

"Okay." Winston stood up. "I paid the bill while you were in the restroom, so we can go."

Tori stood up and would have fallen over if Winston hadn't caught her.

"Ma'am?" their waiter stopped in front of Tori. "Are you okay?"

"She's fine." Winston put one arm around her waist and held her other arm. "I think the wine really got to her, but she'll be fine."

The waiter nodded to them, and Winston walked Tori to his car. Tori had never felt like this. She had been drunk once before, but this felt different. Winston helped her sit in the passenger seat. Tori felt her head wobbling on the headrest of the car.

"Tori," Winston's voice sounded so far away, "I'm gonna walk you to your room since you look exhausted."

"Okay," Tori mumbled, "Thank you Winston."
Winston walked Tori through the lobby quickly. Tori felt like she was gliding instead of walking.

"Tori, are you okay?" Sehoy called out from behind the lobby desk.

"She's fine, just too much to drink," Winston replied, as he hurried her away from Sehoy.

"I'm going to get your key card out of your purse, Beautiful," Winston whispered. "I need it to get on the elevator and get to your room."

Next time Tori opened her eyes, she saw Winston laying on top of her.

"Winston," Tori tried to lift her arms, but they felt like dead weights. Tori glanced down and noticed that her dress and bra were pushed up over her breasts. Winston's hands were painfully squeezing her breasts as leverage while he pushed his pelvic area into her. She could feel pressure in her private area. "What's going on? That hurts."

"Shh," Winston kissed her, "everything is okay. It only hurts for a minute and then you will only feel pleasure."

Tori had a hard time keeping her eyes open. She felt like she was floating and couldn't move any part of her body. She heard Winston grunting and moaning, but she didn't know why. Before she could ask, everything went black.

Tori woke up to banging on her adjoining door. Her head was pounding, and she was having a hard time getting her body to work. Where was Winston?

"Tori," Freya was pounding on her door and yelling her name, "Are you in there?"

"Frey," Tori answered at a normal level.

"Tori, I can barely hear you," Freya pounded again. "Open the door."

"Frey," Tori couldn't move and passed out again.

*** *Freya* ***

Freya could barely hear Tori. She knew something was terribly wrong when Tori wouldn't open the door. Freya remembered leaving the door open, but now it was locked. Freya called Alex.

"Hello?" Alex mumbled, "Frey? What's up?"

"Alex!" Freya shouted into the phone. "Something is going on with Tori. Mom called me to come check on her when she noticed a man holding her up as he walked through the lobby to the elevator. When I knocked on our door, I can barely hear her voice and I can't check on her because the door is locked. It's never locked. We always keep it open."

"What!" Alex must have bolted out of bed because she could hear the commotion he was making, "Why didn't mom call Barrett, Holt, or me?"

"I think she did call you—check your phone."

"Shit, she did. I had it on silent. Fuck!"

"Anyway, I'm sure she called Barrett and Holt, but since I have the adjoining door, she thought it would be better if I went in this way to check on her—it would be quicker. I'm supposed to call her when I see Tori, but I can't get in!"

"Okay. I'll get the key from Barrett's room. I'm on my way."

"Hurry Alex," Freya sounds frantic, "I'm really worried."

A couple of minutes later, Freya heard a knock on her door.

"Come on," Barrett called out, "Alex just went into her room."

Alex

Alex used the master keycard to enter Tori's room. He ran into her bedroom and stopped cold when he saw Tori on the bed. She was lying on the bed with her dress and bra pushed up to her armpits. Her legs spread wide open with a small amount of blood on the sheet. There were bruises on her breasts, arms, and inner thighs.

"Fuck!" Alex couldn't stop his outburst.

He heard Barrett and Freya coming in behind him, so he hurried to the bed and covered her.

"Tori," Alex knelt on the floor next to the bed, cradling her head in his hands, "can you hear me?"

"Alex," Tori could barely hold her head up and squinted, "I don't feel good. What's going on?"

"Oh Baby," Alex looked back to Freya, "Frey, call an ambulance. Barrett, call the police."

"Alex," Freya was shaking, "what's going on?"

"Frey," Alex whispered while Barrett held Freya back, "I think someone drugged and raped her."

"Nooo! Tori," Freya's knees buckled, and she would have fallen if Barrett hadn't held her up.

"Barrett," Alex looked at his brother, "please take Frey into the other room and make those phone calls. I'm gonna stay here with Tori."

"Alex," Tori had tears coming out of her eyes, "what's happening to me? I can't feel my arms and legs."

"Shhh Baby," Alex kissed her forehead, "I have an ambulance coming to see what's going on. Just lay here and stay still. It's gonna be okay. I'll stay with you."

Alex watched Tori come in and out of consciousness. Finally, after what seemed like hours, but was only minutes, the EMTs and police showed up. Alex, Freya, and Barrett stepped out of the way and gave them their statements. The police had to pull back the sheet to take photos for their case. After the photos, the EMTs placed her on a gurney.

"Sir," the EMT called out to Alex, "we need to take her to the hospital. We don't know what drugs she was given, and the doctors need to check her out."

"Of course," Alex walked next to the gurney. Tori was flinching every time the paramedics touched her. "Can I go with her in the ambulance?"

"Are you family?" the paramedic asked.

"No," Alex answered, "I'm a friend and co-worker."

"I'm sorry sir," the Paramedic continued to wheel her to the elevator, "she will be at Sunrise General."

"Alex!" Tori yelled and stuck her hand out toward Alex.

"Just a minute please," Alex spoke to the paramedics. "Baby, I'll be right behind you in my car. I'll see you there." Alex raised her hand to his lips and gave it a gently kiss.

"Sir, we really need to get her to the hospital," the paramedic announced.

Tori nodded as tears streamed down her face, and she watched Alex until the last second before they wheeled her out of the room.

"Okay, sorry," Alex rubbed his hand over his face, "I'll meet you there. Thank you."

Alex turned to his brother. "How did this happen? Didn't mom call you when she saw Tori in the lobby?"

"She did, but by the time I arrived, he was gone. I'm gonna check the cameras. Do you think it was Winston?"

"Well, that's who she was with tonight, so I'd say hell yes."

"Mr. Panther, I'm Officer George Smith and this is my partner, Detective Sean O'Reilly. We are the officers dispatched here when there's trouble in your resort or casino. We've met Barrett and Holt on many previous occasions. They said you and Tori work at the American Indian Cultural Center?" Officer Smith walked up to Alex and shook his hand.

"Yes, I'm their new chef and Tori works with Thunder."

"I'll have to stop by for your fry bread then. Thunder is my mentor and I love to stop by and taste the cuisine. I used to be one of his shelter kids."

"Nice you meet you, Officer Smith. I would love for you to stop by."

"We're done here," Detective O'Reilly interjected, "but we need all of you to come to the station tomorrow and give your statements. Please bring any video footage you might have."

"Of course," Alex nodded, "thank you for coming so quickly."

"Please call us George and Sean," George held Alex's shoulder, "I'm sorry it was under these circumstances, but I promise you we'll do everything we can to figure out what happened to Tori."

"Thank you, George," Alex murmured.

"Alex." Barrett stood next to him. "Let's go to the hospital, so when Tori wakes up, she won't be alone. Come on, I'll drive you."

Alex, Barrett, and Freya followed the police downstairs. Alex felt numb. How could this happen to Tori? *Fuck*. Did Winston do this? *Fucker*. He should've spoken to her and made sure she hadn't gone out with Winston. He should've stopped her when they came to his door. This could've been avoided, and she wouldn't have been hurt. *Shit, this sucked*. His girl was in the hospital after some asshole hurt her. He knew she was dating Winston, but in his heart, she was still his girl. When this clusterfuck of a nightmare ended, he would convince her how much he cared about her.

"I'll let Holt know what happened so he can talk to mom and dad and check video footage," Barrett said as they piled into Barrett's car and headed toward the hospital.

"Do you really think it was Winston?" Freya asked from the back seat.

"If he did," Alex grumbled, "he better run. Because I will fucking kill him for hurting her."

Chapter 23

Where am I?
Tori

Tori woke up with a dry taste in her mouth and a sore body. Looking around, she saw Alex in a chair next to her bed, holding her hand. Freya was on the other side, holding her other hand. What happened? Why was she in the hospital? Just as she was asking these questions, Barrett came into the room with three cups of coffee.

"Hey, Sleeping Beauty," Barrett nudged Alex.

"Hi," Tori mumbled, "Why am I here?"

"Hey Baby," Alex raised her hand to his lips and kissed it, "I'm so glad you're awake."

"Hi Tori," Freya stood up and hugged her, "I'm so glad you're okay."

"What happened?" Tori looked at all of them hoping one of them, would talk to her.

"We'll leave you two to talk." Barrett gave Alex his coffee. "Step out with me for a second, Frey."

Tori saw tears in Freya's eyes before she left. What was going on?

"Alex," Tori sought his eyes, "please tell me why I'm here."

"Tori," Alex waited until Barrett and Freya stepped out and stood up. He leaned over her and held her hand with his right hand while he ran his left hand over her head.

"Were you only with Winston last night?" Alex whispered.

"Yes," Tori was getting agitated, "we went to dinner, and he walked me back to my room."

"Did you willingly have sex with Winston?" Alex whispered.

"No! I wouldn't do that. I don't really know him that well." Tori looked puzzled, thinking about the night before. "I had a couple glasses of wine. I know I wasn't drunk, but I felt woozy."

"Baby," Alex swallowed, "were you a virgin?"

"Alex, what do you mean?" Tori's voice was rising. "I am a virgin. What does this have to do with anything? What are you not telling me?"

"Baby," Alex was going to explain the situation, but he heard a knock on the door and stepped away from the bed as he held her hand.

"Hi Tori. I'm Dr. Wallace and this is Dr. Hansley." Dr. Wallace looked at Alex. "Could you please step out for a minute?"

"No, Alex, please don't go." Tori gripped his hand. "What's going on?" Tori looked at the two doctors.

"Tori," Alex kissed her hand, "I'll be right outside, and I'll come in as soon as the doctors have talked to you."

"Okay," Tori started shaking.

Dr. Wallace stood by the bed while Dr. Hansley sat on the bed and held her hand.

"Tori," Dr. Wallace began, "When you came in last night, someone had drugged and raped you."

"What? No," Tori gasped, "How can that be when I don't remember anything?"

"You don't remember anything at all?" Dr. Hansley asked.

Tori explained when she saw Winston on top of her, but that was all she remembered.

"You came in by ambulance," Dr. Wallace held her shoulder, "we ran some tests that found Rohypnol, the 'date rape drug', in your system. It was possible for us to flush it out of your system. We also noticed that you were assaulted, so we conducted a rape kit. We will not have the DNA results for a few days. I need to know if you want a morning-after pill since they did not find a condom at the scene. I'm sorry to be so blunt, but we need to do this soon. Dr. Smith is a psychiatrist who can help you deal with this situation."

"No, no," Tori released Dr. Hansley's hand, covering her face with both hands while she cried.

"Tori," Dr. Smith gently squeezed her shoulder, "I need to know if the gentleman who was just in here is the one that hurt you. Because if he did, I will not let him in and keep him outside until the police get here."

"No," Tori looked up and shook her head, frantically placing her hands on her chest, "Alex would never do that. I don't remember everything from last night, but I went out on a date with Winston James. Like I told you before, all I remember is him on top of me, but he was still wearing his shirt. I couldn't lift my arms to push him away. I was a virgin." Tori looked away and stared at the wall. How could this happen to her? She had been so careful. *Did Winston do this to her? Why?*

"Okay," Dr. Wallace rubbed Tori's other shoulder, "Alex seemed really worried about you, but we had to ask. The police will be here soon to speak to you. I will begin the release papers, but please make an appointment to speak with Dr. Hansley. She can help you through this.

"Please let Alex back in," Tori mumbled, pleading with them as tears ran down her face.

"Okay," Dr. Hansley patted her hand, "I will add my number to your discharge papers. Please call me anytime."

"Thank you," Tori smiled through her tears.

"Do you want to take the morning-after pill?" Dr. Wallace asked.

"Yes, please," Tori's tears continued to fall, "does that make me a bad person?"

"No Tori," Dr. Smith hugged her, "most women who suffer a traumatic crime like this choose to take the pill as a precautionary step. It doesn't mean you don't value a child's life. You are preventing this pregnancy before there is a heartbeat. However, if the pill doesn't work, you will have to make a tougher decision. Please get checked out by your gynecologist within the next few days."

"Okay," Tori looked to Dr. Wallace, "I will take the pill for now." Then moved her gaze to Dr. Hansley, "And I'll make an appointment with my gynecologist. Thank you."

"I will have the nurse bring you the morning-after pill," Dr. Wallace wrote on her clipboard, "you will not have any long-term risks. However, you might feel nauseous. If you have excessive vomiting or spotting, call me. Also, please make sure you talk to your gynecologist, and let them know what happened; they can help you with anything you might need."

"Okay," Tori leaned her head back against the pillow, "thank you both for helping me."

"Tori," Alex was suddenly by her bed and Tori reached out for him, "I'm so sorry, Baby. The police are here, and they want to talk to you."

"Okay," Tori sensed Alex's arms enveloping her as she experienced excruciating pain in her chest. How had she been so wrong about Winston? *She was too nice and naïve—Alex was right.*

"I got you, Baby," Alex murmured into her hair. "No one will hurt you ever again. I promise."

"Ma'am," two police officers entered her room, "can we please talk to you? We know this is a difficult time and we're sorry, but we're here to help you."

"Yes," Tori wiped her eyes and grabbed Alex's hand, "can Alex please stay?"

"Yes ma'am," the officer nodded, "if it makes you feel safer, absolutely. We haven't met before, but I'm George, a friend of Thunder's. This is my partner, Sean. Can you tell us what you remember from last night?"

"I went on my third date with Winston James. He took me to that steakhouse by the mall."

"I'm sorry to interrupt," Sean asked, "what did you have to drink?"

"I had a glass of wine with dinner. Then I went to the restroom, and Winston ordered another glass of wine for me." Tori noticed George looking at Alex. "When I got back to the table, the waiter had already delivered it. It was after that glass I started feeling tired and woozy. Winston caught me when I stumbled next to our table. Our waiter asked if I was okay, but Winston said he would take care of me. Then he drove me home and took me up to my room. I kept falling asleep. The last thing I remember was him on top of me." Tori looked down, embarrassed to look anyone in the eye. "He was still had his shirt on, and my dress and bra had been pulled up. I couldn't move my arms and legs and I felt pressure between my legs. I asked him what was going on, but I don't remember anything else after that. Well, until I woke up from Freya banging on our adjoining door. I must have fallen asleep again because then I woke up to Alex."

"Okay, we'll look into Winston James," George finished writing the details in his pad, "please stay away from Mr. James until we get your results. Alex, will you be staying with her? I don't think she should be alone."

"Yes," Alex immediately nodded, "I'll stay with her. Thank you."

Alex shook George's and Sean's hands before they left.

"Okay honey," a nurse stepped into the room, "Here are your discharge papers and the pill."

Tori turned her head toward the nurse, taking the pill with a cup of water.

"Please sign here and you can be on your way," the nurse handed over the clipboard, "I can bring you some scrubs for you to wear home."

"That won't be necessary," Alex walked to the closet in her room, "my sister brought her a change of clothes."

"Okay," the nurse nodded, "I will give you a few minutes to change and bring a wheelchair."

"I don't need a wheelchair." Tori stood up too fast to take the clothes from Alex and stumbled into him.

"Baby," Alex caught her and gently helped her sit on the bed, "Take a minute and I'll help you stand up slowly."

"I'm sorry Tori," the nurse said gently, "the wheelchair is hospital policy for all our discharged patients."

"Okay, thank you." Tori took several deep breaths. "I'm ready now."

Alex held her arm and wrapped his other arm around her waist, helping her get off the bed and leading her to the bathroom. "Baby, the wheelchair will make it easier for you to leave. Do you need help with your clothes?"

"No," Tori whispered, "I'll be okay. Just please stay in the room. Don't leave me?"

"I'm not going anywhere, Baby." Alex turned around and crossed his arms in a bodyguard pose.

Tori didn't shut the door all the way. She wanted to look out and see Alex. Once she removed her hospital gown, she looked down at her body and saw the bruises on her breasts, arms, and inner thighs. She couldn't remember the details of what happened and maybe that was for the best. Tori put her bra and panties on and leaned on the sink with her head bowed, crying for her lost innocence that she had promised to the love of her life. She felt empty, as if someone had taken something special away from her.

Tori couldn't stop crying as she crumpled to the floor, her hands catching her before she hit her head on the floor. She was glad she couldn't remember, but Winston's actions devastated her. The betrayal ran deep.

She never wanted to see him again—was afraid to see him again.

"Tori," Alex ran in. "Are you hurt?" Alex sat down on the floor behind her and held her in his arms, curling his body around her tightly.

"Alex," Tori's sobs were heart wrenching, "how could he do this to me? I thought he liked me. He was so nice to me."

"Baby," Alex soothed her with his hand running down her arms gently, "I am so sorry. But you are so strong, you will survive this and be okay. I will help you every step of the way. You're safe now. I won't let him anywhere near you."

Tori turned around and wrapped her arms and legs around Alex. Alex rocked her and held her tight.

"Baby," Alex held her head against his chest and kissed the top of her head, "let's get you dressed and home. Freya and Barrett are waiting for us outside the room to drive us home."

"Okay," Tori mumbled as Alex stood up, holding her. Placing her on her feet, he helped her put on a pair of sweatpants and a t-shirt.

"Tori," Alex gazed into her eyes as he wiped her tears, "you got this."

Tori walked out of the bathroom with Alex's help and saw the wheelchair. The nurse must have left it when they were in the bathroom. Alex helped her sit and wheeled her out. Freya and Barrett pushed away from the wall.

"Hey Tori," Freya grabbed her hand, "let's blow this popsicle stand. We have better food at home."

Tori smiled; she appreciated Freya trying to cheer her up.

Barrett drove them home. They walked in the side door quickly to avoid as many guests as possible. When they reached their floor, Tori noticed the police tape across her door and screamed before her legs gave out.

Chapter 24

Protecting Tori
Alex

Alex barely caught Tori.

"Alex!" Tori cried out, placing her hands on her face, "I can't go in there."

"Baby," Alex pried her hands away from her face, "look at me."

Tori lifted her face and looked him in the eyes, tears streaming down her face.

"You don't have to go in there if you don't want to. Do you want to stay with me in my room?" Tori's pain-filled gaze was killing him. He would do anything to take the pain away from her. "Tori, is that okay with you? I don't want you to be alone. You can stay with Frey if you don't want to stay with me."

"No, I want to stay with you," Tori nodded. "I don't want to be alone, and I feel safe with you."

Alex picked Tori up off the floor. She was killing him. For the millionth time, he wished he had not let her go out with Winston. He should have stopped them when she came to get the keys. Would've, could've, should've, was a game he could play until the end of time, but it wouldn't change anything. Hindsight could have saved her so much heartache and pain, but unfortunately, it was not a trait he possessed. Eventually, he would find Winston and kick his ass, but right now, Tori took precedence.

Barrett opened Alex's door.

"Thanks Barrett," Alex mumbled. Alex carried Tori into his bedroom and laid her down on the bed.

Tori jumped up, "No Alex, I need to take a shower. I feel dirty."

"Okay, do you need my help?"

"No," Tori quickly retorted, "I'll be fine."

Alex nodded, "please don't lock the door."

Tori had already walked into the bathroom and shut the door.

Alex sat on the bed staring at the door and listening for any sounds of distress.

After hearing some crying, he thought it would be best if Frey went in there instead of him. Frey was sitting on the couch with Barrett.

"Frey," Alex approached, "can you please go in there and see if she is okay? That shower is taking longer than normal."

"Sure, I'll check on her."

Alex wasn't sure what they talked about, but when they left the bathroom, Tori had put on his robe and his sister had wrapped herself around Tori. Freya led her to the bed where Tori immediately curled up into a fetal position while Freya covered her with the blanket.

Freya grabbed his arm and led him from the bedroom.

"How is she?" Alex asked after Freya pulled the door slightly closed.

"She's scared. Her skin is raw and red from scrubbing too hard with scalding water. She needs to talk to someone. I know you care a lot about her, but you're not a psychiatrist."

"Yeah, you're right. Dr. Hansley at the hospital gave Tori her business card for her to set up an appointment. I'll talk to her about it."

Alex needed to call Thunder because neither of them were going to work and they were usually there by now. Besides, Thunder would want to know what happened, and he still had to let him know about Winston looking in the folder.

"I need to call Thunder," Alex mumbled. "If she needs anything, can you guys help her until I get off the phone?" Barrett and Freya both said, of course. Alex stepped into the kitchen to make his phone call.

"*Hau*," Thunder grumbled, "Alex, are you okay? Is something wrong at the office? Sorry I got a late start, but I'm on my way."

"I'm sorry I didn't call you earlier Thunder, but I need to let you know what happened to Tori last night."

"What happened to Tori?" Thunder sounded worried, and Alex could hear Isa in the background asking the same question. "Alex, I'm putting you on speaker so Isa can listen also."

"Tori went out last night with an asshole who roofied and raped her," Alex sighed. It was better to rip the bandage off and get to the point so he could get back to Tori.

"Oh my God," Isa cried.

"My mom called Frey and Barrett to check on her. Frey hurried to her room and was surprised to see their adjoining door closed. They always leave the door open. Freya pounded on it, but Tori didn't answer, so she came to get me and get my master key. After we got in, we called the police and an ambulance. We've been at the hospital most of the night, we just got home. I want to kill that fucking bastard."

"Fuck, so do I," Thunder rumbled. "Both of you stay home today. I'll put a closed for family emergency sign on the door. Sarah will probably want to see her. I'll talk to her and fill her in."

"I think Tori would like that. I know she loves Sarah," Alex whispered.

"Have you called Tall Bear? Do you want me to call him?"

"No, I think Tori will want to talk to him herself, but she's sleeping now. I can call you when she wakes up. Just so you know, she doesn't remember everything about the attack."

"Well, I guess that's a plus," Isa sighed.

"Oh, Thunder," Alex just remembered, "Long story, but Frey said Winston, her asshole date, saw the spreadsheet that listed all the items we have for sale in the center for the Unconquered Path Exhibit and he looked fascinated. I just wanted to give you a heads up. I can get Barrett to get a photo of him from our footage. Apparently, he's a regular at our tables."

"If Barrett can do that, I would appreciate it," Thunder said. "We'll be on the lookout for him."

"Also," Alex murmured, "we met George, one of your friends tonight. He was one of the police officers that questioned Tori at the hospital. Barrett and Holt have met George before at the casino, but he said you guys were close. Just wanted to let you know he was great with Tori and very respectful."

"Good to know that George could help," Thunder said. "He was the first shelter boy I mentored. I knew he would have a huge impact in the community. It made me proud when he joined the police force. I'm glad she had him. I'll keep in contact with him and find out any updates on that Winston asshole. Please look after Tori and keep me updated."

"Alex!" Tori was screaming from the bedroom.

"I gotta go. Tori's awake and calling me. Talk to you soon." Alex hurried into the bedroom and ended the call.

"Hey," Alex bent down next to the bed, rubbing his hand over Tori's head, "I'm right here. Sorry, I stepped out to call Thunder. Barrett and Frey are here too. You're not alone."

"Can you lay down with me?" Tori closed her eyes as tears slid down her face.

"Absolutely." Alex crawled under the covers. Pulling Tori back against his chest and holding her tight. "I'm right here, Baby. I got you."

Tori's body was stiff at first, but then she relaxed and held onto his arms.

"Sleep, Baby," Alex kissed the back of her head. When he heard her breathing even out and he thought she was asleep, he slowly extricated himself from around her.

"Where are you going?" Tori bolted upright.

"I was going to get your clothes." Alex gently pushed her back down.

"Can Frey get them?" Tori begged, "Can you just lay here and hold me?"

"Of course," Alex held up his hand, "let me talk to Frey. I'll be right back."

Alex walked out of the room, leaving the door open so Tori could still see him.

"Frey," Alex rubbed the back of his neck, "can you and Barrett please get Tori's clothes and bring them here, so she doesn't have to go into that room?"

"Yes," Freya had tears in her eyes, "Is she going to be okay?"

"Yes," Alex hugged her, "I will do everything in my power to help her be okay."

"Frey, Barrett," Alex heard Holt's voice coming from Barrett's room.

"In here." Barrett hollered and walked into his adjoining door.

"What happened?" Holt stared at Alex. "I found the video footage of Winston with Tori last night. I just woke up to work out when I saw police tape across Tori's door. Frey, are you okay?"

"I'm fine Holt," Freya was hugging herself and rubbing her arms.

"Barrett, I gotta go back in there with Tori. Can you please get all the footage Holt found?"

"Yeah bro, I got this."

"Thank you," Alex walked toward his bedroom. "I'm going to leave both our adjoining and bedroom doors open and let Tori know you guys are here for her."

"Got it, big bro." Barrett walked to his room. "Let me know if you need anything. Holt and I will help Frey get Tori's stuff from her room and bring it in here."

"Thank you."

Alex was relieved Tori wanted his protection and care. He was glad that deep down she was aware of his feelings for her, and she trusted him. It would have been so much harder to protect Tori if she didn't want him around.

"Tori," Alex walked into the room, "do you want to change into pajamas?"

"Yes please," Tori whispered, "can I borrow one of yours and a t-shirt?"

"Of course, Baby," Alex walked into his closet and pulled out some pajama pants and a shirt. She would swim in it, but if that's what she wanted, that's what she got.

"Do you want me to help you?" Alex asked.

"No," Tori put her legs over the side of the bed, "I have to go to the bathroom, anyway. I'll change in there."

Alex helped her walk to the bathroom and handed her the pajamas and shirt before she closed the door. While he waited outside the door, he kept listening in case she needed him. A few minutes later, Tori opened the door, walked to the bed, and climbed in.

"Can you hold me, Alex?" Tori turned on the bed, facing his side.

"Yeah," Alex croaked, "let me change and I'll be right there."

Alex changed into sweatpants, slid into bed, and pulled her into his arms. Exhaustion took over, and they both fell asleep.

Chapter 25

The Bitch Talked
Winston

Winston was relaxing poolside at his parent's mansion when he received a phone call he wasn't expecting.

"Reaper," Winston wondered why he was calling. They did their business last night and Reaper had paid in full.

"Win," Reaper sounded agitated. "Did that girl figure out you were selling drugs to me? I don't need a snitch going to the cops."

"No, she's not really bright." Winston took a sip of his wine. "Besides, I fixed it, so she keeps her mouth shut. She won't be bothering us—trust me I took care of it."

"You better," Reaper sighed, "if this shit goes south, you're a dead man walking."

"Don't threaten me," Winston sat up and growled. "I'm on it. She won't be a problem."

"She'd better not be a problem, Win," Reaper replied and hung up the phone.

Winston stared at his phone. The audacity of that loser hanging up on him. Did he not realize Winston was the boss? That idiot, of course he took care of Tori. Not that it hadn't been harder than he thought. That lady in the lobby looked worried enough to call security. He had to fuck Tori quick. He knew he only had a few minutes before someone was going to go looking for her. In his haste to get her into bed, he gave Tori too much of the drug. He'd wanted her to be conscious when he fucked her, but she was out of it. At least he took her precious virginity.

After what he did, he would have her under his control. She was too stupid to go to the police and by the time she woke up this morning, she might even be pregnant. Once she had his baby, she would be his forever. They would steal from the center and the casino and then move on to get her a job at other places he could rob.

Once he'd fucked her, he heard Freya banging on their adjoining door. He had to get out of there quick before more people came. Running into the stairwell had been ingenious for his escape. He ran down a couple of flights of stairs before he took the elevator the rest of the way down. Then he mixed in with a group of people that were heading out.

Everyone thought he had a lot of money and, in the public eye, he did, but he had a lot of money was invested in stocks, bonds, and a trust fund. The money he had at his disposal was used to pay off the cartel when his dealers were late paying him. Making extra money with Tori would help to offset the months between trust fund payouts. He could continue to lie to his parents about his profession if money was coming in. Winston was an only child, and they believed everything he told them. Hell, they would probably give him more money when they found out they were going to be grandparents. Fucking Tori would not be a hardship.

Finding Tori was a bonus. She was too nice to argue with him and fight him on his decisions. He tested that during their mealtimes, she just went along with him if he told her he was looking out for her. He could charm her and if or when she thought she would leave him, he would have control over their kid, and she could never leave. If she wasn't pregnant by now, she would be soon. He'd picked the best docile woman he could have ever dreamed of.

"Master Winston, the police are here to speak to you," Thomas, his parent's butler, announced as he stood by his lounger.

"Police?" Winston stood up and grabbed his robe. He wondered why the police wanted to talk to him. That bitch better not have snitched. He'd been sure she wouldn't call them. Had she grown a backbone after he left her? Maybe he should have stayed next to her all night? Leaving his drink, he followed Thomas to the front door.

"Gentlemen, to what do I owe the pleasure of this visit?" Winston asked the officers.

"Sir, may we come in?" one officer motioned with his hand, "we have some questions for you."

"Of course," Winston stepped back, "please come in. Would you like something to drink?"

"No sir," one officer spoke while the other took out his pad. "Can you tell us where you were Friday night?"

"I was out on a date with a beautiful young lady and then I came home." Winston closed the door when the officers stepped inside. "Would you like to come have a seat?"

"Sure, thank you," the officers followed Winston into the sitting room. "Mr. James, who was your date with?"

"My date was with Victoria Tall Bear. She works at the American Indian Cultural Center," Winston looked between the two officers, "why?"

"Where did you go for your date?" the officers sat down on the edge of the couch.

"We had dinner reservations at Jack's Steakhouse and then I took her home." Winston sat down in the armchair facing the couch.

"What time did you take her home?" the officer looked around before looking at Winston.

"Our reservation was for 6:30 pm and I dropped her off at 9:00 pm." Winston smiled at the officer.

"Where did you drop her off?" the officer continued, looking around.

"She lives at the Rock 'n' Roll Resort & Casino. I dropped her off in the lobby." Winston looked puzzled. "Why officers? Is Victoria, okay?"

"Did you walk her into the lobby or just drop her off?" the officer stared at Winston.

"I went into the lobby with her and walked her to the elevator," Winston nodded. "She didn't invite me up, and I didn't want to make her uncomfortable. I gave her a kiss on the cheek, she got in the elevator, and I left."

"You say that was around nine at night?" the officer watched Winston's reaction.

"Yes," Winston insisted. "Did something happen to her?"

"Did you see her speak to anyone in the lobby when you left her?" the officer continued to stare at Winston's reaction.

"No. I know she likes to go to the bar sometimes at night for a drink, but I walked her to the elevator like I said before." Winston stayed calm on the outside, while he was seething on the inside. That bitch had given his name. He had to make sure he convinced her not to say anything else about him.

"Okay," the officers looked at each other and stood up, "Would you mind coming down to the station and giving us a DNA sample?"

"No, of course not," Winston nodded, "But I'm confused. Am I a suspect for something?"

"No sir," the officer said, "we just want to clear you of any suspicions."

"Okay," Winston stood. "I'll get dressed and head over."

"Thank you, Mr. James," the officers walked toward the front door. "We'll see you at the station. Please do not leave town in case we have any more questions for you. If you remember anything else about that night, please call us."

"Of course, officers," Winston opened the door for them, "I will help any way I can."

"Have a great day Mr. James," the talkative officer said, then they headed back to their patrol car.

Winston lifted his hand in a quick wave and closed the door. He would NOT give his DNA. *Shit! He'd fucked her without a condom to impregnate her and she had gone to the cops.* Winston never thought she would do that. Drugging her had been so fucking easy since she was too nice and trusting.

Fuck! How had he calculated the situation so wrongly? That lady in the lobby must have called Freya and the police. He'd had to hurry when Freya was banging on that fucking door. He needed to talk to Tori. Jail was not his thing. Maybe he could catch her at the cultural center. There were fewer people there than at the resort or casino.

For now, he needed to pack some stuff and hide out until he could see her again and convince her to tell the police she was confused, and he had nothing to do with it or that it was consensual.

He remembered her opening her eyes and asking what was wrong while he was fucking her, but then she passed out again. At first, he thought he gave her too much, but after the police visit, he regretted not giving her a stronger dose or staying the night to control the situation better. But with a stronger dose, she might have passed out in the car, and he would've had to carry her through the lobby, causing even more people to notice.

In hindsight, he was stupid for taking her home, clearly—he hadn't planned it right. If he had taken her back to his house, he could have threatened or beat her into submission in the morning if she didn't agree to live with him. Now he had to fix what he'd done wrong.

Originally, he'd wanted to compromise her so she would have to help him continue to deal in the casino and rob the center. But since she called the cops, that was off the table. She was not a partner for him—now she was a liability. He had to keep her quiet. It was bad enough the police questioned him. If she said anything about the drugs, then Reaper would be involved.

What a clusterfuck! If Reaper found out about this, he would not only shut her mouth but attempt to shut his. Winston really needed to keep Lucifer's Renegades drugs pipeline flowing in his direction. Tori could have fucked everything up for him. The Bitch had to be shut down.

*** George ***

"That was strange, right?" George asked his partner Sean as he started the car and looked back at the house before driving away.

"Yep," Sean nodded, "he was a little too dramatic for me."

"I agree," George responded. "Pretty sure he won't be coming down to the station for a DNA sample."

"True that," Sean agreed. "Unfortunately, we can't arrest him without more information or a warrant."

"Let's go to Jake's Steakhouse and see if they have any cameras in their establishment. If we can find a video of Tori looking unstable, maybe we can push for that warrant."

"Good idea. You'll be an excellent detective one day."

"Thanks. That's my goal. Moving up to detective status would be an incredible achievement, and I have you to thank for helping me."

"No, thanks needed. I told you when you signed up, I would do anything I could to speed up your process. I'm just glad Captain agreed. We all see your potential. Let's get to Jake's Steakhouse and look at some footage."

"I hope the rape kit comes back with something," George sighed. "Tori is such a nice person. If we can get a positive DNA from the rape kit and her testimony, we can come back and arrest the son of a bitch."

"Agreed."

"After the steakhouse visit, we can go back to the station and see if he showed up. I want to see if we have any updates on the case. Maybe we can convince the captain to let us place some surveillance on him and see what he does."

"Great idea," Sean nodded.

Chapter 26

New Roommate
Tori

Tori felt incredibly comfortable, warm, and safe when she woke up with Alex's arms wrapped around her, with her head resting on his chest. She lifted her head and looked up.

"Hey," Alex mumbled, "How are you feeling?"

"Sad," Tori laid her head back on Alex's chest.

"Baby, I think you should call your mom and dad."

"No! Alex, I can't tell them yet. Maybe after they catch Winston."

"Baby, that could take a while and your parents would want to know. They could help you."

"No, not yet. Please don't make me call them," Tori pleaded with tears streaming down her face.

"Okay, for now. Are you hungry?" Alex ran his hand over her head.

"What time is it?" Tori squeezed Alex with her arms.

Alex lifted his arm from around her and said, "six."

"In the morning?" Tori suddenly sat up.

"No Baby," Alex pulled her back down, "six at night. I can have food brought up for you from either RUSH or Savor. Baby, why are you crying?"

"I missed Girls' Night Out," Tori bolted up. "I know that sounds stupid after what happened, but I was really looking forward to it."

"Baby," Alex sat up and kissed the top of her head, "It's not stupid. Every girl needs her tribe. I'm pretty sure they understand, but if you want, I can get your phone so you can talk to Sarah. I know she really wanted to come over and see you."

"She did?" Tori looked at Alex.

"Yup," Alex reached over and grabbed her phone, "here."

Tori took her phone and called Sarah.

"Tori," Sarah answered, "how are you?"

"I'm sorry I messed up Girls' Night Out," Tori started crying again. She could feel Alex rubbing her back.

"Oh Tori, there are no girls' night without you," Sarah said. "We rescheduled it to the Saturday after the opening. So don't worry about it. Just relax and let me know if you need anything."

"Really?" Tori whispered, "you rescheduled it because of me?"

"Of course, we want you here with us when we do our next girls' night."

Sarah's words overwhelmed Tori. She'd never had any friends postpone anything because she couldn't attend.

"Thank you, Sarah."

"You're welcome, Tori. Now go relax and I'll see you soon."

"Okay, bye Sarah."

"Bye, Tori."

Tori hung up the phone and stared at it while it was on her lap. It was a wonderful feeling to have Sarah as her friend.

"They rescheduled it for next weekend because of what happened last night," Tori laid down on Alex again.

"I figured they wouldn't have it without you." Alex wrapped his arms around her again.

"Wait," Tori sat up again, "Shouldn't you be at work?"

"Clearly, you want to sit up," Alex chuckled, sitting up and leaning against the headboard. "I took the night off. Why don't I order you something and we can eat it out there? Maybe watch a movie."

"That sounds good." Tori crossed her legs. "Can I use your shower?"

"Of course. Please don't lock the door in case you need me. Frey brought your clothes. They're in my closet. If you want to stay in one of my shirts, take your pick from the dresser in the closet."

Tori swung her legs to a sitting position and stood before she walked around the bed toward the bathroom.

"What do you want to eat?" Alex asked when she was facing him.

"Do you think they have soup?" Tori asked, "I don't really feel like eating, but I know I should eat something."

"Yes, they have French Onion and Minestrone," Alex waited for her response. "Which one do you prefer?"

"French Onion, please," Tori gave him a hug, "thank you for asking me. Winston never asked. He just ordered what he felt I should eat."

"Oh Baby." Alex held her tighter. "He was trying to control you. But that's over now. Take your shower and I'll order you some soup. It comes with a roll; would you like one?"

"Yes, please," Tori stared into Alex's eyes, "I'm sorry for treating you so badly Alex. Deep down I knew I could trust you. I was just afraid of dating someone I work with."

"It's okay, Baby," Alex kissed her forehead. "I know you were concerned about us dating. We can take it slow, but you need to know I really like you and want to get to know you. We don't have to decide anything now. I'll order your food and meet you out there after you finish your shower."

Tori nodded. Heading to the bathroom, she turned on the shower. While the water was heating, she walked into Alex's closet for one of his t-shirts. She liked wearing Alex's shirt so she could sleep in it later. It would feel like his arms were wrapped around her. After her shower, Tori joined Alex at the dining room table.

"Tori, have you called Dr. Hansley to set up an appointment?"

"No."

"Baby, I think you should call and schedule something."

"I'm embarrassed and I don't know where my release papers are."

"I have your papers. Don't be embarrassed, you haven't done anything wrong. I think it will help for you to talk to a professional about this. I'll go get the papers and your phone."

Alex came back to the table with the papers and set the phone in front of her.

Tori took a deep breath and dialed the number, setting the phone on speaker.

"Good afternoon, Dr. Hansley's office. How can I help you?"

"Hi, my name is Victoria Tall Bear. I would like to set up an appointment with Dr. Hansley."

"Will this be your first visit with her?"

"Yes, ma'am."

"Okay, can you come in on Thursday, September 28th at nine am?" Tori looked at Alex since he was her driver. Alex nodded.

"Yes, I can make that."

"Great, please come in fifteen minutes early to fill out our new patient paperwork. So, we'll see you at eight forty-five."

"Yes, ma'am. See you then."

Tori hung up the phone and added it to her calendar. Alex scooted up in his chair and cupped the back of her neck to give her a quick kiss.

"I'm proud of you, Baby."

"I'm scared."

"You are going to do great. I think this will help you."

"I agree. Now, can we watch a movie?"

"Absolutely."

Alex was true to his word. They sat in the living room, watched a movie, and ate soup.

Chapter 27

Girls' Day In
Tori

By Saturday night, Tori had finished moving into Alex's room. The center was closed on Sunday and Monday, giving Tori a couple more days off from work. She spent those days in Alex's room, not wanting to see anyone. Monday night, Thunder called her and told her to take the entire week off from work. Tori let him know she would think about it. She really didn't think she could stay in the hotel room for an entire week. There was so much to do at the cultural center and the shelter kids were coming on Friday, and she really wanted to meet them.

Freya took time off and stayed with Tori while Alex switched his shift from dinner to lunch at RUSH because the nights were the hardest for Tori to be away from him. Barrett worked from the family security room to stay close to the girls. They kept Barrett's door open in case they needed him. Frey and Tori curled up on the couch covered with blankets as they ate snacks during the day and watched movies. Relaxing and laughing with Freya helped Tori forget about her current stress. Tori didn't want to be alone; she was still afraid Winston would break in at any moment and hurt her again.

"Someone's having a good time," Tori heard Alex say as he walked into the room carrying a bag and water bottles.

"I brought you girls turkey sandwiches for dinner." Alex placed the bag and waters on the dining room table.

Tori approached the table and gave Alex a kiss on his cheek, "thank you."

"I figured you ladies would be hungry for proper food by now. You can't live on junk food alone." Alex took the sandwiches and chips out of the bag and placed them on the table. "Have a seat. I'm gonna take Barrett his sandwich."

Tori watched Alex walk out of the room.

"Stop drooling over my brother," Freya whispered, and gently shoved her shoulder.

"What?" Tori blushed as she took a bite of her sandwich, knowing she had been caught red-handed.

"I saw you," Freya said while chewing. "Don't play coy with me."

"Oh Frey," Tori sighed, "he's been so wonderful with me. Why did I not want to go out with him? Why did I choose Winston over him?"

"Winston was a real charmer and never showed you his true colors. Forget about him. The police will take care of him. Now you can focus on Alex. Seriously, Alex will never let you down, and I think he truly cares for you."

"Thank you for everything. You are the best friend I've ever had. Sarah was a great friend, but we haven't hung out together since she moved away. I don't know what I would do now without you," Tori stared at Freya with tears in her eyes. "I know Winston was a monster, and when I think about what they said he did to me, I feel so stupid. You and Alex tried to warn me, but I didn't listen." Tori put her sandwich down and wiped her tears.

"Hey Baby," Alex hurried to her side and squatted down next to her, "why are you crying? Frey, what happened?"

"It's not Frey's fault, Alex," Tori grabbed a napkin to wipe her face. "I was just feeling stupid about what I let happen."

"Baby, look at me," Alex held her face in his hands while gazing deeply into her eyes, "you didn't let anything happen. He drugged you. None of this is your fault."

"Thank you for saying that, and thank you for babysitting me today, Frey. It was nice."

"Come on girl," Freya rubbed her back, "it was wonderful having our own Girls' Day In. I love hanging with my new BFF."

"I loved it too," Tori hugged Freya.

"Okay ladies," Alex smiled, "enough mushy stuff. Eat your dinner and we'll watch another movie."

"Alex," Tori grabbed Alex's hand before he walked away, "I want to go to work tomorrow and get some things done. I've been home long enough."

"Are you sure?" Alex squatted down to her level, "Thunder said you could stay home all week."

"I know, but I need to be doing something, and I can't keep Frey from working."

"Hey, I'm enjoying my vacation Tori," Freya said after washing down her mouthful of food. "I could do this for another week."

"No, you couldn't, but thank you for saying that."

"Okay, how about you stay home tomorrow," Alex nodded, "and go back on Friday? That will still give you a week before the opening."

"Okay, that sounds fair. Thank you for understanding, Alex."

"Of course," Alex kissed her forehead and stood up, "finish up your dinner and then come sit with me on the couch. I'm gonna change out of these clothes."

"Okay."

Just as Frey and Tori finished eating, Alex came out of the bedroom wearing sweats and a t-shirt. He picked up their trash and cleaned up the table. Walking to the couch, he sat and pulled Tori's feet onto his lap.

"What are we watching?" Alex asked as he rubbed Tori's socked feet.

"Hey," Freya yelled at Alex, "how come she gets a foot rub, and I don't? I'm your favorite sister."

"You're my only pain in the ass sister," Alex quirked an eyebrow at her.

"Hunh, that's not nice," Freya folded her arms and stared at Alex, "you're my favorite brother."

"Ha, ha, ha, you're funny," Alex smirked at her, "don't let your twin hear you say that. Come here baby sis, I'll rub your feet too if you put on an action movie."

"Done," Freya stood up and moved to the other side of the couch opposite Tori, dropping her feet onto Alex's lap, "you're so easy, but I love you."

Tori chuckled, watching their interaction. Alex was a softie for his family, especially his mom and sister. He pretended to be inconvenienced, but she knew he was enjoying this time with them. Alex massaged Tori's feet with his right hand and Frey's feet with his left as the movie started. An action movie was a small price to pay for his wonderful massages. The movie ended up being very entertaining, with several high-speed muscle car chases.

By the time it was over, Tori was exhausted.

"Okay ladies," Alex patted their calves while the credits came up on the screen, "time to go to bed. Frey, I'll walk you to your room. Tori, I'll be right back."

Tori and Frey swung their legs off Alex and stood up.

"Okay," Tori hugged Freya, "good night, see ya tomorrow."

"Yup." Frey left with Alex while Tori headed to the bedroom.

Tori used the restroom, brushed her teeth and crawled into bed, waiting for Alex.

"I'm back, Baby," Alex announced when he returned. "I need to talk to Barrett for a minute. I'll be right back."

"Okay," Tori yawned and rolled over.

*** Alex ***

"Hey bro," Alex walked into the family security room and took a seat next to Barrett, "have you heard anything from the police about Winston? Tori wants to go back to work tomorrow, but I convinced her to wait another day."

"No," Barrett sighed, "he's gone into hiding after the police went to his house to talk to him. He told them he would go down to the station to give his DNA, but the fucker never showed."

"Of course, he didn't."

"If you take her to work on Friday, stick close to her. I would bet any amount of money we haven't seen the end of Winston James."

"That's not a bet I'm willing to take, because I think you're fucking right. Shit." Alex stood, "I'm gonna go to bed, let me know if you hear anything."

"Will do, bro."

Alex walked into the bedroom and noticed Tori was already asleep. After using the restroom, he turned off the bedroom light and crawled slowly into bed next to Tori.

Chapter 28

Quiet Times…If only
Tori

Tori woke up with Alex's arms wrapped around her. Hanging out with Freya these past few days was just what she needed. She could stop focusing on what happened to her for a few hours and have some fun watching movies. But she was ready to go to work, and she wished Alex would take her. But Thunder and Alex thought she needed more time to relax.

"Good morning, Baby," Alex murmured.

"Good morning, Alex. Are you working today?"

"Nope, I took the whole day off. We can do whatever you want."

"I'm feeling a little couped up. That's why I wanted to go to work."

"How about we hang out by the pool?"

"Oh Alex," Tori sat up, "I would really like that."

"Okay, let me get up and shower, then I'll make you breakfast while you get ready." Alex got up and pulled the blanket up to her chin, tucking her in like a burrito.

"Thank you," Tori smiled dreamily at him.

True to his word, by the time she finished getting ready, Alex had placed two omelets on the table for them.

"This looks delicious, Alex, but it's too much."

"Wow, I didn't know you were making omelets," Barrett strolled into their living room, "thanks, bro."

"Here, have this one," Alex moved his plate to another chair, "I'll share Tori's with her."

"Alex, if that's not enough, I can eat cereal." Tori moved her omelet in front of Alex.

"Absolutely not." Alex moved the omelet back to Tori. "I'll take his away before I take yours."

"Okay, then let's share it."

"Perfect," Alex stood up to get a plate.

"Look at you guys compromising and acting like an old married couple," Barrett blurted out between bites, causing Tori to fidget.

"Really Barrett," Alex stared at him, "keep the commentary to yourself or go eat that in your room. Don't embarrass Tori."

"Sorry Tori, I didn't mean to embarrass you. I'm really just glad you are both getting along."

"It's okay. I know what you meant."

"Barrett, after we eat, we're going down to the pool. Tori would like to leave this room and return to the land of the living by soaking up some sunshine."

"Where's Frey?"

"She's going to work a double today since I took the day off to be with Tori."

"Okay." Barrett picked up his plate and took it to the sink. "I'll continue to work up here. Have fun."

"Thanks." Alex picked up both their plates, followed Barrett to the kitchen. "Tori, are you ready?"

"Yes. See you later, Barrett."

"Yup." Barrett kissed Tori as he walked by her back to his room.

"Hey!" Alex screamed and pulled Tori toward him, "keep your lips to yourself!"

"Sorry!" Barrett laughed and waved when he entered his room. Tori wrapped her arms around Alex, stood up on her tippy toes, and kissed his cheek.

"You know he does that to tease you right," Tori said while Alex held her.

"Yup," Alex kissed her forehead.

Tori was hoping at some point Alex would kiss her. He was giving her time after her rape, but she was ready for some intimacy with Alex. She wanted Alex to erase any lingering feelings or terrible memories.

*** Alex ***

This had not been a good idea. Watching Tori in her bikini was a test of his willpower. Lying next to Tori on the lounge chairs was making him hard. Time to get in the water to cool off.

"I'm going in the water," Alex sat up, "do you wanna come?"

"I'm gonna wait a few minutes," Tori answered with her eyes closed, "and then I'll join you."

"Okay." Alex stood up and walked into the pool. It was time to swim laps to cool off. Alex was on his fifth lap when he saw a bikini body in his way, and it wasn't Tori. He attempted to swim around her, but she moved in front of him again, so he stopped and stood in the pool.

"Hi," a girl in a teeny tiny bikini was standing in front of him. "I'm sorry, I didn't see you."

"Oh," Alex tried to walk around her, "no problem, miss." Unfortunately, every time Alex tried to get around her, she blocked his path.

"So, what's your name?" the girl flipped her hair around her finger. "I'm Sandy."

"Hey Baby," Alex felt arms around his neck and shoulders from behind, "did you make a friend?"

Alex turned and helped Tori wrap her body around his front, holding her ass in his hands while she wrapped her legs around him.

"Hey Baby," Alex crooned, "I did. This is Sandy."

Before Alex could say anything else, Tori planted a kiss on his lips. He was so stunned she could slide her tongue into his mouth. When she ended the kiss, Alex raised his eyebrow at Tori and nodded toward Sandy.

"Hi Sandy." Tori wrapped her arms tighter around Alex's neck, plastering her body against him.

"Uh, hi," Sandy backed away from them. "It was nice meeting you. I, uh, have to go back to my friends."

"Okay, bye Sandy," Tori looked over her shoulder and gave Sandy a little wave.

"Baby," Alex kissed her neck, "that was some first kiss. Were you jealous? You saw me trying to get away from her, right?"

"Yup, you're welcome." Tori turned her head for better access. "And yes, I was jealous and wanted to claim my man before she threw herself at your sexy body. Then I would have had to rip her eyes out."

"Mmm, I like you defending my honor and my body." Alex rubbed his hands down her back, kissing her neck. It seemed Tori was ready to move their relationship forward.

"It's a nice body," Tori squeezed his arms, "are some of your tattoos tribal?"

"Some," Alex gazed into her eyes, "others are just artwork I liked."

"Well, I can't wait to explore all of them." Tori ran her hands over the designs. "Maybe tonight?"

"Anytime, Baby, I'm ready whenever you are," Alex kissed her cheek. "Thanks again for the save. I came in here to cool down after seeing you in your bikini, but now I'm back to standing at attention."

"It's a shame we're not alone," Tori kissed his neck, "it might be fun to do it in the pool."

"Uh, Tori," Alex grumbled, "you're not helping my problem."

"Sorry, not sorry," Tori continued kissing and sucking his neck, "Can we get something to eat, go upstairs and continue this?"

"I like the way you think, but are you sure?"

"I've never been surer."

"Okay." Alex rubbed her ass. "Go ahead and get out. I'm gonna swim a couple more laps or I will shock our guests. Then I'll order us lunch to be delivered in our room."

"You're not afraid of being attacked by another groupie?" Tori raised her eyebrow.

"Nope, I think you took care of that." Alex kissed her long and slow, "pretty sure everyone here now knows I belong to you."

"Okay." Tori gave him a quick peck on the lips. "My work is done." She turned and swam to the steps, climbing them as she stepped out of the pool.

Holy Fuck! Watching her get out with all the water dripping from her delectable body was not helping him in the hardness department, but he couldn't stop watching her until she sat down. Shit, maybe he needed to do three laps and start thinking about ingredients for recipes to get his mind off fucking her. He didn't know when she changed her mind about their relationship, but he was glad she was realizing how much he cared about her.

*** *Tori* ***

That was fun. Tori had felt the green jealousy monster creeping up when she saw that woman in front of Alex. It was good Alex was so receptive, and she didn't have to fight that girl off. At first, she didn't know how Alex would respond. They had never gone beyond holding each other on the couch. But seeing that girl flirting with him had pushed her into claiming her territory.

"Ma'am." A pool waiter was standing next to her chair. "I have this note for you from that gentleman." The waiter pointed toward the bar.

"What?" Tori sat up and reached out to get the note and looked at the bar - her eyes widening.

"Um," Tori looked at the waiter and glance at Winston at the bar, "thank you."

Tori lifted her knees into a fetal position, grabbed her towel, and draped it over her body. She opened the note and read the message from Winston.

I can't believe you told the police about me. You remember that night wrong. You loved every minute of me fucking you. You asked for it. If you tell anyone I drugged and raped you, I will kidnap you and sell you to the Reapers. They love to fuck and share women before they sell them to their highest bidder. Shut the fuck up Bitch!

Upon glancing upwards, Tori noticed Winston raising his glass at her from the bar. Tori looked for Alex, but he was still swimming laps and by the time she looked back for Winston, he was gone. Tori was trembling and ready to go back to their room. She would have to keep the note a secret and keep her mouth shut. Quickly putting on her coverup, she put the note in her pocket and walked to the pool to get Alex's attention.

"Alex," Tori walked to the end of the pool and touched his hand before he turned to go in the other direction. Alex looked up and wiped his face.

"Hey Baby," Alex stared, "what's wrong?"

"Alex," Tori was looking all around the pool, "I'm tired and I want to go back to the room. You can stay here if you want, but I'm leaving."

"Tori," Alex pulled himself out of the water and grabbed her hand, "Baby, wait. I'm coming with you. Do you have our key?"

"Yes," Tori's hand was trembling, "I have it."

"Okay," Alex kept watching her, "let me grab a towel. Baby, you're trembling."

Tori waited for Alex while he grabbed a towel.

"Come on," Alex dried off quickly and wrapped the towel around his waist, "let's go."

Alex guided Tori back to their room.

Chapter 29

The Shark is Circling
Alex

Once they entered the elevator, Alex turned Tori around.

"Baby," Alex held her hands, "what happened?"

"Nothing." Tori would not make eye contact with him. "I just wanted to go back to the room."

Alex stared at her, confused because she was acting nervous.

"Tori," Alex squeezed her hands, "did that girl say something to you?"

"No," Tori's eyes widened, "I just wanted to leave and come upstairs. You can go back down, it's okay. I'll be fine."

"I'm not going down there without you. I want to spend my day with you until I have to go to work."

As soon as the elevator door opened, Tori hurried out of the elevator and opened the door. Not turning to look at him, she hurried into the bathroom.

"I'm gonna take a shower. I'll be out in a minute," Tori said before she shut the door.

"Okay." Alex watched Tori shut him out. What the hell happened? She was fine when she left the pool. She even promised some afternoon delight, which had shocked him. Alex heard the shower turn on and walked to the door to see if it was unlocked. Breathing a sigh of relief when he could turn the knob.

Okay, so she wasn't mad at him. Pacing in front of the bathroom door, he kept thinking about what could've happened. Tori had dropped her coverup on her way to the bathroom. Alex bent down to pick it up and put it in the hamper when a piece of paper fell out of the pocket.

Alex read the note. *Holy shit!* Someone was threatening her. Although the note wasn't signed, he had a good idea who wrote it. He needed to talk to Barrett. Maybe the cameras by the pool had caught Winston. Suddenly, he heard whimpering coming from the bathroom. Alex hurried into the bathroom and found Tori curled up on the shower floor, crying.

Alex quickly stripped and rushed into the shower. Kneeling in front of her, he pulled her into his arms while she cried.

"Baby," Alex whispered in Tori's ear and wiped the hair away from her face, "I got you."

Holding Tori was killing him. He didn't want her to hurt anymore. He needed to be more vigilant.

"Baby," Alex helped her stand when her trembling stopped, "Let's get you washed and in bed. I'll order room service for our lunch."

Alex washed and conditioned her hair. Tori was catatonic while Alex washed her body and turned off the water. While drying her off, he was becoming more worried about her. She was staring into space and did not help at all.

Alex wrapped her hair in a towel and carried her to bed, laying her down and tucking her in.

"Do you want some soup for lunch?" Alex gently rubbed her face.

Tori closed her eyes and nodded while tears leaked out of her eyes.

"Oh Baby," Alex kissed her cheek, "I'll be right back."

Alex's heart was shattering into a million pieces watching Tori. He dried himself off and put on a pair of sweatpants before calling down and ordering soup for Tori and a burger for himself.

"Tori," Alex crawled in behind her, "Baby, I ordered our food. It will be about thirty minutes." Alex gently turned her toward him and held her face in his hands.

"Baby, talk to me." Alex kissed her forehead. "What happened?"

"Alex," Tori hugged him, "just let it go."

"Baby," Alex hugged her tighter against him, "I saw the note in your pocket. What happened?"

"Alex," Tori stiffened in his arms, "I'm scared."

"Please tell me what happened so I can help you." Alex murmured in her hair.

"When I got out of the pool, I was laying down when a waiter came over and said he had a note for me from a gentleman at the bar," Tori looked into his eyes, "Alex, it was Winston, he was looking at me in a really mean way. I'm positive he wrote that note and it scared me."

"Baby, who is Reaper?" Alex held her head and ran his thumb over her cheek.

"I don't know, but that night when I went to get the folder out of your car, Winston was talking to a man that I'm pretty sure is part of a motorcycle club based on what he was wearing. Winston passed him a white brick and some gummy bears, and the man gave him money."

"Did you tell the police?" Alex noticed Tori getting agitated.

"No, I had forgotten about it until now. Do you think that could be Reaper? Did I see something I wasn't supposed to see?"

"I think you might have," Alex kissed her forehead. "I'm gonna call the police and bring Barrett and Holt in on this conversation. I want everyone looking out for you and I want him banned from here."

Alex heard the knock on the door.

"Baby, stay here." Alex sat up and tucked her back in. "I think that's our food. I'll be back."

Alex put the food on the dining room table and walked into Barrett's room.

"Barrett," Alex called out, "You in here, bro?"

When no one answered, Alex texted Barrett and Holt. His second call was to the police.

"Tori," Alex stepped into the bedroom, "your soup is here. I called the police. You may want to get dressed before they get here."

"Okay," Tori sat up and pulled off the towel from her head. Alex watched her grab one of his shirts and walk into the closet. Alex waited for Tori at the dining room table. A few minutes later, she came out wearing his shirt and a pair of sweatpants. He held her chair out for her to sit down. He'd already set up her soup, napkin, and silverware.

"Do you want some water?" Alex rubbed his hand down the back of her head.

"Yes, please." Tori took a sip of her soup.

Alex brought her a bottle of water and headed to the bathroom to grab her hairbrush. He noticed her hair had become tangled from the shower and the towel. Alex ran the brush gently through her hair, getting out all the tangles without hurting her.

"Thank you, Alex," Tori said between bites.

Barrett came running into their room from his.

"Shit, Tori," Barrett was out of breath, "Are you okay? I saw Winston at the pool bar, but by the time I got down there, you guys were all gone. I called Holt and ran to the downstairs security room to see what happened. Holt is in the lobby waiting to escort the police up here. I brought mom."

"Oh Tori," Sehoy whispered as she came from behind Barrett, "my sweet girl. Alex, let me finish that."

"Thanks bro," Alex nodded to his brother and handed his mom the hairbrush after he hugged her, "thanks *chatski*."

Sehoy bent down and hugged Tori.

"Why is this happening to me?" Tori spoke so softly, with tears in her eyes breaking all their hearts.

"I don't know, but the boys will put a stop to this," Sehoy answered. "Now let's finish brushing your hair so it can dry. Alex, I'm going to take Tori into the bedroom to talk."

Alex nodded and moved closer to Barrett. "That's the note given to her," Alex pointed to a baggie on the table, "I'm sure it will have my prints, Tori's and the waiters. I'm also hoping it will have Winston's prints."

"I'm sure it will, since he was holding it when he gave it to the waiter," Barrett commented.

Suddenly, there was a loud knock on the door.

"I'll get it," Barrett walked to answer the door.

"Hello, Sunrise Police," the officer called out when they entered the room.

"Hello, officers," Alex shook their hands, "George, thank you for coming so quickly."

"Where's Tori?" George asked, "can I talk to her?"

"Yes, she's with my mom. I'll go get her." Alex walked into the room and found his mom holding his girl while she cried.

"Baby," Alex walked over and hugged them both. "The police are here to take your statement."

"Okay," Tori wiped her tears.

"Give her a minute to wash her face and we'll come out," Sehoy put her arms around Tori and led her to the bathroom.

Alex left his bedroom to talk to George. "Tori's using the restroom. She'll be right out."

"No problem," George answered and waited.

"Hi, George," Tori said when she came out.

"Hey Tori. Can you tell me what happened today?"

"I was laying out by the pool when I got that note delivered to me by a waiter." Tori pointed toward the note in the baggie. "The waiter said it was from the gentleman by the bar. It was Winston James. He had an evil look on his face and raised his glass as if toasting me. I read the note and looked for Alex in the pool. By the time I looked back at the bar, Winston was gone. I got Alex after that, and we came up here."

"Can we file a restraining order?" Alex squeezed Tori's shoulder.

"Yes, Tori, you can come to the station and file a restraining order." George answered, "I must tell you guys we paid a visit to Mr. James, and he said he walked through the lobby and waited until she got on the elevator. He said he never brought her up to her room and insinuated she enjoyed going to the bar downstairs to drink and hook up. I didn't want to tell him Tori remembered him in her room, because I didn't want to give away too much information. Did you guys find any video footage that can invalidate his statement?"

"Son of a bitch." Alex grumbled and turned around to pace.

"He's lying," Barrett put a hand on his brother's shoulder, "Let's look at our footage from that night. Holt pulled it for us to view."

"I only did that once," Tori mumbled. "It was how I met him."

"Tori," Alex said, "tell the officers about what you saw the night of your date."

Tori repeated everything she saw to the officers.

"Can we look at the video footage now?" George asked Barrett.

"Yes sir," Barrett nodded, "follow me."

"Tori, I'll be right back," Alex stood behind Tori's chair, placing his hands on her shoulders.

"I'll be right here with you." Sehoy sat next to Tori and held her hands.

Alex nodded to his mom and followed Barrett, Holt, George, and Sean to the security monitors. Barrett sat in his chair and queued up the footage from Friday starting at 4:00 pm. They all stood staring at the monitors, hoping to see something from the two cameras near where the family parked.

"There," George pointed to the monitor, "let it play at regular speed."

They saw Tori walking toward Alex's car. Then two men walked in front of the camera and stopped facing each other. You could see clear as day the transaction because the two idiots didn't realize there was a camera next to them.

"Let's keep going and see if you have footage of him entering the resort," George mentioned. "Winston said he dropped her at the elevator. If we can find him on this floor, we know he came to her room."

Barrett fast forwarded to around nine and then slowed it down. They kept looking at the lobby camera near the elevators and the cameras on the family floor. At around nine thirty, they saw Tori being held up by Winston. She was wobbling and stumbling as she walked with him through the lobby. A few minutes later, they watched Winston again, with Tori opening her room door and walking in with her.

"Son of a bitch," Barrett mumbled.

"That's what we need right there," George pointed at the screen. "Barrett, can you also pull up footage from today by the pool?"

"Absolutely." Barrett found the digital file and fast forwarded to when Alex walked out with Tori.

"Shit bro," Barrett said, watching Sandy coming onto Alex. "Oh never mind, go Tori."

"Yup," Alex grinned, "okay, it happened after Tori got out of the pool.

They all watched as Tori accepted the note from the waiter.

"Can you pan over to any cameras by the bar?" George asked.

Barrett pulled up all the cameras by the pool on several monitors.

"There he is!" Alex shouted and pointed to one monitor. Alex wanted to go through the monitor and choke the life out of Winston. Watching the fucker toast Tori made him ill. "What do we do now?"

"Barrett," George tapped him on the shoulder, "can you please put the footage of the drug deal, Winston carrying Tori to her room, and Winston poolside on a flash drive so we can take it down to the station? If I'm correct. Reaper is the one meeting with Mr. James. We have been trying to arrest Lucifer's Renegades for drug trafficking for a while. That footage could help us."

Barrett was copying it while the officers were speaking.

"Here you go, George," Barrett handed him a thumb drive with all the footage he requested. "Let me know if you need anything else. I want that son of a bitch to pay for what he's done to Tori."

"Thank you. We'll take this thumb drive and the note." George grabbed the baggie from the table as he walked through Alex's room. "Do you know who all touched this note?"

"Tori, the waiter, Winston, and me," Alex answered.

"We'll take it in and check DNA," George's partner put his pad away. "We'll need you and the waiter to come in for fingerprinting so we can eliminate your prints from the note. Hopefully, from the note and the results of the rape kit we can arrest him. We asked Mr. James to come in and give his DNA, but we have yet to see him at the station. I'm pretty sure he won't come willingly, but we'll see what we can do. We'll be in touch."

The officers left and Barrett, Holt, and Alex walked back into Alex's room.

Chapter 30

Cooking Lesson
Alex

"Is she okay?" Barrett watched a quiet, slightly hunched over Tori talking to Sehoy.

"Shit Barrett," Alex rubbed his neck, "she better be. I'm gonna take tonight off so I can stay with her. She was doing so well. This is going to set her back.

"Alex," Barrett grabbed his shoulder, "I can stay with her if you have to go downstairs."

"Yeah, man," Holt offered, "I can stay with Tori if that helps you out."

"Thanks guys," Alex placed his hands on his hips and looked down, "I'm gonna go down at five and see what is going on in the kitchen. Can one of you stay here with her until I get back?"

"Yup," Barrett patted Alex's shoulder, "I'm on it. I was off tonight anyway. I'll stay up here with her until you get back. Go back and stay with her until then. I'll be here watching the monitors. Get me when you leave."

"I'll stay on the floor and look out for Winston," Holt mentioned. "I showed his photo to the casino staff, but I'll text it out to the entire staff."

Alex nodded and headed back to Tori.

"Baby," Alex touched her shoulder, "how are you holding up? You hardly had any soup."

"I'm okay. It was nice to have your mom here with me." Tori lifted a corner of her lips into a weak smile. "You should eat your lunch, Alex. It's getting cold. I'm gonna go lay down." Tori and Sehoy stood up.

"Thank you for sitting with me, Sehoy," Tori hugged her.

"You call me anytime you want to talk or need a motherly hug. I know it's not the same as your mom being here, but to me, you are one of my children now."

"Thank you so much," Tori teared up.

They said goodbye to Sehoy and Alex led her into their bedroom.

"I'll bring my food in here and eat it while you relax." Alex stepped out to get his burger from the dining room table and sat down on the bed next to Tori to eat his meal. In all honesty, the food was churning in his stomach. After a few bites, he threw it away. He had a better idea of how to distract Tori.

"Baby," Alex walked to her side of the bed, "I have a surprise for you. Do you trust me?"

"Yes." Tori held his hands while he pulled her out of bed. Alex walked into the closet, put on his flip-flops, and grabbed hers.

"Put these on," he dropped them by her feet.

"Where are we going?" Tori asked, following Alex out of the bedroom.

"It's a surprise," Alex wiggled his eyebrows at her, "I think you will like it. We're heading down to Savor."

"Alex, I don't feel like being around people."

"No one is there now since they don't open up to the public until around five."

"Barrett," Alex walked to the adjoining door, "I'm taking Tori to Savor.

"Okay, let me know when you guys head back up." Barrett said from the security room doorway.

Alex led Tori down to the restaurant and straight into the kitchen. Since it was around one, there wasn't anyone around. Bernie didn't come back until around four to prep for the dinner crowd.

"We are going to cook Indian Fry Bread with some honey and a fruit salad." Alex explained as he grabbed the oil, flour, honey, peaches, cantaloupe, and watermelon, placing them on the counter in a row.

"Alex," Tori watched him place everything on the counter, "believe it or not, I've never made Indian Fry Bread. I've had it. My mom made it for us all the time, but I've never made it."

"Well, no time like the present." Alex grabbed a large bowl and set it down next to his ingredients. "There are a lot of different recipes, but we're going to make the Seminole Fry Bread Recipe my mom taught me. So, can you measure out two cups of flour for me and pour them into this bowl?"

Alex brought a measuring cup and spoons to the counter. Tori measured out the flour and poured it in. He was hoping this would help distract her for a little while.

"Add three teaspoons of baking powder," Alex handed her the teaspoon measuring spoon. "Now add one teaspoon of salt and mix it all together." Alex grabbed the milk from the refrigerator. "Last ingredient is to add one cup of milk. You add the milk gradually, and I'll stir until the dough is stiff."

Alex stirred until the dough was the right consistency.

"Let's wash our hands so we can handle the dough." Alex guided Tori to the sink, and they washed up. Going back to the counter, Alex wiped it down and poured flour onto it. "Knead the dough with your hands so you

can feel the consistency in case you want to make it on your own later."
Alex could tell Tori did not know what he was talking about. Grabbing
half the dough, he stood behind her and guided her hands into the dough,
showing her what to do.

"Baby," Alex kissed her neck, "you smell good."

Tori turned her head and kissed him. Alex was getting way too turned
on, and they had a meal to finish. Not to mention anyone could walk in
on them. "Okay, to be continued." Alex turned her head with his kiss on
her cheek. "Let's separate this in half and flatten it out until it's a half
inch thick. Then we're going to fry it. I'll turn on the burner so it can heat.
Watch what I do with the dough." Alex grabbed the other half and placed it
on the floured counter, and showed Tori what to do. When he flattened his
bread to the right size, he washed his hands and turned on the stove.

"That looks great, Baby. Let's put that aside while the burner heats.
We'll cut up some fruit to go with our fry bread," Alex said as he grabbed
the cantaloupe and cut it in half, handing her one half, a scooping spoon
and a large bowl. "Let's scoop out both sides. Bernie can use it for his
dinner crowd later."

"Okay," Tori smiled while she worked, "this I know how to do."

Alex was glad to see Tori smile. "I love to see your beautiful smile."
Oh Shit, what did I say? Tori's smile suddenly dropped and her eyes grew
haunted. Fuck! Time to change the topic.

"I'm gonna teach you some of our language," Alex said while he
scooped, "these are the words my mom taught me, but there are different
variations depending on which Seminole tribe you are from." Alex pointed
at the cantaloupe, *'famechalatka'*, then he pointed to the watermelon,
'chastalay', and finally pointing at the peach he said, *'pacaneah'*. Tori
repeated the words after him. "After we scoop out the cantaloupe, we'll do
the same to the watermelon. We serve a lot of watermelon—our customers
love it. While you do that, I'll cut up a peach for us to mix into our melon
salad."

"Sounds good," Tori said as she concentrated on her scooping. Alex cut
the watermelon in thirds so she could scoop one as well. Alex placed one of
his pans on the stove and poured oil into it. He cut up the peach while the
oil was heating.

"Alright," Alex grabbed a plate and put both fry breads on it, "the oil is
ready. Come, take a look." Alex picked up the fry bread with his tongs and
placed it into the pan. "You want to make sure your oil is hot and flip it on
both sides until they are both golden brown. I could've also dropped it into
our fryer," Alex pointed to the fryer with the tongs, "but I wasn't sure if
you would want to make this in our room. No fryer there." Alex flipped the
bread with the tongs, removing it when both sides were golden brown.

Pulling out a clean plate, Alex placed the finished fry bread on it.
Holding up the honey, he said, *'foinsampi'*, honey, if you want to pour some
on."

Alex handed her the plate and put the next fry bread in the pan. Tori
poured some honey on it and took it to the counter before continuing to
cut up the watermelon. As soon as Alex's fry bread was done, he noticed

she was waiting for him to eat.

"Here," Alex swapped plates with her, "you take the fresh one."

"No, Alex," Tori tried to hold on to her plate, "it's okay."

"Nope," Alex tugged a little harder, "my girl gets the best one. Go sit at a table out there and I'll bring out our fruit salad. Here's some silverware." Alex pulled open a drawer and handed her a fork and knife. "I'll be right there."

Alex made the fruit salads and grabbed a couple of napkins on his way to the table. Tori must love honey because she had drizzled it all over her fry bread, leaving no piece untouched.

"Mmm, Alex," Tori moaned around a bite, "this is so good. I know you were trying to distract me, but this worked. Thank you."

"You're welcome," Alex would have put a lot less honey on his fry bread. "I'm glad you are feeling a little better. After this, we'll clean-up for Bernie and go upstairs to watch a movie until my shift tonight."

Alex and Tori finished their meal and cleaned up the kitchen. They packed away all the melon they cut up, so Bernie had some prep work done. Bernie would be happy and surprised with their work. Alex led Tori to their room.

"I'm gonna stay with you until five," Alex stretched out on the couch and pulled her against him, "then I gotta check in at work, but Barrett will stay with you. He can stay in his room if you don't want him in here with you."

"I would rather he be in here with me," Tori scooted back between his legs into his arms, "if that's okay with you guys. We can sit on the couch and watch a movie."

"I'm sure Barrett will be fine with that," Alex murmured against her neck. "Do you want to watch a movie or a TV show?"

"Movie, please."

Alex reached back for the remote. "How about a romcom?"

"Wow, are you feeling okay?" Tori reached back and felt his forehead.

"Why?" Alex chuckled, "I can do romance."

"Okay, big guy," Tori snuggled into his arms.

Alex and Tori laid there watching the movie and laughing at the characters' antics until Alex had to leave. Alex got Barrett to sit with Tori and watch movies until he returned. When Alex arrived, Barrett was still awake watching TV while Tori was asleep on the couch. Barrett had covered her with a blanket. Alex thanked Barret and carried her to bed.

Tomorrow would be a tough day for Tori. He knew taking her to the police station to file a restraining order was going to be difficult. Plus, they also had to give their fingerprints and DNA. Alex knew she wanted to go into work, but he was afraid the police station would be emotionally draining. He would leave it up to her. If after the station she needed a work distraction, then he would take her there for a few hours.

He would have to talk to Barrett, Holt, and Freya to see who could watch over her tomorrow night. Alex needed to work at RUSH so Sam could have the night off. Maybe tomorrow night would be a good night to train another chef to help him, Bernie, and Sam.

Tomorrow's problems would come soon enough. Alex curled up to Tori in big spoon style and breathed in her scent. It was a flowery smell, probably given to her by either Freya or his mom. They both those scented shower gels. Breathing in her scent finally lulled him to sleep.

Chapter 31

Mental Health Time
Tori

Tori was up and dressed before the alarm went off. She was nervous about her first therapy appointment, but she would reward herself by meeting the shelter kids Thunder was always talking about.

"Alex," Tori laid down and mumbled into his chest, "are you awake?"

"I am now. What time is it?"

"Time to get up," she giggled. "Will you take me to work today?"

"After your therapy appointment? Are you sure?"

"Yes," Tori sat up and looked down at him, "I'm tired of hiding. The police are after Winston, and I know you'll protect me. I promise I'll listen to everything you tell me to do. I'm really looking forward to meeting the shelter kids and getting to know them."

"Okay."

"Really?" Tori thought she was going to have to convince Alex to take her, but he wasn't fighting her decision at all.

"Yes, just please stay in the center and by either Mark, Thunder, or me."

"I can do that."

"Okay, let me go take a shower, since you are ready to go. I can make you breakfast when I get out." Alex attempted to sit up but stopped when Tori placed her hand on his chest.

"Alex, do you think I'm a tease?"

"No, Baby. Why would you think that?"

"Because I led Winston on and then I flirted with you in the pool but didn't follow through when we came upstairs." Tori looked away.

"Tori, please look at me," Alex gently turned her face toward him. "I really care about you, and I will wait for you for however long it takes for you to be ready to be intimate with me. I don't want to rush you, and I'm not going anywhere."

"Alex, what did I ever do to deserve you?"

"Baby, we deserve each other. I will do anything in my power to make you happy."

"Thank you, Alex. I appreciate and trust you."

"Back at you, Baby," Alex used his hand to reach behind her head and hold her while he kissed her. Tori wrapped her leg around his waist and deepened the kiss, pushing Alex back onto the bed. Releasing his mouth, Tori ran her lips over his neck while her hands wandered over his chest and to his erection, which was growing by the second. Tori stroked it through his sweats.

"Baby," Alex was panting as he held Tori's hand away from his penis, "I really want you, but if you want to get to therapy on time, we really need to stop. Because when we make love the first time, I want to take my time and taste every inch of your beautiful body. I don't want a quickie." Alex kissed her while he tried to remove her from his body.

"I'll be quick in the shower," Alex murmured around their kiss.

"Okay," Tori was breathless as she watched Alex walk into the bathroom.

After his shower, Alex walked into the kitchen and saw Tori making scrambled eggs

"Look at you. I thought you didn't know how to cook?" Alex swiped her hair to one side as he hugged her from behind and rested his head on her shoulder.

"Anyone can cook scrambled eggs."

"Not true. I once saw a chef burn them."

"No." Tori laughed and picked up the pan to separate the eggs into two servings. "There is no way a professional chef burns eggs."

Alex held up his hands. "I'm just saying he did. I'll grab some juice for us while you carry the plates."

"This looks great, Baby. Thank you for breakfast," Alex said, after setting the drinks down.

"I wanted to do something nice for you, since you are constantly doing nice things for me."

"How are you feeling about today?"

"I can't wait to see the shelter kids."

Alex grinned at her. "I know that, but how do you feel about therapy this morning?"

"Scared, embarrassed, humiliated, stupid," Tori sighed.

"Whoa." Alex squatted next to her, gripping her hands in his. "Don't call yourself stupid. I mean, you're entitled to your feelings, but Baby, remember, you are not stupid. None of this is your fault. You gotta start believing me."

"I know everyone keeps telling me that, but I do feel stupid."

"I wish you wouldn't. Talk about it to Dr. Hansley. Maybe she can help you understand you are not stupid."

"I will. Thank you."

Alex kissed her forehead and stood. "Let's finish our breakfast so we can get ready to go."

"Okay."

Tori and Alex sat in silence as they finished their meal. This silence wasn't like their previous uncomfortable silences in the car before the Winston fiasco. This silence was where they both contemplated the day and hoped it would be better than expected.

Alex stood up when they finished and grabbed their plates, rinsing them in the sink. Tori handed him the glasses, and they loaded up the dishwasher.

"I need to talk to Barrett before we leave," Alex informed Tori.

"Okay. I'll come with you, if that's okay."

"Barrett." Alex called out before entering. "I'm with Tori. Can we come in?"

"Yup." Barrett was eating cereal at the table.

"I'm taking Tori with me to the cultural center. We'll be back around five."

"Okay," Barrett looked up, "we'll hold the fort down here."

"Have a good day Barrett," Tori peeked around Alex.

"You too, stay close to Alex or Thunder."

"I will."

Alex grabbed her hand, and they walked to his car. They arrived on time for Tori's appointment. She had to fill out several forms about her health before handing back the clipboard to the receptionist.

"Baby, when they call you back. I'll stay here and wait for you. Take as long as you need, okay?"

"Thank you." Tori held Alex's hand.

"No problem."

"Ms. Tall Bear," a woman called her name from the doorway to the doctor's offices.

"You got this Baby," Alex squeezed her hand before letting her go.

Tori stood up and approached the woman.

"Right this way," the woman waved her hand toward the doctor's office.

The woman led her to an elegantly decorated office with a couch and chair facing each other. Dr. Hansley was seated in the chair. She stood up as soon as Tori stepped inside.

"Tori, I'm so glad you called. Please take a seat." Dr. Hansley walked to the office door and closed it. "How are you doing?"

"I'm a little nervous. I've never visited a therapist. I don't even know the difference between a psychologist, a therapist, or a psychiatrist."

"That's understandable. Few people know the difference. A therapist is a licensed counselor or psychologist who works with patients to treat mental health symptoms and improve how they manage stress and relationships. This is how I want to help you. A psychiatrist is a medical doctor who can prescribe medication to treat mental health disorders. I'm not big on medication. I hope to teach you strategies on how to handle your stress, but if you choose to go a different route, I can put in contact with some good psychiatrists in the area."

"I would rather not go on medication."

"Great, then let's see if by talking to me, I can help you manage the stress you feel from what happened to you."

"Dr. Hansley, I don't feel stress. I just feel scared all the time."

"Stress can manifest itself in different ways. Why don't you tell me what you remember about that day? I know this will be hard, but you will only have to tell me today. We will move forward from there. Please leave nothing out about your thoughts and emotions. If you are open to me and trust me, then I can truly help you. Are you ready?"

"Yes." Tori took a deep breath.

"You can begin whenever you are ready."

Tori began with how she met Winston and how she thought he was such a nice man. Telling Dr. Hansley about her conversations with Alex and Freya was difficult. Dr. Hansley nodded and stayed quiet, taking notes on a legal pad. Talking about being drugged and raped was the hardest part.

"I didn't know what happened until you and Dr. Wallace explained it to me in the hospital. I can't recall waking up in my bed or the ambulance ride. I guess that's for the best, but I feel such a deep sense of loss and I don't know why."

"May I ask if you were you a virgin?"

"I was. And I still feel like I am. Is it wrong to want to get intimate with someone?"

"Everyone reacts differently when they have experienced a traumatic experience. With rape, some women never want a man to touch them. Since you don't remember your rape, maybe you want intimacy with a man you trust to feel like yourself. There is no right or wrong way to react. Only you can decide how you want to heal and be a survivor."

"So, wanting to get close to Alex is not wrong?"

"No. You might feel a sense of loss because you know someone took something from you and you want to regain control of your sexuality. But since you don't remember, your mind is confused. Your parents taught you that making love with someone for the first time is a great gift to be shared with someone you love. Your body may have felt sore, indicating a violation, but your mind had no recollection of the event. When that time comes, you might feel like it's your first time since you don't have a memory of your rape—you still don't remember any part of your rape?"

"No, I just remember seeing him above me, pressure in my woman area, and then nothing."

"That might be for the best. Rape is a very violent crime. Many think it's about sex, but it's about controlling someone. Did Winston ever do things to control you?"

"We only went on three dates. But during those dates, he controlled my food and drink orders."

"Does Alex control you?"

"No." Tori shook her head vehemently. "Alex is the total opposite. He is always looking out for me, asking me what I want, if I'm okay."

"That's good. Let's stop here and we will continue our conversation next week. If that is okay with you?"

"I would like that."

"Great. The one thing I want you to take away from today is to be nice to yourself. You are a wonderful, smart, kind, and caring person. What Winston did is on him and not you. You are a survivor. You will be okay. Alright?"

"Thank you, Dr. Hansley," Tori smiled for the first time during this visit.

"You're welcome." Dr. Hansley stood up and walked Tori to the door. "You can make an appointment with Joan, my receptionist."

"I will. Thank you again."

"See you next week."

Tori walked out to Joan and made another appointment. Then joined Alex in the waiting room. He was sitting with one leg over his lap reading a magazine. Alex put the magazine down and stood up as soon as he saw Tori.

"How did it go?" Alex said as soon as they stepped into the elevator.

"It was good. I made another appointment for next week."

"Baby, that's great." Alex hugged her.

"I gotta say she made me feel better. Not saying I'm fine, but at least I'm understanding my feelings a little better."

"I'm so glad. Do you still want to go to the cultural center?"

"I do. I really want to meet the shelter kids."

"Okay, sounds good. I'll make them some fry bread."

"So now that I know how to make fry bread, do you want some help in the kitchen?" Tori teased Alex.

"You're cute," Alex chuckled as he pulled out into traffic.

"Just saying. My bread might be better than yours."

"Maybe we'll put that to the test," Alex winked at her, "I would love to have you in the kitchen, but I have a feeling you will be busy with the exhibit."

"You're probably right," Tori sighed.

"Tori, seriously, if you get tired or are ready to go early, just let me know." Alex reached his hand out to hold her hand and laid it on her lap.

"Okay, I will."

Chapter 32

Shelter Kids I Spy Winston
Tori

When they arrived, Alex asked her to stay put, and he came around to get her. This was the first time they walked to the entrance together. After they entered, Alex kissed her forehead, acknowledged Mark with a chin lift, and headed toward the kitchen.

"Hey Tori," Mark stood up and came around the lobby desk and hugged her, "I'm so glad to see you. How are you?"

"I'm good, Mark, thank you. Is Thunder in the back?"

"Yes, he's in the warehouse."

"Thanks Mark. I'm gonna go find him."

Tori entered the warehouse and looked for Thunder. He was in the back, rebuilding the boxes they'd broken down last week.

"Thunder, can I help you?"

"Hey, I wasn't sure you were going to come in. How are you feeling?" Thunder walked over and hugged Tori.

"I'm good. What can I do to help you?"

"If you can tape these boxes up, that would be great," Thunder pointed to his stack. "I need to call Tim and find out what time 'Our Kids' are coming."

"Absolutely. I'll work on this here."

"Perfect." Thunder walked to the other side of the warehouse and watched over Tori while he called Tim.

After everything that happened with Winston, Tori knew none of them was going to let her out of their sight.

"Tori, come with me. Let's tell Alex 'Our Kids' are coming at one."

Tori and Thunder walked into the kitchen.

"Alex," Thunder walked up to him, "Our shelter kids are coming at one. Tim said there will be six of them. Can you please make them some of your fry bread tacos or pizzas? I think they would really like that."

"Of course," Alex nodded.

"Oh, and make them some plain fry bread they can take back with them. Grayfeather always made extra for them to take home."

"Yup, I'll work on that too. Do you guys want some for lunch?" Alex asked Thunder and Tori.

"Yes, please," Tori smiled at Alex.

"That sounds great," Thunder clapped him on the back, "I didn't bring lunch, hoping you were coming in."

"I'm on it, Tori, are you doing, okay?"

"Yes," Tori rolled her eyes at Alex, "It's only been thirty minutes. I'm fine."

"Okay, let's let Alex work his magic. We have lots of boxes to build." Thunder placed his arm around Tori and led her out of the kitchen. "Tori, call Sarah. She wants to ask you to our Family Funday Sunday."

"Family what?" Tori wondered what Family Funday Sunday was all about.

"It's what Tommy calls it," Thunder smiled, "really it's just Sarah, Grayhorse, Tommy, Lilly, Isa and I getting together for lunch at Sarah's house."

"That sounds like fun. I'll call her now. If that's okay?"

"Yup, she's expecting your call."

Tori grabbed her phone out of her purse on their way through Thunder's office.

"Hello," Sarah answered.

"Hi Sarah, it's Tori."

"Hey, how are you doing?"

"I'm good, getting better every day," that was Tori's standard answer. She still didn't remember the details of her rape, but it was nice everyone was on alert just in case it slapped her in the face one day and she broke down. "Thunder said something about a Sunday Funday?"

"Yes," Sarah's voice sounded like she was running around and out of breath, "come this Sunday to lunch. You can bring Alex or Frey."

"Okay, I'll ask them but I'm not sure if they have to work. They've taken so much time off babysitting me."

"I've heard. Well, this will just be a relaxing afternoon, and Thunder and Grayhorse will watch over you."

"I would really like to catch up. Can I bring anything?"

"Nope, I got it covered. Can you come around noon?"

"I think so. Let me talk to Alex and Frey since they are my rides."

"Sounds good. If they can't come, let me know, and Grayhorse or Thunder can go pick you up."

"Okay, thank you for the invite."

"Of course, you are welcome any Sunday."

"Thanks Sarah, see you then."

"Bye Tori, have a great day."

Thunder and Tori spent the rest of the morning creating boxes and placing the packing slip inside. They agreed to take down the Red Path Exhibit items on Tuesday of next week and begin to display the Unconquered Path Exhibit.

They meant to stop at noon and eat before their kids arrived, but they lost track of time.

"Thunder!!!!" A boy sung on his way into the center, "we're home!"

"Come on Tori," Thunder interrupted her, "we can stop for now. Time for you to meet 'Our Kids'."

Thunder led Tori out to the lobby.

"Mark, my man." A boy with brown hair and a Marlin's cap worn backward fist bumped Mark. "How's it going?"

"It's going," Mark laughed.

"Who's this beauty, Thunder?" the boy asked while he stared at Tori, and she chuckled.

"This is Tori, my new assistant, and she is taken," Thunder hugged Tim, "Tori, this is Tim, the leader of this pack. It's so good to see you guys."

"Today I brought Luke, Kenny, Jimmy, and Bryce." Tim pointed to them, respectively. "The others couldn't make it. Taken by who?" Tim asked.

"Me." Alex said as he walked toward them.

"Tim, boys," Thunder pointed at Alex, "this is Alex, my new chef. Be nice to him if you want fry bread."

"Ah, dagger to the heart," Tim staggered back and clutched his heart dramatically, "you guys always take the hot ladies."

Tori chuckled at his antics. He reminded her of Lizzy, only younger.

"Well, I may have the hot lady," Alex winked at Tori, "but I have a special fry bread recipe for you guys. Follow me."

"You're gonna love these guys," Thunder gestured for them to follow Alex and took up the rear as they all sat down at a long table that Alex put together for them to enjoy lunch together.

"Wow," Tim stopped at the table when he saw all the different varieties of fry bread, "are these pizzas and tacos made of fry bread?"

"Yup," Alex answered, "please grab a seat and try whichever ones you want. I have more in the kitchen. I'll bring you all some waters. Dig in."

"You don't have to tell me twice," Tim mumbled. "Come on boys, we'll be eating well today."

Tori found out that Tim was leaving the shelter and moving into Thunder's spare room until he made enough money from working at the grocery store to get his own apartment.

"Is Isa, my other favorite hot chick, ready for me to move in?" Tim asked.

"She might be ready," Thunder scowled at Tim, "but if you call her a hot chick again, I won't be ready."

"Aw, you know I love her," Tim smiled, "and I promise to help around the house."

"I know," Thunder nodded, "and for some crazy ass reason, she loves you too."

Tori listened to them tell their stories about Thunder, the younger kids looking at him like he was their hero. Thunder took them into the storytelling room and told them several Lakota stories. He was so good with them. Tori helped Alex clean up and then joined them. As they were walking out, they walked up to Mark at the desk.

"Hey Mark," Tim pointed to the photo next to his monitor, "we saw that guy hanging around in the parking lot. Who is he?"

"His name is Winston James," Mark looked at Thunder, alarmed. "He's been harassing Tori."

"Are you shitting me?" Tim blurted out.

"Language," Thunder grimaced, "you said he was in the parking lot?"

"Yeah, when we got here," Tim nodded, "let's see if he's still there. I'll show you where I saw him."

"Tori, go to Alex in the kitchen. Mark call George," Thunder gave orders as he headed out the door, "Tim, come with me. Everyone else stay with Mark."

Tori hurried into the kitchen and ran up to Alex, hugging him from behind.

"Hey Baby," Alex was at the sink washing the dishes, "miss me already."

"Alex," Tori gripped him harder.

Alex turned off the water and wiped his hands, turning around in her arms.

"What happened?" Alex cupped her face and lifted it up toward him. "You look scared."

"Winston was here."

"Fuck!" Alex attempted to pull her away. "Where's Thunder? Did you see him?"

"No," Tori shivered. "Tim saw him in the parking lot when they arrived. He didn't know who he was until he saw his photo on Mark's desk. He walked outside with Thunder to show him where Winston was standing."

"Okay, come with me. Let's see what they found out." Alex put his arm around Tori and led her out of the kitchen.

"Mark, has Thunder come back inside?" Alex asked.

"No, not yet," Mark shook his head, "but I called George and he's on his way with Sean."

"Okay." Alex stood behind Tori and rubbed her arms.

"Mark," Thunder stormed inside, "did you call George?"

"Yup, he's on his way."

"Did you see him out there?" Alex asked Thunder.

"No, but I still want the police to look around."

They all heard the sirens just as George pulled up in front of the center and left his flashing lights on.

"Thunder," George ran inside, "Mark filled us in. Show us where he was, and we'll look around."

Thunder and Tim walked outside again. Alex attempted to step around Tori.

"Alex," Tori grabbed his arms, "please stay with me."

"Okay Baby," Alex tightened his arms around her and kissed her temple.

After looking around for a while, Thunder and Tim came back inside. George and Sean were going to drive around to see if they could find him.

"Tori, go home with Alex." Thunder walked up to them. "We've done enough for the day and there's not much else to do until we take the exhibit down next week. It's best if you take tomorrow off and come in on Monday when we're closed to the public. We can focus easier without customers."

"Okay," Tori nodded.

"Tori, now that we know who this asshole is, we'll keep an eye out for him too," Tim told her.

"Thank you, Alex. Are you ready to go?"

"I have some dishes to finish. Just give me a minute."

"Alex," Tim looked at him, "We'll be happy to finish your dishes. You can take Tori home."

"Thank you," Alex hugged them. "I really appreciate this. Tim, follow me into the kitchen and I'll show you the fry bread you guys can take home."

"That was so sweet," Tori teared up as she watched the boys follow Alex.

"They are good kids who got the short end of the stick." Thunder wrapped his arm around Tori's shoulder. "If you show them love and respect, they will go above and beyond for you."

"Baby, are you ready?" Alex walked toward them. "Thunder, thank you for letting us cut out early."

"I'll walk out with you guys," Thunder said as he followed them outside and looked around while they drove off.

Chapter 33

Are Frey and Holt a Thing?
Tori

They drove home in silence, both looking around to make sure they didn't see Winston. Tori was so tired of being afraid. The only time she felt safe was when she was with Alex.

"Are you working tonight?" Tori asked Alex as they stepped into their room.

"I need to talk to Sam and see if he can cover me. I'd like to stay with you."

"I'd like for you to stay with me too, but I understand if you can't."

"If I can't, I'll ask Frey to stay with you."

"Okay." Tori walked into the closet to change her clothes into sweats and one of Alex's shirts.

"Baby," Alex held her when she walked out to the living room, "I have to work dinner at RUSH. Sam's wife is pregnant, and she needs him to come home. I'm so sorry. I will try to close up early, around nine. I talked to Frey, and she will switch with another dealer so she can stay here with you."

"Okay," Tori kissed his cheek, "thanks for trying."

Alex bent down and kissed Tori properly, holding her tightly against him when they heard knocking on their door.

"Hey, BFF!" Freya screamed outside the door.

"Gotta love my sister's timing," Alex groaned, released Tori and walked to the door.

"Hey Frey," Alex hugged his sister.

"Hey Bro, where's my BFF?"

"Hi Frey," Tori smiled at Freya.

"Ready for another Girls' Night In Movie Day?" Frey walked up to Tori and grabbed her arm, dragging her to the couch. "Look, I even brought us some popcorn. She's in excellent hands now Alex, you can go do your thang."

Alex shook his head at Freya.

"I'm gonna see if Holt or Barrett can work from up here?"

"Sounds good. What do you want to watch, Tori?" Frey asked, turning on the TV.

"You pick. I'm good with anything." Tori sat next to Frey on the couch so they could share the popcorn.

"Baby, Holt is coming up here to work in the security room," Alex bent down and kissed Tori, "Frey be good."

"Always," Freya smiled with popcorn between her teeth.

"Ladies, I'm here," Holt announced shortly after Alex walked out. "Let me know if you need anything. All the doors will be open."

"Thank you, Holt," Tori smiled at him.

"Yeah, thank you Holtie," Freya smirked.

"You're in rare form, Frey," Holt mumbled and walked away.

Freya had brought them their own popcorn bags, so they moved to their respective couches until the first movie ended.

"So, how are you doing, Tori? I heard Winston was outside the center today?"

"Yeah, the shelter boys saw him. I just want him to get caught so I can relax. No one is safe until he's caught."

"I agree. I'm not gonna lie. I've been feeling scared at night, even though I know our floor is secure," Freya whispered.

"I'm sorry, Frey," Tori sat up facing her, "it's all my fault."

"No, it is not. It's that asshole's fault," Freya moved to sit next to Tori, "you didn't do anything wrong. I started it with that stupid bet."

"Aren't we a pair," Tori smiled at Freya, "here we are both blaming ourselves when neither one of us did anything wrong. If any of this would have happened with a sane man, we wouldn't be in this situation."

"True," Freya sighed, "but then we wouldn't have been able to hang out as much as we have. I have truly loved every minute of our time."

"Me too, Frey," Tori hugged Freya, "now what will we watch?"

"Something funny, please.

Tori chose a movie about how far a girl would go to have a guy dump her in less than two weeks. Before they knew it, they were in their third movie and Alex was coming home.

"Hey ladies, I see you are still in a movie marathon. Did you guys eat dinner?"

"Yes," Tori answered, "we ordered room service."

"Okay. I'm gonna take a shower. I'll be back in a few."

When Alex returned, he helped Tori sit up and sat in the couch's corner.

Tucking her bent legs under her butt on the couch made it more comfortable to move closer to Alex and lean her head on his shoulder. Alex wrapped his arm around her and played with her hair while they watched the movie.

By the middle of the movie Tori's legs were cramping and she must have grunted when she moved them because Alex turned his body and laid down, helping Tori curl up on his chest. Once Tori was comfortably draped over him, Alex covered them with the blanket. Tori noticed Freya was smiling while she laid on the other couch.

"Hey guys," Holt said from Barrett's doorway, "I'm not gonna be switching with Barrett. He's gonna keep walking the floor, and I'll stay in the family security room. Frey, are you working tonight?"

"Nope," Freya hit pause on the movie, "mom gave me the night off."

"Okay," Holt nodded, "if you guys need anything, come get me. Frey, can you come here for a minute?"

"Sure," Freya stood up and started the movie back up, placing the remote by Tori, "just tell me what I miss."

Tori watched Freya go into Barrett's room to talk to Holt. They were whispering so she couldn't hear their conversation.

"Are they dating?" Tori whispered to Alex.

"What?" Alex looked down, "Who?"

"Holt and Frey," Tori nodded toward them.

"I don't know. They've been friends forever. I wouldn't object. Holt is a stand-up guy and is already part of the family, but it would suck if they hooked up and then one of them got their heart broken."

"True." Tori sighed, "but if it worked out, that would be so romantic. I mean, look at us."

"True," Alex kissed the top of her head.

"Okay," Freya jogged back and scrambled under the covers on her couch, "what did I miss?"

Tori hadn't been paying attention because she was watching Freya with Holt.

"Uh, let's just rewind," Tori raised herself up leaning on Alex's chest and rewound the movie, "I think it's best you see it." After she hit play, she laid back down on Alex.

"Smooth, Baby," Alex chuckled in her ear.

"Yup," Tori mumbled. Lying on Alex was torture. His body was so hard, but so comfortable. She was so grateful to Alex and wanted to please him. She knew something had been taken away from her, but thanks to the drugs, she really didn't remember being with Winston. Tori had dreamed about giving her virginity to someone who truly loved her since she found out about sex. And she was feeling those feelings for Alex. She would need to talk to Dr. Hansley about what she was thinking and feeling.

What if she did something with Alex, and it brought back horrible feelings or a terrible memory? She knew sex could be pleasurable. At twenty-seven, she had read about it a lot in her romance novels. She wanted to experience sex with Alex so she could wipe away the sense of loss and forget about seeing Winston on top of her. Was it time to seduce Alex? She had read somewhere that survivors of rape either wanted no sexual contact or might use it as a coping mechanism. Is that what she was doing? She didn't want to give in to this fear of sex. She wanted to be in charge of her body and not lose out on intimacy with Alex.

Tori pulled the blanket higher and roamed her hand over Alex's chest. Wanting to get closer to him, she draped her leg over his hips coming into direct contact with his cock under her inner thigh. She heard him suck in his breath and could feel his cock harden. Alex moved his arm from around her shoulders to her waist, his thumb stroking her side. His other arm stayed behind his head.

Tori looked at Freya to see if she noticed her stroking Alex's chest. Freya smiled at her and got up.

"I think I'm gonna turn in," Freya smirked at Tori, "I'll finish watching the movie another time. Have a good night."

Chapter 34

I Am Woman Hear Me Roar
Tori

"Okay," Tori didn't move off Alex, but placed her hand under Alex's shirt and continued to trace his abs slowly with her fingers, "I'll talk to you tomorrow."

"Yup, I'm gonna close this door since Alex is home, but I'll leave Barrett's door open." Freya said as she pulled Alex's adjoining door closed.

"Tori," Alex murmured, "what are you doing?"

"I don't know," Tori answered honestly, "but I want to please you."

"Baby," Alex closed his eyes, "just being with you pleases me."

"Will you lay back and let me try something?"

"No, Tori. It's too soon." Alex held her hands in his.

"Dammit. Why can't I do something for me? Why does everyone think they know what's best for me? First Winston and now you!" Tori pulled her hands away.

"Are you comparing me to that asshole?" Alex said through gritted teeth.

"No, that's not what I meant."

"Well then, what specifically did you mean?"

"I just wanna feel normal. I want to experience sex and intimacy with you because I trust you. If I ever feel uncomfortable, I trust that you'd respect my boundaries. Basically, I'm using you as my boy toy so I can feel empowered and gain back my sexuality. I know for some women this would be wrong, but it's how I feel. Please Alex, help me gain some semblance of control so I can feel more like a survivor than a victim. Will you help me?"

"Okay." Alex mumbled.

Tori leaned over and pulled Alex's shirt up under his arms. Taking his arm off her waist, she placed it on his chest.

"Hold your shirt up here for me," Tori instructed him. And watched as he looked at her and nodded. Tori straddled him and leaned down, kissing and licking his abs, following his happy trail down to his sweats. Reaching for his sweatpants, she placed her hands inside the back, running her hands down and cupped his ass as she slid the pants down. Once the back was down, she moved her hands around to the front and pulled his sweats down, releasing his cock. Tori heard Alex's breathing speed up.

Alex caught on to what she wanted and shifted his body to help her as she shoved his sweats down to his knees. Leaving them there, she wanted to control his movements.

"Baby," Alex whispered, "are you sure about this?"

"Yes." Tori stared at him wickedly and bit her bottom lip. "But I've never done this before." Tori ran her hands up his thighs and watched him grow even harder, noticing that he was leaking, "I've only read about it in romance novels. Am I doing okay so far?" Tori licked the liquid on his head.

"Yesss," Alex groaned.

"Will you show me or tell me if I do anything wrong?" Tori sucked his head and looked up while his cock was in her mouth.

Alex was panting now and nodded while he stared at her mouth as she swallowed his cock. Tori moved one hand to his cock and the other to his balls and put as much of his cock as she could in her mouth.

"Oh, Fuck!" Alex growled and jerked his hips toward her.

"Did I hurt you?" Tori immediately lifted her mouth off him.

"No, Baby," Alex breathed heavily and held his eyes closed, "do whatever you want. It all feels great."

Tori released his cock and balls and moved her hands around to his ass and cupped him, bringing him closer to her as she swallowed his cock into her mouth.

"Oh Fuck," Alex moaned.

Tori moved her hands again and grasped his hips, pushing him into the couch and holding him in place while she sucked and licked him. Alex tried pushing his hips into her mouth, but she held him down, limiting his movement. Alex grew even harder and longer.

"Baby," Alex whispered, "I can't hold back anymore. If you don't want to swallow, pull off. Shit, that feels so good."

Tori moved one hand off his hip to his cock and firmly stroke him at a quicker pace while she continued to suck his cock.

"Fuck!"

Tori looked up and saw Alex with his eyes closed, head back, gritted teeth. One hand gripped his hair while the other gripped the shirt as he shot off in her mouth. Knowing she had this much control over Alex's orgasm was an empowering feeling. Tori looked back down and swallowed all of it. As Alex tried to control his breathing, she licked him totally dry.

"Baby," Alex whispered, "Come up here." Alex pulled her up into his arms.

"What made you want to do that? You know I'm fine just holding you, right?"

"I know, but I wanted to do something for you where I was in control. Something that would be special to just you and me. I really enjoyed it."

Alex gazed deeply into her eyes. "I need you to know you never have to do anything with me that makes you feel uncomfortable. Whatever and whenever you want to try something, I'm your man."

"Thank you."

"No, Baby, thank you. That felt…abso-fucking-lutely…fantastic."

"So, I did okay for my first time?" Tori said from Alex's chest, waiting for his breathing to regulate.

"Okay? That was…fuck…mind blowing," Alex mumbled when he could form words into sentences. "If you've never done that before, how did you know what to do?"

"Romance novels," Tori kissed his neck, "smutty ones."

"I'll have to read those novels." Alex kissed her head. "On second thought, you read them, and then show me what you learned. I'll happily let you try anything you want."

Tori laughed and smacked him on the chest.

"Okay," Alex chuckled, "I think I can stand up now. Pretty sure we missed the end of the movie. Do you want to watch it?"

"No," Tori snuggled closer, "I want to go to bed."

"Okay," Alex grabbed the remote and turned off the TV, "let's go to bed."

Alex helped Tori up, pulled up his pants, and stood. Grabbing her hand, he twined his fingers with hers and led her to the bedroom.

"I'm gonna take a shower, Baby," Alex pulled her into his arms. "I'll be out in a few minutes." Alex bent down to kiss her.

"Okay, I'll brush my teeth when you get done." Tori pulled back and covered her mouth with her hand.

"No, you don't." Alex pulled her close and kissed her, licking at her bottom lip. "Baby, open your mouth."

"No Alex, my mouth tastes like your release," Tori murmured with her lips closed.

"Baby, I don't care. When I eat you out, you will taste yourself." Alex nipped her bottom lip. "Anything we do, we share. Now open for me."

Tori breathed in his manly scent—she had never kissed a bearded man passionately. Opening her mouth, their tongues clashed together. Each using their dueling tongues to chase and suck each other. Alex tilted her head to the side for a better angle. Feeling his beard rough against her face turned her on even more. Alex released her tongue and gave her a quick kiss on her lips.

"I still have to brush my teeth," Tori smirked after their steamy kiss.

"Okay, come brush your teeth while I get my water hot." Alex turned her around and walked behind her into the bathroom. Tori attempted to brush her teeth while Alex undressed and checked the water.

"Baby," Alex swatted her butt, "you're not brushing, you're watching me."

"Am not," Tori blushed, scrubbed her teeth and spitting out the paste to rinse her mouth.

"Right," Alex stepped into the shower and shouted, "feel free to join me if you want."

Without second guessing herself, Tori stripped, pulled the curtain aside and stepped into the shower. Alex was facing the shower head—Tori had a magnificent view of his long hair and firm ass. Not being able to help herself, she ran her hands down his back, over his ass and around to the front and up over his chest before pressing against him.

"Mmm," Alex wiped his hands down his wet hair, pulling it to the side and turning around in her arms, placing his hands on her hips.

"I love when your hair is down," Tori reached out and ran her hands through it. In her culture, long hair was a sign of strength and virility. "Why do you wear it in a man bun on top of your head all the time?"

"Habit. Since I have to for work," Alex murmured while his gaze wandered over Tori's body. "I don't want my hair in anyone's meal. Baby, you are so fucking beautiful."

Tori stiffened in his arms and withdrew from Alex.

"Baby," Alex loosened his hold, but kept his hands on her hips, "What did I say? What just happened? Did you remember something?"

"Winston's nickname for me was beautiful." Tori looked down. "I guess it brought back awful memories."

"Shit," Alex sighed, "okay. I will use a different word, but I want you to know you are beautiful inside and out. I hate he ruined a perfectly good word to describe you, but he will not win, and I will make sure you know how gorgeous you are daily."

"I'm ready for more, Alex." Tori ran her hand over his hair while she traced his abs. "I want to try." Tori kissed his chest as water drops trailed his chest. "Please Alex, I feel a connection with you, and I trust you. I want to feel everything a man and woman do with you."

"Baby," Alex inhaled sharply, "are you sure? We can stop whenever you want. If there is anything we do that makes you feel uncomfortable or painful, please let me know. I don't want to hurt you."

"About what happened," Tori placed her head on his chest, "I don't remember the details. I don't know if I ever will. I talked to Dr. Hansley about my wanting to do things with you. She said everyone handles trauma differently. I want you to be the first man I remember. I know physically I'm not a virgin anymore, but in my mind I am. Would you be able to be with me after another man has tainted me?" Tori finished her last sentence quietly and nervously.

"Tori, look at me," Alex used his hand to lift her face toward him, "I want to be that man, but I want to take it slow in case you remember anything that scares you. I don't want to make you uncomfortable or scared. I don't give a damn that you're not a virgin. I just wish I could take away what happened. Let me take care of you. I will do anything you want. I just want to make sure you're ready. Turn around, let me wash your hair so you can get used to my hands."

Tori turned around and Alex washed her hair. His hands were so gentle as he massaged her scalp. When it was all shampooed up, he walked around her and gently led her under the showerhead. Running his hands over her hair, he tilted her head back to keep the shampoo out of her eyes. Alex then stepped behind her again and moved her out of the spray of water. Tori felt him rubbing and massaging the conditioner into her hair.

"Can I wash yours?" Tori asked.

"Sure," Alex said, "but first let me wash your gorgeous body so I can rinse out your conditioner. Let me take care of you first."

"Okay," Tori whispered, turning toward Alex. He grabbed a bar of soap and created a lot of lather. Alex started at her neck and moved down her arms. Lathering up again, he focused his attention on her breasts. His hands felt so slippery and sensual over her hardened nipples. "Alex, that feels so good," Tori moaned.

"Baby," Alex groaned, "you have no idea how good you feel."

Tori was not huge in the breasts department, but he could hold a handful. He didn't seem to mind as he massaged and gently squeezed her breast before moving down to her belly. Soaping up again, he washed her back and cupped her ass. Alex's hands were pure torture, and she couldn't wait for him to release some of the pressure building inside her body.

Suddenly, Alex dropped to his knees and washed her legs from her thighs to her ankles. Tori held his shoulders as he took turns lifting her legs to wash each foot. While on his knees, he pulled her toward him and kissed her belly, while one hand cupped her behind and the other went between her legs.

Tori felt Alex making circles around her clit with his finger. Her breath came rapidly now. She placed a hand on the wall and the other on his shoulder. Alex then slowly slid one finger inside her, and Tori couldn't stop her body from undulating into his hand. Alex moved his mouth down toward her throbbing pussy and pressed her against his mouth. Sliding a second finger inside her, Alex circled her clit with his tongue.

Tori's moans grew louder, and she couldn't stop her body from pushing against Alex's face. "Oh my God, Alex."
Tori felt Alex's fingers curl into her and felt a pulsing sensation of pleasure overwhelm her. Tori lost all sense of control and felt her legs weaken as her orgasm exploded through her body. Alex reached around and held her up under her ass with his hands while his tongue lapped up her juices. Alex held her until her heart rate slowed back to normal. Stepping back, he pulled her forward to rinse her legs. Then, turning her around, Alex stood up to rinse the conditioner out of her hair.

"Baby," Alex hugged her tightly and ran his hands down her back, "Are you okay?"

"Yeah." Tori stepped back and looked up at him.

"Why don't you get out?" Alex held her face in his hands. "I'll finish up and meet you in the bedroom."

"But I didn't have time to wash you?" Tori sighed.

"You'll have plenty of time to do that another time," Alex kissed her forehead. "You look tired."

"Tomorrow?" Tori pulled back and asked.

"Sure," Alex nodded, "tomorrow. Now let me get you a towel. Stay here under the water where it's warm."

Alex stepped out of the shower and returned within a few seconds with a towel for Tori. He helped her step out of the shower and dried her off, giving her a quick kiss before dropping his towel and stepping back into the shower.

Tori wrapped the towel around her body and walked into the closet for one of his shirts. After pulling it over her head, she walked back into the bathroom to dry her hair. She heard Alex turn off the water and pull open the curtain.

Tori couldn't stop watching Alex. He was so beautifully built. She hoped they continued the exploration of their bodies when they got to bed.

"Do you sleep naked?" Tori asked while he dried off.

"I do," Alex dried his legs and looked up, "but I don't have to. I've been sleeping in sweats with you."

"You don't have to," Tori hesitated before answering. She was so nervous, but so turned on. "It won't bother me."

Tori's hair was mostly dry, and she wanted to do something for him.

"Will you sit on the toilet seat so I can dry your hair?" Tori watched him from the bathroom mirror.

"Sure," Alex sat down and held her hips while she dried his hair. Alex had long wavy hair down past his shoulders to his nipples. Occasionally, Tori would brush her breast against his face, and he would take in a sharp breath. Tori ran her hands through his hair instead of using a brush. It felt so nice to touch him freely. Tori looked down and noticed him hardening again. Alex rubbed his hands up and down the back of her thighs under the shirt, each time getting closer to her pussy.

"Okay," Tori trembled when Alex cupped the bottom of her ass in both hands and looked up at her. "I think it's dry enough."

Tori stepped back, unplugged the dryer and bent down to put it back under the counter. Suddenly, she felt Alex's hands low on her hips, pulling her back toward him. Alex's tongue licked her from behind. Tori gripped the cabinet doors while Alex continued to play with her pussy.

"Alex," Tori pushed back into his mouth.

"Yum," Alex murmured into her pussy before she felt him put his arms under her legs and pull her up off her feet. Alex carried her into the bedroom and placed her on the bed. Tori grabbed the bottom of his towel, causing it to come off as he backed up. Alex quirked an eyebrow at her.

"Are you sure?" Alex asked. He placed a knee across her on the bed, straddling her while he laid on her, bracing his body weight on his forearms.

"I've never been surer," Tori reached up and caressed his face. Alex dropped his head down, turning his head to better ravage her mouth.

"Baby, look at me," Alex stared into her eyes, "if you want to stop at any time, let me know. We will stop. I will not force you to continue. Okay."

"Okay, Alex."

Chapter 35

Most Important Night of His Life
Alex

Alex scooted back and held the sides of her t-shirt. Tori sat up and raised her hands. Alex knew he needed to go slow and make sure she was okay with everything he did. They had already done some intimate things, but making love might trigger something and he didn't want her to be hurt by anything he did.

Alex followed her down, kissing her neck and inhaling her scent, slowly licking his way down to her beautiful breasts. Wanting to touch her breasts and play while he sucked, licked and plucked her nipples, he straddled her to hold her gently in place. Tori's body writhed in bed, and she placed one of her hands on the back of his head while she rubbed his back with the other. Alex gave equal attention to both breasts before he licked his way down to her pussy.

"Alex," Tori whispered and bucked her hips, "I need you."

"I want to make sure you're ready, Baby," Alex scooted down on the bed and widened her legs. Alex kissed her inner thigh as he slipped his finger inside her pussy.

"Alex," Tori screamed out, "please. Fuck me."

"Tori," Alex looked up, "Baby, I will not fuck you. Not this time. I will make love to you. I just want to see you cum one more time."

Alex inserted two fingers and noticed how wet she was. Spreading her open with his other hand, he dove in and thrust his tongue inside her pussy, excited to taste her. He would love to do this with her every day for the rest of his life. She tasted sweet and tart at the same time. Tweaking her clit, Tori shivered and grabbed the back of his head with both hands, pulling him toward her as she succumbed to her orgasm.

"God Tori, your body is so gorgeous and responsive to me," Alex sat up and reached into his nightstand for a condom. Quickly putting it on, he laid on top of Tori and rolled them over, so she was on top. He recalled Tori's story about seeing Winston above her when she was drugged. Alex didn't want her associating their love making with Winston's rape.

"Alex?" Tori looked at him questioningly.

"Baby," Alex held reached up and brought her face down to his, "when you're ready, guide me in. You set the pace. I will love anything you do, trust me."

Alex smiled at Tori and kissed her slowly, licking and sucking her lips until she opened her mouth, giving him full access. Alex felt Tori grip his cock and pump it a few times before placing it at her entrance. Tori slowly lowered herself onto him while he remained still. She felt like heaven as she wrapped him in her warm, tight pussy. *Oh Fuck*, Alex thought he had died and gone to heaven.

Tori sat unmoving as she became accustomed to his girth and length. Slowly, she lifted and dropped her body onto him, grinding every time he bottomed out.

"Alex," Tori cried out, "I need you to help me."

Alex placed his hands on her hips and moved her forward and back quickly, creating friction. Tori placed her hands on her breasts, plucking her nipples. Alex held her down with one hand, bucking into her while he reached around and played with her clit.

"Alex!" Tori screamed out his name as she ground into him.

Alex felt her muscles clenching him right before her release drenched him. Losing control, Alex pushed up one more time filling the condom with his orgasm before they both collapsed onto the bed and caught their breath. Alex wrapped his arms around her. One arm pressing her chest to his while the other pressed the back of her head into his neck.

"Baby," Alex murmured, kissing the top of her head, "Are you okay?"

"Yeah," Tori sighed, "I never knew that could be so intense and good."

"Baby, you were incredible," Alex rolled them over and kissed her neck, "I have a feeling it will be that good or better with you every time. I'm gonna go clean up, stay here. I'll be right back."

Alex walked into the bathroom to throw away the condom and get a washcloth to clean Tori. As he approached the bed, he saw Tori hadn't moved. Smiling to himself, Alex sat next to her on the bed. Using the warm washcloth, he wiped her between her legs.

"Thank you," Tori yawned.

"I will always take care of you," Alex bent down and kissed her lips before getting up and putting the washcloth in the bathroom sink. Returning, Alex crawled back into bed and helped Tori get under the covers. He pulled her back against his chest, wrapping one arm under her body, holding her breast while his other hand rested on her belly, pulling her tightly to his body.

Alex had never felt so at peace before. Spooning Tori was heaven on earth. She was so brave to want to make love to him. In all honesty, he didn't think she would be ready so soon and he had been ready to wait for her. He was falling in love with her, but he didn't want to tell her yet. Showing her every day would have to be enough for now. He didn't want to scare her off. His strong, beautiful girl was more than he could have ever asked for. He knew he could go to bed every night for the rest of his life just like this.

"Goodnight, Baby," Alex swept her hair off her face and kissed her cheek.

"Night, Alex," Tori held onto his arm across her chest.

Chapter 36

Chillin' with My Bestie
Tori

The relationship with Alex was progressing in the right direction. He made her feel safe and loved. Alex was a generous, tender, and a caring lover. She couldn't have asked for a better partner. Making love with Alex had been the icing on the cake. Neither one had said the "L" word yet, but her feelings were growing stronger every day.

She'd heard about sex and knew the logistics of the act, but being heavily chaperoned, she never came close to anything but a light kiss on the cheek. Sleeping with him had been a enormous risk. She had been nervous it would bring back horrible memories about her rape, but it didn't— which really surprised her. Nothing Alex did reminded her of the rape. Tori thought maybe it didn't happen. Maybe Winston didn't rape her. Even though the doctors told her it happened. *But if they never found DNA, could it not be true?* Her mind played tricks on her when she thought about that night.

She was jumpy around men, but not with Alex. Her mind and body recognized being with him as her safe space. Winston's arrest would help, but she expected to be leery of men she didn't know for a long time, if not forever.

"Hey Baby," Alex ran his hand down her body as he spooned her.

"Good morning," Tori looked over her shoulder and, open mouth, kissed Alex.

"How are you feeling?" Alex murmured on her lips.

"After last night with you, I feel so stupid for not seeing the true Winston. I should have listened to you and Frey. It's okay to tell me you told me so."

"Oh, Baby," Alex turned her onto her back so they could look at each other for this conversation. "I will never say that to you. You are the kindest, most caring person I know. He took advantage of that. You didn't do anything wrong. Never call yourself stupid, because you are not stupid. Inexperienced with assholes, yes, but not stupid."

"Thank you, Alex," Tori reached and ran her hand over his cheek and beard, "you have stood beside me the whole time and I treated you badly."

"Baby," Alex kissed her hand, "I'll always stand beside you and protect you. I'm sorry for how I handled you dating Winston. Let's start over and forget about anything either of us said in the past."

"I would like that," Tori continued to stroke his beard.

"You like my beard, Baby?" Alex smirked.

"I do," Tori smiled, "it's not too full and makes you look like a sexy, badass alpha male."

"Oh yeah," Alex bent down for another kiss.

"Mmmm," Tori ran her hands around his head and stroked his hair, "I also like your hair, and tattoos, and body."

"My little vixen," Alex ran his hands down her body, touching all the parts he mentioned, "I love your eyes, hair, breasts, pussy, and legs. Really everything about you, but my favorite is your heart."

"I love your heart too, Alex. You are such a good, caring man. Can I ask you something?"

"You can ask me anything."

"Sarah invited me to her house tomorrow for lunch. Do you want to come with me?"

"I would love to, Baby, but I need to talk to my kitchen staff and see if they can cover for me tomorrow. I might need to work today in order to switch with Sam tomorrow. Let me send them a text." Alex reached over and grabbed his phone.

Alex: Can either of you switch days with me and work today so I can take tomorrow off?

Sam: I can switch with you. Not a problem.

Bernie: Thanks Sam, I already had plans, but I can change them if you need me.

Alex: Thanks Sam, I'll work lunch and dinner at RUSH today. I appreciate it.

Sam: Yup

"Okay, Baby." Alex placed his phone back on his nightstand. "I'll be working today, and I'll be off tomorrow so I can go with you. On that note, I gotta get up and get ready for work. But not before I please my girlfriend." Alex rolled them over and latched onto her breast.

"Your girlfriend, huh?" Tori ran her hands through his hair. She loved his long hair.

"Mmmhmm," Alex released her breast with a pop and took small nibbles on her nipple. "You're mine now."

"I think I like that," Tori moaned.

"You think?" Alex stopped his seduction, sat up between her legs, and tickled her all over her sides, attempting to find her most ticklish spot.

"Alex, stop!" Tori screamed as she tried to get away from his hands.

"So do you still think you like that or like that?" Alex didn't let up.

"Okay, okay, I like that! I like it!"

Alex immediately stopped and ran his hands up behind her back as he laid down on top of her and held her head to the perfect angle to ravish her mouth.

"I'll talk to Frey, Holt, and Barrett and see who is available today." Alex left her mouth and kissed his way down her body to her tasty pot of liquid gold.

"Alex, don't you have to go?"

"Yup, but not before I eat my breakfast. You know it is the most important meal of the day."

Alex slid his fingers into her pussy into her soaking wet pussy and sucked her clit. After giving her multiple orgasms which caused her to lie on the bed like a limp noodle, he got up and went to take a shower.

*** *Alex* ***

After his shower, Alex saw Tori had burrowed under the covers and fallen back asleep.

"Baby," Alex kissed her cheek, "I'm gonna go talk to Barrett, and then I gotta go."

"Uh, huh," Tori moaned.

Tori looked so comfy all curled up in bed, Alex wished he could climb back in. Unfortunately, he had to work all day and set up who could hang out with her. Thanks to Winston, their schedules were all jumbled. Everyone wanted to help Tori, but it seemed like it was a constant last-minute scheduling. Alex couldn't wait until they could establish a routine and get rid of Winston fucking James.

Alex opened his adjoining door and noticed Barrett's door was already open. Walking into Barrett's bedroom he noticed him still in bed asleep. He hated waking up his brother, but he needed to head downstairs and start prepping food for lunch.

"Barrett," Alex gently laid his hand on his brother's shoulder. Barrett bolted up.

"Is everything okay? Is something wrong with Tori?"

"Sorry, everything is fine. My schedule changed and I have to work today. I wasn't sure if you or Holt could work from up here today?"

"Shit, you scared me," Barrett dropped back down on the bed.

"Sorry, I didn't mean to scare you."

"It's okay. We can make it work, no problem. I can stay up here during the day and I'm sure Holt wouldn't mind working up here when I go downstairs until you finish work. I'll talk to him."

"That sounds great. Do you know if Frey is working today?"

"She has the day off, but is working tonight."

"Okay, maybe she can hang with Tori until she goes to work."

"I'm sure she would love that, then Holt can take over."

"Sounds good. I'll talk to Frey. Thanks, bro. I know this is messing with your schedule, and I appreciate everything you've done for us."

"Of course. We all love you and Tori. I'm so glad you've found such a wonderful girl."

"Thanks." Alex patted his leg over the covers, stood up, and left the room. Alex was so grateful to have such a fantastic, supportive family. Tori was still asleep when Alex grabbed his phone and stepped into the living room to call Freya.

"Mornin' Alex," Freya mumbled.

"Hey, I'm sorry to wake you up, but I gotta go to work. Can you please come over and hang with Tori?"

"Sure," Freya yawned. "I'll be right over."

A few minutes later, Alex opened the door to Freya leaning against the door frame in her pajamas.

"I'm here, you can go," Freya yawned.

"Thanks Frey," Alex hugged her, "call me if you need anything. Tori is still in bed."

"Great, I'm going to join her in a slumber party."

"Okay," Alex chuckled, "see ya later. Holt is going to stay with her when you leave for work."

"Um hmm," Freya walked away and headed to the bedroom.

Alex hoped Tori wouldn't roll over and think it was him next to her. Then again, that would be funny. Alex put in a full day having to work late. By the time he got home, he waved to Holt in the living room and went to take a shower. Trying to stay quiet since Tori was asleep, he slowly crawled into bed when he finished in the bathroom and spooned her while exhaustion took over.

*** *Tori* ***

"Alex," Tori murmured before turning around and seeing Freya, "Hey Frey. Where's Alex?"

"He had to go to work. I'm glad you didn't wake up feeling me up."

"That would've been funny," Tori smiled.

"I think we should tell Alex you did, just to see the look on his face," Freya laughed, "and then add we had a nude pillow fight."

"You are so bad," Tori chuckled.

"What do you want to do today? I'm assuming stay in since there was a Winston sighting yesterday."

"I'm so tired of staying in, but it would be for the best."

"I'm cool with another movie day. Hey, I can get some games from the cabinets in the laundry room. Barrett, Holt and I used to play checkers, Trivial Pursuit, Monopoly, and Apples to Apples. What do you want to play?"

"That sounds fun. I've only played checkers."

"Okay," Freya bounced out of bed, "I'll teach you Trivial Pursuit and Monopoly. It's hard to play Apples to Apples with only two people. We'll play that another night with Alex."

"This sounds like fun. I'm gonna take a shower while you go get those."

"I'll go get the games and be back in five. I'll go through Barrett's room so I can get back in if you are still in the shower."

Tori took a quick shower and waited for Freya in the living room.

"Hey," Tori said when Freya walked in. "What took you so long?"

"I need to talk to you."

"Okaayy, is everything all right?"

Freya placed the games on the kitchen table and walked to Alex and Barrett's adjoining door. She peeked inside and saw Barrett sound asleep.

"Frey, what's going on?" Tori looked worried.

"Let's talk in your bedroom," Freya grabbed Tori's hand on her way there.

"Okay, fess up?" Tori asked as soon as they entered the room.

Freya pulled Tori to the bed. They sat side by side, facing each other.

"I think I'm secretly dating Holt," Freya burst out.

"What? That's great, wait." Tori raised her eyebrow with a puzzled look on her face. "What do you mean, you think?"

"Well, we slept together a few days ago, and I thought everything was great until I saw him with Candy. So, I'm going on a date tonight with Ted to make him jealous."

"Okay, I'm really confused. Start from the beginning and don't leave anything out."

Freya started from when she met Holt in Elementary School and introduced him to Barrett.

"We bonded over bullies. Lucky for him in middle school, he grew tall and exercised, so bullies stopped picking on him. Then he and Barrett both started looking out for me. That's when I fell for him. I crushed hard, but he still looked at me like a little sister. I was heartbroken, but didn't let him know. His friendship was more important. Fast forward to now and he wants to date, but I'm afraid of my family's reaction."

"This is so amazing. I knew he liked you." Tori grinned at her like the Cheshire cat. "I even asked Alex if you guys were into each other."

"You did what? When?" Freya gasped.

"The night we were watching a movie and Holt came to the door to Barrett's room and asked to talk to you."

"Did Alex freak out?"

"Nope, he said you couldn't pick a nicer guy to date. Although I'm pretty sure if Holt was just fucking you with no commitment, Alex would go ballistic."

"Yeah, I get that. I've made such a mess out of this."

"It will be okay. Just go down tonight and let Ted know you are in love with someone else. Then you and Holt will have to talk to Barrett."

"Do you think Alex will help me with Barrett? I think I should keep it a secret until I know if Holt is serious about us. I mean, what if it doesn't work out? Then I could ruin Barrett's relationship with Holt."

"That's true. But I really think it will be better if your relationship is out in the open. I truly believe Alex will help you guys with Barrett."

"I don't know Tori; Barrett could really get hurt."

"Well, so could you. Besides, Barrett is a big boy. I'm sure he could handle you and Holt dating." Tori hugged Freya.

"Maybe," Freya pulled back, "I'll talk to Holt and see what he wants to do, but I'm leaning towards a secret relationship. At least for a little while."

"I don't agree, but I'll support any decision you make. Just talk to Alex before Barrett. This way, Alex can go with you whenever you tell Barrett if you're worried about his reaction."

"That might work," Freya sighed. "Thank you, bestie. I feel better already. I'll talk to Ted first, then Holt. Now, let's play a game so I can distract myself from the shitshow I created."

"You got it." Tori grabbed her hand and pulled her up. "Which one are you going to teach me first?"

"Let's start with Monopoly because it usually lasts longer and if we need a break, we can leave it on the table to finish later."

"Okey dokey."

Chapter 37

Beautiful Way to Start the Day
Tori

"Good morning, Baby," Alex whispered in her ear. "I have a surprise for you. I need you to get up and put on a bathing suit."

"Alex," Tori grumbled, "it's still dark out."

"I know, but you're going to like this," Alex scooted over, gently pushing her out of bed from her side.

"Okay," Tori stood up, rubbed her eyes, and yawned on her way to their closet, "this better be good."

"It will be Baby, trust me."

"Mm," Tori grunted and noticed Alex was already in his bathing suit. "Can you get me a cup of coffee?"

"Coming right up." Alex left the room while Tori headed to the bathroom.

Tori didn't know what he was up to. They'd never gotten up this early unless they were making love. She preferred that to getting up out of a cozy bed. Oh, what she wouldn't give to snuggle up with him again. Walking out of the bathroom, she eyed the bed, ready to get back inside. Just as she pulled the covers up to climb in, Alex walked in.

"Oh, no you don't," Alex wrapped his arm around her waist and redirected her out of the bedroom while he handed her a to go cup of coffee.

"Uh, I was so close," Tori mumbled before taking a drink.

"Come on, you're going to like this," Alex kissed her forehead and led her out the door toward the front of the lobby.

"Why are we going out the front? Where are we going? Why can't we just take your car?"

"So, Winston doesn't recognize the car."

Well, that woke her up. It was so easy to forget about him when she was surrounded by the Panther family. Tori looked around after Alex helped her get up into the passenger side of the truck. She didn't see anyone around, but it was still pitch-black outside.

"Alex," Tori reached out and placed her hand on his thigh, "are you sure it's safe to go somewhere?"

"Baby, we can't stay locked up all the time. Trust me, this will be okay. I got you. Just sit back and relax and enjoy your coffee."

"We are going to be back before Sarah's Funday Sunday?"

"Yup," Alex shook his head as he entered the highway, "we will have plenty of time to get home, take a shower and get ready."

"Can I ask where we are going at this hour?"

"It's a surprise, just relax. If you fall asleep, I'll wake you up when we get there."

Tori sighed, curled her legs up on the seat facing Alex, and closed her eyes. She didn't think she would fall asleep, but it felt good to relax. Looking outside didn't help her know where she was going because she wasn't familiar with the area. But looking at Alex was a special treat. He was so handsome.

"Are you staring at me?"

"Yes, I am," Tori whispered, "I can't believe I'm here with you. After everything I put you through with Winston, I'm just shocked you still like me."

"Baby, that's in the past. There isn't anywhere else I'd rather be right now that here with you."

"You are so sweet."

"Nah, you're the sweet one." Alex covered her hand on his thigh and lifted it up to his lips for a kiss.

Feeling safe, Tori continued the ride in silence. Soon she realized they were parking at the beach. She had never been to a beach, and she couldn't wait to feel the sand between her toes.

"Okay Baby, we're here. This is Fort Lauderdale beach. Let me get our blanket and we can watch the sun rise over the water. You're going to love this."

Tori was clapping and jumping in her seat, waiting for Alex to come around to her door. This was so thoughtful of Alex.

"Come on Baby," Alex smiled and helped her out. "Let's find a good spot by the water."

Tori immediately took off her sandals to walk on the sand as they walked hand in hand through the sand to find a spot. She'd heard the sand was blistering, but in the early morning it felt cool and soft. Tori watched as Alex spread a blanket out far enough away from the tide.

"Come here, Baby," Alex sat down and held out his hand.

Tori sat between his legs, resting her back on his chest while he wrapped his arms around her. Tori loved watching the water lapping on the shore and the small birds running into the water after it receded, leaving little minnows for them. It was so dark out in the ocean until the small waves crested with whitecaps. Wrapped up in Alex's arms and watching the ocean gave her a sense of peace and serenity. Something she needed to settle her mind.

A few minutes later, bright oranges and reds rose into the sky at the horizon line, reflecting those colors into the water, eliminating the darkness. Suddenly Tori could see the sun peeking out of the water. It was so very mesmerizing.

"Hey," Thunder suddenly broke into her thoughts, "what are you guys doing here?"

Tori looked up to see Thunder standing next to them in his running shorts and no shirt.

"I wanted Tori to see our beautiful sunrise from the best place to view it."

"Hi Thunder," Tori looked confused, "what are you doing here?"

"I live a couple of blocks away, and I run on the beach every morning."

"What a great way to wake up," Tori sighed and looked out as the sun rose higher in the sky.

"It sure is. That's why I moved out here. It's just beautiful," Thunder turned toward the beach, "Don't you sometimes come out here to run, Alex?"

"I do, but I mostly use the gym on our floor. It's just more convenient."

"I would love to come out here again, either to run or relax," Tori said as she dug her feet into the sand.

"I didn't know you enjoyed running that much?" Alex glanced at Tori, then looked questioningly at Thunder while pointing at her with his thumb, "Did you know she was an avid runner?"

"Nope," Thunder answered.

"I ran in high school and kept it up on the rez just for fun," Tori stated.

"I will bring you here any morning you want to run," Alex rubbed her back.

"If you want to come down here and run before work, I'll give you a key to the apartment above the cultural center. I used to stay there a lot more than I do now," Thunder shrugged, "you can shower there before work. Hell, you can keep clothes there—if you want. That goes for you too, Alex."

"That sounds great, thank you Thunder," Tori smiled.

"No problem," Thunder nodded. "I'm gonna head home. I'll see you both at Sarah's later?"

"Yes," Tori answered first, "we'll be there."

"Absolutely," Alex dragged Tori back between his legs, "see you later." Thunder waved and continued his run. Tori sat back and laid her head on Alex's shoulder as she continued to watch the sunrise.

"That was nice of him to let us use the apartment." Alex wrapped his arms tightly around her and kissed her cheek.

"He's a nice guy, same as his sister Sarah. They would give you the shirts off their backs if you needed it."

"I have an idea," Alex blurted out. "Let's go in the water. There's nothing like this beach."

"Okay," Tori smiled up at Alex. Placing her hand in his, Alex pulled her up and they walked to the water.

Tori went slowly, expecting it to be cold, but it was just right. The water in the river near the rez was much colder. They walked in until she was waist high. Looking at Alex, she realized he was mostly out of the water because of their height difference.

"Alex, I can go a little deeper, but not much."

"It's okay Baby. I can either squat or carry you deeper, whichever makes you more comfortable in the water. Do you know how to swim?"

"I can doggie paddle, but I never swam in the river near the rez. Can you swim?"

"Yes, growing up here, you learn how to swim really quick. I also learned how to Scuba Dive with Barrett. How about I teach you how to float first?"

"Okay, what do I need to do?"

"I'm gonna put my arms behind your back and legs and slowly let go. Turn sideways."

Tori followed Alex's directions. Once she laid flat on the water, he told her to extend her arms out and relax her body. Alex slowly removed his hands, but stayed next to her. Her head sank a little, but then she felt weightless. Tori floated while Alex remained close to her.

"How does that feel?"

Tori heard Alex talking to her, though it sounded muffled since her ears were under water.

"Can you help me up?"

"Baby, just sit up and drop your legs."

Tori did as he said and realized her feet didn't touch. She yelped and began to doggie paddle as she grabbed Alex.

"I didn't realize we had drifted so far out." Tori looked around.

"We did." Alex pulled her into his arms, and Tori wound her legs around his waist. "But I can still stand, so I wasn't too worried. Besides, there's no riptide today. So, tell me something about you I don't already know. I want to know all about the girl that is twisting me up inside."

"You want to play twenty questions?" Tori asked.

"Sure," Alex winked, "Ladies first?"

"What is your favorite thing to cook for yourself?"

"That's easy," Alex nodded. "Steak, potatoes, and broccoli. What's your favorite thing to eat?"

"My favorite, hmm," Tori pondered her answer, "a burger, but I also would like to eat pizza. I didn't get to eat those at home very often."

"Baby, I make a mean burger and pizza. I'll make you some tomorrow."

"Can I let your hair down?" Tori asked Alex.

"If you want, sure."

Tori slowly released the hair tie from his man bun and put it on her wrist like a bracelet. Alex's hair felt silky soft as she ran her hands over it.

"Tilt your head back." Tori gazed into Alex's eyes and gently guided his head back until his hairline was in the water.

Alex lifted his head up and stared at her. "You are so fucking gorgeous. How have you stayed single so long?"

"My parents were very strict. I usually stayed away from men, well, except when I took the bet with Freya and met Winston. I wanted to do something adventurous and look where that got me."

"Baby, look at me," Alex tilted her head. "I could kill Frey for that stupid bet."

"Alex, it wasn't her fault," Tori interrupted.

"Let me finish, please," Alex kissed her lips, "I love Frey and I know she was being her crazy self, but I wish she hadn't done that. Normally, it wouldn't have been an issue, but Winston is a smooth, calculating asshole who was looking for someone to prey on. I wish you had never met him. If I could take away everything that happened to you, I would do it in a heartbeat. I will make sure nothing like that EVER happens to you again."

"You are so good to me. How are you not married yet?"

"When I was younger, I didn't have time for long relationships. I know that makes me sound like a man whore because I got around. Honestly, I just wanted to have fun with no commitments while I was trying to make a name as a famous chef. I never liked anyone enough to settle down and want to get to know them until I met you. You took my breath away before you even opened your mouth to speak to me. I watched the way you walked through the airport, talking and laughing with your fellow passengers. Your kindness and gentleness came through in the way you carry yourself and speak to others."

"That is the nicest thing anyone has ever said to me." Tori began to tear up.

"Baby, don't cry."

"They're happy tears, Alex. I've waited so long to meet someone who made me feel safe and happy. I'm so sorry I didn't let you in sooner."

"Baby, that's in the past. Now we can focus on our future."

Tori was beaming as she listened to him talk about their future. She leaned in and kissed Alex. Alex cupped the back of her head and tilted it to get a better angle. Kissing Alex was like a wave of euphoria that left her stomach with butterflies and her body tingling.

"We never finished our twenty questions," Tori mumbled against Alex's lips after he released her mouth.

Alex gives Tori more information between kisses. "My favorite color is blue. I love to work out, I enjoy running, I don't gamble, I drink a little, but haven't been drunk in years. I would love to release my stress making love to you. I love how your eyes light up when you look at me. My family is very important to me. I'm grateful to Thunder for giving me the opportunity to get creative with my native cuisine dishes. I love to read but rarely have enough time. My favorite movies have a lot of action. I would love to travel but haven't had much time. My hair has been long since I was a child. I ran and played soccer in high school. I love watching the Panthers play hockey in the arena. I hate shopping but I would do it for you. Holding and kissing you are the best parts of my day. I love surprises, so I never open my presents early before Christmas, even if I know where they are. And I save more money than I spend."

"Wow," Tori laughed when he finished, "that's a lot to process. I'm not sure I can say all that about myself.”

“Baby, just blurt out some stuff about you,” Alex smiled at her.

“Whew, okay, here goes. I love my sister, though she drives me crazy. I didn’t have to cook at home a lot since I worked, and my mom stayed at home. I miss working with preschool aged kids. My favorite color is turquoise. My favorite flowers are tulips because everyone likes roses. I was in an art club in high school and I ran. This is the first time I’ve travelled out of South Dakota. I don’t watch sports but for you I would. The best part of my day is sitting with you on the couch snuggling and watching TV. I love your hair. My hair has also been long since I was a little too. I’ve never fallen in love before. I don’t open my presents early either. I only go shopping when I need something. I don’t know how to swim. I don’t wear a lot of makeup. I love to wear heels. I’m a good driver but I’ve never owned my own car, and I also save more than I spend. Oh, and I love when you touch me, kiss me, and hold me close.”

“Oh Baby, I love to touch, kiss, and hold you close too,” Alex wiggled his eyebrows at her.

Tori groaned as Alex ran his hands under her bathing suit. One hand cupped her ass while the other played with her nipple.

“Alex, I can’t think when you do that.”

“Maybe I don’t want you to think, just feel.”

“Alex, maybe we should stop. Everyone can see.”

“No one is near us. Baby, I need you. Place your head in the crook of my neck and just feel me.”

Tori plastered her body to Alex while he pulled his suit down enough for his cock to slip out. Pulling her suit to the side of her pussy, Alex slid right in. Tori sucked on Alex’s neck while he pulled her onto him with his hands on her hips. Just when Tori was going to scream out, Alex kissed her deep and swallowed her scream. Alex released his orgasm shortly after her. Alex slid out and fixed her bathing suit while Tori controlled her breathing.

“That was amazing, Alex.”

“Yes, it was. Now I think we need to dry off a little and head back home.”

Alex carried Tori until she could put her legs down and walk out on her own. Tori’s legs were a little shaky and Alex didn’t release her hand until she was steady on her feet. They both dropped onto the towel and laid back for a few minutes.

“Baby, let’s get all our stuff. I have a couple more towels in the truck for us to sit on, so we don’t mess up Holt’s seats.”

“Okay, I’m ready. Thank you for this. I’ve really enjoyed it.”

“I’m glad,” Alex leaned over her, “We can do this anytime you want. I love the beach.”

After shaking out their towels to release the sand, they headed to the truck. Alex gave Tori an extra towel before she sat in the truck. Tori knew a little water wouldn’t hurt Holt’s leather seats, but she still sat on the towel.

They drove back to the resort and showered before heading out to Sarah’s.

Chapter 38

Family Funday Sunday
Sarah

Sarah was at the sink filling her tea kettle. She had gotten up early thinking she heard Lilly, but she was wrong and couldn't fall back asleep. Not wanting to wake up Grayhorse, she grabbed a book to read and laid down on the couch in the living room. Now that the sun was rising, she needed some tea.

She was so excited Tori was coming over today. Having a newborn and Tommy took up most of her day. Getting updates from Thunder about Tori was great, but she wanted to see for herself that Tori was doing okay.

"*Hau, wówaštelaka mitáwa,*" Grayhorse came up behind Sarah, wrapped his arms around her, and whispered in her ear. "I woke up, and you weren't there. Are you okay?"

"Yes," Sarah turned into his arms and laid her head on his chest, "I thought I heard Lilly, and I couldn't go back to sleep, so I came out here to read."

"*Wówaštelaka mitáwa,* I could've helped you relax."

"I'm sure you could. Do you want some tea?"

"No, I need coffee." Grayhorse massaged the back of her head while he held her. "I gotta work on that new mare before everyone gets here."

"Mmm, that feels good."

"Why don't you go back to bed…," Grayhorse didn't even finish his sentence before they heard Lilly crying on the Baby monitor, "never mind. Go get her and I'll make you and Tommy some pancakes before I head out."

"*Pilámaya,*" Sarah quickly kissed Grayhorse before going to get Lilly.

Sarah changed Lilly and took her into the kitchen.

"Ah, my two favorite ladies," Grayhorse walked over and kissed them both, "is Tommy still asleep?"

"Yes, I can wrap some on a plate for him. Thank you for making breakfast."

"We're a team, *wówaštelaka mitáwa.*"

"That we are." Sarah heated Lilly's bottle while Grayhorse finished making the pancakes.

"What time is everyone coming today?" Grayhorse placed several pancakes on a plate for him and another plate for Sarah.

"I told them noon. Will you be able to stop then?"

"Yup." Grayhorse poured syrup on Sarah's pancakes and cut them up for her. She only had one hand available because she was feeding Lilly her milk bottle with the other. "Have Thunder find me when they get here, and I'll start the grill. Is Tori bringing Alex?"

"Yes, he cleared his schedule. I'm glad they are finally together."

"My little matchmaker, I bet you're glad," Grayhorse winked at her, "what about Isa's family? Are they coming?"

"Not this time. Gaby's family invited them to their house."

"Okay," Grayhorse picked up his plate, fork and glass, placing them in the sink, "tell Tommy to come see me if he wants to help me with the mare. I know he'll be sad Emmy isn't coming."

"They have become really close," Sarah smiled. Tommy had become close to Isa's brother's oldest daughter. It was so cute how they would ask after each other and beg for playdates.

"Do you need me to prep the burgers before I head out?"

"No, she's almost done. I'll put her down and prep them."

"Okay." Grayhorse gave his girls a kiss on their heads and headed out the kitchen door.

Sarah finished feeding Lilly, burped her and put her to bed. Upon entering the kitchen, she saw Tommy at the kitchen table.

"*Hau, ciŋkší.* Your *até* made you some pancakes." Sarah placed the pancakes on the table for Tommy.

"*Pilámaya, iná,*" Tommy drenched his pancakes in syrup.

"Emmy won't be able to come today, but you can help your dad with that new mare until your aunt and uncle arrive."

"Okay," Tommy's face fell, "I'll help *até.*"

Sarah seasoned the buffalo burgers, made the potato salad, cut up some fruit for dessert, and placed bags of chips on the table. Once she had things under control, she laid on the couch for a quick nap.

It felt like she had just laid her head down when she heard Thunder's booming voice.

"Hello, where is everyone?"

"In here," Sarah sat up from the couch."

"*Hau, taŋkši,*" Thunder walked up to Sarah for a hug.

"Hi, Sarah," Isa hugged her after Thunder.

"How is my future niece or nephew?" Sarah rubbed Isa's little baby bump.

"*El niño* has been calm this morning," Isa said and stared at Sarah.

"Wait, what?"

"It's a boy," Thunder stood up tall with pride and placed his arm around Isa, "we just found out on Friday. I wanted to wait to tell you today."

"Oh my God, Thunder," Sarah had tears in her eyes as she hugged them again, "I am so happy for you. Tommy will be so excited to know it's a boy. He's out back helping Grayhorse tame a mare. Go out there and help him while I get to sit and tell Isa all about how you were as a little boy."

"Honey," Thunder gave her a quick kiss, "remember, I love you and my sister lies."

"Thunder!" Sarah screamed and slapped her brother on his shoulder.

As soon as Thunder walked out, Sarah turned to Isa.

"You know, I'm just teasing Thunder. He was the best big brother any girl could ever have. He will be an exceptionally loving and caring father."

"You guys are so funny," Isa laughed while holding her belly. "You're right. He is pretty incredible."

"Come on, let me get you some water and you can keep me company while I get lunch ready."

"I can help, Sarah."

"Honestly, most of it is done. But you can play with Lilly while I finish."

"Absolutely. I love watching my beautiful niece."

Isa and Sarah worked together, laughing in the kitchen until they heard the doorbell.

"That must be Tori and Alex." Sarah quickly rinsed her hands. "I'll be right back."

"Hi Tori," Sarah hugged Tori. "Hi Alex? Welcome."

"Hi," Alex stepped forward to give Sarah a hug, "It's nice to see you again."

"I'm glad you could get off work and join us. The guys are outside. Tori, follow me to the kitchen. Isa and Lilly are in there."

"I thought I saw Thunder out there. See you later, Baby." Alex kissed Tori on the forehead and headed out with the bag.

Tori smiled and followed Sarah. "I can't wait to see Lilly."

"Wow, so you guys are dating now?" Sarah looked over shoulder with a smirk on her face.

"Yes, he makes me so happy. I'm not sure why I didn't see it before."

"We all make mistakes. Come on."

"Hi," Isa was pacing the kitchen carrying Lilly. "You must be Tori. I'm Isa. It's so nice to meet you."

"It's nice to meet you, too. Thunder says so many wonderful things about you."

"Well, he better," Isa snorted.

"Can I hold Lilly?" Tori asked.

"Absolutely, I love holding her, but being pregnant and holding her is killing my back," Isa grinned and handed Lilly over to Tori.

"Hi again, Lilly," Tori whispered before kissing the top of her head.

"How are you, pretty girl?"

"Isa, sit your butt down, I got this," Sarah led Isa toward the table and pushed her into a chair.

"I was just trying to lessen your load," Isa rolled her eyes.

"Yeah, yeah, yeah," Sarah finished the patties and placed them on a plate. "I'm gonna take these burgers to Grayhorse so he can start cooking them. Do you ladies want to sit outside while they cook?"

"I would love that. I have first dibs on the back porch swing," Isa yelled on her way out.

"She loves that swing. I already told Thunder he needed to buy her one. Come with Lilly. There is plenty of other seating out there."

Tori was loving every minute of holding Lilly. Until holding Lilly, she didn't realize how much she missed the babies at the preschool. Finding a rocking chair, Tori sat near Isa watching the boys playing with the frisbee.

"Where did they get that frisbee from?" Sarah asked, "Are they playing football with that frisbee? Shirtless?"

"Who cares? My man looks hot without a shirt," Isa whispered. "This is better than watching the volleyball game in Top Gun."

"Alex and I bought it for Tommy," Tori interjected.

"Nice, buttering up the kid," Isa laughed. "I like your style."

"I hate to stop the show, but I gotta get Grayhorse to make these burgers. I'm hungry," Sarah sighed.

"Grayhorse, here's the burgers!" Sarah yelled and walked toward the barbeque.

"On my way, *wówaštelaka mitáwa*," Grayhorse stopped playing, pulled on his shirt, and jogged toward her.

"Sarah, do you need help since my slacker girlfriend is holding your beautiful baby girl?" Alex teased Tori while he put his shirt on.

"Oh, the chef wants to help me now when everything is done," Sarah teased. "Thunder said you were an outstanding chef, so next time you cook."

"Deal." Alex smiled and helped Sarah carry everything outside.

"Ugh, shows over," Isa murmured.

"Hold tight Honey." Thunder came over after putting his shirt on, picked up Isa, and carried her to the table. "What show?"

"You know I'm pregnant, not disabled, right?" Isa wrapped her arms around Thunder's neck, rested her head on his shoulder, effectively distracting him from his question.

"Yup, but I just want to hold my beautiful wife," Thunder kissed her, "I live to serve you, honey."

"My hero," Isa sighed.

"*Lekší, inala,*" Tommy ran up to them, "sit next to me!"

They all sat around the outdoor table and enjoyed each other's company and the food. Tori enjoyed being a part of a family. It was great to experience their banter and love.

"Thunder," Tori looked at him, "are you going to work tomorrow even though the center is closed to the public?"

"Thunder goes in every day except Sunday," Isa blurted.

"Isa's right," Thunder nodded, "why did you need something?"

"I was thinking of going since I missed this past week, but I know Alex won't let me go alone."

"Darn right, I won't," Alex murmured, "but I would have gone with you if Thunder wasn't there."

"I know you would, but I also know you usually work at RUSH on Mondays."

"I can pick you up and take you home if you really want to go?" Thunder asked Tori.

"That would be great," Tori answered. "What time?"

"How about I pick you up at ten so you can sleep in?"

"Perfect, thank you Thunder."

"Alex, thank you for my frisbee," Tommy said after he swallowed a bite of his burger. "Will you come back sometime and play with me again?"

"Of course, I would love to." Alex smiled at Tommy and then glanced at Grayhorse and Isa, "maybe sometime your parents will let you visit me at the resort. We can hang out by the pool."

"*Até, iná*, can I visit Alex and swim in his pool?"

"Of course," Sarah answered first. "We'll set something up."

"Alex, can Emmy come with me?" Tommy begged, "Please?"

"Who's Emmy?" Alex looked at Sarah, confused.

"Emmy is my niece," Isa spoke up since Sarah had food in her mouth. "She's the same age as Tommy, and they've become best friends."

"Well then, yes, Emmy is more than welcome to come."

"Now you've opened up a can of worms because Lucy, her younger sister, will also want to come as well," Thunder laughed.

"Well, then you are all welcome to come," Alex threw up his hands, "Come on a Saturday or Sunday and I'll cook you all a meal and you can enjoy the pool and hot tub."

"Nice going," Grayhorse elbowed Tommy, "good job, son."

"Did you just send in our son to do your dirty work?" Sarah slapped Grayhorse on the shoulder.

"No," Grayhorse raised his eyebrows in surprise, "but it worked out well for us, huh?"

They all laughed and finished their meal, taking turns messing with each other. Tori was grateful no one brought up Winston. His whereabouts were constantly on her mind, even though she tried not to dwell on them. Being at Sarah's house with Alex, Thunder, and Grayhorse helped her feel safe.

After lunch, the guys helped clean up the table and load the dishwasher while the ladies sat outside relaxing over coffee. Finally, it was time to go home. They agreed to get together at the resort in two weeks.

Chapter 39

Self-Defense Moves
Alex

On Monday morning, Thunder came to pick up Tori— they worked side by side—taking down and packing the items they needed to ship back. Since Alex was not working today, Thunder had food delivered for Mark, Tori, and himself. By early afternoon, they had put a good dent in their work. Thunder drove her to the resort and left her with Alex.

"*Hau*, Alex," Thunder announced as he and Tori walked into RUSH.

"Hi," Alex looked up from his prep counter. "Have you guys eaten? Hi Baby."

Tori walked up to Alex and gave him a hug. "We already ate."

"I gotta get home. Isa left work early." I'll see you both tomorrow."

"Sounds good," Alex waved.

"Bye Thunder. Thank you for the ride. See you tomorrow."

"Not a problem." Thunder waved and left.

"So," Alex stroked Tori's cheek, "did you get a lot done?"

"We did. It was a good day. Are you almost done?"

"I'm just waiting for Sam since I switched shifts with him. Do you want to help me chop up some veggies?"

"Sure."

"Grab an apron and tie up your hair. I'll grab your supplies." Alex put some veggies next to her cutting board while Tori got ready.

"How do you want me to cut these?"

"Cut the onions and peppers lengthwise. Sam can always chop them if he needs to."

"Alex, can I ask you for a favor?"

"Of course, you can ask me anything. What do you need?"

Tori stopped chopping, turned sideways, and leaned on the counter.

"Will you teach me some self-defense moves?" Tori was looking down and picking at her apron.

Alex grabbed her hand and pulled her into his arms. With one hand, he cupped her face, tipping it up to look into her eyes.

"Yes, I'll get Barret or Holt to help us. What brought this on? Are you okay?"

"I am, but I want to learn some moves so I don't feel so helpless."

"Good afternoon," Sam shouted as he walked into the kitchen.

"Hi Sam," Tori smiled.

"Hey Sam." Alex stepped back and faced Sam. "We cut up some veggies for you. Do you think you'll be okay here? I need to take Tori upstairs."

"Absolutely. I came a little early in case you needed to leave."

"Thanks, Sam." Alex and Tori took off their aprons and washed their hands. "I'll see you tomorrow."

"Sure thing."

"Bye Sam," Tori said over her shoulder as she walked out of the kitchen, following Alex.

"We'll go up and see if Barrett is in his room. If he's not there, I'll text him." Alex guided her into the elevator. After they entered their room, Alex walked to the adjoining door and opened it. Barrett left his door open, and Alex could hear music coming from inside his room.

"Barrett, are you in here?" Alex called out as he walked through Barrett's room into the security room.

"Hey Barrett."

"Hey, what's going on? Is everything okay?" Barrett stood.

"Yeah, but I wanted your help. Tori wants to learn some self-defense moves, and I was wondering if you or Holt could help us out in the gym."

"I'll help you. Holt is working an early shift today."

"Sounds good. We'll go change and meet you in the gym."

"See you there."

Alex walked back into his room. "Baby, Barrett is going to help us. Put on some comfy clothes and we'll meet him in the gym."

Alex put on sweatpants while Tori put on leggings, and they joined Barrett in the gym.

"Hey Tori. Alex said you wanted to learn some moves."

"Yes, I don't want to feel so helpless."

"I get it. Let's go to the mat and try some self-defense moves where you get away from your assailant." Barrett led them to the mat in the center of the gym.

Barrett grabbed Tori's wrist and Tori flinched and pulled back, bumping into Alex's chest.

"Sorry," Tori paled.

"Nothing to be sorry about. I should have known you would be more comfortable with Alex. New Plan. How about I give Alex instructions and he acts as the aggressor?"

"Okay, thank you," Tori nodded.

"Alex, grab Tori's wrist." Alex stepped around Tori and gripped her wrist.

"Are you okay?" Alex whispered.

"Yeah, I'm good. What's next?"

"Tori, look down and see where Alex's fingers meet on your wrist." Barrett stood between them. "Now pull your wrist toward your body fast, applying pressure where his fingers meet. He will not be able to hold on. That is the weakest part of his hold. Alex continue to grip her wrist tightly so she feels resistance. Tori, try it as soon as you are ready."

Alex held tight and watched Tori. Sure as shit, the minute she pulled her wrist away, it broke my hold. Tori stared at me with wide eyed and shocked at the result.

"Great job, Baby," Alex hugged her.

"You didn't make that easy for me, did you?" Tori asked.

"No, Baby. I was holding on tight."

"Way to go Tori, now let's try other moves," Barrett beamed at Tori.

Barrett and Alex spent the rest of the afternoon showing Tori how to defend herself and escape. They weren't trying to teach her how to fight. That would take a lot more days of practice and classes. They just wanted her to get away safely.

"Okay, I've been beaten up enough for one day," Alex groaned as he attempted to shield his groin from Tori's knee. His groin was safe, but his thigh took the hit.

"I like you being the punching bag instead of me," Barrett patted him on the shoulder."

"Alex, I'm so sorry." Tori covered her mouth with both hands.

"That's okay, Baby. You can kiss my bruises and make me feel better when we get to our room." Alex wiggled his eyebrows.

"Anyway, Tori, just remember to act as quickly as you can. You will have the element of surprise for a few minutes. If you can gouge their eyes, insert your fingers in that spot I showed you on the neck, or kick the knees, you'll have a few seconds to get away. So make the most of it and run far and fast. You never want to be taken to a second location if you can help it. We can always practice these moves another day or you can practice with Alex. I'm sure he doesn't mind being battered and bruised by you." Barrett laughed at his own joke.

"Thanks, asshole."

"Alex, be nice to Barrett. He's just trying to help me."

"Yeah Alex," Barrett smirked.

"Come on Baby, let's go shower and watch a movie," Alex turned Tori and led her to the door while giving Barrett the middle finger behind his back.

"Bye Barrett. Thank you," Tori yelled.

"Bye Tori. See you later."

Chapter 40

Monster Sighting
Tori

Tuesday, the center was closed while they switched exhibits. Opening night for the Unconquered Path Exhibit was on Thursday and they had a lot to do in two days. Alex drove her to work and went into the kitchen, leaving her with Thunder and Mark.

After lunch, Tori was walking back to the museum when she saw police officers at the door.

"George, Sean," Tori opened the door and held it open for them, "Have you been out here long?"

"No ma'am," Sean smiled at her, "We just knocked. We're lucky you saw us so quickly."

"Hey Tori," George hugged her, "how are you?"

"Did you need something?" Tori stepped back.

"George, Sean," Thunder came out from his office, "Can we help you?"

"We just wanted to let Tori know we received the results from the DNA testing and Mr. James is our suspect. We also went to Jake's Steakhouse and retrieved the video footage showing Tori stumbling out with Winston."

Tori suddenly held her stomach, bent over and threw up.

"Mark," Thunder called out before stepping around Tori to rub her back, "get Alex!"

Tori was trembling and covering her mouth, "Thunder, I'm so sorry."

"Don't worry about it. I'll clean it up."

"I'm so sorry, Tori," George stated.

"What's going on?" Alex ran out of the kitchen after Mark.

Tori felt Alex's arms wrap around her from behind.

"He really did rape me. I was hoping it was a mistake. That maybe he was just laying on me but never followed through," Tori mumbled.

"What happened?" Alex's squinty eyes looked between Thunder, George, and Sean.

"Positive DNA on Winston," Thunder replied.

"Oh Shit," Alex held Tori tighter.

"I'll get the mop and clean this up," Mark said.

"Tori," George bent down to look at her, "we just wanted to give you an update. We went to his house to serve a warrant, but he wasn't there. We've been looking for him with no success. Just wanted to let you know in case you see him. I know Tim saw him here last week, but we couldn't find him. If any of you see him, please call us."

"Okay," Alex turned Tori in his arms, "thank you, George. I'm gonna take Tori to the restroom. We'll be back."

George gently touched Tori's shoulder. "I promise you we won't stop until we find him." George looked at Alex and then at Thunder. "You all be careful and be vigilant."

"Shit," Thunder grumbled.

Tori heard Thunder thank George and Sean. Alex went into the bathroom with her and turned on the faucet.

"Baby, rinse your mouth. I'm gonna run to the kitchen and get you a bottle of water. I'll be right back."

Tori leaned her hands on either side of the sink and stared at herself in the mirror. *How could he have done this to me?* She thought. And how could she not remember such a horrible act? Alex must have run to the kitchen because, just as she finished her thoughts, he was bursting through the door with a water bottle.

"Here, drink this. You need to stay hydrated."

"Thank you."

Walking out of the bathroom, they saw Thunder outside the door.

"Tori, I know you are getting tired of having one of us with you, but word will get back to Winston about the DNA results. Now more than ever, you don't go anywhere alone. If Alex can't be with you, Grayhorse or myself will go with you."

"I also have Barrett and Holt watching over her at the resort," Alex told Thunder.

"Why is this happening to me?" Tori lifted her tear-stained face from Alex's chest and wiped her face.

"Have you told your father what happened?" Thunder asked.

"No, I'm too embarrassed. He'll be so heartbroken and mad," Tori whispered as she stepped away from Alex, "he's been protecting me since I was born. He put his trust in me. I let him down by letting this happen. I was hoping to call and tell him after Winston was arrested."

"Tori," Thunder gently held her and bent down to look at her, "you didn't let any of this happen. Winston drugged you, and he took advantage of you. Please call Tall Bear and your mom. If you don't, I'll have to call him. He needs to know, and it would be best if he heard it from you. He's already going to be angry since it happened two weeks ago."

"You're right," Tori nodded, "will you both come with me while I call him?"

"Of course," Thunder nodded, "Let's do this in my office."

"I'm gonna go back to cleaning the exhibit room," Mark pointed in that direction, "let me know if you need anything."

"Thanks Mark," Thunder nodded, and they walked toward his office.

Tori called her dad and put it on speakerphone.

"*Hau, cuŋkší*," Tall Bear answered the phone, "it's good to hear your voice."

"*Hau, ató*," Tori stood by the phone on the desk fidgeting with her hands, "it's nice to hear yours too."

"How are you?" Tall Bear asked, "I put you on speakerphone so your mom can hear your voice, too."

"*Hau, cuŋwítku*," her mother's voice came through the phone.

"I'm okay," Tori sighed, "but there is something I need to tell you both."

"Okay," Tall Bear sounded weary, "What's going on? You know you can tell us anything."

"*Ató, iná*, I wasn't careful, and I went on a date with an evil man," Tori said and rambled the entire story of what happened to her and how she was drugged and couldn't remember the rape.

"*Hiyááá*," Tori had tears streaming down her face as she heard her mother yelling in the background.

"Tall Bear," Alex jumped in as he held Tori, "this is Alex Panther. I'm here with Thunder on this call. We are doing everything in our power to catch this asshole and get him arrested for what he did."

"How did this happen, Thunder?" Tall Bear yelled into the phone, "you were supposed to watch over her. First Rachel and now my daughter. I trusted you. And Alex, she was under your family's care at the resort. Tori, I'm bringing you home. NOW!"

"*Hiyá, ató*," Tori cried, "it's not their fault. I went willingly with a person I thought was a nice man. They didn't even know when I left with him. It's my fault, not theirs. I don't want to leave. Please don't make me go."

"Shh," Alex whispered in Tori's ear, "You got this Baby. Your dad just loves you and wants to keep you safe."

"Tori," Tall Bear spoke, "Put me off speaker and let me talk to Thunder."

"Okay, *ató*, but don't get mad at him," Tori spoke quickly. "Thunder and Alex are doing everything they can to keep me safe since the incident. Thunder at work and Alex at the resort, along with his siblings. I can get through this with their help." Tori touched the speaker button on her cell phone and put the phone against her ear. "You are off speaker. Yes, I'll call *iná* later. Okay. Here's Thunder."

Tori handed her phone over to Thunder and mouthed "I'm sorry". Thunder touched the 'mute' button.

"Tori, it will be fine," Thunder said to her, "don't worry about what Tall Bear says to me. I'm a big boy, I can handle it. Everything will be okay."

"But I don't want you to get in trouble because of me."

"I'm not in trouble," Thunder smiled, "I got this. Alex, why don't you take Tori into the kitchen for a drink of water?"

"No," Tori answered, "I'm fine. I just need to use the restroom. I'll be right back."

Tori did her business, washed her hands, and stepped out. She had a strange feeling and looked toward the front door. Winston was standing outside the door with his finger up to his mouth, silently saying keep your mouth shut. Then he moved his fingers like a gun and pointed them at her. Tori stood frozen to the spot until he pretended to shoot her. Tori ran into Thunder's office, swinging in around the door frame. Thunder has already hung up with her father.

"He's here, Winston's here," Tori screamed in a panic. "He's going to kill me!"

Alex stood up and Tori ran to him while Thunder ran out of his office.

"Hehehe, wawawaasss at thethethe dddoorrr," Tori was trembling and stuttering into Alex's chest.

"Tori, calm down Baby," Alex rubbed her back, "take a deep breath. Winston was at the door?"

"He's gone," Thunder came back in. "Where did you see him?"

Tori stepped away from Alex and placed her palm flat on his chest and gulped some air, placing her hand on her heart.

"He was right outside the door," Tori pointed outside. "I was coming out of the bathroom, and he was standing outside staring at me.

"George," Thunder spoke into his phone, "Winston was just here. Can you come over and talk to Tori?"

"Great, see you soon," Thunder hung up and turned toward Tori, "George will be here in a few minutes to take your statement. They weren't far away."

"I should have kept my mouth shut," Tori backed away from them. "I involved all of you in my stupidity. I am so sorry."

Alex reached out, but Tori was too quick as she pivoted and ran out of the office.

"Catch her, Alex," Thunder pointed at her, "don't let her leave."

"I'm on it," Alex ran out of the office and caught up to Tori, "Tori, don't go out there. Stay here with me. I've got you."

Alex pulled her into his arms while Tori cried and pounded on his chest.

"Alex," Tori cried, "I can't. What if he hurts you? Maybe it is better if I leave and go home. I've made a mess of this."

"That fucker will not hurt me," Alex wrapped one arm around her waist and the other on the back of her head, pressing her against his body, "or you. I'm gonna be stuck to you like glue. You did the right thing coming to us. The police will be here soon." Alex pulled her away from his chest and bent down to look her in the eyes. "He is a coward who is trying to scare you, but you are stronger than that. You are not a victim—you are a survivor—from his cowardly act. You have done nothing wrong, and you have every right to make decisions about your own life. If you want to stay here, then stay here. I want you here with me if that is what you want. He is the asshole, he is the coward, he is at fault. You are stronger than you think. Go into the restroom and straighten your crown, my strong, gorgeous, independent princess. I know you can do this. I will be right here beside you if you need me."

Tori straightened up and wiped her face. Alex's words and confidence in her gave her the strength she needed to fight back and show everyone she was an adult and could handle the tough times. There was nothing wrong with being nice, and she was tired of people taking advantage of her. Just because she was nice didn't mean she was a pushover, and people could treat her bad. She was not a victim; she was a survivor, and she was ready to stand tall and proud. Winston would rue the day he messed with her.

"You're right," Tori nodded. "I can do this. I do not need to run home. I can fight back. I'll be right back."

*** Alex ***

"Nice going," Thunder said from behind Alex. "I was afraid she was going to bolt."

"She needs to be reminded she is a strong, independent woman who can do anything," Alex faced the bathroom. "I don't think she hears that enough. But she will from now on. I know her parents love her, but they coddled her too much when she was at home, not allowing her to do things on her own. I don't want her second guessing her decisions. She is so nice that assholes think she is stupid and naive and take advantage of her. Not anymore. She can still be her nice self, but she needs to feel empowered."

"It's good she has you, Alex," Thunder slapped him on the back.

George knocked on the door and they heard Mark yell, "I'll get it!"

"Hey George," Mark let him in, "you got some news?"

"I came to talk to Tori," George said. "Thunder just called me."

"Mark," Thunder walked toward them, "Winston was just outside, and Tori saw him."

"Oh Shit!" Mark cursed. "What's with this guy?"

"Hey Thunder, long time no see," George greeted him sarcastically, "Where's Tori? How is she doing?"

"I'm here George," Tori walked right up to him, "thank you for coming back."

Alex stood back with his legs spread and arms crossed, impressed by Tori's newfound backbone. That was his girl, fuck she was so damn hot when she let her confidence shine.

"Tori," George turned toward her and pulled out his pad, "can you tell me what just happened? I gotta tell you, this asshole is really pissing me off. He must have been nearby when we left."

"Yes," Tori stood up tall, "I was coming out of the restroom, and I saw Winston standing outside the door. He looked right at me and ran his fingers over his lips, telling me to shut my mouth. Then he made a gun with his hand and pointed it at me, pretending to shoot me. That's when I ran into Thunder's office to get him and Alex."

Alex could barely contain his anger; he didn't know Winston had threatened Tori. He walked up to Tori, placing his hand on her lower back, he whispered in her ear, "You did good, princess. You got this."

"When I ran outside," Thunder continued, "he was already gone."

"Okay," George nodded, "I'll add this to your case. Tori, don't go anywhere alone. We haven't been able to find him. He's on the run and dangerous. You all need to be on alert; please call me if you need anything. I'll be in touch. We'll drive around and see if he's still in the area."

"I'll walk George out," Mark said. "I wanted to talk to him about something."

"Thanks again George," Thunder shook his hand.

"Tori," Thunder walked over and touched her arm, "Why don't you stay in the exhibit away from the windows? I will bring in the artifacts and you and Mark can work in that room."

"Thunder," Alex wanted to help, "I can help you guys. I'm done in the kitchen."

"Sounds good," Thunder nodded, "with your help we can get done quicker and you can take her home sooner."

Alex, Thunder, Mark, and Tori worked together, putting up the new exhibit and packing up the old one.

Chapter 41

The Calm Before the Storm
Tori

For the past couple of days, Tori, Alex, Thunder, and Mark worked their butts off to display everything needed for Opening Night. Things had been quiet on the Winston front, and everyone was on edge. It was strange he hadn't made a move. Everyone hoped he'd left the area and was on the run in another state.

Tonight was opening night and Tori wore her white doeskin, knee length dress trimmed with silver and small turquoise accents along with her matching knee-high white doe skin moccasin boots. She placed a matching beaded headband with feathers hanging down on her head, leaving her hair flowing down her back. She added two thin braids to the sides, interwoven with a strand of beads.

As a final touch, Tori put on her personally designed long beaded earrings. They were not totally visible with her hair down, but she loved them. While she was applying her mascara, Freya came into her bathroom.

"Wow, Tori," Freya stood in the doorway in her traditional brightly colored patchwork dress," Alex let me in. You look absolutely beautiful in your Lakota clothing. Want to borrow my red lipstick?" Freya pulled it out of her purse and showed it to her.

"Frey, you look stunning yourself," Tori looked at her from the mirror. "That lipstick has horrible memories for me."

"Nope," Freya shook her head, "this is a different one. I threw that one away— good riddance. This is a deeper red that will look phenomenal on you."

"Thanks, Frey," Tori whispered, all teary-eyed. She knew Freya had liked that lipstick color based on her excitement when they spoke the night of the bet. Anyone else would have kept the color—after all, lipsticks were expensive. But not Freya. She would have hated to hurt Tori. Freya felt like family to her in such a short time.

"No, no, no," Freya started waving her hands wildly, "no crying. You'll ruin your makeup, and Alex will kill me."

Tori grabbed her hands, and they laughed together.

"So," Freya held up the lipstick again, "finishing touches before Alex sees you."

Tori smiled and nodded, allowing Freya to apply her lipstick.

"Perfect. Rub your lips together." Freya stood next to her and looked at Tori in the mirror. "Now go out there and take my brother's breath away."

"Thank you." Tori hugged Freya and walked out into the living room.

Alex was standing by the adjoining door, talking to Barrett. Freya cleared her throat behind Tori, and Alex turned around, his mouth hanging open as he stared at Tori from head to toe.

"Wow, Princess," Alex faced Tori with one hand against the door frame and the other against his stomach, "you look absolutely exquisite."

Tori looked at Alex. He normally wore his Chef shirt and slacks, but Thunder had asked them all to wear their cultural traditional regalia for their openings. Alex was wearing a red and yellow headband around his head, with his hair in two long braids adorned with feathers. His red, yellow, and black striped shirt belted with fabric at his waist, which ended directly above his knees. He wore buckskin pants with fringes down the side and a beaded band with a hanging feather under each knee paired with his moccasins.

"You look exquisite," Tori mumbled as she ran her gaze back up his body. "I mean handsome." Tori blushed while Alex walked up to her, kissed her cheek, and whispered in her ear.

"You're lucky there are other people in this room, or I would be dragging you back into our bed to ravish you."

Tori's blush deepened as she looked down.

"Alex," Freya slapped him on the shoulder, "I don't know what you said, TMI, but don't embarrass the girl."

"Why not?" Alex placed his hand on Tori's face and lifted it. "She looks great with a little pink in her cheeks. My princess looks great tonight."

"Okay, lover boy," Barrett announced, entering his room. "Let's get going."

"You look great too, Barrett," Tori smiled.

"Hah, see big brother?" Barrett shoved Alex and bent down to kiss Tori on her cheek. "I look hot."

"She didn't say hot," Alex shoved him back, "and get your paws off my girl."

"You're a lucky man, bro," Barrett hugged Alex.

"I sure am," Alex grabbed Tori's hand in a firm grip. "Let's go. I need to get some last-minute prep work done at the center."

"I can help you," Freya said on their way out, "I just texted mom and dad to let them know we're on our way down."

"Thanks, Frey," Alex waited until everyone entered the elevator and pushed the down button.

Walking out of the elevator, Tori stopped short in the lobby when she saw Osceola and Sehoy standing with Tall Bear, Spirit-of-the-Eagle, and two Seminole tribal council members.

"*Até*," Tori ran to her dad, "I'm so happy to see you. I didn't know you were coming. This is such a great surprise."

"*Cuŋkší*," Tall Bar hugged Tori tightly, "I've missed you and needed to see you. How is my beautiful little girl?"

"Better now," Tori stood on her tippy toes and kissed Tall Bear, "I've missed you too. Did *iná* and Lizzy come?"

"Due to what happened to you and that coward still being on the run," Tall Bear hugged her, "she stayed with your sister on the rez. But as soon as the coast is clear, we will all come down to visit."

"Sir," Alex walked to them and put his hand out for a handshake, "It's a pleasure to see you again."

"*Pilámaya*, Alex," Tall Bear shook his hand, "Tori told me you two are dating and that you've been taking good care of her after what happened. I appreciate that, son."

"I called my dad after that last conversation in Thunder's office," Tori looked at Alex. "I wanted him to know how important you are to me."

"Of course, sir. I will take care of her and do everything in my power to keep her safe. I love her," Alex stated.

"What?" Tori whispered, stunned by his declaration as she stared at Alex. He hadn't told her he loved her before.

"I should have told you sooner Tori," Alex took Tori's hand and pulled her toward him as he stood facing her, "I love you, Tori. I love your kindness toward others, your inner strength to move forward and be the exceptional woman you are. You're smart, gorgeous, and I want us to have a future together. I won't rush you, but I want us to spend more time together getting to know each other. It may be sudden, but deep down in my heart, I know you're my soulmate. I will protect you with my life."

"Oh my God," Tori's tears ran down her face, "I love you, Alex."

Alex held her face and kissed Tori a little longer than her father probably would have liked.

"Okay, okay, enough of that," Freya split them apart, "we need to go. Save some of that sugar for later," Freya turned and looked at Tall Bear's expression, "or not. Tori, here's a tissue to dab on your face."

They all started laughing, and Osceola directed everyone to the cars. "Alex, you go with Tori, Frey, and Barrett. Everyone else will come with me in the company van. Let's limit the number of cars so we don't fill up Thunder's parking lot. We will meet you there, Alex."

"Holt," Freya watched him standing in his suit with his hands in his pocket, "Are you coming?"

"No," Osceola answered, "I need Holt to stay here and hold down the fort in case Winston makes an appearance."

"Sounds good, *chacteka*," Alex responded, leading Tori towards the front of the resort.

"Alex," Tori stopped and grabbed his hand, "aren't you parked out back?"

"No princess," Alex kissed her forehead, "I moved the car and parked it out front next to the company van."

"Hey," Holt grabbed Freya's hand when everyone walked off, "you look beautiful. Be careful."

"Thanks. I'll be fine," Freya smiled and hurried to catch up.

Everyone got into their respective cars and drove to the cultural center. Thunder greeted them at the door when they arrived. Tori noticed when she walked in that Thunder, Grayhorse, Sarah, and Tommy all wore a braid in their hair down the side. The only ones who weren't wearing braids were the non-natives (Mark, Gaby, Matteo, Maggie, Lucy, and Emmy). They wore a nice white dress shirt and black slacks.

"*Hau*, Uncle Spirit," Thunder exclaimed, "I'm so glad you came. It's good to see you."

"*Wakíyaŋ Hotóŋpi*, I couldn't miss the opportunity to come see you," Uncle Spirit hugged Thunder. "Besides, someone needs to keep Tall Bear in line at the casino, since Swift Antelope couldn't come. Now, where are the beautiful women in your family and my adoptive daughters?"

"Isa just went into the bathroom," Thunder puffed up his chest, "our child is apparently sitting on her bladder."

"Is it a boy or girl?" Uncle Spirit asked.

"A boy," Thunder smiled.

"Congratulations *Zintkála Wakíyaŋ Hotóŋpi!*" Uncle Spirit slapped him on the back. "I am so happy for you both. I know you will be a remarkable father."

"Uncle Spirit," Sarah screamed and ran toward him as quick as she could while carrying Lilly on a cradleboard on her back like the old days. Isa followed her out of the restroom. "I've missed you."

"*Wíŋyaŋ mitáwa*," Grayhorse placed his hands on his hips and shook his head at his wife, "please do not run with our child on your back."

"Sorry, *higná*," after giving Uncle Spirit a hug, Sarah walked to Grayhorse and wrapped her arms around him.

"*Wíŋyaŋ mitáwa*," Grayhorse held Sarah by her hips, "If she gets heavy, let me know and I will carry her."

"Okay," Sarah kissed Grayhorse.

"Hi Uncle Spirit," Isa hugged him after Sarah let him go.

"Isa, you are glowing," Uncle Spirit placed his hand on her belly and chanted a quick prayer.

"I am now, not a few weeks ago," Isa grinned, "then I was pale from all my throwing up."

"Well," Uncle Spirit draped his arm around her, "you look absolutely beautiful."

"Thunder," Tall Bear interrupted all the introductions, "do you have any news about the case?

"No, Tall Bear. They are still searching for Winston. We need to be on the lookout for him." Thunder pulled out his phone and turned it around for all to see. "Here is a picture of him. I will text it to all of you. If you see him tonight, please let me know ASAP, and I'll call George."

"Sounds good." Tall Bear hugged his daughter. "Thunder, where do you want us?"

"First, thank you all for coming to help us," Thunder introduced everyone to each other, then lifted his clipboard to check his notes, "Mark, you and Maggie will be in the gift shop. Isa, I want you to stay off your feet and sit behind the lobby desk to help anyone that needs directions or has questions. Barrett, Tori, and Sarah can walk around serving wine. Please put some white and red on your tray. Freya, Tommy, and Emmy can carry the food appetizer trays. Aurora, can you please help Alex in the kitchen? Matteo can be the host and Gaby can waitress, or vice versa. Osceola, you and your tribal council can decide who wants to tell stories in the storytelling room and who wants to be in the exhibit room in case anyone has questions about your artifacts. You can tell as many stories as you want. Tall Bear and Uncle Spirit, you can roam wherever you want. I will also roam and talk to our guests. Oh, and Grayhorse you can be our greeter like usual. Any questions?"

"*Lekší*," Lucy walked up to Thunder and pulled on his pants to get his attention. Looking up at him with a very sad look on her face, she asked, "What can I do?"

"You," Thunder squatted down and picked her up, "are my special worker. Would you please stay in the storytelling room and help any little girls who want to learn about the different American Indian outfits at the little girls changing station? It is my most important job and I need a special person to do it."

"*Haŋ, lekší*," Lucy hugged Thunder tightly and gave him a peck on the cheek, "*pilámaya*. I can do that."

"Your niece has him wrapped around her finger," Sarah whispered to Isa, "God help you if you ever have a little girl."

Isa chuckled, "yup."

"Okay everyone," Grayhorse clapped his hands, "take your places so Thunder can do his checklist before his OCD makes him grumpy."

"Before we do that," Uncle Spirit interrupted, "Can we all please go into the storytelling room and ask *Wakaŋ Táŋka* to bless us tonight?"

"Of course," Thunder, along with everyone else, nodded and headed into the room.

All the tribal council members from the Lakota and Seminole tribes said prayers and asked for blessings, not only for the opening, but for finding Winston and ending Tori's terror. After the prayers, everyone took their places while Thunder went around with his checklist.

"I'm off to the kitchen," Alex bent down and kissed Tori, "with my magnificent team." Alex, Aurora, Gaby and Matteo headed off with him.

The Seminole Tribe of Florida council members stayed in the room and decided where they would each go. Meanwhile, Mark and Maggie walked into the Gift Shop. Mark wanted to show Maggie the location and prices of all the items that were for sale.

"Barrett, Sarah, Tommy, Emmy, and Frey, come with me," Tori called out. "Let's go into the lobby to figure out who is carrying what."

"Honey," Thunder whispered in Isa's ear, "stay away from the Indian

Fry Bread with honey."

"Hey," Isa smacked Thunder, "You might like it if I spill something on myself."

"Very true," Thunder kissed her inappropriately as he walked her backwards out of the room.

"What is that about?" Freya asked Sarah.

"Funny story." Sarah wound her arm around Freya and followed Tori out of the room with Grayhorse chuckling as he trailed behind. "Isa's a little clumsy and they kept hooking up every time Isa spilled food on her clothes."

"Tommy, you can carry the Indian Fry Bread Pizza bites; Emmy, you can carry the Indian Fry Bread Taco. Frey, you can carry the Indian Fry Bread with honey. Sarah and I will carry the wine glasses. And Barrett, can you carry the glasses of water just in case someone doesn't want to drink alcohol? Does that work for everyone?" Tori looked at them as they nodded.

"Here are your trays." Gaby placed six empty trays on a table in the restaurant.

"I got the red wine and glasses." Matteo set them down. "I'll get more glasses and you guys can pour the red wine. Alex said to pour the white and water when the doors open so they stay cold."

Everyone settled into their jobs, and they opened the doors at 6:30 pm. Tori walked to the front door when they first opened and stood next to Grayhorse when he opened the door for a couple and greeted them.

Chapter 42

Unconquered Path Exhibit Opening Night
Tori

"Welcome. My name is Grayhorse. Let me give you a brief description of what we have tonight. To my left is the entrance to the museum room, which has the exhibit 'Unconquered Path'. In the back is the storytelling room, where you can hear a great story from a member of the Seminole Tribe of Florida. Stories will begin at seven and eight. Next to that is the Gift Shop. You may purchase any paintings, sculptures, jewelry and/or pottery that have a price tag. Most of which are in the gift shop. Items without price tags are not for sale. The artifacts enclosed in the glass cases in the museum are considered holy and can't be sold. Between the gift shop and the restaurant are our restrooms. If you are hungry and want more than finger goods," he pointed behind them to the restaurant, "Our restaurant is open tonight and is serving American Indian cuisine. If you need any help, please do not hesitate to ask someone dressed like me," he smiled as he pointed to himself. "We are dressed in our traditional clothing and are here to assist you. Again, welcome and have a pleasant evening," Grayhorse smiled as he finished his spiel and the couple walked into the exhibit.

"I'm going to stand with you for just a few minutes. If that's okay."

"Tori, I'd rather you stay inside—away from the door—in case we spot Winston."

"Okay, you're right. Thank you for looking out for me."

"Of course."

Tori left Grayhorse by the front door and grabbed a wine tray. She strolled the lobby comfortably interacting with their guests as they wandered around the cultural center. Their interest and excitement in learning about the exhibit was infectious. Wrapped up in their joy, she followed a group toward the storytelling room to hear a Seminole Tribe of Florida story.

"Barrett, can you please take this wine tray? I'm going to check the storytelling room."

"Of course," Barrett held out his other hand, "give it here."

Tori thanked him and strode into the room. She saw Lucy in the back asking the other little girls to quiet down because Billy Jones, a descendant of one of the original members of the Seminole Tribe of Florida and council member, sat on the bench on the stage to tell his story.

"Hello everyone, my name is Billy Jones, and I am a direct descendant from Abiaka— Sam Jones to the Americans. Abiaka was a well-respected medicine man, strategist, warrior, and leader of the Miccosukee tribe. His voice was the strongest in opposing removal, and when American leaders talked about forcing the Seminole to leave Florida, the words 'Sam Jones and his group will never agree to leave' were a constant. During the wars, he regularly stayed away from negotiations with the American military, instead sending trusted lieutenants such as Coacoochee and Osceola in his stead. He would then go into the American camps as a fisherman selling his catch, observing and learning all he could while being comfortably overlooked. At the end of the wars, Abiaka led the last Seminole remaining in Florida into the deep wetlands, far away from American forces and settlers. The Seminole Tribe of Florida survives today because of him.

We followed Abiaka, who the Americans knew as Sam Jones, into the swamps of Florida, remaining free and unconquered. We kept our ways and our traditions. As the years went by, more and more people settled in Florida. They built cities and drained the wetlands. We talked to and traded with these settlers as they filled our old lands. They built roads and railways throughout the state, bringing new travelers to our lands. We greeted these travelers and shared with them our culture and sold them our crafts.

We continue to grow and prosper, from the two hundred who followed Abiaki, to over five thousand tribal members today. We continue to fight for our freedom but have moved the war from the battlefield to the courtroom. We are a sovereign government with our own schools, police, and courts. We run one of the largest cattle operations in the United States. We own the guitar shaped resorts and hotels like the one near here. They are an international business with locations in 74 countries. We continue our traditions of sewing, patchwork, chickee building, and alligator wrestling. The world has changed, as it always will, and we have adapted, as we always have—while keeping our ways, our culture, and our lives to remain the Unconquered Seminole Tribe of Florida. Sam Tiger will now tell you a story he heard from Betty Mae Tiger Jumper."

Billy gestured to Sam to take the stage.

"Hello everyone, my name is Sam Tiger. I am a descendant of Betty Mae Tiger Jumper. This is a story I heard from Betty Mae Jumper, also known as Potackee. She was the first and, so far, the only female chairperson of the Seminole Tribe of Florida. She was a nurse, newspaper editor,

Communications Director for the tribe, a superb storyteller, and was the first Florida Seminole to learn to read and write English. Her first languages were Miccosukee and Creek. She came from the Muscogee of Creek origins and spoke the Miccosukee language. Betty Mae Tiger Jumper died on January 14, 2011, at the age of 87. However, when she was alive, she would attend the Florida Folk Festival and other such gatherings; she enthralled crowds with Seminole legends she first heard as a child around the campfire. The following story is an excerpt from her book 'Legends of the Seminoles.'

This story was told to me by my grandmother when I was just a baby. Where we lived, the sounds in the woods were very important to us. We were always asking, 'What is that sound from?' A lot of times we were answered with a story such as this one."

The little green frog was sitting on the edge of the water lilies sleeping away. A big ol' rabbit came hopping along, came upon the frog and said, 'Hi there! Why are you sleeping? It's too pretty a day to sleep. Wake up! Wake up!'

'I don't have to do anything,' said the irritated little frog. But that pretty ol' pesky rabbit kept it up until the little frog got really mad and told him, 'I'll fix you up.'

So little frog started singing his funny little song or the noise he makes to call the rain. Within a few minutes, the black cloud came and the wind started blowing. Then the rains came and soaked the ol' rabbit so much he got cold and ran home.

Whenever you hear the frogs singing away today, better be near shelter, because they are warning you that rain is coming soon.

Tori was in the room longer than she planned, but the history of Alex's tribe and their stories were so interesting. She loved learning about his people and their culture. She tiptoed out of the room and was immediately pulled into Thunder's office.

"Whaaa…," Tori felt a cloth with a strange odor placed over her mouth as another hand wrapped around her waist from behind, dragging her across the office. The last thing she saw was Reaper closing Thunder's office door with an evil twinkle in his eyes. No, not again—Alex!

Chapter 43

Time to Quiet the Witness
Winston

Winston pulled Tori into the office, kicking the door when he saw a furious American Indian man running toward him.

"Lock the door quick!" Winston yelled at Reaper. "I'll take care of her, go to the car and start it. We'll be right behind you. Go, hurry!"

Reaper locked the door and ran past Winston. Winston held the cloth over her nose and mouth until Tori went limp in his arms. Then he carried her fireman style through the warehouse and out the back door. He had to hurry, before that man caught up to them. Going by the angry look on his face, the locked door wouldn't keep him out for long. Luckily, not only was Reaper waiting with the car running, but he'd left the front and back door open for them.

"That went off better than expected," Reaper said when Winston threw Tori in the backseat and slammed the door before getting into the front passenger seat. "How'd you get the car so fast?"

"I texted Numbers after the staff got here and asked him to move the car for me," Reaper answered as he pulled out of the parking lot. "All I had to do was pull it out of the parking spot and open the doors."

"Good thinking, Reaper."

"Well, it wouldn't have gone smooth if you hadn't gotten all the info about the center from the bitch in the back," Reaper laughed. "By the way, since they hadn't sealed all the boxed jewelry, I grabbed some."

"Yeah, I grabbed some too," Winston nodded. "It helped that Tori told me all about her job. Stupid Bitch. Little did she know telling me about the reflective glass in that office was going to help our cause. Unfortunately, I think the owner saw us." Winston was looking around outside the car.

"Shit, they just ran out the front. Go, go, go! Hurry the fuck up!"

"Sneaking into the warehouse during the food delivery was a genius idea. Can I have her now?" Reaper looked back salivating, "You've already fucked her. I think now it's my turn now, especially since I've had to hide out in the warehouse for the past six hours."

"Not yet. Stop your whining, and drive. Besides, I had to wait in there with you," Winston reprimanded Reaper. "Oh shit, they're following us. Lose them and head to the marina. Did you remember to call one of your brothers and tell them to have the boat running when we get there?"

"I did, but I need to text him our ETA," Reaper looked in his rearview mirror. "Get my phone and text Bull. Tell him to get his ass there and get the boat started now."

*** *Grayhorse* ***

Shit! Grayhorse heard Thunder's 'we have a problem' whistle. Thunder and Grayhorse had their own special versions of whistles from when they trained horses on the rez. It was quicker to ask for help with a whistle than yelling.

Grayhorse turned around and watched Thunder run to his office. He tried the door and when it didn't budge—he kicked it in. Barrett set down his trays and ran to Thunder's side. They spoke, and Grayhorse saw Thunder signal him to head out as Barrett ran toward him. Grayhorse noticed Freya ran to the kitchen. Something must have happened to Tori.

"We gotta go," Barrett mumbled when he reached Grayhorse.

"What's going on?" Grayhorse asked as they ran out of the building.

"They took Tori," Barrett ran behind Grayhorse, "Thunder thinks it was Winston, but he had brown hair. Probably colored his hair since he's on the run. By the time Thunder burst into his office, they were gone. Thunder's phone alerted him that the warehouse's back door was opened."

"Fuck!" Grayhorse saw a car screeching out of the parking lot. "Follow me. We'll take my truck. Did you see her in the car?"

"I only saw two men in the front," Barrett hollered as he ran to the truck. "One looked like a biker and the other had brown hair. I hope she's in the backseat and not in the trunk."

Barrett buckled in and slammed his door. Just as they were pulling out, they saw Alex running toward them. Grayhorse braked and unlocked the door.

"Sorry," Alex jumped in quickly and slammed the door, "Someone tell me what the hell is going on. Frey came running into the kitchen saying I needed to hurry and get in the truck with you guys. Frey doesn't usually panic, so I ran out as fast as I could."

"Barrett!" Grayhorse focused on the road and shouted, "you fill him in while I try to catch up to that car. When you finish, call 911."

"Winston took Tori," Barrett turned around in the front passenger seat and stared at Alex.

"What the fuck!" Alex screamed. "How?"

"We don't know how he got in," Barrett responded, "But Thunder saw a brown-haired man pull Tori into his office. By the time he got there, his door was locked, then he heard his phone go off, informing him that the warehouse's back door had been opened. We're positive they're in the car Grayhorse is trying to follow ahead of us. Because why else would someone peel out of the center's parking lot?"

"Fucker!" Alex cussed. "How did this happen? I should've kept her in the kitchen with me."

Alex scooted closer to Grayhorse and Barrett from the backseat, leaning over the center console.

"Barrett," Grayhorse glanced over to Barrett, "call the police. Use my phone so it goes through my car speakers."

"911, where's your emergency?" they heard the operator's voice.

"Hi, this is Jake Grayhorse and I would like to report a kidnapping," Grayhorse spoke while he drove.

"Who has been kidnapped? Where are you?" the operator asked.

"I am following the kidnapper's car, and I would love for someone to assist me," Grayhorse answered. "We are heading north on I-595. I'm not sure where he is heading."

"Can you tell me what happened?" the operator asked.

"Tori Tall Bear was working at the American Indian Cultural Center when a man dragged her away. She has a restraining order against this person named Winston James. He drugged and raped her about three weeks ago." Grayhorse tried to give her the information while concentrating on the road.

"I have police on the way. Can you tell me the make, model, color, and license plate?" the operator tried to get as much information as possible.

"I have two other people in the car with me," Grayhorse informed her. "They will give you the information. I don't want to lose them. We just got off the highway, and it looks like he's heading toward the marina. Please hurry."

Barrett gave the operator all the information she requested. Alex was still leaning over the console with his elbows on the two front seats while covering his mouth with his hand.

"I just got a text from Thunder," Alex said, looking at his phone, "he said he called George. George is in pursuit—he heard the police call go out. He also said he was going to check his security cameras to find out how they got in."

"Sir, our police officers are on their way," the operator informed them. "Please do not engage with the kidnapper, help is on the way."

"Thank you." Grayhorse disconnected the call. "I'm glad George will be there, since he knows us."

"Alex," Grayhorse turned into the marina, "text Thunder back and tell him we just pulled into the Sunshine Marina so he can tell George where we are."

*** *Thunder* ***

"Thunder," Isa ran toward Thunder, "what just happened?"

"I think Winston just took Tori," Thunder ran his hand over his head, "Fuck! Why does shit keep happening during my openings? Shit! I gotta pull footage and see how the fuckers got in. I only heard the warehouse alarm when they were leaving."

"Thunder," Isa rubbed his arm, "this is not your fault. We couldn't have had more people here watching Tori if we tried. We'll figure out what happened, and we'll get Tori back."

"I know honey," Thunder hugged her, "I love you. I need to talk to Tall Bear."

"Good luck. I love you too," Isa kissed him and walked back to the lobby desk.

Thunder calmed a few people who saw him kick in the door and told them it was no big deal. He'd locked his keys in there and needed something. He laughed it off and changed the subject. Luckily, most of the guests were in the storytelling room or the exhibit room. He didn't want his guests to panic. Winston was gone, and there was no threat to any of them.

Thunder was glad he had installed the security cameras and alarms. However, that hadn't been enough. From now on, he was going to consider having security guards. He would have to talk to Barrett and see how it worked at the casino. Thunder walked up to Freya.

"Thank you for getting Alex," Thunder placed his arm on her back.

"Do you think they'll catch them?" Freya was wheezing.

"I'm sure they will," Thunder looked directly into her eyes, "Frey, I need you to stay calm. I trust that Grayhorse will catch up to them and call the police. We have a lot of guests here, most of which, do not know what happened. We need to pretend everything is okay until we hear otherwise. If you need help serving wine, please ask Gaby or Matteo for help."

"Thunder?" Sarah walked up to them while he was talking to Freya.

"I know Sarah," Thunder pinched the bridge of his nose, "I'm worried too, but we can't kick everyone out. We only have another thirty minutes to go. As soon as I hear from Grayhorse, I'll let you all know what's going on." Thunder led them to the lobby desk by Isa.

"Isa in twenty minutes, please lock the front door so no one else comes in." Thunder gave her his keys, "just tell them we are at capacity and ask them to come back tomorrow."

Thunder texted George.

Thunder: Tori kidnapped, please help.

George: On it. Already heard it on the radio.

"George is on the call," Thunder told them all. "I need to find Tall Bear. Has anyone seen him?"

"Last time I saw him, he was walking toward the exhibit room with

Uncle Spirit," Isa replied.

Thunder's phone buzzed.

Alex: Headed to Sunshine Marina, tell George.

Thunder: Got it.

Thunder: Headed to Sunshine Marina

George: Got it.

"Okay," Thunder sighed, "Alex just texted that they were headed to the Sunshine Marina. I texted George. I'll be back after I talk to Tall Bear."

Thunder walked into the exhibit room and found Tall Bear with Uncle Spirit, just like Isa said.

"Tall Bear," Thunder approached them, "Can you come with me to my office, please?"

"Is something wrong?" Tall Bear asked, concerned.

"Let's discuss this in my office, please," Thunder gestured for him to walk ahead of him.

"I'm going with you," Uncle Spirit announced as he followed them, "*Wakíyaŋ Hotóŋpi*, why is your door broken?"

Thunder made sure they were all in his office before he shut the door as best he could. This was going to be a tough conversation that should not be overheard. Thunder got to the point.

"They took Tori," Thunder blurted out.

"What? How?" Tall Bear shouted while Uncle Spirit placed his arm around his friend's shoulders.

"I don't know." Thunder answered, "He didn't come in the front door and the back door alarm only went off after he left the building. I'm not sure how he got in. But Grayhorse, Barrett, and Alex are following the car. Alex texted me. They are headed to Sunshine Marina. The police have been notified. They are in pursuit."

"I want to go there now," Tall Bear announced, "take me there, Thunder. That is my little girl that's in trouble."

"I don't know if that's a good idea. It's an active scene and I don't want anything to happen to you or for us to get in the way."

"I. don't. care." Tall Bear shouted, "take me there NOW!"

"Okay," Thunder tried to calm Tall Bear, "Let me tell Isa that we are leaving. She can close and lock up for me."

Thunder, Tall Bear, and Uncle Spirit approached Isa.

"Honey," Thunder rubbed Isa's back as she sat in the chair, "I'm going to take Tall Bear to the Sunshine Marina. That's where Alex mentioned they were heading. Can you please close for me? Once all the guests leave, please let our volunteers know what happened and do not stay here alone. Go home with Sarah. I'll get you from their house."

"Okay," Isa kissed him, "please be careful. I love you."

"I will honey," Thunder kissed her forehead, "I love you too."

Thunder, Tall Bear and Uncle Spirit headed toward Thunder's truck.

*** *Tori* ***

Tori woke up to Winston yelling at Reaper.

"Dammit Reaper," Winston screamed, "I told you to lose them!"

"Look Asshole!" Reaper yelled back, "I'm trying. At least we've already contacted Bull and he will have the boat running when we get there."

Tori was trying to control her trembling and even out her breathing. *Shit, I was taken to a second location.* She needed to think and get away from them. She thought it might be easier to pretend to still be passed out and make a run for it when they stopped. It sounded like they were heading towards a marina. It would be a lot harder to escape once she was on a boat. Tori didn't know how to swim.

Whatever they gave her to knock her out was still in her system. She felt sluggish, but knew it would be better to run on solid ground than to stay afloat in the water. Biding her time, she relaxed her breathing and listened to their conversation, knowing she had to make it harder for them to take her.

Tori waited and as soon as the car stopped, she bolted out of the car. Unfortunately, she was still out of it and was stumbling instead of running at full speed. Winston easily caught up to her from behind and grabbed her around the waist, pulling her with him toward the dock. Tori continued to fight him and struggled to get out of his arms.

Tori could hear police sirens and watched as Alex and Barrett jumped out of a truck and ran toward her.

"Alex!" Tori tried to yell, but due to being chloroformed her voice didn't come out as strong as she would have liked.

"Tori!" Alex frantically screamed as he ran toward them, "Let her go, asshole!"

Suddenly, Winston came to a stop. Next thing she knew, she was flying, landing hard on her side and gasping for air. Jerk. He threw her in a boat. *Now, what was she going to do?*

"Tori, hang on, I'm coming," Tori heard Alex scream. She sat up and watched in horror as Winston leapt into the boat, pulled a gun out from the back of his pants and pointed it toward her head.

"Back away or I'll kill her," Winston yelled. "Reaper, hurry the fuck up. We need to go NOW!" Bull was untying the dock lines while Reaper manned the helm of the boat.

"We can't go anywhere," Reaper hollered back. "That boat is in our way."

"Well, do something!" Winston yelled back.

Tori knew she had to do something even though her body was in pain, and she had a gun pointed at her head. She couldn't let them take her. Alex wouldn't be able to follow her on water. She looked around and noticed there was an empty boat dock to the right of the boat they were on. She was terrified of drowning, but she would rather die in the water than stay on this boat with these despicable men. The way they spoke about her in the car, she knew they would rape her repeatedly. Suddenly, the water wasn't so scary.

If she could get away from them here, Alex could get to her. He was only a few feet away from her, trying to talk to Winston. Tori hoped that if she pushed his hand away from her head and kicked Winston on the side of his knees, he would stumble. Hopefully not firing the gun at her. Playing it out in her head, she moved her legs around so she could deliver her kick. Tori looked at Alex and shifted her eyes toward Winston. She wanted Alex to distract Winston so she could make her move.

"You won't get away with this," Alex shouted, "I will find you, and kill you if you harm a hair on her head."

"Yeah, yeah, yeah," Winston snorted, "like you protected her from me before. By the way, she was a virgin, and I loved every moment of initiating her into sex. Last time she was a little out of it, but next time she will be an active participant. I can't wait to have her mouth on my cock as Reaper fucks her from behind."

Tori could see Alex breathing heavy with his hands gripped into fists on either side.

"Fucker," Alex spoke through gritted teeth, "put the fucking gun down so I can kick your ass."

Winston threw his head back and laughed. His relaxed pose was just what Tori had been waiting for.

She pushed his hand up and away from her while she kicked his knees on the side with both legs. Winston was stunned when his legs buckled, dropping the gun. Time seemed to slow down, and everything happened at once.

"Tori!" Alex shouted, looking at her with wide eyes.

"Fucking Bitch!" Winston shouted from the floor, trying to reach out to grab her.

"Fuck!" Bull ran toward the gun.

"Shit!" Barrett screamed.

"Police!" the officer yelled. "freeze!"

Tori knew she had to make a split-second decision. By trying to get away from Winston, her back was up against the side of the boat. Tori used the side to stand up and sat on the edge while she watched them yelling at each other. It was now or never. Once she made eye contact with Alex, she mouthed 'I love you' before she swung her legs around and pushed off the boat into the water.

"Fuck!" Tori heard Winston yell at the same time she heard a gunshot. Then she went under, and everything became silent.

Chapter 44

My Future Flashed Right Before Me
Alex

Alex and Barrett bolted out of the truck as soon as they arrived at the boat dock, while Grayhorse parked his truck. Getting to Tori was his priority. Alex was pissed beyond reason when he saw Winston toss Tori into the boat like a bag of trash and put a gun to her head. He was going to kill him. The boat was running but couldn't pull out because there was another boat leaving the marina at the same time. Winston seemed unstable as he yelled at his accomplices. This could buy him time to get to Tori.

Alex heard the police officers behind him.

"Police!" the officer yelled. "Freeze!"

Alex and Barrett immediately stopped and raised their hands. Alex heard footsteps coming closer. Shit, he had to stop. He didn't want the police to think he was on the side of the kidnappers.

"Alex?" George asked, and Alex turned around. "You can put your hands down. Please stay here and we'll take care of this."

Suddenly, Alex watched in horror as Tori jumped overboard. Living in South Florida, Alex and Barrett were both excellent swimmers. They were also dive buddies. Alex took a few steps and dove into the water after Tori. He could hear yelling, but tuned it out to focus on finding Tori in the water.

When he took the diving classes, his instructor would mess with him underwater to teach him how to not panic underwater and hold his breath for as long as possible. Little did he know how helpful those lessons would be years later. Alex was swimming around, trying to find Tori underwater. Finally, he had to come up for another breath of air, which turned out to be a great idea when he saw Tori wrapped around one of the pilings directly under the dock like a koala on a tree.

Alex swam underwater toward her.

"Princess," Alex mumbled into her hair as soon as he held her tightly, "how are you doing?"

"Alex," Tori cried, "I'm so happy to see you. I thought I was going to die."

"No Baby," Alex pulled her into his arms. Now he was her koala tree as he treaded water holding her. "I will not let you die. Can you swim?"

"Not very well," Tori was shaking, "but I will do my best."

"Okay," Alex smiled and gave her a quick kiss, "get on your back like I taught you. I'll put my arms under your arms and pull you to shore. We're gonna stay under this dock so they don't see us."

"Okay." Tori grabbed his arm and Alex helped her onto her back. Alex placed his hands under her arms, keeping her head above water as he swam backwards using his legs.

Alex could hear the stand-off on the deck and heard a splash. He didn't know who had gone in the water, but he had to get Tori to shore in case he encountered Winston or one of the other two guys under the dock. Before he went into the water after Tori, one of those guys had the gun. Alex swam quickly and pulled them up from the piling closest to shore.

"Barrett," Alex called out to his brother, "here."

Barrett ran toward them and grabbed Tori. "Nice kick to the knees. I love a student that listens."

"It was all I could think to do."

"You did great Tori," Barrett side hugged her.

"I saw her jump overboard, so I grabbed the blanket in my truck." Grayhorse held it out for Tori. "Here, wrap this around you. This blanket seems to love females in distress."

"Thank you," Tori gave Grayhorse a puzzled look, "what?"

"Never mind, it's a long story," Grayhorse chuckled. "Let's go. That police officer is waving us over."

They all turned and headed toward a police officer who was standing by an ambulance.

"Princess," Alex held her tight against him, "we need to get you checked out."

Alex walked Tori to the ambulance and turned around when he heard a commotion coming from the marina dock.

"Alex," Tori screamed to get his attention, "check his pockets and Reapers. They stole some jewelry from the center."

"Take your hands off me!" Winston screamed. "Do you know who I am? Who my father is? I will sue you and you will all lose your jobs."

"Sir, there is a warrant out for your arrest," George said as he pulled him with his hands cuffed behind his back. "You have the right to remain silent. Anything you say can and will be used against you in a court of law. You have the right to an attorney. If you cannot afford an attorney, one will be provided for you. Do you understand these rights as they have been said to you?"

"I want my lawyer, NOW!" Winston was yelling so loud his face was red and distorted and spittle flew from his mouth, "this was all Reaper's idea. Did you arrest him?"

"You," Winston tried pulling George toward the ambulance when he saw Tori, "you will pay for this bitch!"

"Fucker!" Alex blocked Tori's path and yelled, heading toward Winston, "Shut the fuck up and leave her alone. George, check their pockets. Apparently, Reaper and Winston stole some jewelry from Thunder."

Alex was close to Winston when he felt a set of hands holding each of his arms.

"Alex," Grayhorse whispered and placed one of his hands on Alex's chest, "don't say anything else. The police will handle this."

George reached into Winston's pockets and pulled out the jewelry he had stolen.

"Well, well, well, look at what we have here," George pulled several pieces of jewelry out of Winston's pocket. "We got it from here. Sean!" George shouted behind him, "check Reaper's pockets after you arrest him."

George pulled Winston toward his car, opened the door, pushed his head down and shoved him in the backseat.

"Where are the other two perps?" Barrett asked George.

"Both went into the water," another officer said. "We caught Reaper, but not Bull. But we'll keep looking. Bull is a member of Lucifer's Renegades MC. We know the location of his clubhouse. We'll find him."

"This is what Reaper had in his pocket," Sean opened his hand. "Unfortunately, we must enter it into evidence for this case. If we find anything else, we'll let Thunder know. We'll release all the jewelry to Thunder as soon as we can."

"Thank you," Alex looked down and saw it was mostly items from the Red Path Exhibit that still needed to me mailed to the original artists.

"Alex," George walked toward him, "If Tori is okay, take her home. We can take her statement tomorrow at the station."

"Thank you, George," Alex shook his hand. "We'll see you tomorrow."

"No problem," George stepped back, "Grayhorse call Thunder. He must be beside himself. I'll have my hands full with Mr. James and Reaper at the station."

"Will do," Grayhorse stepped closer to George, "thank you so much, George."

"No problem," George shook his hand, "see you all tomorrow."

"We'll be there," Grayhorse said. "I'll bring Thunder since he witnessed the initial abduction."

"Perfect," George nodded, "See ya."

They all waved goodbye to George and Sean, who took off with Winston in the back. Another officer took Reaper away in his police cruiser. Other officers on land and the police officers on the boat continued to search for Bull. Alex headed toward Tori in the ambulance.

"Hey," Alex addressed a paramedic, "how is she? Does she need to go to the hospital?"

"No sir," the paramedic finished, checking her heart rate and pulse, "they only used chloroform once. Her heart rate sounds normal, and her pulse is strong. She might experience dizziness and drowsiness, but she should be okay. I would monitor her overnight, and if she had any vomiting, please bring her to the hospital immediately."

"Okay." Alex put his hands under Tori's armpits and carried her down from the ambulance. "She lives with me, so I'll watch her. Thank you for checking her out."

Alex put his arm under Tori's legs and picked her up as soon as she stood on the ground. Tori wound her arms around his neck and put her head on his chest.

"Tori," Grayhorse ran his hand over her head, "How are you holding up?"

"I'm glad you guys are here." Tori looked at Grayhorse with tears in her eyes. Grayhorse bent down and kissed her forehead.

"I'm glad we're here too." Grayhorse mumbled. "Alex, stay here. I'll get the truck and drive you all back to the resort."

"Thanks, man," Alex sighed, holding Tori tightly against his chest.

"Tori," Barrett rubbed her arm, "Sweetheart, you scared us to death. I'm so glad you are okay. That was quick thinking and very brave, but I just about had a heartache when you jumped overboard."

"Tori!" Tori looked up when she saw her father running toward her.

Alex placed Tori on the ground so she could hug her dad. Tori started crying while her father held her.

"Alex saved me *até*," Tori mumbled into his chest, "when I jumped into the water, Alex jumped in to save me."

"Tori," Tall Bear held her face in his hands, "why would you do that? You can't swim."

"I had to get away *até*," Tori whispered. "I would rather die than go with them. But Alex saved me." Tori turned around and went back to Alex.

"Thank you, Alex," Tall Bear shook his hand. "I can never thank you enough for saving my baby girl."

"It was my pleasure, sir." Alex kissed Tori on her forehead. "I love your daughter, and I plan to marry her whenever she's ready."

Tori didn't have time to answer because just as she was going to say yes to Alex, Grayhorse pulled up his truck.

"Alex," Grayhorse screamed out of his truck, "Come on, I'll drive you, Tori, and Barrett to the resort. Thunder, I called Sarah. Isa went back to the resort with her. Can you take Uncle Spirit and Tall Bear?"

"Yup," Thunder called out.

"Sounds good," Alex walked Tori toward the truck, "we'll see you guys at the resort."

Alex placed Tori in the back seat and buckled her in. He then went to the other side and sat in the middle of the back bench seat to be close to her. As soon as Alex buckled in, he watched Tori unbuckle and sit on his lap sideways. Alex didn't have the heart to put her back in her seat, so he held her tightly with one arm wrapped around her waist and the other pushing her head into the crook of his neck and shoulder. Tori was breaking his heart as she cried into his chest. He could have lost her tonight, and he didn't know how he could live without her in his life.

Chapter 45

My Hero
Tori

As soon as they arrived at the resort, Barrett gave Freya, his parents, and Holt a recap of everything that happened.

"Grayhorse," Sarah ran to her husband.

"*Wíŋyaŋ mitáwa*," Grayhorse caught his wife and spun her around, "I'm fine."

"Thunder," not one to be outdone, Isa ran toward him.

"Honey," Thunder placed his hands on his hips and shook his head at his wife, "please do not run. What if you trip and fall?"

"Then I know you will catch me," Isa kissed her husband.

"I'm going to get Tori upstairs," Alex announced, "we'll see you all in the morning?"

"Yes," Tall Bear answered first and walked over to Tori, "I'll see you in the morning *cuŋkší*. I love you."

"I love you too, *até*," Tori kissed his cheek.

Alex nodded to all of them and walked past them to get Tori up to their room. Once in their room, Alex carried Tori to their bathroom and sat her down on the counter.

"Princess," Alex put his hands on her face and with his thumbs lifted her head to look at him, "I'm going to get you some pajamas to sleep in. I just didn't want to lay you down on the bed while your clothes were wet. Sit tight, I'll be right back."

Alex gently unlaced her tall moccasin boots and slipped them off her feet, while Tori stared at him silently.

"Alex," Tori whispered, "I'm okay. Can you bring me one of your shirts?"

"Of course, Baby," Alex kissed her forehead, "you love my shirts, don't you?"

"I feel safe as if your arms were wrapped around me," Tori stared at him, "it's even better when it's the shirt you had on previously because then I can smell your scent and it comforts me."

"Oh Baby," Alex pressed his forehead to hers, "I will gladly wear one under my chef shirt every day and you can wear it at night to sleep in. I love that you feel comforted in my shirts. Besides, they look better on you than me."

Alex grinned and walked away to grab one of his t-shirts from his dresser and handed it to her.

"Thank you," Tori half-smiled. "I'll be out in a minute. I'm gonna take a shower to get the salt water out of my hair."

"Okay," Alex hesitated, but left the bathroom, not fully closing the door in case she needed him.

Alex changed into his pajama bottoms and sat on the bed waiting for Tori with his hands hanging between his knees. He was listening for signs of distress from the bathroom. Soon Tori walked out in his t-shirt and walked to her side of the bed.

"Baby," Alex stood up, "let me dry your hair before you go to bed."

"Okay." Tori walked back into the bathroom.

Alex took out the blow dryer and ran his hands through her hair until it was dry. Watching her through the bathroom mirror. He loved running his hands through her hair and she did too, because she closed her eyes and sighed, leaning against the counter. When he finished, he spun her around and kissed her.

"I'm gonna take a quick shower." Alex kissed her cheek.

"Okay," Tori left the bathroom.

Alex showered and dried his hair before he joined Tori in bed. Tori was facing him in bed with her hands prayer style under her head. She smiled at him when he came toward the bed. Alex turned off the lights, sliding into bed and pulling her into his arms.

"Baby," Alex covered her and tucked her in, "do you need anything?"

"Yes," Tori looked at him, "can you please hold me?"

Tori looked so sad and lost.

"Of course, princess," Alex laid flat on his back and pulled her into his arms.

Tori draped her arm around Alex's waist, bent her knee across his hips, and laid her head on his chest. As Alex rubbed her back and leg, he realized she was naked under his shirt. He would not push himself onto her. She needed rest and cuddling. He was open to making love to her, but he left that decision in her court. He was just happy to have her in his arms, safe and sound.

"Alex," Tori kissed his neck, "will you make love to me?"

"Baby," Alex groaned, "do you think this is a good idea? You hit the deck hard when he threw you. I know they gave you some ibuprofen, but I don't want to hurt you."

"Alex," Tori ran her hand down Alex's chest until she reached his pajama pants, slid her hand inside, and gripped his cock.

"Tori," Alex sighed and kissed her, "are you sure about this?"

"Yes. I could've died today. I need you to remind me we are alive, in love, and have our future to look forward to."

Clearly Tori knew what she wanted because she continued to massage his cock and chase his tongue with hers. Alex tried hard to stay still and enjoy her attention, but it became hard when she pushed the waist of his pajama pants down to release his cock.

Tori stopped kissing him and sucked on his neck, pretty sure she marked him from how hard she was sucking his neck. Alex grinned. He loved her marking her territory. He would have to mark his territory soon. Tori then kissed her way down his chest.

"Lift up, Alex," Tori murmured against his lower chest.

Alex lifted his hips off the bed and Tori put her hands under the sides of his pants and pushed them down to his knees, holding his legs together. She straddled his thighs and lowered her mouth slowly onto his cock. Tori went as far down as she could without gagging. Alex could feel her throat right before she pulled off and placed her hand on the base of his shaft, stroking while she sucked on his head. As if that wasn't enough to shoot out, he felt her hand massaging his balls. Oh fuck! He needed to stop her before he came too early.

Alex moaned and placed his hands under her arms, raising her up and sliding down on the bed low enough to place her mound over his mouth.

"Hold on Baby," Alex groaned, "it's my turn to please you."

"Oh Alex," Tori moaned.

Alex licked her from her opening to her clit. Licking, sucking, and nibbling her clit. He could feel Tori's juices flowing into his mouth. He loved her taste. She was so sweet. Alex looked up and noticed Tori was trying to keep her weight off his face by balancing on her thighs and holding the wall for support. Alex chuckled. She wouldn't be able to hold off much longer.

While holding her hip with one hand, Alex entered her pussy with one finger and heard Tori moan. Not good enough. He wanted her to go crazy and cum all over his face. Alex inserted his second finger and moved his finger in and out, emulating the way he wanted to fuck her.

"Ohhh, Alex," Tori's breathing sounded erratic.

Alex hummed against her clit and started swirling his tongue around it while his fingers curled inside of her, applying pressure to her g-spot. Tori was moaning louder and trying to push away from his face, but between Alex's hand on her hip and his fingers inside her, she had nowhere to go. Alex was loving every minute of driving her crazy with his tongue and fingers.

She was so wet, Alex moved his other hand off her hips and toward her pussy. He wet his fingers with her cum and rubbed it all the way to her ass. He rubbed her puckered hole with her juices.

"Alexxx!" Tori screamed.

He knew she was close to cuming when he felt her grind her pussy into his face. Alex increased his intensity, driving her crazy with his mouth and fingers. He heard Tori pound on the wall twice right before she screamed and released her orgasm onto his face.

Alex licked her one last time, lifted her off his face, and dragged her down his body to his cock. Placing her atop him and pushing himself inside her. Tori went wild on his cock, pushing as hard and quick as she could, grinding herself onto him. She placed her hands on his chest and pounded onto him while he raised his hips to meet her thrusts.

Tori sat up, found her clit and rubbed herself.

"Oh fuck, Baby," Alex moaned, "that is so sexy."

"Alex, I'm so close," Tori groaned, "help me."

Alex grabbed her hips and set a quick deep in and out pace until Tori screamed her orgasm and gripped his forearms. Alex could feel her gripping his cock and lost the fight with his self-control, shooting the longest stream of cum he'd ever had in his life. Tori dropped onto his chest.

"Thank you, Alex," Tori murmured against his chest before she yawned.

"No princess," Alex sighed, "thank you. I love you. Go to sleep and rest now."

"I love you too, Alex." Tori whispered.

Alex stayed awake for a few minutes, listening to Tori sleep. He gently placed her on her side so he could clean himself and her. Alex grabbed a washcloth from the bathroom, wet it, and cleaned up Tori. She was so tired she didn't even stir while he wiped their orgasm from between her legs. When he finished, he jumped in the shower and cleaned himself up.

When he walked out of the bathroom, Tori was still sound asleep. Alex didn't bother with clothes. He just slid under the covers and spooned Tori. This is where he wanted to be for the rest of his life. Tori was his home, and he was going to do everything in his power to keep her happy and safe.

Chapter 46

I Got This!
Tori

Tori woke up to Alex spooning her. Last night had been exhilarating with the exhibit and terrifying with Winston. But laying in Alex's arms was like heaven. She could feel his hardness pressing up against her back. Tori pushed back against him.

"Mmm," Alex mumbled into the back of her head, "how do you feel?"

"I'm okay." Tori pushed back again and ran her hand along the back of his thighs.

"Keep doing that," Alex kissed her neck and ran his hand over her belly and mound, "and you're going to feel better than okay."

"I'd like that," Tori moaned and pushed back again.

"Yeah." Alex ran his hand over her pussy and slipped his finger inside. "Does that feel okay?"

"Uh, huh," Tori was moving back and forth between his cock and his finger, "Alex, please."

"I got you, Baby," Alex moved his one arm totally around her, cupping her breast and tweaking her nipple while inserting a second finger into her pussy. "I promise I'll take care of you. You are so wet for me. I love that."

Tori was reaching a state of euphoria, everything Alex did turned her on. She turned her body, her breasts pressed on the bed to trap his hand under her. Alex slid into her pussy and continued to play with her clit.

"Alexxx," Tori screamed into the pillow. Her body undulating between the bed and Alex until her orgasm broke free.

"That's it, Baby," Alex moved her hair and rained kisses down her back, "I love making love to you. Your body is so responsive."

Tori was shivering from her release. Alex held her tightly against him with one hand still on her breast while the other continued to stroke her clit as he pumped into her. *Oh, My Goodness*, she felt so good.

Alex sat back on his haunches and pulled Tori up onto his lap, keeping her legs outside of his. She was wide open to him. This position allowed him to play with her while he pumped into her. It also allowed him to play with her breasts. Tori could hear their bodies slapping into each other. As soon as she started contracting her muscles before her orgasm, Alex moved forward and laid on top of her again, holding her in place while he pumped into her until they both orgasmed at the same time.

Tori was winded and couldn't move if she tried.

"Baby," Alex moved the hair away from her face and kissed her cheek, "join me in the shower?"

"Okay," Tori murmured, "if I can move."

"I'll get the water started," Alex chuckled, "if it's too far to walk, I'll come get you."

"Mmm, okay." Tori felt the bed dip when Alex left it. Then she heard the shower. She felt boneless and didn't want to move.

"Come on Baby," Alex rolled her over and picked her up, "I got you." Alex carried her to the bathroom and helped her into the shower. "I'm gonna call Thunder and let him know you won't be in today."

"No, Alex," Tori looked up at him, "I want to go in. We have the shelter kids coming in today. Winston is in jail, please I can't just stay here and do nothing."

"Okay, turn around." Alex grabbed the shampoo. "I'll wash your hair. Change of plans. I'll let him know we'll be there after we go by the police station."

"Mmm, that feels fantastic," Tori moaned while his fingers were massaging her scalp.

"Don't distract me, woman," Alex groaned, "I'm gonna wash you, and you can dry yourself and get dressed while I finish my shower."

"I can help you." Tori turned around and stroked his cock.

"Baby," Alex sighed, "as much as I would love to continue this, we really have to get to the police station and then work."

"Tonight?" Tori smirked at him.

"Abso-fucking-lutely," Alex kissed her thoroughly before turning her around to rinse, condition, and wash her body.

"I'll call Thunder," Tori said as she stepped out of the shower and dried herself off. "I'll be done before you, party pooper." Tori winked, dropped her towel and sassily walked into the closet.

"I'll show you party pooper tonight, woman!" Alex hollered from the shower.

Tori laughed while she dressed in the closet. Tori had never been playful with a partner, especially not when she was naked. Knowing Winston was in jail helped her relax. Tori stepped out, grabbed her phone, and called Thunder.

"*Hau*, Tori," Thunder answered his phone, "how are you this morning?"

"*Hau*, Thunder," Tori sat on the bed to put on her shoes, "Alex and I are going to the police station but heading to work afterward."

"Tori," Thunder sighed, "you don't have to come in."

"I know," Tori looked at Alex as he got dressed, "but I want to. I enjoy talking to 'Our Kids'."

"Okay, but the shelter boys usually come every Friday. You could talk to them another time."

"I still want to go in Thunder. I really feel okay."

"Alright, it's totally your call. I'll see you around lunchtime?"

"Yes," Tori answered. Alex motioned for her to follow him.

"Can you ask Alex to make extra fry bread for the kids? I don't want to forget, and the boys really look forward to it."

"I'll let him know," Tori stood and followed Alex out.

"Okay, see you soon."

"Bye, Thunder." Tori hung up and put her phone in her purse.

"Ready?" Alex asked from the front door with keys in his hand.

"Yup," Tori smiled and walked out with Alex, "Thunder wants you to make some fry bread for the shelter kids."

"I can do that," Alex nodded. "If we get there in time, I'll even make them tacos and pizzas with plenty of bread for them to take home."

"You are so sweet." Tori leaned up and kissed him.

"Mmhmm, Baby," Alex continued to kiss her in the elevator, "you are the sweet one."

"Get a room," Tori heard as soon as the elevator doors opened, and Freya was standing on the other side.

"What are you doing up?" Alex asked his sister.

"I have the day off," Freya smiled. "Are you guys going to work? I would've thought Thunder would give you the day off."

"He did," Tori hugged her, "but I wanted to go in."

"Okay," Freya grabbed her arm, "I talked to Sarah and Isa yesterday while we were hanging out waiting for you about Girls' Night Out. They said if you were up for it, we could do it tomorrow night. What do you think?"

"I would love that." Tori grasped her hand. "Can you let them know? We are on our way to the police station."

"Yup, I'll call Sarah," Freya squeezed her hand back. "Are you really okay?"

"I will be, Frey." Tori looked at Alex, "your brother has been a great help."

"Okay," Freya hugged Alex, "take care of our girl."

"You know it," Alex took Tori's hand, bringing it up to his lips and kissed the back. "Let's go. See you later, Frey."

"Bye guys," Freya waved before disappearing into the elevator.

Tori and Alex went to the police station and met with George and Sean. George informed them Grayhorse, Thunder, and Barrett had already come in and given their statements. George made everything easy for them and they were only there for about an hour.

George let them know Winston was still in jail for robbery, kidnapping, rape, and attempted murder. The maritime police had sent divers after

Bull and found him. Bull was being accused of kidnapping and attempted murder since he shot at Tori when she went overboard. The authorities charged the final suspect, Reaper, with robbery, kidnapping, and being an accessory to commit murder.

George informed them once they had all the stolen jewelry photographed, they would return it to the cultural center.

They thanked George for all his help and headed to the American Indian Cultural Center. Thunder spent most of the morning fixing his door. When he finished, he asked Mark and Tori to come into his office for a quick meeting before the shelter kids arrived.

"I called this meeting because I've been trying to figure out how to make this center safer," Thunder pointed to Mark and Tori to sit on the couch while he sat in his armchair. "I'm tired of people stealing from me. After what happened to Isa, I installed security cameras, but obviously that's not enough. So, I want to hire either a couple of police officers or a couple of security guards. The tribal council is on board, especially after what happened to you, Tori. What do you all think?"

"I think it's a great idea," Tori stated.

"I have a proposition for you," Mark looked unsure and was fidgeting, "you know I love working here." Tori looked between Mark and Thunder.

"I want to do more than what I'm doing now," Mark took a deep breath and continued, "I spoke to George about becoming a police officer. He said he would give me a recommendation, but I still wanted to work here. George also said if I became an officer, it's not guaranteed that I would be assigned to the cultural center. Especially not on a daily basis. I would need to patrol the city. Which I totally understand. So, I started looking into becoming a security guard for you specifically. I spoke to Barrett Panther, and he told me I could take a 40-hour training course. I wouldn't be able to arrest anyone, but I could detain them until the police arrived. What do you think?"

"That sounds great," Thunder smiled broadly, "you really researched this, didn't you?"

"I did," Mark nodded. "I really want to do this."

"Okay," Thunder agreed, "I can work with that. Once you're trained or in your training, if you think we need another guard, we'll interview. If not, then you will be our only security guard. I'll see if I can get someone to fill in for your position. I might have an idea about that."

"Thank you, Thunder," Mark and Thunder shook hands.

"I will do whatever I can to pick up extra work so you can go to your training." Tori hugged Mark. "Thank you for wanting to keep us safe."

"I'll go find out when the next class starts. Until then, and even after my training I can help until you find someone." Mark seemed so excited Tori was happy for him.

Tori went back into the warehouse to finish checking the inventory and log the items that were missing. Working helped Tori get back to normal. She could finally put her terror to rest. Tori's phone buzzed uncontrollably on the warehouse table with incoming texts.

Sarah: Okay ladies, let's try this again. GNO tomorrow, my house @5

Freya: Woohoo, can't wait.

Maggie: I'm in.

Isa: Sounds good.

Gaby: I'll be there.

Tori: Thank you, guys, for rescheduling. I'm so excited.

Sarah: See you all then.

Tori: Can I bring anything?

Sarah: Just yourself.

Tori was ecstatic the girls still wanted to have their Girls' Night Out. Sure, they had talked about it, but now it was a reality. She could now enjoy it and relax, not having to worry about Winston.

Chapter 47

Girls' Night Out
Tori

When Saturday came around, Tori couldn't wait for the day to end. Thunder let her go home at four so she could change and get to Sarah's house by five. Freya worked a day shift so she would be ready to go when Tori finished work. Asking Alex to drive her and Freya allowed them to drink without worrying about driving. Alex jumped at the chance to drive them. He hadn't let Tori out of his sight, even though Winston was still in jail. Tori realized Alex would do anything to make her happy, something she had never had from any previous dates.

"Are you ladies ready to go?" Alex stepped into his bathroom, which was filled with makeup, hairspray, and perfume fumes.

"Yep," Freya grabbed Tori by her shoulders from behind and turned her toward Alex, "Doesn't Tori look great."

"You look gorgeous," Alex mumbled as he gazed into her eyes.

"Thanks Alex." Tori kept her gaze on his chest.

"All right," Freya clapped her hands, "Let's get this show on the road. I've never been to a girls' night out, and I can't wait." Leave it to Freya to lighten the mood and make everyone feel better.

"You've never been to a girls' night out?" Tori asked, quirking her eyebrow at Freya.

"Nope," Freya wrapped her arm around Tori's arm, "with two hot looking brothers who had so many girls drooling over them, I never really knew who wanted to be my friend and who wanted in my brother's pants. Soooo, I pestered them and their cute friends, leaving me no time to have girlfriends."

"Hot, huh?" Alex shoulder bumped Freya in the elevator, "thanks sis.

You are so good for my ego."

"Don't let it get to your head," Freya bumped him back, "I don't think you're hot, just the crazy ass girls that seemed to like you and Barrett. Their words, not mine."

"Brat," Alex laughed at Freya, "It's okay if you think I'm hot. I think my little sister is beautiful; inside and out."

Tori enjoyed watching them banter with each other. The love they had for each other gave her a warm fuzzy feeling inside. Seeing Alex being affectionate with his family was so sweet. She missed her sister. Lizzy made her smile when times were tough, or dates went bad.

Tori, Freya, and Alex headed through the side door to the car.

"Tori," Alex opened the doors for his sister and Tori, "Can you text me Sarah's address?"

"I would, but I don't have your number," Tori replied sassily with her hand on her cocked hip.

"I see you've been hanging out with Frey too long," Alex quirked an eyebrow. "Frey, stop corrupting her. I blame her sassiness on you. I can't believe I haven't given you my number."

Alex pointed a finger at Freya before he gave Tori his number. Tori quickly added it into her contacts and texted him Sarah's address as soon as she sat down.

"So, Tori," Freya began her embarrassing stories of Alex, "did you know Alex was a skinny, wimpy kid in high school bullied by all the popular kids because he loved to read comic books?"

"Oh Shit," Alex swore from the front seat, "Frey really? Are you telling this story because I can't reach you from the front seat?"

"Yup," Freya laughed and continued, "they even stuffed him in a trash can once."

Tori was trying not to laugh at Alex. Bullying is not okay, but the look on his face of pure mortification was funny.

"Frey," Alex stopped at a light, turned around and pointed at Freya, "If you don't stop, I will pull over and make you stop. I will tickle you so long you will pee your pants. How are you going to explain that to your new Girls' Night Out girlfriends?"

"You wouldn't dare," Freya immediately stopped laughing and looked horrified.

"I would so dare," Alex put on his blinker, acting as if he was going to pull over.

"Okay, okay," Freya raised her hands up, "I do not want to be embarrassed on my first girls' night out. I'll shut up."

"Thank you," Alex sighed.

"But I'm not promising to not tell her the rest of your high school stories another time." Freya smiled from the back seat.

"Of course you're not," Alex smirked. "Little sisters, gotta love them."

"When you meet my sister, Lizzy," Tori interjected, "she will probably tell you stories about me, too."

"Oooh, awesome," Freya said excitedly. "I can't wait to meet her. Do you know when she might come down?"

"No," Tori turned to look at Freya, "I think my dad will wait a while before he lets her come. Especially after what happened to me. But I'm hoping since Winston is in jail, he'll let her come soon."

The mood changed in the car, going from joking to pensive, but leave it to Freya to lighten it again.

"They used to give Alex wedgies in the hallway too," Freya shouted out of nowhere.

Alex sighed and shook his head. Tori smiled and looked out the window as Freya continued to shout out things the high school bullies did to Alex.

"Well, would you look at that," Alex interrupted Freya, "we're here, Frey. You can stop the stories now. I think Tori has heard enough."

"I'll stop for now," Freya patted his shoulder from the back seat, "come on Tori, let's go."

Alex walked the girls to the front door. Tori laughed, watching Freya's antics as she jumped around Tori, singing Girls' Night Out. Tori didn't miss when Alex mouthed to Freya, "thank you".

"Tori!" Sarah opened the door before Tori knocked. "How are you?" Sarah whispered in her ear. "Listen, you do not have to talk about what happened. But if you want some girls to lean on, this is a safe space, and we love you."

"Thank you," Tori whispered.

"Of course," Sarah nodded, "Come in. Alex, the guys are getting ready to take the kids to the park if you want to go with them."

"Tori," Alex looked questioningly, "will you be okay if I go with the guys?"

"Yes," Tori hugged him and whispered, "thank you for asking."

"Of course, Baby," Alex kissed her cheek and gazed into her eyes, "call me if you need me."

Tori smiled and nodded at Alex.

"Sarah, you remember Freya, Alex's sister, from opening night," Tori turned to introduce Frey, "Frey, Sarah is a great friend from back home."

"Hi Frey," Sarah hugged her, "can I call you Frey?"

"Absolutely," Freya nodded.

"Great. We didn't really have time to get to know each other that night, so I'm glad you came." Sarah gestured with her hand, "follow me into the living room so you can get to know everyone else."

Tori saw Thunder walking toward them.

"Thunder, long time no see," Tori waved to him.

"Right?" Thunder side hugged Tori, "glad you are getting a chance to hang out with the girls."

"Freya," Thunder hugged Freya, "nice to see you under better circumstances."

"I totally agree," Freya said after Thunder released her, "it's good to see you as well."

"Alex," Thunder patted Alex on his back, "are you coming with us to the park?"

"Sure," Alex nodded, "thanks for the invite."

"Lucy!" Thunder yelled.

"*Haŋ lekší*," Lucy, learning some Lakota from Tommy, screamed and came running into the foyer.

Thunder grabbed her and swung her around before holding her in his arms.

"You have a new customer for Lucy's Hair Salon. Grab your scrunchies and hair ties," Thunder kissed her cheek and pointed at Alex's man bun.

"Yay!!!" Thunder put her down, and she ran to grab supplies.

"Uh, what did you do?" Alex turned his head and looked around. "What did that mean? Why was she staring at me with so much happiness and interest?"

"You are going to look spectacular when we return you to Tori," Thunder slapped him on the back.

"What?" Alex still looked confused.

"Gentlemen and kids, let's rock and roll!" Thunder ignored Alex and yelled. Finding Isa, he gave her a kiss.

Grayhorse kissed Sarah and picked up Lilly. Tommy and Emmy yelled goodbye while they ran out of the house. Matteo kissed Gaby and Lucy ran up to Alex, grabbed his hand and pulled him to the car. Alex turned to Tori with a look on his face which asked if she knew what the hell was going on and Tori shrugged her shoulders.

"I'll drive 'Mom's Taxi', Sarah's van, since Lilly's car seat is in there." Grayhorse announced on his way out.

"So, what's your name?" Lucy pulled Alex along.

The ladies all waved goodbye and laughed.

"Alex is in for a treat," Sarah said when Gaby, Isa, and Aurora laughed.

"Anyway, Frey and Tori," Sarah pointed at them and then pointed to the other ladies, "you remember Isa (Thunder's wife and my sister-in-law), Aurora (Isa's mom), and Gaby (Isa's sister-in-law), and Maggie who works with Isa. We were all introduced at the opening but didn't really get a chance to talk to each other.

Everyone greeted each other, and they all walked into the kitchen for drinks. Isa had water while the others had wine. Sarah had outdone herself. She had white wine in an ice bucket and a bottle of red on the counter. Next to the wine was a charcuterie board with different types of cheese, grapes, crackers, and sliced salami. After grabbing drinks and filling up their plates, they went into the living room to get cozy and chat.

"So, what form of torture will Alex endure in Lucy's Hair Salon?" Freya asked Sarah.

Sarah, Gaby, Aurora, and Isa all laughed.

"At this point," Isa spoke up first, "I think it's sort of an initiation. Lucy loves to braid long hair. She did Grayhorse's first when I spoke with Thunder in the park a few months ago. Then Lucy got her hands on Thunder's on a Sunday Funday, and now it's Alex's turn. You don't think he'll mind, do you?"

"No," Freya chuckled, "Alex loves kids. He'll let her have her fun."

"Matteo has gotten out of it," Gaby grinned, "since he doesn't have long hair."

"Yeah, but he's had to endure Lucy's Nail Salon," Isa laughed.

"So true," Gaby laughed.

"Oh," Sarah jumped up off the couch, placing her drink and plate on the coffee table, "I have photos of Grayhorse and Thunder's hair style. Let me get my phone." Sarah reached into her back pocket, found the photos, and handed it to Tori and Frey, who were sitting side by side on the couch.

"Oh wow," Tori laughed, "this is remarkable. I've never seen so many braids. At least Grayhorse's braids were pulled back on the side, but Thunder's braids make him look like a peacock with feathers. How did she get them to stand up like that?"

"Grayhorse's hairdo was very impromptu at the park. Lucy didn't have all her supplies," Isa laughed loudly, "but for Thunder's hair, she was ready. She used pipe cleaners. My niece is very creative."

"I wonder what she'll do with Alex's hair," Freya took a sip of her wine. "I hope she goes all out."

"Do you think Alex will have the braids when he comes home?" Tori asked Gaby.

"Grayhorse pulled his out before he came home," Sarah took a sip of wine, "but my lovely baby boy took photos so I could see his daddy's new hairstyle. I'm sure one of the guys will photograph Lucy's masterpiece if he doesn't wear it home."

"What makes you say that?" Freya asked Sarah.

"Uh, Lucy has a wall in her room only for her Lucy's Hair Salon customers." Gaby slapped her hand on her leg, laughing. "Grayhorse and Thunder have several photos. They have been her customers several times. She has them wrapped around her little finger."

"Those boys," Aurora shook her head up and down, "are so good to Lucy about her salon."

"Oh wow," Tori laughed with them, "they are pretty terrific. I'm gonna have to see this wall if my man is going to be on it."

Everyone froze and stared at Tori.

"Your man?" Freya raised an eyebrow at her.

"Uh, you know," Tori tried to laugh it off, "my best friend, man."

"Oh, no," Freya waved her finger from side to side to her, "you said your man. Right, ladies? I knew you guys were together now. Especially after he gave his undying love vow to you in front of your father. It's about time you admitted it to all of us."

"Undying love vow?" Sarah asked.

"Alex told Tall Bear he loved her and hoped to spend the rest of his life with her."

"Wow, that's so romantic," Maggie sighed. "I need a man like that."

"Well, if you would stop dating bikers and losers, you might meet a nice guy," Isa mumbled.

"Okay," Tori blushed, "he is my man."

"Well duh," Freya patted her leg, "In case you haven't noticed the way he looks at you, he is undeniably your man."

"Mags," Isa blurted out, "What's up with you and Ryan? You haven't talked to me about him in a while."

"Well," Maggie took a sip of wine, "It didn't work out. I need more excitement in my life."

"Mags," Isa sighed, "you are so crazy. He's a really nice guy."

"I know, Isa. But I need a little something more."

"Whatever," Isa rolled her eyes at Maggie.

After a couple of hours of drinking and laughing at their bad dating stories, Sarah pulled out the nail polish.

"Sarah, are you sure you guys should be painting your nails after drinking?" Isa asked while she chose one of the colors Sarah had placed on her cocktail table.

"What do you mean?" Sarah asked Isa.

"Uh, you guys aren't exactly sober," Isa informed them as they giggled. "I'm not worried about myself. I'm pregnant and sober. But you guys are giggle pots."

That comment caused a round of giggles as the girls selected their colors.

"We are women, we can multitask! We can drink and paint nails!" Sarah screamed with her fist up in the air as her war cry.

"Yeah!" all the ladies repeated Sarah's war cry, holding up their nail colors.

"Okey, dokey," Isa raised her eyebrows at them.

"Hey," Maggie yelled, "let's do every nail a different color!"

"Yes, Mags," Freya screeched, "great idea!"

After a few hours of much drinking, swapping colors to paint a nail, gossiping and much laughter, the guys arrived with the kids.

Chapter 48

The big Reveal
Tori

"Honey," Grayhorse yelled, holding Lilly while the kids ran inside, "we're home!"

The ladies stood up from the living room and ran toward the front door.

"Woohoo!" Freya screamed and pointed toward the front door. "Sexy!"

Alex came in with at least 20 braids sticking straight out all over his head. To make it even funnier, he had two Princess Leia braid buns over his ears.

"Oh, my God!" Tori stood up and walked over to him, and poked the buns lightly on each side of his head. "You are the manliest and sexiest Leia I've ever seen." Tori kissed him smack on the lips.

"I guess you figured out Lucy is in a Star Wars phase," Gaby laughed and hugged Matteo. "She wants to dress up as Princess Leia for Halloween and have Matteo be her Chewbacca."

"That would be so cute," Isa stated, "or she could be Snow White, and the guys could be the seven dwarfs: Matteo, Grayhorse, Thunder, Alex, Barrett, Mark, and Tommy."

"Uh," Thunder interrupted, "I like the Star Wars idea better."

"This is better than the official photo for the wall," Freya said as she snapped a photo.

"What wall?" Alex turned around and looked at Thunder and Grayhorse who were snickering behind his back.

"I usually take a photo of the customer and then you can take the braids out." Tommy smiled at Alex. "Then I send it to Lucy for her to print and frame it on her wall in her room."

"Wait," Alex holds up his hand, "I could have taken this down after Tommy took the photo?"

"Well, yes," Aurora joined the conversation while hugging Lucy, "but then we wouldn't have had the pleasure of seeing your beautiful hairstyle."

"That's what I said, *abuela*," Lucy beamed at her grandmother. "He wanted to take it down when we went into McDonalds, but we told him he couldn't so you could see it in person."

"Oh, wow," Freya guffawed and was holding her stomach, "you wore that in public."

"Yup," Alex sucked his lips and nodded, "sure did."

Thunder and Grayhorse lost it while Sarah and Isa smacked them on the arms.

"Isa, what did you spill on your shirt?" Thunder grinned. "You were supposed to be drinking water."

"I was," Isa looked down, "Oh hell, I think that's hummus." Thunder wrapped his arms around her and kissed her with lots of tongue.

"Come on Alex," Tori kissed his cheek and led him to the bathroom, "I'll help you get all the braids out."

"Lucy," Alex squatted down and waved her to him, "Thank you for my hairstyle, honey."

"You're welcome, Alex," Lucy hugged him. "I can't wait to put you on my wall."

Alex gave her a kiss on the cheek. Tori melted with the interaction. Alex was such a good sport with Lucy and the guys. Tori grabbed his hand and pulled him into the bathroom.

"That was really nice of you," Tori said after he shut the door.

"Wow," Alex stared at himself from all angles in the mirror, "sexy, huh?"

"Very," Tori grinned, "Sit on the toilet so I can reach your head."

Alex obeyed and sat on the toilet. He opened his legs and pulled Tori between them, placing his hands behind her thighs. He held her the entire time she took out the braids.

"Stay still," Tori mumbled, focusing on not pulling his hair.

"Baby," Alex muttered, "I'm not going anywhere. You're the one that's not steady. How much did you drink, anyway?"

Tori chuckled and continued to undo the braids and run her fingers through his long hair, sometimes touching his face with her breast. She could feel her nipples harden. Alex ran his hand up and down the back of her thighs, coming closer to her pussy each time while he kissed her breasts when she leaned in close.

"Done," Tori smiled down at Alex. As she gazed into his eyes, she felt drawn to him until their lips met and Alex gently kissed her. Tori placed her hands on either side of his face and pulled away.

"Alex," Tori whispered, staring at his lips, "we can't do this right now."

"Tori," Alex grabbed her hands and kissed them, "I wish we were home right now so I could place you on that counter and eat you out."

"I wish we were home too," Tori pulled him up, "come on, my sexy man. Let's finish this at home.

"Uh, Tori, what did you do to your nails?" Alex turned and opened his hands as he stared at Tori's fingers.

"We gave each other manicures." Tori looked down.

"Um, maybe you guys shouldn't have been drinking when you did that." Alex saw how each nail was a different color and the color was not only on the nails, but on the skin around the nails. It looked like a two-year-old painted her nails. "How many drinks did you have?"

"I only had three," Tori looked at her nails, "I think they look great."

"Okay Baby," Alex opened the door and pulled her out, "I think it's time to go home."

"Frey, time to go," Tori sang down the hallway.

"Okey dokey," Freya walked over to them and fluffed up Alex's hair, "Nice fro bro." Freya and Tori couldn't stop laughing.

"This is going to be a long night," Alex sighed and put his arms around both of their waists, "thanks guys. Lucy, can I please borrow a hair tie for my man bun?"

"Yes!" Lucy ran to the bathroom and came back with all the hair ties previously in his hair.

"Thank you honey," Alex released his sister and Tori while he put his hair up, "say goodbye ladies and let's go."

"Goodbye Ladies and let's go," Tori and Freya both screamed in a fit of giggles.

"Bye," everyone yelled back.

Alex walked to the car ahead of the ladies. He opened the back door for Freya and the front door for Tori.

"No Tori," Freya grabbed Tori, "sit with me in the backkk!"

Tori would have tripped if Alex had not held her up.

"Go ahead and sit with Frey," Alex closed the front door.

Tori kissed him before he closed the back door.

"Ooooohhh, smootchie smootchie," Freya started making kissing noises as they both giggled in the back.

Alex got in the car and called Barrett.

"Hey bro," Barrett answered, "everything okay?"

"Yup, but the ladies tied one on." Alex pulled out of the driveway. "I need your help to get them upstairs."

"Hi Bare!" Freya shouted.

"Wow," Barrett sighed, "she only calls me that when she either wants something or she's drunk. Text me when you get here. I'll come get Frey so you can focus on Tori."

"Thanks bro," Alex hung up and shook his head at the two giggly girls in the back seat.

Chapter 49

The Private Party after Girls' Night Out
Alex

When they arrived at the resort, Holt came out.

"Barrett told me they had some fun," Holt helped Freya out of the car. "He had something he had to deal with and asked me to come get her."

"Thanks man," Alex helped Tori out of the car on the other side, "I appreciate it."

"Hi Holtie," Freya fell into his arms, "how you doin'?"

"Apparently," Holt bent down and picked up Freya, "better than you. Put your arms around my neck, Frey."

"Okey dokey," Freya sighed and rested her head on his chest, giving him a tight squeeze around his neck.

Alex and Holt carried the ladies into the resort. Alex didn't think they were as drunk as they were acting. A drunk woman would be more passed out, not moaning and feeling up their chests.

"Are they okay?" Sehoy asked from the Lobby Desk.

"Yup," Alex replied, "just had a little too much fun with Sarah."

Tori waved at Sehoy and held on as Alex and Holt carried her and Frey into the elevator.

"What's up with the nails?" Holt commented when he looked at Tori's hand.

"They decided to give themselves manicures while drunk," Alex smirked.

"I hope they have nail polish remover," Holt laughed. "I think they'll need it tomorrow after they wake up."

"What do you mean, Holtie?" Freya pulled her arms from around Holt's neck and looked at her hands. "I think they look great, right Tori?"

"Holtie?" Alex raised an inquisitive eyebrow at Holt.

"Ugh," Holt grunted, "please don't call me that, Frey. I will never live that down now."

"I think our nails look wonderful!" Tori exclaimed while she looked at hers.

"See you tomorrow, Alex," Holt said as he walked out of the elevator and headed to Freya's door.

"Yup." Alex stepped outside the elevator and looked at Holt. "Thank you again Holtie for coming to get Frey. I couldn't have gotten them up here on my own." Alex laughed while Holt gave him the middle finger.

"No problem, fucker," Holt opened Freya's door. Since Holt worked in security, he carried a master key to all the rooms in the resort. "I'll get her to her room and go back down to work. Have a good night."

"You too," Alex opened his door, laughing as he walked in. Tori held onto Alex's neck with one hand while she continuously ran her other hand up and down his chest while he carried her to the bedroom. Alex stood her up by the bed.

"Baby," Alex held her by her arms, "why don't you change into either my shirt or pajamas?"

"Okay," Tori slowly began undressing Alex.

"I take it you want this one?" Alex helped her take off his shirt. Tori took it and sashayed into the bathroom.

"Alex," Tori hollered, "where are you?"

"Baby," Alex came into the bedroom and held out his hand, "it's okay. I'm right here. I just went to get you some water and ibuprofen. Here, drink this entire glass of water and take these."

"I'll drink it," Tori winked at him, "if you come lay down with me."

"Deal." Alex handed it all to her. "Let me change my clothes."

"I think you should strip and sleep naked," Tori said between gulps of water.

"You're cute when you're drunk."

Tori finished drinking her water and taking the pills while Alex took off his clothes in front of her. Tori was acting very sassy. He would need to stay on his toes because she was up to something. Alex used the restroom, turned off the lights and slid into bed, facing her.

"Alex," they laid on their sides facing each other, "thank you for tonight. Can I ask you something?"

"You can ask me anything." Alex ran his hand over her arm and pulled her into his arms.

"Will you be mine?" Tori kissed him.

"Duh," Alex licked her bottom lip and sucked it into his mouth. Tori opened her mouth and deepened the kiss as their tongues and teeth clashed in their make-out session. Tori wanted to touch and please Alex. She reached her hand down until she ran her hand down his cock.

"Can you lay down for me and hold the headboard?" Tori watched as Alex stayed quiet and lifted his arms to grab the slats on the headboard.

"You look so sexy." Tori placed her hands on either side of his hips and looked up at Alex.

"So do you," Alex groaned.

Tori ran her hands up his legs and watched him harden the closer her hands travelled to his cock. Tori scooted on her knees between his legs.

"Can you widen your legs so I fit on my knees?" Tori whispered. Alex widened his legs and moaned when Tori leaned over and her hair skimmed his thighs. Tori looked up into his smoldering eyes.

"Do you enjoy when I do this?" Tori ran her hands on his thighs and watched him grow even harder, noticing that he was leaking. Tori bent down and licked his head.

"Fuck, Yess," Alex hissed, holding the slats so hard his knuckles were white.

"Will you do something for me?" Tori sucked his head and looked up while it was in her mouth.

Alex gasped and nodded while he stared at her mouth as she swallowed his cock down her throat. Tori moved one hand to his cock and the other to his balls and put as much of his cock as she could in her mouth.

"Oh Fuck!" Alex growled, trying to stay still, "I'll do anything for you."

"Will you fuck me missionary style?" Tori asked while she licked his cock.

"Are you sure?" Alex asked through gritted teeth and pulled himself up to look at her. "Tori, Baby, this is important. Look at me, please."

Tori let his cock pop out of her mouth and gazed into his eyes.

"Yes, I want to see you when you lose control," Tori said before taking his cock back in her mouth. Tori alternated between licking, sucking, stroking, and taking him as far as she could down her throat.

"Baby," Alex pumped into her mouth and removed his hands from the headboard, pulling her off him and rolling them over.

"Are you okay?" Alex looked down into her eyes. "We don't have to do this."

"I'm okay, Alex. Now move and fuck me."

"Shit Tori," Alex bent down and swallowed her moan as he entered her, fucking her with a purpose just like she wanted. He would give his woman anything she wanted anytime. It didn't take long for either of them to reach an explosive orgasm. Both watching each other until the last moment.

"Oh Fuck," Alex collapsed on her, "Baby, you are amazing. I love you."

"I love you too, Alex." Tori murmured.

Alex rolled off, cleaned them up, climbed back into bed and spooned Tori. Life was good. He knew he wanted to marry Tori, but he would give her some time to adjust to their normal schedule before he proposed. Wanting to be ready with a ring, he would ask Barrett and Frey to go shopping with him.

Chapter 50

Halloween…A few weeks later
Tori

"Alex, we're going to be late to Lucy's house," Tori said from their living room. Freya and Tori had been waiting for Barrett and Alex to change into jeans and a polo shirt with the logo for 'Lucy's Hair Salon'. In the end, Lucy didn't want to be Princess Leia or Snow White. She wanted to go as a hair stylist and have the boys be her customers and bodyguards.

The girls were all going because they were not about to miss out on this opportunity. Aurora was going to give out candy at Gaby and Matteo's house while they Trick-or-Treated.

"Okay," Alex came out of the bathroom, "I'm ready. How do I look?"

"Sexy," Tori and Freya rose from the couch.

"You'll look so much sexier once your hair is done," Freya smirked.

"Okay," Barrett stepped into the room, "let's do this."

"I can't wait to see what she does to your hair," Freya pointed at Barrett.

"It won't be too crazy, since my hair isn't as long as Alex's," Barrett grinned.

"Oh, Lucy is very creative," Freya ran her hand through Barrett's hair, "I bet she can get at least 25 small braids in here." Barrett smirked at her.

"Yeah, yeah, yeah," Alex walked toward his door and opened it, "let's go. I'm sure Lucy is chomping at the bit to see us in her salon."

They all left work early so they could get to Gaby and Matteo's house by five. Grayhorse and Thunder should already be there getting their hair done. Since they didn't need seven dwarfs, the only boys getting their hair done were Grayhorse, Thunder, Alex, and Barrett. Tommy was thrilled to not be a dwarf. He was excited to be dressed as a duo with Emmy. Peanut Butter and Jelly were the perfect costume combo for them. Not only did those foods complement each other, but Tommy and Emmy were best friends.

Before they exited the car, Tori turned to Alex and Barrett in the back seat.

"Thank you, guys, for humoring Lucy with this Halloween costume."

"Not a problem," Barrett commented. "How much damage can she do to my hair?"

"We'll see," Alex looked at Barrett. Then turned around and stared at Tori.

"Baby," Alex placed his hand on her thigh, "That little girl is so stinking cute and sweet, how could we not do this for her?"

"Well, thank you." Tori leaned over and gave him what was supposed to be a quick kiss, but Alex snuck his tongue in her mouth.

"Okay, okay," Freya groaned, "enough of that. Let's get this show on the road. I can't wait to see your new do's."

They stepped out of the car, walked to the door, and Tori knocked.

"Hi," Isa welcomed them, "come in. Go straight to Lucy's room. Follow this hallway and make a left after the kitchen. You can't miss it. She has her door open, waiting for you guys. She already finished Grayhorse and was putting the last-minute touches on Thunder. Frey and Tori, come with me. The ladies are happily drinking in the living room waiting for the 'Lucy's Hairstylist Show.'"

"See you later, gorgeous," Alex kissed Tori, "let's go Barrett."

"Hi," Tori and Freya announced when they entered the room. Everyone repeated their greeting.

"Come get a glass of wine," Gaby walked to the kitchen island. "What do you want, white or red?"

"White for me, please," Tori answered while Gaby poured.

"Oh Sarah, you brought Lilly," Tori walked to Sarah and held her hands out to cradle Lilly, "she looks so cute in her little pumpkin outfit."

"Minnie offered to watch her," Sarah handed Lilly to Tori, "but I think she will be okay, plus she is our little pumpkin."

"I'll take red," Freya waited while Gaby set down Tori's wine, "so what hairstyle do you think Lucy is giving the guys?"

"It's a secret," Isa motioned her finger in front of her lips, "Lucy doesn't want us to see them until she is done. Emmy is in there with her as her assistant and Tommy is photographing the event."

"It's my house," Gaby handed Freya her glass of wine, "and I'm not even allowed in there."

The girls continued to guess which hairstyles Lucy would come up with. They knew it would not be neither dwarfs nor Star Wars - themed. Guessing was fun until their guesses became out of control.

"Oh, my goodness," Isa screamed out, "there are four of them. What if they are the Teletubbies." Everyone busted out laughing.

"They would be the buffest Teletubbies I've ever seen," Sarah wiggled her eyebrows."

"No, no," Freya blurted out, "ninja turtles."

"You've had too much to drink," Tori shoulder bumped her, "they don't have any hair."

"True," Freya stopped to think, "buff reggae musicians with dreadlocks."

"I hope not," Isa sighed. "Dreads are difficult to get out. You must cut your hair and Thunder would NOT want to do that."

"I got it," Maggie hollered, "sexy male strippers."

"Get your head out of the gutter, Mags," Isa smirked at her. "Lucy doesn't know what male strippers are. Right Gaby?"

"She better not," Gaby harrumphed, "Matteo would lose it."

"Okay ladies, Lucy's Hairstyle Show is about to start," Emmy said from the hallway entrance that led to Lucy's bedroom. "Tommy, cue the music."

All the ladies faced Emmy, ready to see the boys.

"This is so exciting," Freya clapped her hands with enthusiasm.

"Remember boys, strut your stuff," Emmy said and stepped aside so she could introduce the hair models.

"Our male models will represent animals and nature or animals in nature." Emmy announced, pretending to hold a microphone in her hand.

"Wait, Emmy," Tommy shouted, "I have to get out there to take my photos."

"Okay, now that Tommy is set, we can start. First, we have Thunder sporting a beautiful animal in nature look. Uncle Thunder, come on out."

Thunder walked out with his sexy stroll, swaying his hips like a female model would. He walked all the way in and pivoted, stopping to give everyone an eyeful. Thunder's hair was braided and wound up to resemble a bird's nest. Resting on top of the nest was a fake bird with lots of leaves sticking out of the braids. All the girls were hooting and hollering. Thunder winked at Isa on his way out.

"Next, we have Grayhorse representing the woman who can turn you into stone with one look. Grayhorse, come on out, ladies be careful of looking him in the eyes."

Grayhorse bent down and put his hands out with his fingers spread in a creepy way as he walked by the ladies, saying boo. His hair was also all in braids that were randomly held to his scalp, with fake snakes coming out from everywhere. Sarah stood up and kissed at him as he walked by her. All the other ladies pretended to look away and encouraged him to scare them.

"Our third customer is Alex, who will represent the sea world. Some people like to eat these, but I think they are gross. Not that you're gross, Alex," Emmy shook her head vehemently.

"No problem, Emmy." Alex stepped out and kissed her cheek.

Alex sashayed out, wiggling his arms like an octopus in the ocean, with his hair all braided. However, most of it was in a bun at the top of his head with two large googly eyes attached. He also had eight long braids hanging down for the tentacles. He walked by all the ladies and attempted to tickle them with his hands. Frey had received the brunt of it since Tori was still holding Lilly.

"And finally, our last customer is Barrett. He didn't think Lucy could do anything to his hair, but she proved him wrong. Barrett represents what some animals live in…a tree. Come on out Barrett."

Barrett strolled in with his arms bent upward and fingers spread. He stopped and stared up at the sky in a stiff pose. Lucy had managed to braid all his hair and used brown pipe cleaners to hold it up like baby branches growing out in all different directions.

"Now we will bring everyone out with our special hairstyle designer Lucy!"

"Woohoo," all the ladies were hooting and hollering as the men walked out and surrounded Lucy. The ladies stood up for a standing ovation.

"Oh my God, great job Lucy," Gaby wiped a tear from her eyes from laughing so hard as she checked the time, "it's getting late, we have got to go."

"*¡Ay! ¡Dios mío!*" Aurora opened her mouth and covered it with her hands. "*Qué guapos!*"

"What did we miss?" Matteo said, as he walked through the door after Aurora. He usually worked late, but today he left work early to pick up his mom before they all went trick-or-treating. "Wow, you guys look great." Matteo chuckled and bent down to pick up Lucy. "You outdid yourself, baby girl." Matteo kissed her cheek before setting her down.

"Emmy and Tommy helped me," Lucy cheerfully ran to Emmy for a hug, then Tommy.

Everyone hugged and congratulated Lucy, Emmy, and Tommy before the kids went to grab their trick-or-treat bags.

"Sexy huh," Alex wrapped his arms around Tori and Lilly, pretending to gobble up her neck while he lightly tickled her with one hand. Alex stopped when Lilly pulled one of his braids.

"Oh Lilly, don't pull Alex's hair," Tori laughed and tried to pry Lilly's fingers off Alex's hair.

"Cock blocked by a baby," Alex grinned, "that's a new one for me."

"Language!" Sarah screamed at Alex.

"It won't be the first time a baby blocks you," Grayhorse smirked. "Trust me."

"Damn…darn," Alex shouted after Tori slapped his arm, "sorry. She has good hearing."

"She's a mom." Tori held Lilly's fingers so she couldn't grab Alex's hair again. "She also has eyes on the back of her head and can multitask."

"So, what was that about Lucy not being able to braid your hair?" Freya tapped Barrett's spiky braids.

"That little girl has a very creative mind," Alex chuckled. "She, beyond a doubt, proved me wrong."

"A bird," Isa said as she made sure to tuck the leaves into the braids, "I like it Mr. Thunderbird."

"Yeah," Thunder kissed her cheek, "she did good."

"*Wówaštelaka mitáwa*, come here and look at me," Grayhorse was trying to drag Sarah's face toward his.

"I don't want to turn to stone," Sarah said, smiling as Grayhorse finally turned her face, but she closed her eyes.

"*Wówaštelaka mitáwa*," Grayhorse became serious, "I'm the one that will turn to stone if you don't look at me. You are the light of my life."

"Oh Grayhorse," Sarah immediately opened her eyes and gazed into his, "I would not survive life without you. How did I get so lucky? I love you."

"*Mitáwicu çaŋté thečhíhila*," Grayhorse kissed his wife gently, "I'm the lucky one."

"Yuck," Tommy blared from across the room, "can you guys stop so we can go get candy?"

"Someday *ciŋkší*," Grayhorse continued to gaze into his wife's eyes, "I hope you are blessed to marry a wonderful woman like your mom."
Sarah smiled and hugged her husband.

"*Mitáwa*, give me the baby carrier," Grayhorse reached out to take it. "I can carry Lilly."

"I'll carry her until she falls asleep." Sarah grabbed his hand and held it, "I don't want her to pull on your braids like she did Alex."

"Okay," Grayhorse brought her hand to his lips and kissed her, "but if she gets too heavy, I'll take her. I'll be fine."

Tori walked toward Sarah and helped Lilly into the Baby carrier Sarah wore on her front. Sarah turned her around so Lilly could watch the action. The carrier Sarah wore on her back or front was nice, and it allowed Lilly to face in either direction. Tori liked that. Maybe someday that would be something she could get to carry Alex and her child. Tori jumped when Thunder whistled.

"Okay, the sun is down, and it is time to get this show on the road," Thunder hollered. "Let's roll."

"You, okay?" Alex held her against his side. "You jumped."

"I'm fine," Tori smiled at Alex. "I was just startled out of my daydream."

"About what?" Alex looked down at her.

"Our future," Tori leaned her head on his shoulder.

"Sounds good." Alex hugged her. "You can tell me later."

"*Mami*," Matteo came out of the kitchen with a bowl of candy, "here is the candy. *Gracias* for staying to hand it out so we can both go with Emmy and Lucy."

"*Por nada, mi niño*," Aurora kissed his cheek, "you all go have fun."

Everyone except Aurora headed out the door. The guys took their job seriously and stayed with Lucy, Emmy, and Tommy as they approached every door. It's a good thing they had such funny hairstyles because without them, they looked very imposing as they stood behind the kids with their arms crossed in a wide stance.

They went several blocks so the kids could get a lot of candy. The ladies kept giving other women the evil eye if they stood or walked too close to their men. Several women would stop and turn around to stare at them as they walked by with the kids. The men, however, were oblivious to their looks. Their sole focus was on watching the kids and ensuring their safety.

Tori was having such a good time—Best Halloween EVER!

Seminole Fry Bread Recipe

INGREDIENTS
- 2 cups flour
- 3 tsp. baking powder
- 1 tsp. salt
- 1 cup milk

DIRECTIONS

Mix flour, baking powder and salt. Add milk gradually making sure the dough is stiff. Put on floured bread board and pat it out with your hands until it is 1/2 inch thick. Cut into strips with a slit in the center. Fry in hot oil until both sides are golden brown.

Traditional Fry Bread Recipe

INGREDIENTS
- 1 pkg. dry yeast
- 3 cups warm water
- 1 tbsp. salt
- 1 tbsp. sugar
- 6 cups flour
- 2 tbsp. oil
- 1/2 cup cornmeal

DIRECTIONS

Dissolve yeast in warm water then add salt and sugar. Let stand for 5 minutes covered with a towel. Add flour and oil to liquid mixture. Mix and put on floured bread board and knead until mixture is smooth. Put dough in a greased bowl, cover with towel and let it rise for 1 1/2 hours. Remove from bowl and put on bread board, knead in the 1/2 cornmeal. Make dough into 2 balls rolling each into 12-inch circles 1/2 inch thick. Cut into 2-inch squares and drop into hot cooking oil. (Works best with cast iron skillet.) Fry 5 to 6 pieces at a time for only a few moments. Drain on paper towel and sprinkle with white powdered sugar.

Old Fashioned Fry Bread Recipe

INGREDIENTS
- 4 cups flour
- 2 tbsp. baking powder
- 1 tsp. salt
- 1/2 cup shortening
- 1 cup warm water

DIRECTIONS

Mix flour, baking powder and salt. Gradually add in the shortening and water. Add only enough water to make dough stick together. Knead dough until smooth, make into fist-sized balls. Cover them with a towel for 10 minutes then pat them out into circles about the size of a pancake. Fry in hot cooking oil in cast iron skillet until brown on both sides. Drain on paper towels, serve with jam.

Recipes from: https://www.crazycrow.com/site/fry-bread-recipes-from-various-tribes/

Indian Fried Bread

- Oil
- Self-Rising Flour
- Water

Put flour in large bowl, use one hand to mix the flour while slowly adding water with other hand. You don't need to measure anything. Add the water till the mixture is slightly sticky (you don't want it really wet) If you added to much water just add some more flour.

Once you have your dough you need to heat up your oil. This is important! Your oil has to be very hot. Put the oil in a large deep pan. You need enough oil (like 2 1\2 inches deep) the bread should be able to float. Once you have heated your oil up, flour your hands and tear off some of your dough (you can make them as big or as small as you like) Knead the dough in your hands so it's like a pancake. Keep adding flour to your hands so it's not sticking.

Carefully add the dough to the oil. Remember the oil is hot so don't drop it in. It should only take like 5 seconds on each side. Use a fork to pick it up and turn it over. It should be golden brown color. Place on a paper towel to drain excess oil.

Making fry bread takes a lot of practice. You probably won't make the best fry bread the first time. Just keep trying.

Erica Miner, Seminole Tribe of Florida website

Sofkee

- 2 quarts of water
- 1 teaspoon baking soda
- 2 cups of white rice
- 3 tablespoon cornstarch

Bring 2 quarts of water to a boil; add 2 cups of rice and 3 tablespoons of cornstarch, stirring occasionally to prevent rice from sticking to the bottom. Boil for approximately 12 minutes, lower heat then add teaspoon of baking soda stir frequently until rice is tender. Set and cool until tolerable temperature.

Seminole Tribe of Florida website

Special Thanks

I was fascinated to find out the Seminole Tribe of Florida were unconquered. They are a Federally Recognized Indian Tribe. The only Tribe in America who never signed a peace treaty. The fact that 300 Seminoles were able to hide out in wetlands in Chickee's (log cabin-type homes, logo used at the beginning of every chapter) is incredible and shows their fortitude and love for their culture.

I tried to do the Seminole Tribe of Florida justice in my novel. It was hard to find a lot of words in their language which is why I don't have a lot of translations. I'm sorry if I got something wrong. My characters and locations are fictional. I truly enjoyed learning about this strong, creative, and smart tribe. If you are interested in learning about them, please go to: www.semtribe.com.

Since Alex was a chef, I added several fry bread recipes. Finding so many on the internet, I wanted to include a few different options. I added at the bottom where I found these if anyone is interested in looking up other types of foods. I love Indian Fry Bread; I buy it at every pow wow or festival I attend. The last pow wow I attended was at the Moundville Native American Festival in Moundville, Alabama in the beginning of October. It was my first time attending this festival where I met and saw a great array of American Indian artists. I was also able to try Indian Fry Bread Tacos and plain fry bread with honey - both were delicious.

Any discrepancies on my interpretation of Tori's rape are mine. I apologize if anyone felt that I didn't describe it adequately. In no way did I mean to trivialize such a heinous crime. I wanted to place more focus on her being a survivor than a victim.

Thank you also to my reading circle, my husband, daughter, and friends (Michelle, Catherine and Amy). I would also like to thank Detective Joe for answering my police officer questions. I would be remiss if I didn't thank my 4th child by choice and favorite book editor McKenzie Gibel. You truly pushed me to write a better book. I couldn't have done it without you. Our family is blessed to have you in our lives.